Kinsella's Man

···

Western Literature Series

Kinsella's Man

■ ■ ■

RICHARD STOOKEY

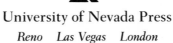

University of Nevada Press

Reno   Las Vegas   London

Western Literature Series

Editor: John H. Irsfeld

A list of books in the series appears at the end of this volume.

The paper used in this book meets the requirements of
American National Standard for Information Sciences—
Permanence of Paper for Printed Library Materials, ANSI Z39.48-1984.
Binding materials were selected for strength and durability.

Library of Congress Cataloging-in-Publication Data
Stookey, Richard.
Kinsella's man / Richard Stookey.
p.   cm. — (Western literature series)
ISBN 0-87417-248-9 (acid-free)
1. Nevada—Fiction.   I. Title.   II. Series.
PS3569.T646K56   1994
813′.54—dc20   94-4859
CIP

University of Nevada Press, Reno, Nevada 89557 USA
Copyright © 1994 by Richard Stookey
All rights reserved
Book design by Kaelin Chappell
Printed in the United States of America

2 4 6 8 9 7 5 3 1

To M.

PART ONE

•••

1954

CHAPTER 1

1

The salt flats lay like a frozen puddle of milk, stretching beyond the limit of the eye in every direction, as a venerable Model A roadster, bright blue in color, made its chuckling way westward over the desert highway. It had rained during the night, and here and there on the white surface glassy sheets of water gathered the morning sun into brilliant patches of light. Off to the south, mounds of spent clouds lay in gray disorder against the knees of the distant mountains, patiently waiting to be dispersed by the sun. The air was cool and fresh, sharp with the tang of the sea.

The two men had been riding in silence for more than an hour—since soon after the driver, in accordance with previous arrangements, had picked up the other at the Ogden hotel where he had passed the night. It was not, however, an uneasy silence, a vacuum to be filled by conversation, but a condition with which both seemed quite comfortable. There was a sense that talk, when it came, would not be unwelcome, but there was no reason to seek it out.

The passenger, a dark, heavy-browed young man of twenty-five or so, sat quietly erect beside the window, large, bony hands folded in his lap like a pair of sleeping rabbits. His features were rather sharp and angular, with high cheekbones and a decidedly prominent nose, but the impression was hardly one of ferocity. On the contrary, he seemed utterly calm and untroubled, content to be driven—yet at the same time there was an extreme, almost exaggerated sense of watchfulness about him, as though he had long made it his business to be wholly aware of his physical surroundings. His dark gaze, although it came to rest now and then upon the unbending line of highway, for the most part reached out toward the mountains, not only the cloud-clotted range to the south but those to his right as well, looming like bright, floating islands on the level seafloor of the desert.

Perched atop his head, at an angle that might lead one to believe it a recent acquisition, was a stiff yellow straw hat; huddled at his feet, its brown eyes glancing upward only now and then, was a small, silent, particolored dog.

The man at the wheel seemed somewhat older; it was difficult to say for sure. Very tall and broad through the shoulders, he also wore a hat—the customary tan felt, brim slightly rolled, long-established stains about the sweatband—and the hair visible beneath it, dark, woolly curls lying close against the skull, showed no trace of gray. The skin at the corners of his eyes, however, was gathered into a faint nest of wrinkles, which as he peered out at the dazzling white landscape—the linear, featureless highway like a string laid straight upon the salt—seemed to deepen into faint, intersecting canyons. The man's full lips, when they parted, revealed a magnificent set of even white teeth—excepting a single long eyetooth of gold.

The driver was black, very black—his skin the precise color of a new cast-iron stove.

"Where you from, John?"

The words, coming as they did after such long silence, seemed to materialize like an image out of shadows, then reverberate within the small space of the cab like a soft chime. The voice that spoke them was rather high in pitch, but with a breathy, smooth quality about it that made one think of folds of fabric rubbing together. The one spoken to, stiffening slightly, reached down to touch the head of the dog, which had stirred at the sound, then glanced quickly over at the still, ebony features to his left.

"You mean where I work, you mean Harignordoquy?" came the hesitant answer after a few seconds. The accent was heavy, dense, distinct.

"No, before. I mean originally."

"France," the young man said, not offering to elaborate further.

The driver did not take his eyes from the road, nor did he immediately respond. After several minutes the other, apparently convinced that the conversation was at an end, turned his attention back to the horizon, which had just begun to show the dim shape of mountains to the west. Straining to make them out, he had just located what seemed to be the highest point when the smooth, high voice spoke again.

"Nice place, is it? France, I mean. I never been there."

Again the young man turned, his eyes dwelling more openly now on the dark contours of the face beside him. The driver, eyes forward on the roadway, did not return his gaze.

"Pretty nice, 'least the part I come from." The word "pretty," as the young man spoke it, seemed made of "putty" and "sooty."

The driver, receiving this information in silence, seemed to withdraw once more into his study of the highway.

The one he had called John, again feeling the dog stir at his feet, reached down to reassure it with a touch, then looked off toward the western mountains, which now emerged like a bright, floating promise in the early sunlight. The slightest trace of a smile had begun to suggest itself about the corners of his eyes when the soft voice again was there.

" 'Lot different from here, I'll bet—that place you come from. Plenty good water and grass. Your sheep must be real happy over there." This time the dark man turned, his brilliant, gold-accented smile seeming to radiate like a flash of sunlight.

"It's different," John said uncertainly, turning away. "This country better for sheep, really. We never had that many."

Once more it seemed that the conversation was at an end—and indeed it almost was. It was only after some fifteen minutes had passed, the buildings of a town now looming in the distance at the western edge of the salt flats, that the driver spoke again. It was as if the interregnum had not occurred.

"Well, you'll have quite a few with us—at least if the boss has his way."

John, who could not imagine why the boss would not have his way, looked out the window and was silent.

Passing through the little town, its low white buildings blending perfectly with the desolate scene over which they presided, they left the salt flats behind and turned abruptly to the south. Soon they were angling gently upward toward the bench at the base of the mountains and, reaching it, continued for some fifteen miles along the eastern flank. It was only when they began to climb up toward the first pass that the cheerful tone of the engine altered, notes of effort being subtly but increasingly added until at last, when it seemed that the old car's good humor was about to be exhausted, they emerged on the flat near the top and, passing the signpost at the summit, started down the other side.

The descent from the pass was gentle and brief, into a shallow, arid valley some six or seven miles wide, really little more than a depression at the base of the higher hills beyond. Although the forbidding expanses of salt were now behind them, the vegetation remained sparse and tentative, with little besides an occasional patch of greasewood or dry, stunted sage to do battle with the alkaline soil. Soon, however, as they began to move upward through a broad, open canyon, the character of the land began to take on a wholly different aspect. Stands of cedar darkened the hillsides, and here and there amid the sage, increasingly taller and greener as they ascended, a few bunches of timid grass appeared. Over the brim of the pass the tip of a darkly wooded mountain loomed up before them, apparently the first in a long range extending southward—and far in the distance beyond it a great snowy bulk of peaks gleamed against the sunny morning sky.

Soon, however, these bright ones were lost from sight, shouldered from the stage by the dark shape of their nearer rival. Indeed, the skies themselves appeared to conspire, for as the Model A topped the second summit, drifting easily downward now through a sea of lush, frost-green sage, a bank of clouds moved heavily across the eye of the sun, smothering the last trace of brightness with a sudden, peremptory air. It was like an announcement, a territorial declaration, and as they continued the gentle descent across the sage plain the brooding peak rose ever higher above them, as if intent upon establishing the fact of its dominion over everything spread out at its feet.

"Big mountain," the young man said suddenly, decisively. They had not spoken since passing through the town, and the words seemed to hang in the air between them. Once more the dog stirred, looking up as if to assure itself that the words were directed elsewhere.

The man at the wheel again turned; the smile this time was more subdued, even sympathetic. "Not as big as some, maybe, but big enough, I reckon."

John, smiling himself now, shook his head but said nothing. For a moment only the bright sound of the Model A, fulsome now as it reached the bottom of the gentle descent, filled the silence.

"Name's Molly," the big man said at last. "Molly Peak. You'll get to know her real well the next few months. Me too, I guess, from what the boss tells me."

John, refusing even to think about what this last remark might mean, looked up and smiled faintly but said nothing. Again he glanced up at the mountain, assessing it differently now. Little snow remained, but among the upper, darkly wooded portions below the crest he could make out the softer shapes of broad, high meadows—which all at once emerged into bright sunlight as the passing cloud, resuming its journey, moved off to the north.

Soon the road had bent off to the west and another, gentler range of mountains, sides aglow in the morning sun, rose up before them in the distance—the dark mountain and its brothers now off to their left. Then, as the road turned south once more, both ranges came into view at once, running on either side of a long, narrow valley. They passed a crossroads, joining a road coming in from the northwest, then continued into the valley along the base of the dark mountains.

Again the country had become dryer, with dark, volcanic outcroppings rising like great dinosaur backs here and there on the plain. Off to the right the land descended toward a marshy bottomland, apparently the remains of an old, shrinking lake. Here and there were small fenced areas, expanses of wild hay, and beyond them the dark line of a railroad coming up from the south. Beyond this, perhaps ten miles distant, rose the western mountains, their dry, sandy-colored flanks fluted with canyons. There among the foothills John thought he could make out an occasional ranch house, or at least a windmill and corral, but here, on this side, he could see nothing to indicate a human presence. The sage-strewn plain, unmarked by even the suggestion of a fenceline, rose gently upward for no more than a mile before, gathering a sprinkling of cedars, it angled abruptly upward, soon to be lost in the patchwork of meadows and dark forests of the mountain.

It was only after they had gone some distance, perhaps ten

2

"Take your things in there and wait for me. I have to put the car away." They had driven through the shadow of the great house and continued toward the outbuildings, where they now came to a stop beside the bunkhouse. John, getting out, held the door for the dog, who hopped to the ground and shook its coat violently, as one would knock the dust from one's hat after a long horseback ride. The two, man and dog, then walked together to the rear of the car. John drew open the rumble seat, lifted out a single rope-bound suitcase, and watched the blue Model A move off, then disappear around the corner of the barn.

He mounted the low porch of the bunkhouse and, putting down his bag, looked about him for a moment. Aside from the house itself, the rest seemed ordinary enough. The barn was perhaps a bit bigger than most, but it had the same weathered, well-used look about it as any other. Directly across from him, but apparently extending around the other side of the barn as well, was a big, well-kept corral, eight or ten horses gathered in one corner. Beyond it, along a little weed-choked ditch, was a tall row of poplars, their graceful, pointed tips gently waving in the morning sunlight; a battered house trailer was parked beneath. There were a few sheds and buildings as well, but only one that caught his eye, a dilapidated little cabin set back against the row of poplars further down, not far from the looming shape of the big house itself.

He had seen such houses before—not only in Salt Lake City but in Cambo, a town not far from his own where rich people from Paris and Bordeaux came to take the cure—but never had he been quite this close to one. Then, on those other occasions, there had always been a substantial fence or wall of some kind—and behind that an expanse of well-tended lawn—proper reminders of the immutable and impermeable barrier between him and the exalted personages who lived in the great dwelling they protected. Now, here, there was nothing like a proper

fence—unless one were to count the sagging picket affair enclosing the yard at the back—and if there had ever been a lawn,
it was now reduced to a few wispy clumps of green along the
narrow ditch passing through.

These differences, however, hardly seemed to alter his reaction. There was the same sense of otherness, the same vague
feeling of intimidation he had experienced before—and besides,
in addition to them there was now something else, something
about this particular house, in this particular place, that both
troubled and, in a way he could not quite understand, uplifted
him at the same time. Again, inexplicably, the long-ago vision of
those high castle ruins, lit by a sudden shaft of Spanish sunlight,
passed quickly before him—and again, fleetingly, he sensed the
same violent struggle between awe and affront, inspiration and
outrage, that had brought those sudden tears. Now, however, he
simply lowered his eyes and, speaking with unwonted sharpness
to the dog, turned and went into the bunkhouse alone.

It was really quite luxurious as these things went. At the
far end, beneath a row of dirty windows, stood a long table
covered with oilcloth, and in a small room off to one side he
could see a stove, sink, and refrigerator. At the opposite end of
the table was another doorway, leading to an indoor toilet and
washroom. Between lay eight narrow beds, each with its own
plain wooden dresser, and several side tables made of wooden
fruit boxes filled with magazines and newspapers. Tacked here
and there on the wall, a reminder that cowboys here assayed
about the same as elsewhere, were the usual variety of Vargas
girls, rodeo schedules, and newspaper clippings.

He had just lowered his suitcase to the floor when he heard
the heavy thump of boots on the porch. "You'll stay here until
the sheep come," the black man said as he came in, ducking his
head to make it through the doorway. "Take any bed that isn't
made." He motioned vaguely toward the other end of the room,
then turned to go. "Leave your bag here for now. Come on along
with me."

Speaking again to the dog as he passed, John followed the tall, broad-shouldered form out of the bunkhouse, through the picket gate, and across the unkempt yard at the rear of the house. Flowers grew in bunches beside the fenceposts, and the hum of bees filled the warm morning air. Almost to the house, beside the little weed-choked ditch, stood a child's wheelbarrow. Seated upright in its bed was a worn stuffed bear in bathing trunks, one eye missing. The big man mounted a low porch and disappeared through a screen door, calling to someone inside.

John came to a stop, wondering whether he was expected to proceed inside as well. It was difficult for him to get used to, the way this big black acted toward him. He was friendly enough, and even thoughtful in his own way, but there was something . . . unnatural in the way he ordered one about, especially now that they had arrived. It was as though he thought he owned the place, which he certainly did not. John didn't remember just what name the man had given when they met at the hotel, but he knew one thing for certain: it was not C. Kinsella.

He hesitated a moment longer before at last he mounted the porch, pulled open the screen door, and went in. Passing through a kind of large utility room, its walls festooned with a variety of raincoats, hats, and harnesses, he emerged into the kitchen, where he again paused near the doorway, deciding it would be best to wait.

Hardly the first working ranch kitchen he had seen, this one was in many ways like the others. The pair of large stoves (one wood, one butane), the oilcloth-covered table ringed by high-backed chairs, the long wooden sinkboards and hanging cast-iron pots and pans, the yellow spirals of flypaper in various stages of occupation, the wide-bladed ceiling fan—all of these he might have expected anywhere, and as he looked about him he felt vaguely reassured by this basic sameness, this familiar arrangement of objects and functions. Yet in other ways it was utterly unlike the others, this kitchen—and again he seemed to feel rising up within him, as it had on the bunkhouse porch

not ten minutes before, that strange, confusing blend of awe
and affront, outrage and envy. For one thing it was enormously,
even unnecessarily large, for it occupied almost the whole of the
east side of the house. Much longer than it was wide, even its
breadth could not have been much less than twenty feet. Tall
windows, five of them, ran all along the east side, opening on a
view of the sage flats, cedar-strewn foothills, and mountains beyond. At the far end of the room, perhaps fifty feet from where
he stood, squatted the two stoves—from one of which, at this
moment, rose comforting smells of cooking—while before them
the long wooden table extended almost half the length of the
room. At the near end was a tall dish cabinet, and lower cabinets of the same kind lined the entire width of the wall facing
the windows, excepting only the portals of two doorways—one
near the stoves leading to a large open pantry, the other just
across from him opening into a hallway.

It was not only the sheer size of the room, however, that
made it so . . . different. The rest—indeed, the aspect that
most affected him—was simply a matter of quality, of care and
workmanship. Here, unlike in those other kitchens, the pots
and pans hung not from simple nails or hooks but from neat
wooden pegs—and the corners of the sinkboard troughs, now
gleaming in a flood of sunlight, were not nailed or screwed but
smoothly joined with dowels. Indeed, so far as he could make
out, there was not a nail or screw in the whole kitchen, if exception were made for those in the hinges of the door beside him.
Even the curtain rods, from which now depended some rather
stained and disreputable chintz curtains, were made of wood,
not metal, as were the towel racks beside the sinks. It was as
though a master cabinetmaker had built the whole room to the
order of a man who intended it to last forever.

Occupied with such thoughts, he gave a gentle start as, quite
suddenly, the tall black reappeared through the doorway opposite, this time followed by an old, bent Indian in faded Levi's
and slippers, a pillow and some linens over his arm.

"Here," the black said, taking the things from the Indian and handing them to him. "By the time you've made up your bed it'll be time for dinner. The boss wants to talk to you afterward."

The old Indian smiled toothlessly across the table, deep crow's-feet gathered about the corners of his soft brown eyes. John, nodding curtly in the big man's direction, returned the Indian's smile as he turned to go.

Carrying the fresh linens and pillow, he started back across the yard toward the bunkhouse, where his dog sat waiting beside the porch. The small wheelbarrow and its burden again caught his eye, and he paused for a moment beside it. The ragged bear, its monocular gaze directed wistfully up toward the mountains, was about to lose one of its ears, and its nose had been subjected to unmerciful chewing, but its modest bathing costume appeared to be quite new, sewn by hand. He was about to reach down and touch it when the sound of a hoarse, deep voice, shouting or calling to someone inside, inspired him to continue on his way.

This time the bunkhouse was not empty. Seated at the long table, smoking a curved pipe as he perused an issue of the *Police Gazette,* was a thin, bald-headed old man with heroic white mustaches. John, not wishing to disturb him, walked quietly to one of the three unmade beds and deposited his burden there. As he walked back to fetch his suitcase from its place near the doorway, however, he could feel the man's gaze on his back, and when he turned he was met with two very pale gray eyes and a reedy voice.

"Hi. I'm Carl Withers." The pipe remained firmly clenched between Carl Withers's teeth.

John spoke his own name and smiled, then carried the suitcase to his bed. The gray eyes, unblinking, did not leave him for an instant.

"You the sheepherder?" It was not quite a question, not quite a statement, but something between the two.

John nodded.

The old man remained silent for a moment, sucking softly on his pipe while he continued to look John up and down. "Take that bed over there," he said at last, motioning vaguely toward one in the corner. "It's better," he added.

John did as he was bid, carrying the pillow and linens in one arm and his bag in the other. When he looked up again the old man had gone back to his magazine. He made his bed in silence and had just finished transferring the contents of his bag into the dresser when he heard the sound of a truck arriving, then loud voices and the thud of boots on the porch.

Four men burst into the room—each with hat in hand, each exhibiting the tanned cheeks and pale forehead characteristic of their common profession. The first two, engaged in a heated dispute over some matter of baseball tactics, promptly threw their hats on their beds and went on with their discussion. The remaining pair, however, having nothing so weighty to distract them, soon noticed the thin, dark figure seated on the corner bed, the old suitcase resting on his knees. Two they were, but John, as he looked warily over at them, had some difficulty convincing himself of the fact, for they looked like two copies of one—identical whitish-blond hair, whitish eyebrows, blue eyes, small nose, protruding ears, powerful build. These, he would soon find, were the twin Lindsay brothers, distinguishable to the uninitiated only by the convenient fact that one was missing the index finger of his right hand. Now they stood in identical postures, each with the same curious expression on his face, each with his hat in his left hand, each utterly still.

"This here's the sheepman," Carl Withers said softly in his high, gentle voice. "Name's John."

With the disagreement continuing to rage in the background, the Lindsay brothers approached one by one and, speaking their names, shook John's hand—thereby providing him ample means for distinguishing between them. Nat Lindsay, he of the missing finger, would turn out to be somewhat garrulous—as garrulous as his brother was laconic; he had already begun to inquire into

John's origins, preparatory to probing his intentions, when all at once the baseball *cognoscenti*, having at last noticed the foreign body in their midst, fell silent. The voice of Carl Withers again announced John by profession and Christian name as they, the disputants, approached.

Lonnie Wilson was short and rather slight, with a narrow face surmounted by a mop of black, curly hair. He seemed somewhat younger than the Lindsays, perhaps twenty-two or three, but he had an air of confidence, even arrogance, and an extremely firm grip. The other man, Orson Darnell by name, was tall and broad, an ample belly overhanging his large brass belt buckle. His face was round and florid, no stranger to drink it seemed, but the impression was nevertheless of great power, like an irascible bear. He did not smile as he took John's hand, but carefully looked him over from crown to toe as if considering how much he would bring at auction.

"He's from over to Brigham City," announced Nat Lindsay, proudly sharing his early findings.

"Who'd ya work for over there?" asked Orson Darnell, scowling.

"Peter Harignordoquy."

"Peter who?"

"Harignordoquy."

"Basco," Orson Darnell said under his breath, but quite loud enough for everyone to hear. "Never heard of 'im," he added after a moment, and, taking a red bandanna handkerchief from his back pocket, loudly blew his nose.

"I have," put in Lonnie Wilson. "Big outfit. Runs near twenty thousand head of sheep. That right?"

John warily nodded.

Orson Darnell headed for the washroom. "Never heard of 'im," he muttered as he went.

"You bet," continued Lonnie Wilson loudly, pressing the point. "When I was over to Logan two years ago I heard about that guy all the time. Big, I mean b-i-i-g, outfit."

"Well," said Nat Lindsay, sitting down on a bed, "he's gonna have a pretty small outfit here. We don't even have one sheep around here that I know of."

"S'pos'ta come next week," John said quietly.

"How many?"

"Dunno," John said. "Less'n twenny thousand, I think." He watched with satisfaction as the faces of the Lindsay brothers, then that of Lonnie Wilson, broadened into smiles.

"More like twenny," came the reedy voice of Carl Withers, laughing past the pipe still gripped in his teeth.

"Well, John," added Lonnie Wilson, "I don't give a damn how many you have—long as you keep 'em way the hell up on the mountain."

A muttering of general assent ran through the company, cut short by a bitter voice from behind them. "And how in hell do you think he's gonna do that? D'ya think those woolly bastards are going to winter up on Molly? Ol' Thunder'll have 'em right down here on top of us. You won't be able to walk out the door without smelling the *stink* of 'em." All eyes turned to Orson Darnell, whose big form now choked the doorway to the washroom.

"Why don'cha just leave that to the boss?" Lonnie Wilson said sharply, his small green eyes flashing. "You aren't in charge around here yet, far as I know."

Just at that moment a bell sounded from the direction of the big house. Orson Darnell, casting a malevolent glance about him, stood aside as the others filed into the washroom, leaving John standing alone beside his bed.

"Better wash up," Orson Darnell said, not unkindly, when the others were gone, and strode heavily out of the bunkhouse.

Following the others, John retraced his steps across the yard to the back door of the big house. Inside, the long kitchen table was set for the meal. As the old Indian, laden with steaming bowls and platters, slippered from stove to table and back again, the men seated themselves and began to fill their plates with slices of pot roast and mounds of steaming mashed potatoes. John, seated between the Lindsay brothers, did the same, carefully watching the others to make sure that his portions were neither too large nor too small.

The place set at the head of the table was empty, as was the one at its right hand and one other, down near the far end of the table. No one, however, seemed in the least concerned about this; all set to work in silence, the only sound being the clatter of knives and forks and an occasional muffled demand that something be passed or refilled. The old Indian, silently moving back and forth, seemed almost invisible, the platters appearing and disappearing as if of their own will. Perhaps five minutes had passed in this fashion, the more avid beginning to look about for seconds, when there came the sound of footsteps, accompanied by low tones of conversation, approaching down the hall. The tall, wiry form of an old man, his white, close-cropped hair gleaming in a ray of sunlight, appeared in the doorway, followed like a looming shadow by the big black.

John, looking up, felt the old man's gaze settle briefly on him, then quickly look away as he moved with what seemed a slight limp to the head of the table. He was dressed like the others, in faded denim work clothes, and as he eased into the chair they absently began to move platters in his direction. The black, for his part, crossed to the outer doorway, where he was met by the old Indian with a wicker lunch hamper. Taking it, he continued out the door, and a moment later there was the sound of a truck starting and driving away.

No greeting was exchanged—indeed, it seemed that no one had really noted the new arrival at the table but John himself. Lonnie Wilson and Carroll Lindsay had begun a desultory conversation on the treatment of lame horses, but no one else seemed inclined to join it. John warily attended to his eating, watching out of the corner of his eye as Orson Darnell, seated across from him, spooned a great puddle of strawberry preserves onto a piece of bread. At the other end of the table Carl Withers, who had now been joined by a small, dark Mexican of about fifty, negotiated a spoonful of mashed potatoes and peas past his epic, tobacco-stained mustaches.

"Where's Book off to now?" Orson Darnell said, somehow producing this inquiry from the midst of an enormous mouthful.

For a moment it seemed that the question was going to be ignored, the man at the head of the table continuing to serve himself as if it had not been asked. Then, very slowly, he raised his eyes and looked about the table, lingering only a moment longer on John than on the others. The voice when it came was quiet, yet at the same time deep and harsh, rumbling out like distant thunder on a still and silent afternoon.

"Chokecherry."

This point established, the parties returned to the principal matter at hand. Lonnie Wilson and Carroll Lindsay, content to let the matter of lame horses remain unresolved for the moment, prepared slices of bread and preserves in the manner of Orson Darnell—who for his own part had fallen once more on the meat and potatoes, apparently making a new beginning at this point. When moments later the Indian produced a pair of pies from the oven, however, even he, to protect his share, was obliged to abandon the main course in favor of dessert.

"You get fixed up, son?" The deep, hoarse voice, seeming again to come from a distance, reverberated in the air. John, pie-laden fork midway between plate and mouth, abruptly realized that it was he who was being spoken to. He could feel himself stiffening in his chair as, slowly lowering the fork, he turned toward the head of the table.

It was the first time John had really looked at the man, whom he took to be the foreman. He seemed about sixty-five, a few years younger than Carl Withers, certainly, but it was rather difficult to say for sure. Although his hair was almost completely white, the bushy eyebrows remained quite dark, with wiry tufts of gray and even black still predominating. His eyes, a pale, hard blue, had a crystalline quality about them, and as the young herder felt their even gaze upon him he had a momentary instinct to bolt.

"Yessir," John said, mastering it. His own voice sounded unfamiliar to him, as if another had really spoken the words.

"You get acquainted with everybody?"

"Yessir." A vague murmur of accord rose from around the table.

"John'll stay with you in the bunkhouse," the man said to them. "For just a couple weeks, until the sheep and his wagon arrive." He lit a cigarette and pushed his coffee cup an inch forward, toward the center of the table. The old Indian immediately materialized to fill it.

Orson Darnell cleared his throat and, with a loud scrape, pushed his chair back from the table. The others' eyes turned briefly toward him, but he said nothing.

"You guys about finished up there?" the old man said sharply, impaling Darnell with his glance.

"Yep." The voice was soft, almost unrecognizable. "Today should about do it."

"Good. There's about ten miles of fence needs looking after." The man paused, taking a deep pull on his cigarette, before he added: "Book'll be out sometime this afternoon to show you."

Again there was a brief, uncomfortable silence. The ice-blue gaze remained on Darnell for a moment, then abruptly came to rest again on John. "While we're waiting for your sheep—and the wagon too, guy over in Chokecherry's sending one—while we're waiting you'll be working with Tabby, something he needs a hand with." The Indian, seated now with a cup of coffee, smiled his toothless, wrinkled smile.

"This afternoon you and I'll go up and look over some of your range. Give me ten minutes—I'll meet you at the barn."

"Lonnie," he added, looking down the table, "you stick around for a minute."

A general scraping of chairs signaled the conclusion of the meal. While Lonnie followed the old man down the hall and

Darnell lingered to say something to the Indian, John followed
the others out onto the porch. The small Mexican, who so far
as he could tell had not yet noticed his presence, took off immediately on his own, heading toward the battered house trailer
beneath the poplars. The three others, moreover, seemed to
have forgotten about him entirely, immediately becoming involved in an animated conversation he could neither follow nor
understand. Hanging back a moment, he watched as they descended the stair and, wholly caught up in their discussion, set
off together toward the bunkhouse.

After a moment he too went down the stair and started across
the yard, again pausing beside the one-eyed bear in the wheelbarrow beside the ditch. This time, however, he reached down
to pick it up, cradling it in one of his large, callused hands as
he assessed the damage. He was standing thus, the bear's single
eye staring wistfully up at him, when he heard the screen door
slam. Orson Darnell, his heavy body swaying from side to side
as he came down the stairs, started across the yard toward him.

"Pretty beat up, eh?" the big man said roughly, but with a
cautious note of congeniality in his voice.

"Yeah, pretty much," John agreed, carefully returning the
bear to the precise position in which he had found it.

"Needs a new one," Darnell added vaguely as, side by side,
they continued toward the bunkhouse. They did not speak, but
John sensed a subtle softening in the big man's demeanor, as
though the brief chastening received at dinner had humbled
him. They had almost reached the low stair of the bunkhouse
when Darnell abruptly drew up.

"That your dog?" he said.

The small, watchful animal, lying in the shade of the bunkhouse a few feet from the stair, had risen to its haunches as they
crossed the yard.

"Yep," John said.

"Looks smart. You can tell by their eyes."

The dog, sensing that it was being talked about, looked earnestly at John and uttered a low, eager whimper.

"Yeah, pretty smart." Again, as always, the "pretty" had a bit of "putty" to it.

"I like dogs," the big man said. "Especially smart ones." And immediately he took a slow step forward, extending his broad, fleshy hand before him.

"Yes, you're a smart one; no dummy you," Darnell murmured, advancing. The dog looked once, very quickly, at John, then settled lower and began, very softly, to growl.

"He's not friendly," John said as the broad form slowed, then stopped. "He's not used to people much."

Darnell, turning, seemed crestfallen. "But if you say something to him." A faint note of menace had crept into his voice by the time he added, "I'm not going to hurt him, you know."

John, shrugging, shook his head. "Don' matter what I say. He's jus' not used to it."

"Not used to it," Darnell murmured as he lowered his hand. "One-man dog, I guess," he added after a moment, seemingly resigned. "Some of 'em are like that."

"I guess so," John said softly before he added, once more: "He's jus' not used to people."

"Yeah, I understand," the big man muttered. Then, turning, he walked quickly to the porch and mounted the stair.

John spoke a word to the dog and it came to him, settling at his heel. Darnell looked down at them briefly, then started toward the door.

"'Scuse me," John said suddenly. "Could I ask you jus' one thing?"

Again stopping, the big man turned back toward him. The face seemed a bit redder than before, but the small brown eyes betrayed nothing.

"Sure," Darnell said evenly, a note of forced equability in his voice.

"Well, that big guy who brought me, the n- . . .—well, you know the one. Book, did you call him?"

"That's right."

"Well, he said Mr. Kinsella wanted to talk to me right

after dinner. But now the old white-haired guy, you know—he nodded behind him, in the direction of the house—"he says I should go with him. Maybe . . . maybe somebody oughtta tell Mr. Kinsella, jus' in case . . . ?"

Darnell hesitated a moment before he answered, his eyes narrowing imperceptibly as he gazed down. Then, slowly, a faint, cordial smile flickered across his heavy features.

"Sure, I'll take care of it," he said, and disappeared inside.

John glanced back toward the big house, its shadow now reaching out toward him, but no one else had yet emerged. Sighing once, he turned and set out toward the barn, the dog following eagerly behind.

3

The two horses moved easily through the cedars, following the course of a bright, narrow stream along the uphill border of the hayfield. The smaller of them, a neat, short-coupled pinto mare with a white rump, led the way; following close behind, the tall old gray shook its head and snorted from time to time, as if protesting an insult. Bringing up the rear, seemingly oblivious to the dust, was a small, particolored dog.

As the group moved along, an occasional jackrabbit peered out of the brush, long ears erect like antennae, then turned and loped lazily away. The smell of cedars and blooming sage was strong and pungent.

In the field below, visible through the occasional breaks in the trees, were several wheeled sprinklers of enormous length, their showery spray catching rainbows in the sun. At the far end of one of them, leaning against the fender of an old yellow truck, a small, dark figure looked along its length.

As they neared the furthest, most northerly tip of the hayfield the two horses came abreast, moving side by side now up a broad, rocky track which, coming up from the field and crossing over a narrow bridge, led away from the creekbed toward the northeast where two tall cottonwoods rose against the hillside. The big gray seemed to calm somewhat, and for a time there was heard only the soft clop of hooves on the porous earth, the lazy squeak of saddle leather. Several hundred yards short of the cottonwoods, however, the pinto again turned, leading the way up a narrow trail through the cedars. The gray, obviously averse to leaving the main track, stalled—and only after some firm encouragement did it set out again in second place, from time to time shaking its head and snorting as before. Soon the cedars thinned, and the wooded flank of a mountain could be seen rising darkly against the afternoon sky.

At the ridge the two horses paused, their sleek sides heaving gently as they waited. Now the men were talking, the one on the dainty pinto raising his arm to describe a vast semicircle extending from the two cottonwoods, whose shimmering tops could be seen in the hollow below, all the way to the high mountains beyond them and down their sloping flanks to the south. The other man sat motionless atop the great blowing gray, big hands resting lightly on the pommel of his saddle. From time to time he seemed to ask a brief question, but for the most part he was silent, his dark eyes following the other's gestures with grave attention.

After a time, when the horses had caught their wind, they again set off, the pinto leading the way up the spine of the ridge to the south. Soon, the dog faithfully following in the dust behind, they entered a stand of pinyons and were lost from sight.

It was perhaps an hour later when they returned, moving slowly down the ridge toward the place where the trail from below emerged. The old gray, preceded now by the dog, had led the way coming back; indeed, John had found it difficult to hold it back in a walk. It was a very powerful horse, more powerful even than its appearance would indicate, and remarkably headstrong in the bargain. John, drawing it back once more, was more than a little puzzled why such a horse, given its age and disposition, should be kept on at a working ranch such as this, where quick obedience and reliability were at a premium. The docile young pinto, padding deliberately behind, provided a ready contrast.

Reaching the bottom of the trail, where it intersected the track below, John drew up to wait for the pinto, which had fallen some distance behind. Again, however, the big gray seemed disinclined to obey and, turning to the right, sought to head up in the direction of the two tall cottonwoods. Curbing it forcibly, John was in the difficult process of turning it about when the pinto and its rider appeared.

"He's very strong," John said apologetically when he had at last succeeded and the horse, defeated, stood snorting but flat-footed beneath him. The wiry old man, who had watched the performance in silence, sat slumped in his saddle, icy blue eyes glowering from beneath dark eyebrows.

"He's ruined," the old man said at last, spitting into the dust. "Used to be a damn good horse, but now . . . I don't know why in hell they saddled him up for you."

"What happened? To the horse, I mean."

"Happened?" Watching, John saw the furrowed face abruptly soften. For a moment there was silence—then a dark rumbling as the old man coughed, just once. "Nothing really," the rough voice added after a moment, seeming to come to itself once more. "He's just old, that's all—and nobody rides him anymore."

"I'll ride him," John said simply.

The other regarded him evenly for a moment, then said at last: "So you will."

Again the horse stirred and tried to turn; again John, with some effort, held him back. "Why does he want to go up there?" John said, motioning over his shoulder in the direction of the tall cottonwoods.

"The spring," the old man said. Then, after a moment: "You probably should see it anyway."

The young herder, nodding, waited while the other, a wholly blank look settled over his face now, looked past him up the wide trail. "You go on," he said at last. "I'll wait for you here." John watched him draw a cigarette from his pocket and light it, then released the gray and headed briskly upstream.

Soon they had reached a small, marshy meadow, the trail continuing along the uphill side, above the numerous seeping rivulets that had brought it into being. It was quite green here already, with little clumps of flowers showing bright against the coppery trunks of the water birches. On the far side was the main body of the stream, quite narrow and rapid at this point, while up to the right the two cottonwoods shimmered softly in the pale afternoon sun. The gray, moving with smooth, steady power now, continued briskly up the trail, mounting the dry hillside. Finally, after crossing a low saddle, they came in sight of the spring. Here, for a moment, they stopped, the horse snorting with impatience while John, suddenly pensive, surveyed what lay before him.

He had seen many springs before, but never one quite like this. The springs he knew emerged from rocky clefts or oozed up out of meadow hillsides; often they occurred in groups, combining the strength of several small openings to produce a respectable stream. This one, however, would have none of that. Nestled in a little pocket in the hillside, the broad trunks of the two cottonwoods hulking up at the far side, it covered an area perhaps twenty feet across—the water bubbling vigorously, miraculously up as if eager to reach the light. All about the edges, and here and there in the center as well, were great clumps of watercress, their dark green bulk forming a strange contrast with the ebullient waters that nourished them.

Nudging the horse into motion, he descended the hundred feet remaining and stopped at the spring's edge. There, while the horse drank deeply, he dismounted, kneeling on the spongy bank to gather up a handful of watercress. He had just raised it to his mouth when, looking across the bubbling expanse of water to the other side, his glance wandered up to a kind of grassy depression beneath the roots of the larger cottonwood. There, just at the far end, stood a smooth, unmarked marble shaft, about two feet in height—and all about it, in a profligate confusion of faded color, a scattered heap of wilted flowers. Rising slowly to his feet, he stood looking across at it for a moment before, turning, he slowly raised himself into the saddle and urged the big gray back down the trail.

They did not speak again for the next half hour, until at last they drew up at the corner of the corral.

"Put up my horse, if you would," the old man said. "I have something to take care of."

John nodded, dismounting, and patted the haunch of the big gray before, passing under its head, he reached out to take the bridle of the pinto. The old man gingerly stepped down, handed him the reins, and was about to turn and go when John spoke.

"D'ya think Mr. Kinsella gonna want to see me tonight? Or maybe I should jus' wait 'til morning." The old man stopped. Remaining quite still, he looked into John's face, the pale blue eyes intent, seeming to examine every pore and hair. There was a sudden air of fatigue, of sadness, of some great and oppressive regret about those eyes as the long moment passed, then was abruptly, finally gone.

"I'm Kinsella," he said. Then, after a moment, reaching out to touch John on the shoulder: "I'm sorry."

John watched in silence as the tall form turned and, striding stiffly, crossed to the corner of the barn and disappeared.

4

Quickly, with the efficiency of long habit, John unsaddled first the pinto, then the big gray, and turned them out into the corral. Then, draping the bridles over his shoulder, he picked up the two saddles, grasping each behind the pommel, and started toward the barn, the dog at his heel.

There was a refreshing coolness in the air now, and he breathed in deeply, drawing it to the bottom of his dusty lungs. The late afternoon sky, streaked with curdled skeins of cirrus cloud, had washed the landscape in soft tones of blue and gray, and the air was alive with swallows. He watched them as he went, following with his eye as they veered and swooped, open-mouthed, above the steep roof of the barn.

Entering through the high main doorway, he stood for a moment while his eyes adjusted to the darkness. Then, making out what seemed to be a dim light at the far end, he set out toward it. As he drew nearer, the weight of the saddles tugging at his shoulders, he could hear the soft sound of a radio. At last he reached an open doorway and, mounting the single step, gently lowered his burdens to the floor.

Inside, leaning over the high workbench, was the big black man, wholly intent upon a piece of harness he was repairing. A single bare lightbulb burned over his head. John stood silently for a moment, listening to the low drone of the radio and watching as the long, coal-black hands removed a piece of glued leather from the vise, then placed it on the anvil and, taking up the hammer, began to apply small copper rivets. It was not until the piece was finished, the dark, sure hands setting it aside to take up another, that he thought to announce himself.

" 'Scuse me."

Slowly, deliberately, the big man looked up. An expression akin to confusion passed briefly across his face until, eyes adjusting to the distance and the light, his lips at last opened into a broad, generous smile.

"Well, it's John. You'll have to excuse *me*. My mind was a thousand miles away—or a couple hundred at least. How's it going?"

"Okay," John said, faintly smiling. "The . . . Mr. Kinsella and me, we jus' got back. Could you tell me where to put these?" He nodded toward the saddles at his feet.

"Surely. Did you lug them all the way across the barn?"

"Yes. I didn' know."

"Well, there's a shorter way." Leaving his harness on the bench, the tall form moved toward the doorway where, towering over John, he bent down to take one of the saddles in a smooth, easy motion. "This way," he said, and strode through an adjoining doorway.

Telling the dog to wait, John picked up the remaining saddle and followed into a dark, high-ceilinged room—its air heavy with the smell of leather and saddle soap, neat's-foot oil, and harness wax. He could make out eight or ten saddles resting on wooden racks along the wall, while beyond them another half-dozen hung by their pommels from lariats attached to a long beam. In a far corner he could see the long shadow swinging its saddle to an upper rack. Then, again, that high, smooth voice: "Put yours on the bottom there, the rack just to your right." Doing as he was bid, he turned to find the big man close beside him.

"See that door?" he said, pointing toward the far end of the room.

"Yes."

"Well, it leads straight out into this end of the corral. A little easier that way."

"Thanks," John said softly. "Thanks . . . Book."

There was a long, low chuckle. "Funny name, sure enough, but that's what they mostly seem to call me around here. Like they could read me or something—and maybe they can. But I'll tell you one thing sure: my mamma'd have a conniption fit."

"What did she call you?" John said.

Again came the soft, easy laugh, bright teeth flashing in the dusky light. "Why, she called me by my name, that's all. '*Booker!*' she'd holler. '*You, Booker Goodman, get on in here, and I mean now!*' Lord, wouldn't she holler . . ."

Turning, the two moved together back toward the shop. They had almost reached it, the light filtering in toward them, when all at once John felt a hand on his sleeve.

"Tell you what, John." The voice this time was soft, subdued.

"Why don't you just call me Booker too? Make my mama happy, bless her soul. Maybe it'll catch on."

Back at the workbench now, Booker Goodman had taken up the broken harness—and with it a rambling, lazy account of what Kinsella seemed to have in mind. John, seated on a nail keg in the corner, sat in silence vaguely listening, watching, submerging his thoughts in the soft drone of the other's voice, the low murmur of the radio, as the dark hands moved deftly from vise to anvil, glue pot to hammer, under the glare of the hanging lightbulb.

Across the room, where a dirty, cobwebbed window looked out into the gathering dusk, a large black blowfly hummed urgently against the pane.

It had happened too quickly, far too quickly, all this. Two days before, just returned to the home ranch after lambing, he had been thinking of nothing more than returning to the mountains—their mountains, above Logan, where he and the others had spent the last seven summers with the sheep. Then Harignordoquy had paid his visit, saying that he wanted to help out a friend and it would be a good opportunity and all that—and here he was. Here he was. No, it was too soon, far too soon to try to make any sense of it. For now he wanted nothing more than to sit here, on this keg of nails, and allow the drone, the murmur, the hum to surround and warm him, feeding a deep inner silence.

"Well, if it isn't the little princess!"

Vaguely startled, John looked up at the big man's face, which had flowered once more into that brilliant smile of greeting. This time, however, the eyes and voice were directed past him, toward someone standing in the doorway. Touching the head of the dog, who now lay at his feet, John turned slowly about. Standing on the threshold, her shadow cast backward on the barn floor like a felt cutout, was a small blonde girl of six or seven with very large slate-blue eyes. Her hair was somewhat disheveled, and in her right arm she carried a worn, buff-colored, one-eyed bear.

"How's my helper today?"

The little visitor, whose gaze had gone directly to the dog, now smiled vaguely in Booker's direction.

"Nice," she said. The great blue eyes swung about and came to rest on John, whom they proceeded to scrutinize with great and unabashed curiosity before, at last satisfied, they returned their attention to the dog.

"Do you know who this is?"

The blonde head nodded no, then slowly raised itself to John's face, the eyes again regarding him with bold aplomb. John, at first returning the glance with a smile, was at last compelled to take refuge in an examination of the backs of his large hands.

"Well, it's John, that's who. He's come to take care of your daddy's sheep."

The little girl, unsmiling, again regarded John for a moment before she said, very solemnly: "Daddy don't have any sheep."

"But he's going to *get* some, missy, you know that. And when they get here . . . why, John here'll be waiting to take care of 'em."

All of this information having no visible effect on the little girl, Booker at last turned to John.

"And this is Deirdre. Miss Deirdre Kinsella, if you please."

John rose from the nail keg and, approaching the doorway, reached his right hand down to the girl. She looked down at the hand for a moment before, carefully shifting the bear to her left arm, she reached out to grasp two of the extended fingers in a cool, firm grip. Then, withdrawing, she shifted the bear back to her right arm and again, raised her eyes to the young herder's face.

"Are you going to help me out again today?" Booker said at last. "I need pl-enty of help here, missy, that's for sure."

At first it seemed she had not heard, so entranced was she by the newcomer and his dog—but then, after a long moment, the blonde head slowly turned, directing its cool blue gaze upward toward the workbench.

"I can't," she said, a stern note in her small voice. "Daddy wants to see you."

Booker Goodman looked quickly at his watch and, pursing his lips, tapped home the last rivet. "Well," he said slowly, "guess that means we'll have to put it off until tomorrow, don't it." Holding the harness up to the light, he looked gravely at it for a moment before crossing the room to hang it on a worn wooden peg on the far wall. When he turned, however, he was smiling.

"I guess you'll just have to settle for talking to John," he said. "I'll bet he can tell you plenty about all the little lambs we'll have." With a smooth, graceful stride the big man moved to the doorway and, reaching down as he passed to lay a large dark hand on the small bright head, disappeared into the shadows of the tackroom. There was the closing of a door, and then only silence.

"What's your bear's name?" John said at last.

The little girl, having now exchanged audacity for reserve, intently regarded the floor at her feet.

"Buff," she answered softly, still not raising her eyes.

"Buff. Like a buffalo?"

The blue eyes glanced up quickly, their expression a blend of puzzlement and scorn, then just as quickly looked away.

Silently John looked down on the silent golden head.

"He could use some fixing."

Again she looked up—but this time there was interest. Slowly, carefully, he bent down.

"This ear going to fall off," he said, reaching out to touch it with one long finger. "An' he can't see too well with jus' one eye."

Now, for the first time, a shy, curious smile crept over the little girl's face, where it remained until he added: "You oughtta tell your mama."

Suddenly, like a light switched off, the smile disappeared. Again she looked at the floor.

"Well how 'bout that old Indian? Bet he could fix your bear. Buff."

For a moment there was nothing. Then, in a muffled tone: "He don't know how."

"Don' know how, eh? Well, I bet that big guy, that Booker fellow, does. The way he fixes those harnesses and bridles."

"He don't know either."

"Don' know either. Well, I wonder who else 'round here might know. Must be somebody," he added, smiling.

Again there was silence, but slowly, slowly, the small head turned upward once more, the blue eyes, darkly grave now, coming to rest on his face.

"Now if it was a sheep or a dog, I might be able to do it myself. A bear, though. Don' know much about bears, 'cept I was chased by one once."

Unblinking and silent, she looked up at him. At last, after a long moment: "I'll bet you could, though. I'll bet *you* could."

"Well, maybe. If I tried real hard."

This time the smile was bright and warm—and all for him.

5

At the southeast corner of the house, beneath the windows of a small sitting room, lay a broad flat area, perhaps thirty feet square, surrounded by a low stone wall. Overgrown now, it still bore the vague tracery, paths and raised beds, of a garden—indeed, judging by the care with which all appeared to have been laid out, a fine and meticulously tended one. Now, however, the only reminder of that former glory was a unkempt patch of flowers, all of the meanest but most hardy sort, which grew bravely in one corner.

As for the rest, to call it a weed bed would have been far too generous. On one side, where a large portion of the stone wall, pried apart by the winter cold, lay collapsed in rubble, a patch of sage had begun to take vigorous hold, and in a far corner the familiar yellow-green of rabbitbrush could be seen among a scattering of less invasive volunteers. There could be little doubt that Nature, left to her own implacable devices, would require but a few more seasons to dismantle the wall entirely and reclaim this plot as her own.

Until quite recently—no more than a week, in fact, before the young sheepherder's arrival—there had been absolutely nothing to suggest that Nature's plan might meet with interference. Even Tabby Weepup, who apparently was responsible for the patch of coarse flowers in the corner, seemed oblivious to the remainder of the plot; it was simply a place to grow his few flowers, nothing more, and the notion of reclaiming the place as a proper garden would never have occurred to him. All this had changed, however, on that warm afternoon the preceding week when the child had discovered, in a remote corner of the barn, an old, half-deteriorated gardening magazine. Booker being absent, she had gone directly with it to her father—intruding unbidden into his gloomy study in a manner no one else would have dared—and a few minutes more had found them seated together in his big chair by the window, slowing turning the fragile pages one by one. The very next day the order had issued: dahlias and roses and chrysanthemums, just like those whose faded replicas still glowed from those pages, were to grow at Phoenix Ranch—as once before they had.

John, to be truthful, would have been hard-pressed to call this work at all. It was a long time since he had had his hands in the dirt, at least with a view to growing something out of it, and the change from his normal existence of sheep and dogs and Dutch ovens would have been refreshing even had there been no companionship at all. But companionship there was— not only in the person of Tabby Weepup, who spent most of his afternoons (for he still had the cooking and other household chores to do) leaning on the handle of his hoe, but also in the form of regular visits from others as well—including, of course, Deirdre, the newly repaired Buff tucked under one arm.

Booker Goodman, needless to say, was often there—the ultimate responsibility for this, as apparently for most other things, having settled on his ample shoulders—but the frequent visits of the other cowboys were more difficult to explain. And yet they came, and nearly every day—sometimes alone, sometimes two or three together, wandering over to stand in silence for a few minutes before, remembering some more pressing business, they turned without a word and walked away. And then there was Levi Mondragon, the shy, reclusive little Mexican who worked the hay; every day at precisely five o'clock his battered yellow pickup would appear around the corner of the corral and come to a stop beside his trailer, and every day at precisely five-fifteen he could be seen walking, alone as always, along the bank of the ditch to the garden wall where, always stopping behind it, he surveyed the day's progress with obvious interest.

Levi Mondragon, John came to learn, himself had a flower garden at his home in New Mexico, to which he regularly returned for the winter on the twentieth day of September every year.

"Then there are the apples," Levi Mondragon had told him one day, his hushed tone suggesting an important confidence. "The apples of Taos are the best in the world."

There was only one who never visited. Indeed it sometimes seemed that Kinsella, on whose order, after all, the project had been undertaken, went out of his way to avoid the place entirely. More than once the young sheepherder, kneeling among the emerging flowerbeds, had looked up to see the tall, stooped form moving toward him from the direction of the barn—only to turn aside at the last instant and disappear into the house. Nor were there any inquiries about progress—at least not directly from the master. It was Booker, always Booker, who made such inquiries, who himself approved or amended John's ideas, just as he brought what was needed to carry them out.

And yet John sensed nothing personal in all this—at least nothing having to do with him. Every day, as on that first day, they gathered in the long, sunny kitchen for the midday meal, and although the master did not always appear—and usually had very little to say even when he did—he often called John aside afterward. Always, however, it was about the sheep— when they were expected, what would be needed when they arrived, how long it would take to outfit the wagon when it came. Never, never a single word about what John was doing, how he was progressing. It was, or seemed to be, something about the garden itself—something which, as one day followed upon another, he decided he was not yet meant to understand.

For even then, during those few short weeks before the sheep reclaimed him, he had begun the process, the task of understanding—gathering up the first few of those threads which, woven together, might someday begin to reveal the true outlines of the tapestry into which he himself was now being added. He asked no questions, or very few, but he had learned well how to listen. The endless conversations in the bunkhouse, the soft, sometimes almost wistful inflections of Booker Goodman as he looked out over the reemerging garden, even the increasingly voluble remarks of the little girl—all these added to the mix from which, little by little, he began to draw out the threads, and then at last to weave.

But most of all it was simply Tabby—the ancient, loquacious Indian, yellow-white locks leaking out from beneath the crown of his ragged hat, darkly wrinkled cheeks gleaming like elephant hide in the sun, knotted hands cupped over the top of the hoe handle as, leaning heavily upon it, he droned on through the long afternoon, his soft, singsong voice emerging through barely moving lips like a wind among the trees. Every day he had come, emerging on the back porch precisely at one-thirty, stepping gingerly down the stairs to take up his hoe, making a few desultory prods at the earth with it before drawing himself upright, laying his hands atop the handle, and beginning to talk.

Every day, that is, but one: the day he had spoken to Nat Lindsay at breakfast.

"You'll bring my mule?" the old Indian had said, leaning over Nat's shoulder. It had seemed more reminder than request; only the form was a question.

"What, is it the first of the month already?"

Nodding gravely, Tabby had returned to the sink, where he remained scrubbing a pot until at last he saw the stocky, tow-headed form moving out toward the corrals. Only then had he stirred, taking a long knife and a large wicker basket from the pantry before descending to the garden, where John was already hard at work.

"You're early," John had said, but the old man had simply nodded as he passed, stopping only when he reached the ragged patch of flowers in the corner, which he had sternly forbidden John to touch. He had almost filled the basket when Nat appeared with the white mule, snubbing the reins short to a fencepost before he turned to go.

"There you are, old man. John can help you up."

And so he had, then watched as the fragile figure and his basket of flowers, the white mule ambling placidly beneath, disappeared around the corner of the barn and headed up the creek, not to return until after three o'clock, when, without a word, he climbed the porch and disappeared into the house.

Yes, it had been a pleasant time, those few weeks, a time of relaxation and learning all at once, but then at last the day had come, that final afternoon. Fresh-painted sheep wagon parked beside the barn, a thousand fresh-sheared yearlings bawling in the furthest corral, he had stood alone outside the renewed stone wall and looked out over the paths and low, fresh-seeded flower beds. It was a good beginning, he thought, and as the shadow of the big house slowly extended itself outward, settling once more over his handiwork like the wing of some great bird, a deep satisfaction settled over him as well.

Perhaps it was merely that—the feeling of accomplishment, of consummation—or perhaps it was something else as well that had caused him then, for the first time, to raise his eyes, moving them slowly upward over the soaring stone walls until just below the roofline, behind the panes of a small window, they encountered the pair of pale, tired blue eyes which, he was quite sure, had been there very often all the days before.

CHAPTER 2

To the people of the ranches across the valley—some of whose families had been here, living in those same dilapidated but seemingly indestructible dwellings huddled at the base of the western mountains since the middle of the last century—the advent of Cyril Kinsella had come as a blessing, a perplexity, and an everlasting entertainment. There was no one, down to the youngest toddler, who had not heard it discussed at one time or another, and there were some who, gathered about those venerable hearths, still looked upon it as the central drama of their lives—who when they spoke of it together, as remarkably many of them still did, adopted the unmistakable tone of intimacy and mutual understanding that marked them as members of the chorus.

Of his origins little was known, at least with any certainty. A faintly nasal accent marked him for an easterner—that much, at least, had been clear from the outset; some with sharper hearing went so far as to insist on Boston. In any case it seemed to be taken for granted that he had or had had some uncertain connection with the copper people in Creighton, the mining and mill town at the south end of the valley—an assumption that seemed to be borne out, to some degree at least, by certain subsequent events. There were even one or two who claimed, at least in the beginning, to see some resemblance to a certain New York lawyer, Kincaid by name, who Dan Blickendorf himself had sent out to do a bit of sharp business for him. That, however, had been in 1926—long ago even by the standards of these resourceful memorists—and in any case this theory had long since run aground on some rather hard and intractable facts.

It all amounted, in short, to little more than rank speculation. If plain, hard facts were to be the order of the day, well, frankly there were none—none, that is, beyond what had been too obvious for anyone to fail to see and understand. The first of these—in time if not in significance—was simply that one bright morning in the fall of 1928, he, Kinsella, had appeared on the landscape of the old Wilkerson property with a wagon and a pair of mules, and before any appreciable portion of the farflung neighborhood (if such it was: six families, twenty-eight souls in all, spread unevenly over the face of five hundred square miles) was properly apprised of his presence had begun to raise a passable cedar-post cabin on the creekbank.

No one really questioned his right to be there. It had been only a matter of time, they knew, before someone with enough ready cash showed up to buy that property out of the old Indian fighter's estate—and now, with the new national highway coming and due to cut right through the northwest corner of it, they had come to expect it day by day. The surprising thing, though, was that there should have been a cabin—at least one as substantial as this was getting to be. A fence crew they had fully expected—followed in short order by a few thousand head of cattle owned by some Creighton mining baron or San Francisco financier. (No lesser personage could have afforded it, that much was clear—or had quickly become clear when several of them, observing a decent interval after Uncle Billy's funeral, had made inquiry of his Denver daughter, who promptly advised them that all sixty-one sections, or almost forty thousand acres of it, were indeed for sale, but she was not going to part with an acre short of that.)

Perhaps, then, this cabin was for a kind of caretaker or foreman—so the thinking had begun, and had continued, until the man made his first trip for supplies.

Wilson, the laconic proprietor of the Chokecherry Creek store, had made it clear enough for anyone to understand: "Said his name's Kinsella and it's his and he's aiming to live there. Didn't have much else to say—unless you want to count when I asked him where he's from. 'Out east,' he says real soft, leastways them were his words. What he meant was that it's none of my damn business. Or yours either, I reckon."

So it was that when the first snow flew—and the newcomer, having topped off his creekside cabin the week before, had departed with his mules and wagon for the winter—so it was that the mills of conjecture, which ground exceeding fine around those winter fires, were straightaway set in motion. For the men the matter was of some practical concern. They had, after all, become accustomed to treating the Wilkerson property as open range. Uncle Billy had once been a stickler about such things— to the point of winging off a shot now and then—but it was nearly ten years now since he had gone to stay with the Denver daughter, and things had taken their natural course. All the old fences were down, their stock ranged over it freely, and to put it plain they had come to rely on it just a bit. Would this man Kinsella, they wondered, be willing to take on a few ground leases at a reasonable price—or would it be, as it had been with Uncle Billy during his sterner years . . . none of their damn business? They muttered and they worried. They hoped for the best.

There were others, however, whose winter speculations ran along somewhat different lines—women and children, these.

To the wives and elder daughters one thing could not have been clearer: that a man who could buy the Wilkerson property, all sixty-one sections of it, was not a man who would long abide a cedar-pole cabin. Such a man—and none of them had really seen him, you understand, they simply judged by what they had heard—such a man would build a proper house. And a proper house, the kind of house he would build, would surely be one requiring the presence of . . . a suitable wife. Not that any of them (the daughters) might have presumed to imagine themselves in that office (besides, they had not seen him, only heard)—not to suppose that at all, only that it was more than enough to while away the winter hours, something to get them from the morning milking to the evening's chores and beyond, far beyond.

They could see her clear enough, thick golden hair swept back dramatically over delicate ivory ears—or better yet cut short, in one of those perky styles which announced that its wearer was not to be trifled with, surely not to be told to carry out the slops or silence the newest baby. Patiently she waited, abided, this chosen woman, in Salt Lake or Denver or San Francisco, patiently, constantly rereading his many letters for news to feed her dreams—news of the house, the plans, the hoped-for schedule which soon, so soon, would see her packing, planning, ordering, choosing whatever her heart desired. And beyond this, a woman of refinement and breeding, surely, one who could, without seeming at all haughty or aloof, make it her affair to show them, instruct them, guide them in the way a woman of the 1920s ought to think and act and feel. Yes, that was what they needed in this valley. Yes, *she* was what they needed.

And the children? Well, they simply wondered if there would be other children.

And so it was that when spring came to melt the land (the spring of 1929 this would be) there had been great and mounting anticipation in every heart, twenty-nine in all (a fine, dark-eyed boy having been born to the Murchisons, just north of Paiute Creek, on New Year's Day)—and when a sharp-eyed but truant

schoolboy at last espied the bright new Model A, the first that
he or any other boy of the neighborhood had ever seen, proceeding at a sensible pace up the winter-rutted road from Creighton
and, after coming to a full stop in the middle of the deserted
roadway, turning smartly to the right between the cedar gate-
posts that had been the cabin builder's last project before his
autumn departure, there had been many to question him on his
report. No, the boy assured them, no there were no others; the
man had come alone, alone in that marvelous blue automobile.
Standing tiptoe in his stirrups, he had seen it draw to a stop
beside the cabin—and that was all.

And yet not quite all, for a few days later there had come
a second report, this by a rival scholar sent home on account
of toothache: the mule-drawn wagon had returned, but this
time bearing three dour-faced Goshute Indians, an assortment
of tools, a pair of strange-looking and (to this boy at least) un-
identifiable machines, and at the reins a towering, yellow-haired
Swede.

They straightaway set to work. About a half mile east of the
cabin, above what was known throughout the neighborhood as
the "first" spring, lay a jumbled slide of rosy-red porous stones,
and it was here that the strange implements were unloaded.
While the Swede and his Indians set about dressing the stones,
Kinsella himself remained below, where with sextant, shovel,
ax, stakes, and twine he laid out an outline on the sagebrush-
choked flat south of the cabin. Then, abruptly, he was gone
again—he and the bright blue Model A. The Swede and his
Indians, however, remained, and soon a neat pile of dressed
stones had begun to rise beside the staked outline in the brush,
two of the Indians bringing them down on a wide cedar sledge
with the mules. A few more days and, quite miraculously, two
more Indians had appeared—five in all now, their tents pitched
out along the creek just below the cabin. And while these, the
newcomers, set about clearing and trenching the site, the bringing of the stones went on—until one afternoon these last two

had gone up to the quarry as well. The following day, at an hour past dawn, the towering Swede was at work below, he and a single helper, and stone by stone the structure began to raise itself above the sage-strewn landscape.

It was only a few days later when another outfit arrived, a rough bunch from nobody knew quite where, who, setting up a little tent city down by the main road, vigorously turned their teams and wagons and scrapers, not to mention their collective attention, to the task of making something better of that track out through the sagebrush, which up to then had served as the driveway.

All that spring and summer the work went on—stone dressers above, masons below, road builders pressing steadily up the rise and over—until late in the summer the state highway crews moving up from the south had passed through on their way to Wendover, leaving behind them a wide gravel track all the way to Creighton. And soon—so soon indeed that some were heard to wonder whether such public improvements might have been scheduled for Kinsella's personal convenience—there had occurred the first of what in time was to become a seemingly endless if not positively monotonous succession of similar events: the arrival down that elegant roadway—and subsequent disappearance up what was already coming to be called the lane—of yet another wagon or even from time to time a motor truck bearing not only mortar and cement but huge planks and beams and barrels of nails and nuts and bolts and bundles of dull blue slate.

Some of these vehicles, it was said, had come not simply from Creighton but much further, across the old Pony Express route through Dalley and Lost Creek and Claymore, all the way from Salt Lake—while others carried burdens not even the last-named metropolis could supply, bringing them direct from the railroad siding at Chokecherry Creek, to which they had been expedited from distant venues too exotic to relate. In any case, one August evening not one but three vagrant boys were able to report with pride on their attendance at a signal event: the second-story beams, raised by means of a mule-powered hoist, were settled into place. Sad to say, neither these boys nor any others were there to witness when, precisely two months later, the third-story beams did the same—for they, reluctant scholars, had once again departed to their books.

Two weeks more and the first snow flew; loading into their now-empty wagon, the Swede once more at the reins, the builders had rolled away, the broad new road to Creighton stretching out before them like a smooth gravel carpet.

Another weary winter, another yawning space of time; the engines of conjecture, having idled through the long summer, began once more to grind in earnest. It was indeed to be a house, that rosy shell looming up on the snow-covered horizon—there could no longer be any real doubt of that. But what kind of house was this? Not the house of a peer among peers, the men reasoned. Hardly the house of one with any call to be neighborly. The women, burdened as they were with hopeful visions, were even more perplexed. Clearly, they murmured, this was to be more than the proper house they had had in mind. This was grandeur, even ostentation. The woman who would come, be brought here, to live in this great mansion, would such a woman bring with her the open and generous heart they so badly needed? The more they looked at the soaring shape across the valley, the less they were inclined to think so. And as for teaching them, as for showing—the lady would very likely wish to have nothing to do with them at all. Besides, they reasoned, the ways of the gentry were not the ways they longed to know. There was nothing left then but to despise her—and thus anticipate her view of them.

Only the children took the broader view: any child would be better than none.

Again spring came, the spring of 1930, and again he too came . . . alone. The blue Model A, parked beside the cabin, gleamed like a jewel against the smoky green of sage as for two days he tramped about, always returning early in the evening to stand once more within those soaring walls and look up at the sky. Then, on the morning of the third day, the wagon was there as well—and again the work began. This time, however, the cherished automobile did not depart (although it did disappear—beneath a canvas tarpaulin), and when the parade of wagons and trucks resumed, bearing their various burdens up the now-completed lane, it was Kinsella himself who met them, withdrawing from his pocket a small pair of gold-rimmed spectacles through which he meticulously examined the batch of invoices in his hand.

This, however, the boys affirmed, was not all that he did; no, far from it, very far indeed. Mounting the high scaffolds with the fearless Swede, he straightaway took to working there alongside him, laying the stones at almost the selfsame pace. He had a strange kind of energy, did Kinsella, which made things very different now that he was about. On warmer days he would take off his shirt, the white of his skin in strident contrast with the coal black of his hair, and when it came to climbing out on a rafter to perform some dangerous operation, three full stories high in the azure sky, why Kinsella himself was the man for the job!

Soon there was noticed what appeared to be a marked tendency on the part of certain boys of the neighborhood to walk slightly pigeon-toed, with the weight forward on the ball of the foot. This was the way that Cyril Kinsella himself walked.

In late August they began on the roof. The five Indians had departed now, taking the stonecutting equipment with them in the wagon, and the Swede and Kinsella worked alone, laying the dull blue slate in even rows from the eaves, over the gables, and up to the high peak. Then at last that too was done, and they turned to the windows and doors, leaving until last the great oaken front door, which, rumor had it, had come all the way from Michigan.

Recently, the boys noticed, the burdens coming up the lane

had begun to change. Still there were the barrels of nails, still the stacks of lumber—but where before it had been massive beams and planks (once, they remembered, brought by an actual logging team, thirty-two mules, with a flagman in the lead), now it was fine redwood siding (all the way from California, it was said), milled trim in all shapes and sizes, doors and banisters and window sashes and cabinets. For they had begun inside now, working from dawn to dark at a feverish pace—still just the two of them, Kinsella and the Swede.

Then one day up rumbled an enormous truck, and inside it, unloaded into the sagebrush as if they had been sacks of wheat, fine white porcelain sinks and toilets and, yes, bathtubs, *three* of them; and last of all, carried inside in great iron pieces, an enormous woodstove. Yes, that indeed had been a banner day, most particularly for the two boys who happened to be present— for Kinsella himself had spoken to them and, what was more, asked them to carry one of the stove pieces inside and, what was meant to be even more but somehow was not, gave each of them a shiny new Indian head nickel.

It was shortly after this important day, when the children were all safely in their schools and the first bite of fall had been felt in the air, that three of the men of the neighborhood, sharing a top rail at the Murray stockyards, reached an important, even momentous decision. The hour had come, the moment was propitious, the iron was hot: a solemn delegation took shape. Cementing their resolve in the nearby saloon, they had proceeded together to the place and, if their report could be credited, "confronted" the grave Kinsella outside his oaken front door.

This fact established, however, the remainder of their report had not been nearly so martial in tone. A pleasant enough fellow, they said; quite amiable, in fact, "once you got to know him." And no, he had no immediate plans to use the whole of his range and would be quite willing to entertain the notion of leasing some it, the lower portions at least, when he got settled

in. In the meantime, he had said—"for next year at least"—
they were welcome to continue using it as they had.

It was accounted, in short, an untarnished triumph—and so
it had remained for the space of several minutes, until cross-
examination commenced. No, they had not thought to inquire
about his family or if he had any—about just who was going to
be filling those three claw-footed bathtubs. "It was no time to
get personal, Alice."

For this unfortunate default the men paid dearly, in various
ways, subtle and cunning, for several weeks thereafter.

Again the snow flew, piling in great dimpled drifts up to the
new-painted windowsills. This time, however, there was to be
no hasty departure; Kinsella and the Swede, sharing the cabin
by the creek, continued their labors into the winter. Sometimes
late at night a soft glow could be seen in one of the upper
windows, suggesting that even darkness had failed to still their
hammers. Then, one mid-January morning, the blue Model A
was seen to emerge from its canvas cocoon and, after a bit of
coaxing, ground down to the snow-strewn highway and set off
in the direction of Creighton. They, both of them, were gone.

Spring was well under way, the willows beside the springs
beginning to redden with new buds, when at last, long last, the
first sign of their return appeared. The blue Model A it was not,
however; it was only the wagon, the very same wagon—and in it
the very same Swede and three Goshutes, who straightaway set
to work on the barn. Again the parade commenced, once more
bringing lumber, heaps of it, and great casks of nails.

The boys were disconsolate. Barns they had seen; barns they
had even worked on themselves, although never one quite so
large as this. It was not, in short, something that fired their
imaginations. Kinsella, they muttered to one another, Kinsella
would never come for this.

They had not yet learned, these backward boys, to expect
the unexpected. Their vigilance declined to a dangerous and
demoralizing level. They began to play baseball.

And so it was really little more than happenstance, the merest fluke of coincidence, that brought his arrival to their notice at all—at least on the mid-June Saturday (this would be 1931 now) that it occurred. As it happened, however, the scion of a nearby ranch, plodding homeward from another dispirited contest astride his somnambulant horse, had been commissioned by his mother to pick up a certain canning kettle from her sister— this requiring the detour of a mile or so to his aunt's house in the hills. Surely it had not been curiosity about the progress of a mere barn that had caused him, upon mounting that little rise, to cast that lazy glance across the valley; surely it had been something more akin to nostalgia, cousin to vague longing. In any case he had at first doubted the report of his eyes: that tiny patch of brightest blue just then coming to rest . . .

The unfortunate horse, rudely awakened, found its legs and began to run.

He had indeed returned, and with him the parade. Now, however, it was no longer open wagons, open trucks, but covered vans, high and square and filled with inconceivable riches. There were elegant chairs and couches, all covered in dark blue velvet—or what the boys took for such, their only acquaintance with that fabric having been through certain forbidden novels which, passed hand to hand, were customarily kept hidden in the granary. There were long, paper-covered cylinders, thick as nail casks, which could only have contained rugs—the splendor of which was necessarily left to the imagination. There were tables and desks of dark polished wood, so bright in the sun that they seemed cut from flint. There were marvelous beds, one a four-poster with legs like telegraph poles. There were chests of drawers with marble tops, vanity dressers with tall, gleaming mirrors, cedar chests banded with copper . . . and box after box, crate after crate, with stern admonitory legends stenciled on their sides.

It was indeed a treasure-house, a mine of opulence. It was as if the great stone structure were being fitted out not as a dwelling place at all but as a hotel, a mansion of dalliance. And yet how, why, should such an establishment be here, alone in this endless plain of sagebrush? For this there were no answers, only a great and growing perplexity about the whole affair—a perplexity that was thought to have suffered its ultimate provocation when one day there arrived in a tall crate an enormous grandfather clock with a face the color of the sun. Was thought to, it bears repeating, for the very next day, late in the afternoon, the wonderstruck boys saw emerge from the van, then from its massive crate . . . an actual grand piano!

Yes, they were sure. No, they were not mistaken. Well, perhaps it was to be a dance hall, then. But a dance hall with a barn?

Then, as mysteriously as he had come, the grave Kinsella had dropped from sight once more, the famous blue automobile disappearing as if dissolved by the moon. For a few days the furniture kept coming—the Swede, it was said, had a map to show where it went—and then, very suddenly, it too ceased, all swallowed up by those rosy stone walls. Then, again, there was only the barn. The doldrums descended once more.

It was almost a month later, toward the end of July, that there came to pass an event which, it was thought, would at last lay to rest the more outlandish of those tremors of speculation that by then had begun to proliferate throughout the countryside.

It was again young Bobby Fisk, the boy of the somnambulant horse, who saw it, witnessed it from a distance that brooked no quibbling. He had wearied of the national sport a bit early that day and, leaving two or three others at "the diamond"— as they generously referred to the dreary patch of ground out in the sagebrush where they gathered—had set out along the edge of the new highway in the hope of catching a glimpse of a certain Wanda Murchison, who often passed that way in her father's gig when she went, as often she did, to visit a sick aunt in Chokecherry Creek. Whether she actually passed that day or not, however, was never known for certain, for just as her secret admirer, feeling the first weary pangs of discouragement, had been about to turn aside on a more direct route to his home, he had spied on the southern horizon, proceeding over a distant rise in the roadway, the one vehicle that had the power to banish any lingering thoughts of the Murchison one-horse shay.

It was indeed, unmistakably, the fabulous blue Model A, the eagerly anticipated harbinger-conveyance. Drawing his own conveyance to a twitching stop, the boy had remained in awed silence as it approached, as it passed, as it proceeded merrily down the quarter mile remaining and, after coming to a full stop as always on the deserted roadway, turned up the lane and soon was lost from sight.

Afterward, in the face of a withering cross-examination, Bobby Fisk had stood his ground. Yes, he was sure not only that it was Kinsella (no one, really, was about to challenge that), not only that he had not been alone (he wasn't blind, was he?), not only that it had been a woman (yes, he had repeated endlessly, yes, young and slim and beautiful, with cool green eyes and a cloud of chestnut hair, yes), not only all that but yes, colored streamers too, and tin cans and old shoes tied to the bumper.

At last, no chink appearing in the boy's perceptive armor, his testimony was accepted—whereupon consternation once more had its day. After all, they were not so benighted as they might seem; they, all of them, read the *Creighton Transcript* every week (the very Wednesday it came out, most of them) and certainly would have seen any announcement. Even if the wedding had taken place elsewhere, surely . . . Kinsella, after all, did live here, and in that sense, at least, was one of them. It was not proper. It was not right. It was upsetting. It was . . . a scandal.

Mercifully, this state of agitation did not long endure—the next day but one being Wednesday. There it was, not on the front page, to be sure, not even at the top of the page where such things normally were found, but nevertheless quite respectably if modestly placed, about halfway down the right-hand column. Which, all things considered, was no more than appropriate—

for it was not really the usual wedding report at all but a sort of formal notice, now more than three weeks after the fact. "In Guadalajara, State of Jalisco, Mexico," it said, "the former Abigail Reston, of a distinguished San Francisco family formerly resident in this city . . ." Still, some objected, one might have expected a larger article, especially considering just which "distinguished family" was involved; and certainly, certainly there should have been some mention of their future home. "For all it says here," Gladys Fisk was heard to bitterly observe, "they might as well be living in Guadalajara, State of Jalisco, Mexico." And as for the groom—"Mr. Cyril Kinsella, late of Salt Lake City," and not a word more.

Smoothing their ruffled feathers, however, the ladies of the neighborhood convened to plan their visit. It had never been their intention, of course, to "go rushing in on the young folks," surely not "before they'd had a chance to settle in." A week, they agreed, would be too little, but two weeks seemed altogether too much. Ten days, then. Ten days. They would all go together in a body, so as to allow their acceptance or rejection to be felt as a common benefit or burden, as the case might be. There were some things, they agreed, that one simply had to carry through on, that was all. These things decided, they had washed out the teacups and departed their separate ways.

For all its spirit, all its pluck, however, it was, sad to say, a resolution not fated to be tested, for the next day but one the news arrived—and all was set to naught. Abigail, the dread and fabled Abigail, had flown away in the night . . . and was gone, never to return.

It was too much, altogether too much to take in all at once. Perhaps, some ventured, it was simply the prospect of such loneliness, such isolation. A mine superintendent's daughter, let alone one of Mark Reston's, accustomed since birth to a life of elegance and gaiety and excitement . . . but why then had she consented, why come out here at all? As for that other circumstance—that the Swede, quite mysteriously, had disappeared as well, although the barn and corrals were still not quite completed—only the suspicious, indeed the low-minded, would seek to draw any connection. It was a perfect conundrum—and at last they decided that they would never know the answer. Only one thing was clear: she was gone—and the grave Cyril Kinsella, late of Salt Lake City, had been left in complete and utter charge of a luxuriously furnished three-story stone mansion, sixty-one square miles of Nevada rangeland, and three Goshute Indians.

Inside of a week the Indians too were gone . . . and Cyril Kinsella was alone.

They all knew who Mark Reston was—or had been.

Indeed, it would have been difficult in those days for anyone *not* to know, at least anyone who paid the slightest bit of attention to the news. From the first day he arrived in Creighton—late in 1924 that would have been—until the day he departed three years later, hardly a single edition of the weekly paper had failed to have some story or other about him and his doings. Often there had been pictures too—at the site of the proposed mill, with the surveying party along the railroad right-of-way, cutting the ribbon at the new library—so that to most of them he was not only a name but a face as well.

Not that it was exactly what you would call a handsome face, not with that shiny bald pate and hawkish glance, but it was a face that got your attention all the same. There was a certain energy and confidence in it, a calm intelligence that could inspire others to deeds beyond themselves.

He had come on the scene like a whirlwind, dropping out of nowhere, it seemed, to buy up all the available copper claims in the canyon west of Creighton, then combining them in the hands of a new company, Nevada Copper as it was called. Only later was it learned that not only he but his father before him (a well-known Comstock engineer, as it turned out) had been interested in the area for some time, that he had secretly commissioned a firm of consulting engineers to report on it the year before—and that his abrupt appearance was simply the final step in a carefully executed plan.

In any case, things had gone quickly at first. The buying of water rights, the announcement of plans for the mill and smelter, the letting of contracts on the railroad—all these had taken place within a year of his arrival. Soon Mark Reston was spoken of as one to be reckoned with in the county, if not in the entire western mining community.

What was more, he had turned out to be a real asset to the town. His was an old San Francisco family, and the principal offices of the family engineering firm remained there. No one would have been particularly surprised to learn that he would be little more than a visitor here, staying only as much as the business demanded. From the beginning, however, he had let it be known that his lot was thrown in with Nevada Copper— and with Creighton. The whole family—wife, two girls, three servants—arrived from San Francisco, setting up at first in a plain little brick house behind the school, then moving to the principal banker's former residence while construction began on something more permanent. The girls, eighteen and sixteen then, even attended the local high school briefly—before setting out for their fancy colleges in the East—while Mrs. Reston (or Juanita as she insisted on being called, having descended from an old and apparently thoroughly democratic Texas cattle family) eagerly set to work on the local Miner's Aid Society. As for Reston himself, he was soon elected warden of the new Episcopal church, and a post on the school board came not long after. It had seemed, in short, a true commitment to the life of the community.

As Reston himself then liked to express it, his sole aim was to "share in the awakening of the jewel city of the West."

Afterward, when that dream had slipped through his fingers and he and his, in vast confusion and disarray, had retreated to their safe San Francisco harbor; afterward, when all that could have been said and done was said and done and the new people were firmly, finally in control; afterward, afterward, there were more than a few who wondered if there was really any way it— or at least the business part of it—could have turned out otherwise. The ore deposit was indeed as huge as predicted, but it would remain in the ground unless there was money to bring it out, mill it, transport it to the main line, and all the rest. Four million, Reston thought, would be enough, but where was Nevada Copper to find that kind of cash? The stock market was grudging, and the few private investors who at first showed interest soon cooled when faced with the facts. It was, after all, only 2 percent ore, no matter how much there was of it. There was money to be made, of course, but only by the patient, the long-suffering, the strong . . .

And so indeed it may have been inevitable from the first— that one cold New York winter day, his prospects few and dwindling, he should have found himself on that creaky elevator, going up. "A. H. Blickendorf & Sons," the door announced; he removed his galoshes and stepped inside.

And yes, perhaps he should have known better, looked further, hoped harder. But the fact was he was tired. And there seemed no other choice.

It had, in fact, been rather like a play—well rehearsed, frequently performed. First, a week after he had laid the reports before them, came the opening, cautious and circumspect, the pleas of penury ("Looks good, Mark, but we've just got too many irons in the fire right now, way too many to do justice to something like this; for the present, suppose we just take on some of your bonds, enough to help you get the railroad started. Then perhaps later, as things go along . . ."). And yet already the rest was under way—the discreet private inquiries and acquisitions, the forming of a new company to hold the properties, the secret, methodical acquisition of stock in Nevada Copper. Then, when all was in readiness, a word in the right place and the news was out: "It's the Blickendorfs behind that new Creighton Consolidated outfit! And if it's good enough for them . . ." Yes, until only the denouement remained.

There were still one or two in the valley who remembered, or at least claimed to remember, the day he had arrived—the young New York lawyer they called Kincaid. It would soon be twenty-eight years ago now, that autumn of 1926, but some things, these confident retrospectors asserted, stay with you forever. One of these things, apparently, was the look of this Kincaid's face as he stood on the new railroad platform—the strange, weary smile that settled over his features as, elegant tooled-leather briefcase in hand, he surveyed the skyline, if such it could be called, of East Creighton, Nevada (the railroad still lacking a mile or two of reaching the city itself). He had remained there for several minutes, the same smile imprinted on his face, until at last the small party sent to meet him, including Reston himself (who was to be his host, the big new house having been finished just that summer), had straggled up the platform.

It was then, if these reports can be credited, that a very curious thing occurred. As the little party approached, the courtly Reston in the lead, this fellow Kincaid had removed his well-brushed bowler hat, revealing a head of jet-black hair, and, carefully lowering his tooled-leather briefcase to the ground, sailed that well-brushed bowler hat over the roof of the new station and into the train yard beyond. Then, greeting the astonished welcoming party as if nothing at all had happened, he had accompanied them bareheaded down the platform to the waiting car, where he was met by a small boy who had retrieved his hat.

In any case he had made quite an impression, this Kincaid—and not only in matters of business and finance. More than a few pretty heads were turned by that tall, graceful figure, more than a few hearts pierced by that penetrating ice-blue gaze. The local copper people, apparently considering their guest to warrant festivity, had even hosted a fancy dress ball at the high school (the new hotel not being finished quite yet), and tales of

that young man's dancing—especially with his lively and per-
sonable hostess—continued to echo about the countryside long
after he had packed his elegant tooled-leather briefcase for the
last time, settled his well-brushed bowler hat, this time quite
securely, on his handsome, well-shaped head, and, turning to
bestow one last smile on the little bon voyage party gathered on
the platform, stepped aboard the train which then bore him,
some said forever, away.

And yes, there were even some who remembered, or claimed
to remember, that last smile—although again their vantage
point at the crucial moment was never made wholly clear. The
librarian Maud Sharpley, for example, who apparently had been
among those skewered by that disarming gaze, remained ada-
mant ever after in her claim that it had been quite different,
this smile—different from all of those that had come before.
"There was a kind of wistfulness about it," she was often heard
to say, "as though some part of him, some irreplaceable segment
of his heart" (Maud always did have a certain way of expressing
herself) "had been left behind there on the platform as, very
slowly, the train moved away and was at last swallowed up in
the distance."

The more likely explanation for that smile, however, if there
was anything different about it at all, just might have been a
trace of embarrassment, or perhaps even just a tinge of guilt.
For among those on the platform had been Mark Reston, who,
though his wife was unfortunately indisposed, had brought
along their two daughters, both lately returned from their first
trip to Europe. And the Mark Reston who then stood on the
platform was not the same man who, just six days earlier, had
watched with the astonished others as that elegant bowler hat
arched gracefully up over the roof of the new railroad station
and disappeared into the train yard beyond.

There really had been little to it—the groundwork had been
laid so well. The board of Nevada Copper were reasonable, if
needy, men, and Reston was only one of seven. Nevada Copper

needed money, and that was one thing that Creighton Consolidated, its stock now soaring, had in great abundance. What could be more reasonable, more sane, than a merger of the two? As for the matter of real value—the inconvenient fact that the new company's mineral claims were marginal to say the least, amounting to little more than what Reston had passed over and rejected—well, that was an unfortunate reality to be sure. Nevada Copper's shareholders might have some understandable reluctance to share the pie, but at least there would be a pie . . .

"They have us where they want us, Mark. A bitter pill, but let's swallow hard and be done with it."

In the goodly crowd of dignitaries who gathered below the Creighton courthouse on that Saturday morning five weeks later, their faces already bright with sunshine and libation as they looked up at the two confronting flag-draped locomotives and listened to the playing of the brass band, there were relatively few who knew that the tall, bald, smiling man who took the hammer and then, after a few well-chosen words, ceremoniously drove home the final and appropriately copper spike, was there and then performing his last official act. And as the events of that memorable day proceeded, the dignitaries joined now by a swelling crowd of celebrants drawn from all the countryside for a hundred miles around—the courthouse square transformed into a great and glorious picnic ground, where whole beeves turned glumly on their spits as drink and speeches flowed with equal fervor on into the evening, until and even after, in the still-unfinished hotel, the dancing had begun—yes, as all this unfolded, there were fewer still who might have thought that the smiling recipient of so many grateful toasts, one glowing daughter on each arm, held the smallest note of sadness in his heart. And so it was that when Sunday morning came, the sun rising all too early over the sleeping, stupefied town, there were none at all to notice as the long, black Packard, its four somber-faced occupants looking straight before them, made its smooth, sure way out of town.

Over the course of the next few years there were a few articles about them in the paper. Nothing like what had been there before, of course, but at least something to show that the town still cared—for in spite of all that had happened, all that had failed to happen, still the town remained grateful for all they had done. As for Reston himself, he had returned to the family engineering firm in San Francisco, where his life at first resumed in much the same fashion as before. Then, however, a month or so after their departure from Creighton, his dear Juanita had suddenly and rather mysteriously died, leaving him quite alone when the girls later went their own ways—Marcella, the younger, to a highly advantageous marriage in Cleveland, and Abigail—until just recently, of course—to a prominent New York publishing firm. The current reports, it was said, suggested that his health was failing; some even mentioned a stroke of some kind. All of which evoked widespread feelings of sympathy among the townspeople, and not a few of them were known to have sent letters of encouragement and condolence.

As for the lawyer Kincaid, it was difficult to say just what had become of him. He seemed to be a man who gathered rumors about him—until at last one came to wonder whether there was really any man at all beneath the wrapping. One week it seemed that he had become the talk of Denver, compromising socialites as he engineered bank takeovers—but the following week (after the next trucker or traveling salesman had had his say) all this was declared a big mistake, for Kincaid had all the while been in Panama, where he was either in the hospital recovering from a gunshot wound or preparing to defend some labor agitators at trial, or both. Soon it seemed that the townsfolk were willing to believe anything about him, absolutely anything at all—until at last some who claimed to be in a position to know were even heard to maintain that he had never really left at all, being actually one and the same as a certain darkly bearded Mr. Black, who, a month or so after the Restons' departure, had showed up as the resident manager of the Daisy, a notorious Runcietown crib, before eight months later dropping completely and permanently from sight. With this outlandish claim, however, the rumors appeared to have ceased—even the most imaginative sensing that they might have gone too far. A year passed, and then another, and talk of the lawyer Kincaid was heard no more.

No more, that is, until those bizarre events of the summer of 1931 in the shadow of Molly Peak—and then it amounted to little more than a passing mention of the name. For if there were a hundred things that the strange doings at Phoenix Ranch had made less clear, there was one at least which no one, not even somebody as pigheaded as old Ira Murchison, who had punched cattle for Uncle Billy himself, could any longer afford to dispute.

"So maybe we'll have some rest now from your harebrained Kincaid theories—unless, of course, you want to tell us that the man who stole Mark Reston's mining company just married his prettiest daughter."

"Just keep your mind on the dishes, Alice. I'll be out doing the chores."

He was not expected to stay long.

What indeed, the neighbors reasoned, remained to hold him now that his plan—that audacious, magnificent design—had come to such a sorry end? Surely not the land, which even in the best of times was good for little more than a few resourceful cattle. Even supposing that had been his intention in the beginning, it was hardly likely that he would have the heart for it now. Besides, the men confided, he didn't have the look of a real stockman anyway.

But what of the house? the women asked. What was to become of that awesome monument, that soaring testimony to his love, so cruelly betrayed? What of it indeed? the men replied, ever the realists. Now, today, tomorrow, and ever afterward it would stand there as a mute reminder of his folly. He would soon be no more than a memory here, returned to the life that made him. And that enormous rosy tower out on the sage flat would stand empty and forlorn until the winter winds, hard about their remorseless errands, had slowly dismantled it, stone by stone, and returned it once more to the porous earth whence it had sprung.

Thus the sober, level-headed men. Their ever-attentive wives and daughters, however, were only half convinced. To be sure it was a shame, they said among themselves—not to mention a delicious scandal, "right here in our valley." Just the notion was enough to make your heart stop: that he should have loved her that much, enough to build her such a monument, a temple to house her sacred presence, and then be betrayed, rejected in favor of, of . . . of a common carpenter! (This theory, it must be understood, had in spite of its common, even low, origins quickly taken root and flourished, soon overcoming all less hardy competition.) And yet, and yet, could it really be so final, so irreversible as all that? A soul as grand and capacious as his, would it not also have room for compassion? Surely, then, when she had recognized the folly of her actions, as most certainly she would . . . surely when she came to him, chastened by the knowledge of her error, and humbly sought forgiveness . . . oh surely, surely she would find it, and then, then . . .

And even if not, even if no, then surely there were other pebbles, surely for such a man as that, on the beach. And so perhaps there might be another; perhaps indeed another would be far better—not only for him but for them as well. Another who, though of lesser plumage, might have a kinder and more generous heart. Surely that was not too much to hope.

All nonsense, the men replied, when they became aware of this vain chatter. A proud man such as that, they pointed out, would neither accept back damaged goods nor trifle with substitutes. ("No more than would I," some of the more circumspect were seen to add with a nod.) No, the ultimate result was a foregone conclusion: He would be gone, departed, disappeared long before the first snowflake flew. Any day now, they intoned, any day the parade would begin once more—but this time in reverse, the vans and wagons and trucks coming empty and going away full, with every stick and stitch of it down to the bare walls.

"Mark my words," the men concluded gravely, "any day now, you'll see."

They were still speaking in this fashion when, one day toward the end of August, the three Goshutes reappeared and began to put in wood for the winter. All hypotheses were abruptly placed in suspense—a state in which they yet remained when, one week later, the Swede and his stone-laying apprentice arrived and promptly resumed work on the barn. At this point all theoreticians, man and dame, retired in disarray from the field.

And so he stayed—stayed 'til the snow flew and Swede and Indians departed, having not only finished the barn and corrals and a bunkhouse to boot but planted a neat row of poplars on the north side along the ditch; stayed all through the winter, he alone in that great lonely house with his silent piano and velvet settees; stayed into the spring when, as soon as the sun had thawed the ground, the Indians again appeared and set to work on the fences—a task which as it turned out was to occupy them for two years to come; stayed until, a few sections enclosed, the first of the cattle began to arrive . . .

Indeed he stayed, did Cyril Kinsella, and for the next sixteen years he stayed alone—unless, of course, one wished to count the cowboys, of whom there were sometimes as many as nine or ten, and the toothless old Indian who had showed up to cook and clean for him. There were a good number of rooms in the big house, of course, which never felt the tread of his or anyone else's foot—rooms that remained always shuttered and closed, furniture carefully draped in muslin while dust accumulated in layers on the floor—and yet it was hardly in the style of a hermit that he lived: far from it. The grand master bedroom at the head of the stair, its broad-legged four-poster placed to give a morning view of Molly Peak—that was where he slept and took his morning coffee. The library too was kept open, its shelves slowly filling with books sent from the East; there, at one end was his broad oaken desk, and the chair where often he sat up late, very late, into the night. The noon meal he customarily took in the long kitchen with the cowboys, but in the evening, quite alone, it was to the formal dining room that he went for his late supper, the old Indian moving from kitchen to table like a silent, helpful owl.

Not only did he stay; he prospered—and this though the first several years seemed cunningly designed to drive him out. This, after all, was the decade of the thirties, and the smell of dust was in the air. That first winter itself, the winter of 1931, was an unusually dry one, bringing little snow even on the higher mountains, and the spring had added no rain at all. When summer arrived the hay crops were very thin, and the other ranchers had begun shipping cattle early—just as he, Kinsella, was bringing the first of his cattle in. A hundred prime Herefords, that was all, and enough feed to take them through any winter. Soon a half dozen more Indians had appeared—these in addition to the three already stringing fences—and inspired by the Swede's capable apprentice promptly set to work clearing land, two great tracts at the base of the hills to the north and east, where the two fine springs had continued to run full throughout that dry, dry summer and fall. By the time the snow flew more than three hundred acres was ready for seed, and more to come next year.

And how it flew, that winter—the grim, punishing winter of 1932. Devastation all about him, stranded cattle perishing in thousands on the range, Kinsella himself had stayed close to the hearth—and his pampered hundred, fat and sleek, remained safe in the barn and corrals. Spring came, and with it general financial collapse. Cattle prices dropping, mortgages foreclosing, banks failing, Kinsella had continued his methodical course, slowly building his herd and developing his irrigated hayfields year after grim, dry year until, when at last the first dim signs of recovery began to be felt, all had to agree that it was fully accomplished: Cyril Kinsella, neophyte rancher, had emerged from the midst of gloom and desolation with one of the finest livestock operations in all of east-central Nevada.

And still he was alone, immured in that great rosy-walled castle like some misplaced feudal baron. Not to say, of course, that he never showed himself; indeed, as time passed his came to be a well-known face in the immediate neighborhood, not only at the Murray stockyards but up in Chokecherry Creek as well. And then there were the times when he would simply disappear for a week or so, the blue Model A emerging from its garage and heading north. Then, it was supposed, he spent his time in Salt Lake or in Denver, wherever the fortunes of a successful and enterprising stockman might take him. As for the past, there seemed little doubt that he had put it far, far behind him.

Still, as the thirties implacably unraveled toward the forties, and talk of famine gradually gave way to talk of war, there were few in the neighborhood who failed to notice how he had changed. The reserve and shrewdness that had won their respect and even grudging admiration in the young man had subtly altered to a kind of brooding, unforgiving cynicism, as though his successes had only served to confirm some dark truth that he had suspected all along. His appearance as well had changed markedly—and for the worse, most would agree. Where once there had been a quiet, almost dangerous vigor about him, now there was a strange yet cunning kind of lassitude. His face seemed to have grown thinner, more concentrated, the lines deep and pronounced below the fast-graying mane of once coal-black hair.

Now, as always, there were the silences—those moments of utter stillness that seemed to come upon him without warning, withdrawing him from the midst of an apparently normal conversation as though a leak had suddenly sprung in his consciousness—but now they too were different. Gone were the days when something resembling apology might have graced his speech or manner when such a moment had passed; in its place they had come to expect some bitter, dismissive remark or gesture, sometimes no more than a wave of the hand as he turned to go. The audience was at an end.

It was Mrs. Tipton—the station agent's wife at Murray—who put it best. "The richer he gets," she said, "the meaner he gets."

Then, in the fall of 1945, the impossible happened: Cyril Kinsella fell in love.

No one knew just where or how he had met her, but the signs were there from the beginning. All at once it came to be noticed that the blue Model A, which formerly would have remained in its garage for weeks at a time, had become a decidedly more frequent sight on the highway. Twice, sometimes three times a month now it could be seen heading north of a Thursday or Friday afternoon, often not returning until the following Monday. What was more, as many soon came to remark, on the days immediately following these expeditions his gaze invariably gained an inexplicable softness, his manner an inexplicable mildness. Unfortunately, however, this pliant mood proved rather short-lived, degenerating within a day or two into a petulant irascibility of monumental proportions. And thus it was that everyone—and most especially the handful of cowboys who had to deal with him on a daily basis—was visibly relieved when they saw the blue Model A emerge once more from its trim garage, move slowly down the lane, and, coming to a full stop as always at its intersection with the deserted highway, head off to the north at its customary sensible pace.

It was, to give her due credit, Mrs. Tipton herself who first identified the condition by name.

"Love?" her husband had said, pushing the green eyeshade back on his forehead. "Molly, whatever have you been putting in your tea? Have you ever seen a buzzard in love?"

"Just never you mind that, Wilbur," Mrs. Tipton had coolly replied. "Remember where you heard it, that's all. One of these days when he comes back, one of these fine days he won't be alone."

And so when that day actually arrived, on a crisp Tuesday in March, the year now 1946, there was vindication in plenty for that oracular lady. For it was the station agent himself who, as fate or justice would have it, was the first to see them, he having gone out to the crossing to look at a balky switch. And it was he as well who, a few short minutes later, stood before his smiling wife and, eyes downcast, dutifully tendered his report, then opened the meeting to questions.

"Small, blonde, kind of pretty I suppose—like a kid almost, but maybe not quite that young."

"Young enough, though," Mr. Tipton added, a sly, meditative smile settling over his grizzled features. "One thing you'll have to admit, Molly, that old buzzard isn't easy to figure."

Margaret Kinsella, formerly Wilvert, née Devereaux, was then almost three years a widow, having lost her husband to a sniper's bullet on the beaches of southern Sicily. She had married quite young, wanting children, but none had come—and when the war took her husband of four years from her she had done what seemed the only thing left to her. Moving to an apartment not far from her parents, she immersed herself wholly in her work, which, as it happened, was the designing of children's books. Indeed, until her meeting with Cyril Kinsella, a man nearly thirty years her senior, she had never considered remarriage; she had her work, made enough to provide for her simple needs, and, it seemed to her, was relatively satisfied and content. But when they did meet—at one of her father's dinner parties, as it happened—the matter seemed immediately decided otherwise. His formal proposal, when three weeks later it came, arrived less as a surprise than as a command of fate. She had accepted freely, gladly, even eagerly, but with the strange intuition that she had no other choice.

Perhaps it was this sense of helpless assent, perhaps simply something arising from the losses she had suffered, but ever afterward her eyes were never quite without a certain wistfulness—the same soft wistfulness that played about them on that chilly March afternoon as, standing on the half-frozen ground before her new home, she gazed up at the chimneys and gables outlined against the cloud-streaked sky. She was, to put it plainly, a most delicate and beautiful woman—her face a halo of pink and gold and white and blue, her tiny but finely made body reminiscent of a young deer—and as at last, that day, she lowered her eyes from the towering front of the great house to rest them on the confused but somehow rejuvenated (or rejuvenating) features of its builder, Cyril Kinsella felt his heart swell with the joy of inexpressible . . . privilege.

As well it might. There are certain human creatures—the word *person* seems somehow inappropriate, as if possessing too much weight and definition, too many assumptions of human obligation—whose very being seems but a prelude to their passing, whose earthly form sits so lightly on them that each breath of wind seems to threaten their right to stay. It is not a matter of sickness or frailty—Margaret Kinsella's aura had neither of these about it—but rather an aspect of the spirit, a quality which when communicated to those around it gives rise to a half-understood longing, an inexpressible need to sustain and nourish, even to pamper and indulge, in the expectancy of its early departure.

Thus the word *privilege*. Although Cyril Kinsella would never have confessed to a sense of the ephemeral in his new wife, still he was betrayed by his attitude toward her. No, it was not just the simple joy and relief of a man who had been alone too long, a man who finds himself not quite able to believe his good luck—for his was a joy tinged with anxiety, even fretfulness. Indeed, if Margaret had not been willful enough to insist on her freedom she would surely have been smothered in the protections with which he everlastingly sought to surround her. As it was, however, she went her own way, a bit of gentle scolding being quite enough to disarm Cyril Kinsella and leave him with his nameless fears.

She loved to ride alone, insisting that only then could she truly sense what was about her. Perversely, perhaps, her horse was the biggest that Kinsella owned, a long-legged gray who combined the greatest reliability with an almost unbelievable reserve of stamina. She was a capable rider, although perhaps not so capable as she herself thought, and had a deceptive strength that allowed her to go for many hours without seeming to tire. Often she would stay away the entire day, riding to the remotest corners of her husband's extended domain. On these occasions, at least at the beginning, the cowboys sometimes thought they could hear raised voices from the big house when she at last returned.

Perhaps her favorite destination was what was known as the "second" spring—simply because it was beyond and upstream from the first, the site of the stone quarry. On summer afternoons the cowboys would sometimes catch a glimpse of her across the creek, the big gray threading its implacable way among the cedars as it carried her upstream. It gave them a strange feeling of contentment, security even, to see her so, to know that as the long afternoon passed they could from time to time look up at the nodding tops of the two cottonwoods on the hillside and know that she was there, her narrow back resting against a root as she read her book and nibbled on a bit of watercress.

For the cowboys adored her too—from young, black Booker Goodman, the astonishing harvest of a Denver business trip two years before, to white-haired Carl Withers, who had broken his first horse on the day Kinsella was born. A good part of it, perhaps, was her independence, that gentle stubbornness by which she always seemed to succeed in having her own way. But beyond that lay something much, much more important. Her presence, it seemed, had added a dimension to their lives that none had known before. It was not simply that she was a woman, and a very pretty one at that; all of them had known women, even pretty ones now and then. Nor was it just a matter of balance, of counterweight against the harshness of their normal existence, whose essence was Kinsella himself. Rather it was a kind of equilibrium, a creative tension. Whereas before there had been but a single pole, a single center around which their lives had revolved like dependent moons, now that had been matched by another, an opposite but somehow harmonious center, which, engaging the other in a kind of silent dialectic, seemed to cast all their workaday tasks into a larger, more generous frame of reference. It was as though their lives had achieved a new focus in which long-forgotten possibilities might at any time loom up. There was talk in the bunkhouse of sweetwater ranches, memories exchanged of girls left behind.

It was so brief, so cruelly brief. There was one spring and one summer, one fall and one winter—one full turn of the year. And then it was nearly spring again, the spring of 1947, and as the land quickened in the warming sun, so did the womb of Margaret Kinsella begin to stir. Suddenly the cowboys noticed that she had stopped riding, spending most of her time now reading or playing the big piano or simply pottering about in the rock-walled flower garden Kinsella had made for her behind the house. And it was not long before, their suspicions apparently confirmed, they felt free to nod meaningfully to one another as she passed, her tiny shape now strangely weighted forward, drawing her along the path between garden and house.

Until at last it seemed that Kinsella's protective instincts had found an ally in their object; by the end of the summer she was rarely seen outside the house. Even the soft sound of the piano echoed less frequently from the front parlor. The cowboys began to look for her, treasuring and reporting on each brief glimpse— the weary face at the window, the tiny but grotesquely over-balanced figure moving slowly down the hallway—as if by so doing they could keep at bay the evergrowing sense of danger and imminent loss that dragged at their hearts. The result of this, however, was the precise opposite of what they intended:

each fleeting sight of her, each gentle, calm word from her, only served to reinforce their mounting dread.

And so when at last the day came, coalescing out of the shadows of October like an advancing figure in the mist, it seemed more a fulfillment than an event. The doctor and a nurse arrived at noon, their pinched faces seeming to acknowledge that they too were merely actors playing out their parts. Booker Goodman irritably banged about the bunkhouse for a time, then abruptly announced that he was going to take a look at some fences on the north side. The others stayed behind, playing a dispirited game of cards as they gazed out the open doorway at the big house. It was almost four o'clock when they saw the nurse emerge and, going to the car, return with another black satchel—and soon after that the screaming began. For a moment they listened intently, as if none of them really knew what it was, then one by one they silently put their cards on the table, stood up, and walked out toward the far corrals. The last of them had gone when Tabby Weepup emerged through the kitchen doorway, ran awkwardly to his cabin, shut the door behind him, and pulled the ragged curtains closed.

Booker Goodman, returning at dusk, had been just in time to catch a glimpse of the ambulance heading slowly out the lane. He was still looking after it, his dark, smooth face utterly immobile in the fading light, when the great front door had suddenly swung open and the doctor and nurse emerged on the porch, the latter carrying a tiny, blanket-wrapped bundle in her arms. Remaining on his horse by the barn, he had watched them descend to the car, the doctor holding the door as she stepped gingerly inside. It was only when they too were gone, the green Nash moving like some great exotic beetle down toward the highway, that he slowly dismounted and, with a last glance upward at the darkened house, unsaddled his horse and went inside.

CHAPTER 3

1

It was high summer in the mountains. The mornings were fresh and clear, the afternoons long and warm, and when at last the sun descended to touch the ridges across the valley the evening chill came on surely, swiftly, enveloping like an icy glove as the night emerged, a theater of stars. The drumming of grouse, the cry of a hawk, the hum of insects, the querulous conversation of the coyotes—these were the sounds of the place, these and the sobbing sigh of the evening wind moving up through the trees from the warmth of the valley below.

There were other sounds as well, of course, but they were of one's own making, one's own importation. The horses, the sheep, even the saddles and pots and pans, all had their own voices, their own complaints and exclamations. And if sometimes a sudden hush descended, sometimes in the heat of a long and weary afternoon, one needed only look in the shade of the wagon for the dogs, who were always eager for human conversation in any form.

It was a calm, ordered life—one little troubled by conscious longings and ambitions. Sometimes in the mornings, when two hours before dawn he would rise to a cold breakfast and, saddling the picketed horse, set off toward the bedground, he seemed to sense an inkling of some vague destiny, but always this passed, was effaced like the stars themselves as in the gray of first light he began the long, loose circling of the now stirring herd, gently guiding it in the direction he wished it to travel, shaping it with his presence, until at last the first warming glow appeared in the east, over the ridge of peaks whose arid backs sloped down to the great desert beyond, and, sensing a moment before they themselves did that the time and place had come to stop, he began to turn the leaders back, gently, gently, until the realization took hold and the herd began to turn back upon itself, of its own will. The day's progress was ended.

The rest of the day was largely his own, to spend entirely as he wished. It had been a generous spring, and the succulent shrubs and grasses still had enough moisture to keep the sheep from wandering in search of water; except for a brief afternoon visit—just to see that all was well—or an occasional trip to spread salt at the next night's bedground, he was usually free to ignore his charges until the following morning. Returning to the camp, he would catch the second horse, which often had wandered a good distance in spite of its hobbles, and picket it, releasing the one he had ridden. Then, making a small fire, he would prepare his morning meal—a substantial affair of potatoes and ham, cheese, sometimes an egg or two, with black coffee and red wine—which he would eat sitting in the sun, on the steps of the wagon. Afterward there were the dishes, the dogs, perhaps the making of some bread, the iron Dutch oven nestled in the coals—and the long day ahead.

There were some he had known who found it very difficult,

the passing of these hours. There was always hunting or fishing, of course, and he too had found a good deal of pleasure—not to mention fresh meat—in such expeditions. Sometimes late in the afternoon he would lock the dogs in the wagon and, taking the new .22 Kinsella had provided, walk up to a stand of pinyons on the ridge. The grouse were often there, dull-witted and plump, sometimes five or six in a single tree, and he would methodically shoot their heads off, one by one, starting from the bottom so as not to startle those above.

But this was only an occasional diversion; one could eat only so much grouse, even in a start-up year when there were no lambs to supplement it. There were countless hours left to fill, long stretches of time which to many of his countrymen, especially at first, had seemed an unbearable anguish. Some of them took up whittling, some (much to their dogs' dismay) twanged on a guitar, some tried to remember how their uncles and grandfathers in the old country had spun wool with a wooden bob. As for the others, the aspen groves were full of their elaborate bark carvings, the rocky ridges littered with their carefully erected "stone boys." And then, of course, there were the naps, the endless, pointless naps.

He too had tried all these things, at least during the first few years. He too had had moments when his mind seemed to begin racing, running wildly backward to that other time, that other place, and dwelling there upon the pleasant and the fearful, the things that had bound him as well as those from which he had fled. But at last, mercifully, that time had passed. The long summer afternoons lost their terror and he was at peace, or relatively so.

For the past several summers he had been working on his English. In the beginning it was no more than reading—and laboriously writing out—the text of tin-can labels, but by now he had progressed far beyond that. He was, in fact, the proud owner of six actual books, only one of which—the small French New Testament, a First Communion gift from his mother—

had come with him to America. There were three dictionaries, one all in English, one French to English and back again, and one French to Basque (but not back again, there being none of that kind so far as he knew). Two of these he had found in the dusty corner of a winter shack, and the last he had bought from another herder at the cost of a dozen fishhooks.

The other two books, however, had come as outright gifts. The first, presented to him by the owner of a Basque hotel in Ogden, was a ponderous volume bound in faded blue leather, the shattered spine of which announced, in what once had been stamped gold letters, *Men and Skins—A History of the Canadian Fur Trade*. The other, and the book to which his current efforts were directed, was almost new, its dust jacket hardly soiled. It was Lindbergh's *Spirit of St. Louis,* the Book of the Month Club edition. This had come to him just recently, a going-away gift, in fact, from Harignordoquy's widowed sister, who was always deeply moved by any effort toward self-improvement on the part of one of her brother's herders, whom she considered generally beneath contempt.

And so it was that when the morning's chores were done, the dogs already snoozing beneath the wagon, he would disappear inside, draw down his table, and set to work. The routine of his devotions never varied. Taking down his text from the shelf, selecting a sharp pencil from the soup can at his side, he would laboriously copy out several sentences into the tall pages of a warped, half-filled financial ledger he had long ago retrieved from a trash heap behind the Brigham City bus station. Then, putting down his pencil, he would read the sentences aloud— or at least sound them out—several times until they seemed right. This done, he would proceed, by a diverse combination of checking and cross-checking among his reference works, to de- termine the meaning—or what he deduced to be the meaning, which was not always the same—of each of the words he did not know. Next he would enter these words, along with their definitions or what he took to be such, in French or sometimes now English, in the pages at the back of the ledger reserved solely for this purpose. Finally, fortified by this fresh knowledge, he would read the sentences once again—then proceed on as before, if strength remained, with those that followed.

He had thus far in this manner copied out 19 pages of *The Spirit of St. Louis,* a not inconsiderable sum given the short time he had owned the book. Preceding these in the old ledger, in the small, meticulous hand of a French schoolboy, were 182 pencil-written pages of *Men and Skins—A History of the Canadian Fur Trade.*

It was curious how important it had become for him, the learning of English. In the beginning certainly, during those first few years here, it had not been so. On the contrary, he had avoided it, hiding behind a helpless smile or a willing countryman whenever that was possible. Besides, everyone he had anything much to do with—his employer, the camptenders, the other herders—was either Basque or at least spoke some French or Spanish. There had simply been no need for English, especially for one who, like himself and so many of the others, thought of nothing beyond the amassing of enough money to return home on his own terms. But then something had happened to him.

It was difficult to say just how it had begun. The sudden marriage of his sister almost two years ago, the arrival of her new young husband at the family farmstead, yes, all that had had something to do with it; but even that had not been all, or perhaps even the most important part. For there were those others too, the ones who had come back, their eyes now hollow with grief and disappointment, now bright with the joy of reunion, as they told the tale of how it had been. The girls who did not wait, the imperious elder brothers, the spiteful, even greedy relatives, the uncanny . . . smallness of it all.

"Yes, that was the hardest part," he remembered Patchi saying the day he arrived back—Patchi, who had been the first of them to go back home, his pockets full of money, his heart full of

hope; Patchi, who eight months later was back, eager to return
to the mountains and the sheep. "It was all like a miniature—
little hills, little trees, little people, little skies. Not like here,"
and Patchi raised his eyes to the far horizon.

In any case it had happened—and now, eight years after his
arrival, he rarely thought of it anymore. More than that, he
found that he had lost patience with those who did think of it,
did speak of it, rarely spoke of anything else. For more than
a year now he had found himself avoiding them, their gatherings—as they avoided him. He had become an American. What
he wanted was not a ticket home but one to remain. All he
needed was a foothold; he would take care of the rest.

He was enormously pleased with the way the wagon, his
sheepcamp, had turned out. When it had first arrived—he
ankle-deep in manure, bent over a rake in the flower bed, Tabby
lisping like a willow beside him as the big cattle truck moved
slowly up the lane, that frayed canvas top swaying mournfully
from side to side on the bed as the truck came around the big
house, then lurched to a stop beside the barn—he had not been
so sure. It was basically sound, a good set of wheels and springs
and undercarriage, but he had never seen one quite so old and
dilapidated. Perhaps it was Kinsella's obvious dismay—the old
man standing a few steps back, slowly shaking his head from
side to side as they moved it down the ramp—yes, perhaps it
was that which had determined him to make something of it
regardless.

"Don' worry, sir," he had said. "A little paint, a little canvas,
it'll be okay, it'll be jus' fine." And so it was. Better than fine.

Not to say he had had no help. Tabby, Booker, the Lindsays,
old Carl, even Levi Mondragon one afternoon, they all had
seemed eager to lend a hand. And there were some things—
putting on the new canvas, for example—that he could not have
done without them. For the most part, however, he had done it
alone—he and little Deirdre.

It was amazing to him, the way she had taken to it. The first few days, when the sight of him spending his late afternoons there instead of in the garden was something of a novelty, that he had been able to understand. She had never seen a sheep-camp before, or anything like it, and the thought of a little house on wheels appealed to her—she whose room in the big house, so Tabby had told him, was fully five times as large. But when after two weeks she was still there, even coming to the garden at three o'clock to remind him it was time to go, he had begun to wonder. She never seemed to tire of it. The scrubbing, the sanding, the painting and polishing and mending—it was all the same blissful business to her.

"When does this go back inside?" she would ask, her bright eyes turned up toward him as she rubbed a bit of steel wool on a rusty stove lid. They had taken out the little woodstove and stovepipe, setting it on the ground to one side as the interior work proceeded.

"That's the last thing. When everything else is done, then we put it back."

"Then we'll *really* be ready," she would say. "*Really* ready to go."

Unfortunately she had quickly, almost immediately, formed the notion that she would be going too. She insisted on it—even after not only he but Tabby and her father as well had told her repeatedly that it could not be so.

"I'll go anyway," she would say. "I'll run away." Her great blue eyes, when she threatened this, always seemed to grow a bit smaller and harder, the pupils contracting into tiny, intractable specks of flint.

In the end he had given up, remaining blandly noncommittal when she talked that way. It was not his affair, he decided. He had done his best, now it must be a matter for her father, for Tabby and her father.

And so they had labored together, each afternoon until Tabby came to call her for supper. What was more, she had acted as

his decorator on at least one occasion—this when he had asked
Booker to get him some oilcloth to line the ceiling. As often
happened she had gone along, coming back with eight yards of
the most colorful material Creighton Mercantile could boast of.
Red strawberries with green leaves and white blossoms, all set
against a butter-yellow background—it was quite lovely, they
agreed, especially tacked up there behind the hooped wooden
beams, which themselves bore a fresh new coat of blue-green
paint.

"That should keep me nice and warm," he had said, "even
when the wind blows up on the mountain."

"Yes," Deirdre said, scrubbing on another stove lid—"yes,
we'll make a fire in the stove and cook some popcorn."

And then at last it was done, gleaming blue and white against
the barn—and time to go. Food bins filled, pots and pans and
all the rest aboard—time to go. And yes, even Kinsella had
seemed pleased then, and the next morning he had been there
too, standing with Booker against the top rail of the corral as the
sheep began to file out—John atop the big gray, the dogs (for
there were two now, a Fina to comfort Pastor) moving eagerly to
his commands, gently coaxing, molding, as the herd took shape,
the air filled with dust and bawling and the hollow sound of
bells—then slowly, compactly, began to move off toward the
waiting mountain.

No, he had thought nothing of it, not even enough to notice
that she had not been there that morning, waving with the
others as he set off. There had been too many other things to
concern him—a thousand skittish Rambouillet yearlings, to be
precise—and perhaps too his mind had already gone on ahead,
above. But no, he had noticed nothing, certainly nothing of the
sheepcamp trailing far behind—or the small, grave figure seated
beside Booker on the box, her little suitcase propped up between
her knees, the trusty Buff clutched beneath her arm . . .

"Why did you let her come?" he had asked Booker when, ten
days later, the big man arrived again, this time alone, with the

mules and provisions. "Another time, when things were more settled . . . but that day? After what she'd been saying . . . you knew there'd be trouble."

The gentle foreman, eyetooth glinting in the noonday sun, had smiled his most innocent smile.

"Course I knew. Boss knew too, I guess. But she gets her way with him, you know."

"Yes, I suppose she does," he had replied—recalling yet again the dark looks, the little foot stamping in the dust, the recriminations and bitter tears. Then, silently, he had turned and walked away, to finish hitching up the team.

2

He had never dreamed that Booker's visits would come to mean so much to him. The arrival of the camptender, of course, was always, under any circumstances, an important event; there was no one he knew, not even the most hardened and misanthropic of his countrymen, who did not look forward to it. Cheerful or surly, generous or miserly, the camptender was still a man— which made him very different from a horse or a dog or a coyote. Or a sheep. And when the supplies were unloaded there was always the half hour or so, sometimes a good deal longer, for the bringing of news, the exchange of small talk, and, if one were very lucky, a few precious moments of low laughter.

He had not doubted that Booker, even Booker, would be able to provide this basic human solace, at least on a certain rudimentary level. The nearly four weeks spent below had been more than enough to convince him that the big black foreman, aware as he seemed of John's lingering wariness, still regarded him with a certain indulgent generosity and goodwill. At the same time, however, it seemed unlikely that anything beyond this could ever exist between them. There were too many memories, too many myths.

And then, of course, there was the matter of experience and background, or lack of it. He was used to camptenders who knew a good deal more than he did—who had herded on the same range before him and knew just where to look for strays. This one, however, could be no help at all.

And yet all of these, myths and misgivings alike, seemed to have faded away with the first few visits. There was something about this place, something about this mountain, that made them different with one another, not as they had been below. The greatest of Kinsella's servants and the least, here they seemed somehow equals—yet more than that. Here they seemed somehow . . . in league. Against what? That he could not have begun to say.

No, it was not something he felt able to understand, nor did he waste time trying. He had no talent for puzzles. All he knew was that in spite of, perhaps in some way because of it all they got on well, very well—and that what had begun as brief, almost perfunctory visits, little more than a hasty delivery and a single gulped cup of coffee, had soon swelled into something entirely different, the minutes becoming an hour, then two, until sometimes it was only the great glowing orb of the sun, beginning its remorseless fall toward the ragged western peaks, which at last brought the big man grumbling to his feet.

As that first long summer wore on, and the tone of those fortnightly visits pursued its subtle but ineluctable course, they had spoken of many, many things. Booker, at the cost of a good deal of persistence at first, had gradually learned something of the young herder's background—the years in France as well as those here—and John, with a bit less effort perhaps, had filled in the broader gaps in what Tabby, during their sweet, long afternoons in the garden, had told him of the black foreman's past.

"I couldn't believe it when he came up to me," Booker had said, invoking the moment, almost ten years ago now, when Kinsella had approached him at the Denver stockyard. "I'd been working there more than a year, since the army let me go, and I'd seen him a few times, but he hardly talked to anybody, least of all me. He was dark in those days, his hair with just the beginning of some gray, and he seemed always mad—you know, angry. Worse than now maybe . . . maybe. Anyway, there I was, minding my own business, and here he comes, right at me. 'How'd you like to work for me?' he says, first words out of his mouth. How'd I like to work for him, me black and broke and skinny and still thinking about the war too much. How'd I like it? I'd like it fine. Sometimes now, though, I wonder . . . Sometimes."

No, Tabby had not told him of that. For Tabby, it seemed, Booker had not really begun to exist until that day a year later when the incumbent foreman, a stringy little Arkansan who had come away from the christening bowl with the name of Abner Pick, announced his firm intention to "teach that big buck a lesson." Why he had supposed that it would be he who would teach and the other absorb, rather than vice versa, was never entirely clear, but in any case the following morning had found the redoubtable Abner Pick, his head expertly bandaged, in the back seat of the Salt Lake bus, while Booker Goodman, having succeeded to his position, shared an elaborate breakfast with Kinsella in the dining room of the big house. Yes, for Tabby, who had served that breakfast, it was at this precise moment, no earlier, that Booker Goodman had emerged from the mists of nonbeing.

But if there was one subject that consistently arose to fill those warm mountain afternoons, one theme that regularly recurred, there could not be the slightest question what, or who, it was. And in that respect, at least, this particular afternoon late in July was like all the rest.

"I don't know that I can take it much longer," Booker had begun, the last dregs of the coffee cooling in his cup. His voice had suddenly grown almost shrill, with that particular hard edge of impatience it always had when he had been stewing over something all the way up. "One of these times, when he's in the muck of one of those broods of his, I'm just going to have enough of it. I don't *have* to stay, you know. He can get somebody else to hold his hand."

Booker often complained about these episodes—the "broods" as he called them. John had never been near the master's library, where all this seemed to take place, but he could by this time visualize the kind of dark, forbidding place it must be. This was Kinsella's haunt, the place where he seemed to spend many of his waking and a good number of what should have been his sleeping hours—and where, it seemed, he all too often, day and night, summoned good Booker Goodman.

"Not that I mind going in there when he has something to say. That's my business, after all, to do his business. But when he starts in on that same old stuff again, when he shows up outside my door in the middle of the night, saying it just can't wait, and then the same old thing . . . Lord, I just don't know."

It had been a particularly bad session, the one the night before. Earlier that day, watching the old man at lunch, Booker had sensed that it would come, the summons, and he had remained close to home, expecting and dreading it, all the remainder of the day. When ten o'clock arrived without it, however—only a deep, heavy silence emanating from the big house—he had begun to think he might be wrong. Nevertheless it was with a distinct feeling of futility that he had gone to bed—so that when at last it did come, the soft, insistent knocking on his outer door, the deep, tobacco-and-whiskey voice rumbling outside, it was with a strange mixture of chagrin and vindication that he had drawn on his trousers once again, then followed blear-eyed across the dew-soaked yard.

"It was the wife again, that first one. That's always what it seems to be now—when he really, *really* gets going."

John already knew something about "that first one." Tabby had talked about her too, at least the basic outlines. For even Tabby had not yet been there, in the fall of 1931, when she had come . . . and gone. And yet doubtless the old Indian knew a great deal more about her than he had let on—perhaps, like Booker, more than he had ever wished to know. For her hasty departure, a mere six days after that triumphant entry, had by no means been complete. Not that she had ever returned herself—physically, that is; and yet in many ways, one in particular, she had refused to become truly absent. For there had been a child.

Why she waited those five years to tell him, why after all that time she had bothered to tell him at all, none of this was ever really clear. But the fact was that early in 1936, on the first of March to be precise, she had taken it upon herself to write a letter, her first. The reasons she gave—that she was to remarry and her new husband wished to adopt and give the child his name, that she thought it right in these circumstances that he, Kinsella, know—were clear enough, even in some way sensible, perhaps, but why she acted as she did was another matter. Certainly the motive was not financial; her father, although less active in business following his stroke, had managed his investments wisely, and the new husband, a doctor of some kind, was certainly no pauper. No, there had been no request for money, not then or at any other time—not even when five years later the doctor, pleading neglect, had asked for a quiet divorce. As for the matter of visits, that simply had never come up. Why then the letters had continued, why even after that initial announcement evoked no response they still went on, detailing each childish accomplishment and misfortune with a care and faithfulness that would have satisfied the most doting of absent fathers—that was what seemed impossible to understand.

Unless all she wanted after all—and as the years passed and her insistence mounted this seemed all the more probable—was to someday wrest from him a response, some form of acknowledgment of, if not his responsibility, then at least his complicity in the child's existence. Legally, of course, there could be no doubt of it, there being no one who could prove anyone else had been involved. Factually it was almost as certain—or as certain as the question of paternity could ever be, the matter of the Swedish carpenter having long since been laid to rest. And so in the end it seemed no more than stubbornness—on her part in insisting, on his part in refusing to affirm.

"When you have two people that pigheaded," Booker said, "nothing's going to change."

No, he had never answered the letters, not that first one or any of those that followed. For indeed they had followed, continued to follow, one upon the other, sometimes ten or more a year—and there had now been almost twenty years. Yet he had insisted on reading them, poring over each in turn not once but many times before at last, sometimes days later, he would rise from his desk and carefully, even ceremoniously, lay it in the grate, then watch it burn to ash. Yes, why he insisted on all this was perhaps the greatest mystery of all. At least it was to Booker, who for the past five years had all too often served as witness for these morbid incendiary rites.

"Why he doesn't just burn them first, or better yet just tell me to chuck 'em when they come—I'd even burn 'em if he wanted, right out behind the barn—that's what I can't figure out for the life of me. But oh no, he's got to have it all, the whole miserable thing, and then all the rest that goes with it." For after the burning—which somehow seemed to soothe him—there always remained the talking, that deep, rough voice murmuring on, on into the night until at last, mercifully, the whiskey and exhaustion combined to claim him.

"And that's how I leave him, almost every time now. Head down on the desk, glass of whiskey still there by his hand. I get up, put out the cigarette in the ashtray, and go. Two, three in the morning, usually. Last night it was nearly four."

Abruptly the big man got up, his broad form stretching upward like a dusky Goliath. Then, releasing a long, weary sigh, he set out quickly toward the wagon, where he gingerly deposited his cup on the stair.

"Well, let's get your buggy moved," he said as, whistling shrilly at the mules, he set off toward them with a long, loose-jointed stride.

He had gone no more than twenty feet, however, when suddenly he drew up and, after standing quite still for a moment, turned to look back. The weary expression of the moment before was gone; in its place was a broad, open smile.

"You know what, John boy? It might be getting just about time for a little Saturday night visit in town, you and me—and anyone else who wants to come along."

"Oh?" was all he could think of to say.

"Yes, indeed. I know some young ladies who would definitely, *most definitely* like to make your acquaintance."

Feeling his face redden, John looked down. "Well I dunno. Maybe in six weeks or so, after I take 'em down again, but then there's the breeding. I dunno." Slowly he raised his head, eyes squinting as he looked up.

But Booker's smile was even broader than before. For a moment the big man said nothing. Then, quickly, he turned away, slapping his thigh with a bright "Yup, yup" as he set out again, whistling up the mules as he went.

3

It had been a dry, blazing August, even for this country. Everything—the trees, the rocks, the sheep, the dogs and horses, even he himself—seemed coated with a fine, powdery dust, and when at last the sun went down, dropping like a ball of molten lead behind the jagged ridge across the valley, the sky glowed red for half an hour like the inside of a forge.

"No, I've seen nothing to compare with it," Booker testified, "not in my nine years, at least. After that fine spring, a good June, a decent July . . . Yes, even Tabby says so, even the boss.

And if anyone ought to know . . . Anyway, if you think it's hot up here you oughtta be down below."

John had no desire to be down below, nor did his thousand virgins, but it appeared that some concessions were in order. There were four small springs on the north side of the mountain, two of which in time past had been dug out and set up with pipes and troughs. During July and even early August these had seemed enough, but as the month blazed on toward September the sheep wanted something more. That could only be the creek, which even in this weather ran full and cold—but that was a long journey, especially if undertaken twice a week as they now seemed to require. And so, little by little, he had begun to move them down the mountain, each half mile seeming to raise the temperature another degree.

At least there had been a bit of rain from time to time, though hardly enough to help. Early in the afternoon, after a stretch of particularly hot, dusty days, he would see the clouds building high and steep against the mountains to the west, their bruised undersides threatening what they could not deliver, at least to him and his charges, and soon the air would take on a sharp, electric smell as the first oblique bars of rain, often ending before they reached the ground, appeared across the valley. The dogs, panting beneath the wagon, would begin to whine, until at last he relented and put them inside. Then, sitting beside his still-smoldering fire, he would watch it come, listening to the dogs' low whimpering as the darkness marched toward him, then their sudden silence as the sky was split by a bright, jagged flash, the air erupting with a cracking report like the sound of brittle twigs breaking beside his ear, then only the low, hollow rumble, lingering, lingering, long after it should have been gone, until . . . another flash, another crack, and again the long, low rumbling sound. Sometimes, too often, there would be nothing more than that. The spent clouds, breaking open before him, would simply disperse and pass out of sight. Now

and then, however, a little would remain for them as well—
a violent spattering that briefly rattled the dusty leaves of the
aspens before proceeding on up the mountain. And then, once
more, it was done.

The sheep, unlike his dogs, seemed but little impressed by
these late-summer fireworks, simply taking cover in the trees
until it all had passed. Neither, however, were they refreshed;
a day or two more and again they would become restless, longing once more to go down. Then, especially then, he had to
be alert—for they would only wait so long. And not a moment
longer.

The day had been very warm, the sheep retreating into the
shade of the groves before the morning chill had truly passed.
And there they had remained until late afternoon, when at last
the sun began to sink in the sky. Now, he knew, they would want
to begin, and by the time he reached them they were already
on their feet, impatiently milling beneath the trees. There was
little need to use the dogs, and soon he had them on their way,
the hollow clatter of the leaders' bells like moving buoys in the
dust.

It took little more than an hour now, this journey; hardly had
they set out, it seemed, when the leaders began to hurry, smelling water. He remembered the first time he had brought them
down, from high on the mountain among the pines; then, in
late July, it had taken more than twice as long. He sorely missed
that country, with its high, clear air and open sky—but perhaps
it was just as well. Within a month's time these summer days
would be giving way to autumn, the dusty leaves of the aspens
beginning to yellow on the hillsides, the sheep growing fretful,
and they would be coming down for the last time—until next
year. Now, at least, they would not have far to go.

He waited until they were settled, some standing knee-deep
in the stream, the others ranged perhaps a hundred yards along
the bank, before he turned the big gray horse upstream, heading

toward the second spring. It was the first time he had done this.
Always before he had remained with them, seated in the shade
with his book until, an hour and a half later perhaps, they had
had their fill and were ready to depart. The last time they had
come, however—three days ago it was now—it had occurred to
him that he really was not needed, at least not until they began
to want to move again. The dogs would keep them from crossing
to the other side, could even keep the leaders from departing for
a time. As long as he was back then, ready to move with them,
why indeed should he stay? In any case he would not be far. And
so in the end he had resolved to go, if only for an hour this first
time.

Reaching the low saddle, he drew the gray to a stop, just as
he had before. Five months had passed now since that first visit,
and the big horse had since put aside most of his bad habits, but
even now there was the suggestion of impatience in his manner as, fidgeting from foot to foot, he stood looking down at
the spring. John thought to reprimand him, then let it pass,
touching him to go on.

Somehow he forgave the horse, for even he, who had never
known Margaret Kinsella, was immensely moved by the sight.
There was something miraculous about it, an unsought-for gift,
and as they slowly descended, the horse moving carefully, gingerly, as though some rider other than himself bestrode him,
John felt a vague sense of . . . election, as if he were somehow
awaited. He was a good Catholic—or once had been—and well
schooled in the avoidance of such proud thoughts, but the sense
of elation would not leave him, no, not even after he had allowed
the horse to proceed up the swale beside the trunks of the two
great cottonwoods and come to a stop. Dismounting, he cast a
brief glance upward toward the marble marker, its heap of faded
flowers now almost obscuring it from sight, then settled into the
grass and opened his Lindbergh book.

When next he raised his eyes he knew he had stayed too long.
Indeed, he had suspected it much earlier, when the visit to the

San Diego airplane factory was just beginning; now, the visit done, there was no longer room for doubt. Yes, they would long ago have begun, the leaders, growing first impatient, then fractious, then enlisting enough of the others behind them to at last break free, heading upward, leaving the dogs, disheartened, to keep what control they could over the ever-diminishing number left behind. Yes, and soon the whole band would be scattered, spread over half the mountain, each of them wondering—if a sheep could truly wonder—why he had not yet arrived to gather them together for the night. Yes, for those two small pages there would be a heavy price to pay.

Getting to his feet, he walked quickly toward the grazing horse. Even now, however—even in light of what awaited him below . . . and above—it was very difficult to leave this place. One or two early nighthawks, precursors of many more to come, wheeled among the upper branches of the cottonwoods, plunging and weaving in the light, cool breeze that had arisen. Behind, all about him it seemed, the spring continued its seductive song. At last, reaching the big gray's side, he bent down to gather up the reins, then hesitated and turned to look once more. For one brief parting moment he gazed down at the spring, its troubled surface now shot with shadows. Then, for no reason he could have named, he found himself looking beyond it, beyond the plain marble marker with its mound of flowers, beyond and up the hillside, his eyes rising slowly, steadily, until at last the shadows ended in brilliant sunlight against the stony bluff above.

It was then, at that moment, that he saw it: a thin, uneven stream of small dark forms issuing from a rubble of gray, shiny rocks high on the bluff, soaring upward to top the cottonwoods, and then, turning abruptly south, trailing off into the azure sky. He stood very still, watching, for several minutes, waiting for it to end. Yet end it would not; on they came, streaming from the same rocky place like a trail of airborne ants—as indeed they had streamed for fully half an hour before he had taken notice. As indeed they were still streaming when, five more precious minutes passed, he let the reins slip from his hand and, dropping his book into the saddlebag, started up the hillside.

At first it did not seem very steep, although the rocky ground made the going difficult nevertheless. Soon, however—just as he emerged from the shade into full sunlight—the angle increased, until at last it became necessary to use his hands as well, from time to time taking hold of one of the brittle little shrubs that grew out of the cracks in the rocks. Small lizards with bright yellow throats peered down, then scattered recklessly before him as he went on. And still the ribbon of dark shapes continued, rising in the same gentle arc upward and over the treetops, until at last, just as he reached the base of the heap of rocks from which they came, it suddenly slackened, then stopped. For a moment there seemed a kind of a confusion, as a few of the small creatures continued to mill about above him; then, quite suddenly, all had dispersed—and it was as if the thing had never been.

For a moment he stood still, wiping the sweat from his face as he looked upward toward the place he had marked with his eye. Thirty feet, surely no more than that remained, but he did not at all like the idea of scaling that stony heap of rubble. Soon, however, he had begun, scrambling upward on all fours, stones slipping and shifting beneath his feet, hands grasping at the warm, slippery-looking surfaces, sweat stinging the corners of his eyes—until at last he was there.

Perhaps he had expected something larger, more dramatic, even something he could have walked into. In any case he felt disappointment at what he saw: a short, narrow shelf of rock and earth below, a sort of stone overhang or roof above, the opening between hardly large enough to admit one of his dogs. Kneeling down, he felt a breath of cool air on his face. Beyond, far off in the darkness, he could hear a soft yet urgent fluttering, and now and then a kind of high squeaking.

From below, beside the spring, there came the urgent whinny

of the horse; the old gray, it seemed, had now taken to remind-
ing him of his obligations. Ignoring the reproof, he took a small
stone in his hand and, reaching inside as far as he could, tossed
it in. There was brief, hollow clattering, then—nothing. Or
what he thought was nothing, for just as he was about to rise
from his knees there came another sound—a kind of striking, a
. . . thump.

Again the horse issued its warning, which he rewarded with
a soft, onerous Basque curse as he reached for a second stone,
this a good deal larger than the first. Again the same experiment, but this time, when the silence came, he began to count.
Exactly on the number six it came, more solid now—the thump.

Smiling, John rose to his feet, just as the third impatient call
came up from below. But this time there was no curse. Still
smiling, he quickly turned away and started down.

4

The mountain known as Molly Peak, well over ten thousand
feet in height, stands like a massive bookend at the northern
tip of a long range which, extending some eighty miles to the
south, rises gradually toward even higher peaks before, southeast of the little city of Creighton, it gradually descends to a low
pass, then proceeds to lose itself in the desert. Here on the north
end, however, the termination is much more abrupt. The exposed face of the mountain drops swiftly, steeply, through dense
pine and fir forests to emerge, about halfway down, on a broad,
rolling meadow—the same, in fact, where John and his sheep
had begun that first summer. Beyond the northerly edge of this
meadow, however, the mountain again drops steeply, this time
through forests in which the high-country pine and fir gradually
thin and give way first to pinyon and aspen, then at last to that
gnarled, stringy-barked juniper which, the botanist notwithstanding, is known by all hereabouts as cedar. The earth seems

to dry, the soil become more powdery, as the descent continues, then at last relents in a range of low sage-and-cedar hills which, lowering ever more gently toward the north, at last expire into the arid flat below.

It was in these hills that John had located a place for the fall breeding—and one morning in mid-September, just as the aspens on the ridges were beginning to approach their most luminous gold, he gathered up his fretful young *troupeau* and headed down, Booker and the sheepcamp bringing up the rear. The place had apparently been used before—not for the breeding of sheep, presumably, but for something having to do with the cattle—for there was a kind of temporary corral of cedar posts and rusted barbed wire. This he had no use for, but it was a good place nevertheless. There was water—a small, shallow stream descending from the east and a few old troughs scattered here and there. It would certainly do—at least until something better appeared for next year.

Here he would remain for more than a month, until the cooler weather began to make its presence felt in earnest and it was time to work gradually northward, his thousand no longer virgin, toward the desert, where together they would pass the long, lonely winter.

It was good now to be here, not only for the fleeting sense of permanence but because the place was relatively accessible. The former users had left behind a rutted but still usable dirt road that mounted steeply from the highway, and up this road, gears grinding, came not only Harignordoquy's truck with the rams— two dozen burly and eager Rambouillets, exactly as promised— but actual visitors too, a positive stream of them, in fact.

There was Booker, of course, every few days now—even though the actual need for him had lessened now that the camp could stay put for a time. Still he came, bringing a few groceries as his excuse, and often two or three hours would pass before the orange '47 Ford once more lurched into motion across the flat and, having gathered a goodly cloud of dust behind it, disappeared down the rutted track toward the highway. John sensed a growing restlessness in the big foreman, perhaps merely in anticipation of the long winter to come, but their long conversations beside the campfire, though often composed of little more than thoughtful silence, seemed to calm him somehow, and he always seemed in better spirits when he departed than when he had arrived.

The others, however, had been a good deal less expected— Lonnie Wilson came once with the supplies, the two Lindsays with a crate of chickens, and even, very briefly, Levi Mondragon, the shy little Mexican fellow who worked the hay.

"*Es hora de irme*," Levi Mondragon had said, his small, dark face alight with greeting and anticipation as, extending his hand, he stepped down from the cab of his battered, yet obviously freshly washed, yellow truck. "The apples of Taos are waiting."

And then, of course, there had been that other visit; yes, that as well . . .

It had been a cold, cloudy morning, the day they came, but about one the sky cleared off and a warm sun emerged through the lingering mist, setting the blooming rabbitbrush ablaze. The rams, thirsty as usual, had emptied the troughs again, and he had just finished refilling them, carrying buckets from the little stream, when he made out the familiar groan of Booker's pickup laboring up the road. Returning to the camp, he stoked the fire and put on another pot of coffee.

It was indeed Booker's truck, but even from a distance, as it hove into view over the ridge and began to make its way across the flat, it was apparent that he was not the driver. Although Booker was hardly noted for abusing his machinery, even he had learned to navigate this last stretch of the so-called road with relative dispatch. And indeed, *navigate* seemed the proper word, for the way across the flat, although not nearly so rough as the section leading up from the highway, passed over a series of uneven swales and ridges which made an approaching vehicle resemble a sea vessel more than one confined to land. If Booker, however, had so far perfected his technique as to permit an approach like that of a tugboat in a choppy sea, the present driver seemed determined to emulate a docking ferry— the orange prow of the pickup breasting each low ridge with a mournful creaking sound, then slowly moving over the top in a motion reminiscent of a camel retiring for the night. Observing this meditative approach, John fell to wondering just who the driver might be.

He had his answer long before the faithful orange craft lurched though the final pothole and shuddered to a stop. Indeed, he had been occupied with an entirely different question for the concluding hundred yards of the voyage—for at least since then it had been evident to him, even through the dust-streaked windshield pitching toward him, that there was at least one other in the cab, a somber, white-haired figure sitting stiffly upright by the far window. And as the truck drew nearer, its orange body creaking like old masts in the wind, he had discovered a third form as well—this one immediately recognizable to him. The small blonde head in the middle, bobbing up and down over the dashboard with each bump, seemed to be smiling back at him—or perhaps that was only what he hoped. For when at last the vessel came to rest, the thin white plume of steam slipping out as always from beneath the hood, the smile, if such it had ever really been, had turned to a grave, self-conscious frown.

If both passengers thus greeted him with a somber expression, however, it soon became apparent that for the larger of them at least that condition was only temporary. Tabby Weepup had never liked or trusted automobiles, and this ride had confirmed in him a resolution never to set off in one again. As soon as his foot touched the earth, however, the grim expression began to melt away, and when five minutes later he took the seat offered him by the fire, the old Indian seemed utterly at ease.

As for Deirdre, however, it was clear that she was determined to exact some further price for John's betrayal, or what she continued to regard as such. She had been reluctant to come at all—so Booker later told him—and only Tabby's insistence had persuaded her to relent. Now, sulking on the other side of the fire, she gazed darkly out toward the far hillside—where the rams, moving with silent, determined energy from one ewe to the next, were grimly at their work.

This visit, it seemed, was all of Tabby's making; indeed, he had demanded it, or came as close to actual demanding as ever he had before. Kinsella, although not going so far as to offer outright opposition, had shown little patience for the idea, at least at first. It was a busy season just then, in the midst of fall shipping, and Booker's last supply run had been only a few days earlier. The more the master thought of it, however—and the more Tabby, in his own subtle fashion, had continued to insist—the more it seemed just the thing to do. The old Indian asked for little enough, and besides he, Kinsella, had not once seen his herder or his sheep since that early morning more than three months ago when, leaning on the top rail of the corral, he had watched them set off for the mountains. Yes, it was time. And so they had come, the master himself at the helm.

"Are they good rams? Harignordoquy promised the best."

"Yes, they're good," John had said, standing beside the open truck door with him as they looked out at the distant hillside. "The best—I dunno 'bout that."

Kinsella looked over at him and scowled. Then, taking Deirdre by the hand, he silently set off with her across the flat, toward the hillside.

Yes, it was now more than three months since he had seen Kinsella, but he had thought of him often, very often. Indeed, he had been more than a little disappointed by the master's failure to pay him a visit on the mountain. He had almost come to expect it, what with the old man's apparent interest in the sheep and all, those first weeks. Once, only once, he had even gone so far as to mention it to Booker.

"Oh, he'll show up," the big man had assured him, a grim, faintly ironic smile flickering about his lips. "Just when you wish he wouldn't."

Well what, John wondered, had he expected? Why indeed had he expected anything? He could not begin to answer. But the fact was that he *had* expected something—something—from the first moment he had seen Kinsella. Sometimes it almost seemed that he had a claim on Kinsella—one the old man was perhaps still not aware of but soon, any moment, would be. But that, of course, was ridiculous. The only claim he had on the old man was his wages, and maybe a ride to the bus station when he was turned out. No, he could not begin to figure it out. All he knew was that he felt it, this . . . something.

"Don' let 'im bother you," Tabby said, raising the cup to his mouth with both hands. "S'been a bad mood for weeks." The old Indian looked over at him and smiled with his eyes, the cup still raised to his lips. "Have a l'il more sugar?"

John reached down for the can and poured another spoonful into the outstretched cup.

"'Nudder?" The old man's eyes twinkled up at him like two smooth brown stones in shallow water.

At last it was enough; John returned the can to the upended orange crate that was its daytime home by the fire. Then, retrieving the coffeepot from the corner of the grill, he added a bit more first to Tabby's cup, then to his own. He looked out across the flat, where the two figures, the tall seeming drawn along by the small, moved slowly off toward the hillside. They reached the little stream, lingered for a moment, then crossed the low bridge and continued on their way.

"He talks 'bout you sometime," the swishing voice said from behind him. "Likes you, I t'ink."

John felt a thrill of pleasure move up his spine, then spend itself in his scalp. But he did not answer or, for a moment, turn. When he did, moving the few steps which brought him back to the edge of the fire, there was a soft smile on his lips.

"How you been, Tabby?" he said quietly.

"Been okay," the old man said, again raising the cup to his wrinkled, toothless mouth. "Been jus' fine."

"You look fine. Maybe a little older."

"Little older," Tabby agreed, smiling broadly. "You too."

"S'pose so," John said. "How 'bout a cookie?"

"Don' mind."

John set off walking toward the wagon. The dogs, dozing beneath it, roused themselves and came to meet him—then when he ignored them, returned to their places and lay down. He stepped inside and took the tin down from the shelf.

Out across the flat, at the base of the hill, Kinsella and the little girl had stopped; still hand in hand, they looked up at the sheep. Then, as John hesitated on the step, the tall, stooped form of the old man bent down and, pointing upward, began explaining something to her. John watched a moment, then pulled the half-door closed behind him and set off once more toward the fire.

"Here," he said, offering the open tin.

"T'anks," Tabby said. Extending his smoothly wrinkled hand, he reached inside to take a single biscuit.

"You need more'n that," John said, and slipped three more into the old man's hand.

"T'anks," Tabby said, nibbling at the edge of one. "I got sumpin' f'you too."

John smiled, replaced the lid on the can, and put it away in the orange crate. "You don' say."

It was an expression he had heard Booker use. He was amazed to hear it coming from his own lips.

"Don' say," the old man repeated, and slowly opened his left hand. Inside, lying lightly on the shiny palm, was a small, bright cross and chain, silver and coral stones. Tabby looked up from it into John's face, then gravely held it out to him.

John made no move to take it. "What is it?" he muttered weakly, having no idea how he was meant to react. As soon as the words were out he realized how absurd they sounded.

"It's the ol' missy's," Tabby said. "She tole me to keep it."

John, continuing to look down at it, did not reply.

"Take it," the old man said. "You keep it now."

"Keep it," John muttered, still at a loss how to respond.

"Yah, you keep it, jus' like me—for the li'l missy when she get married."

"Married . . ."

"Yah, you keep it for her—jus' like the ol' missy said."

At last John reached out and, taking the chain between the tips of his fingers, lifted it to rest in his own palm.

"Good," Tabby said, with his broad, toothless smile. "Have 'nuzzer cookie?"

John, ignoring the last question, looked down at the small cross. The red stones, catching the light, seemed like drops of blood against his palm. Then, very quickly, he reached down to take the old man's hand and, holding it open, gently replaced the cross where it had been. "Best give it to Booker," John said. "He's sure to be here then. Me . . ."

The old man's soft brown eyes looked up at him in disbelief, then seemed to darken, harden.

"No, not Booker," he said abruptly, closing his fingers tightly over the cross. For a moment Tabby continued to look up at him, puzzlement imperceptibly giving way to utter disbelief. Then, very slowly, he lowered his gaze to the still-closed left fist resting on his lap; slowly the grip began to loosen, then opened like the petals of a flower.

"Look how it shine," he murmured. "I kep' it shined up real good."

"It's nice," John said. "But why don' you jus' keep it? Later, if you don' want Booker to keep it . . . if I'm here . . ." He heard his voice trail off weakly, for already the old man's eyes had begun to darken once again.

"No!" Tabby said sharply with a violent shake of his head. "Mus' be *now!*" And once more he thrust his hand forward, half rising to his feet as he did so. "Mus' be *you!*"

Glancing over the old Indian's rigid shoulder, avoiding the growing insistence in those shadowed eyes, he saw that Kinsella and Deirdre were heading back toward them. Still hand in hand, still engaged in some sort of quiet conversation, they had crossed over the little bridge now and would soon be here. The master's face, inclined, wore a tender, almost vulnerable expression that John had never thought to see there. The child— although somehow he had already ceased to think of her as a child, this though she was but six years old—the child looked up at her aged, silver-maned father with that curious, skeptical expression that she so often wore. Her fine blonde hair, roughly tousled now, shone like spun gold in the waning light of the sun.

"Okay," he said softly. "Okay." Reaching down once more to the smooth brown palm before him, he gathered up the cross and slipped it into his shirt pocket.

"Good," Tabby said for the second time, delaying his smile until he was absolutely certain. "'Nuzzer cookie?" he said at last.

Afterward, when they, all three, had gone—the orange pickup lurching over the final ridge and dropping from sight— afterward he remained for a long time beside the still-smoldering fire. He was not a person much given to moments of reflective self-examination. Indeed, like many others of his race, he viewed such things as largely a waste of time, if not positively to be shunned as self-indulgence. He did what was expected of him as well as he was capable, he tried to take advantage of the opportunities that came his way—and the rest generally took good care of itself. The visit just concluded, however, seemed somehow freighted with importance—yet there was nothing specific in it that he could identify as the cause. The result was a strange uneasiness—a feeling which through its very rarity seemed enhanced beyond itself.

The matter of Tabby and his cross, well that was not really

something to get bothered about. There had been no point in opposing the old man, after all, and when the time came for him to move on . . . then would be time enough to leave the thing with Booker.

It was strange about Tabby and Booker, though. He had never noticed any problem between the two of them—the opposite, if anything—and the big foreman had mentioned nothing over the summer that suggested any change of heart. In any case it had not seemed a matter of animosity, really—not even one of preference.

As for the little girl, well, as the afternoon proceeded she had seemed to soften toward him a bit. Not much, but a bit. That certain hint of a smile when, offering the cookies once again, he had given her three instead of one. And then, when it was time to leave, that soft "Bye, John."

No, the source of his uneasiness was Kinsella. Of that he was very, very sure.

"What's that?" the old man had said sharply, the frost-blue eyes narrowing with sudden interest. They were standing beside the open door of the sheepcamp then, just the two of them, the old man having asked to see his arrangements.

"The book?"

Responding to the curt nod, he had hurried inside to fetch it from the table, gathering up the big ledger as well.

"What I thought," Kinsella had said, ruffling through the bright, still-stiff pages. "I heard it was out." Slowly turning it over, looking down at the photograph on the back of the dust cover—the young, slim Lindbergh, the silver airplane—his eyes had seemed to lose their focus for a brief moment, then suddenly hardened to blue diamonds once again as, handing it back, he turned to go.

"I'm studying it for my English," John had heard himself chatter, the sound of his eager voice at once surprising and distasteful to him. "Mrs. Ithurria—Mr. Harignordoquy's sister—

she give it to me, almos' new. I read sixty-six pages already . . ."
And then, as though he lacked all power to stop: "But *you* must
remember—the day he flew."

The master had begun to turn away, his boot raised to return
to the others by the fire. But very suddenly he had stopped,
drawing back as though reined. For a moment he stood very,
very still, then looked back into John's eyes.

"Yes, I remember." The voice, when it came, was quiet,
almost gentle. The face too . . . no, it had not been that soft
expression he had earlier turned toward Deirdre, but there was
something like it in the tilt of the wiry eyebrows, the soft set of
the mouth.

"Were you here then?" John had heard himself, emboldened,
murmur.

"No, not yet. Not quite yet. I was still . . . somewhere else."

The old man fell silent, his gaze still strangely softened,
almost gentle, as he stood looking out toward the rams on the
hillside. And John, at last, had managed to keep his tongue,
simply watching until all at once the white-thatched, weary
head was turned toward him once again.

"Sixty-five pages did you say?"

Breathless, John burst out: "No, sixty-six—almos' sixty-
seven. Would you like to see 'em?"

A puzzled, vague smile had settled over the old man's face.
"See them?"

"Yes!" The single word, as he himself had heard it, seemed
almost shouted. It was with a conscious effort that he softened his tone. "Yes, sir. I have 'em right here, all wrote out."
Timidly, fearfully, he had opened the ledger and held it out.

For the briefest of moments he felt Kinsella's eyes, their hard,
crystalline quality returned, dwelling on the words—but then,
again, the old man had turned away, looking off toward the
hillside.

"No," he had said at last, the word coming softly, bathed in a kind of distant sadness. "Another time." And slowly he had set off alone, back toward the fire.

All the remainder of that evening, and long into the breathless night, John Siloa could not dispel the feeling that he had been allowed a glimpse into the windows of Kinsella's soul.

CHAPTER 4

1

On the first day of October the good Tabby Weepup, in accordance with his customary practice, ordered the white mule made ready and, filling his basket with the year's last chrysanthemums, set out after breakfast for the second spring. It was a chill, blustery day; wispy clouds scudded high above, and the boughs of the cedars creaked in the wind as he passed. Out across the dry, stubbled hayfield the dust made swirling phantoms against the sky. The cowboys, watching his slow, steady progress from the flat below, smiled secretly to one another, then returned to their work. All was as it should be.

When four-thirty came, however, with no sign of the old Indian, there was an apprehensive remark or two; and after an hour more passed the Lindsay brothers loaded two horses into a trailer and headed off, raising a great cloud of dust behind them. Parking at the upper edge of the hayfield, they proceeded on horseback up the stream until they reached the small, marshy meadow, where at the far end they found the white mule standing quietly beside the trunk of a willow. Seated against the base of the tree, his sheepskin coat buttoned up to his chin, the wicker basket by his side, was Tabby Weepup. He was quite dead.

Lifting the light, brittle body to the back of the mule, the two cowboys headed back to the truck where, after loading one of the horses, they parted—Nat returning in the truck while Carroll, leading the mule, set off down the streambank trail toward the ranch.

That evening, after the mortal remains of Tabby Weepup, laid in solemn state on the parlor table, had been viewed for the last time by all the denizens of Phoenix Ranch (excepting only the shepherd, whom Lonnie Wilson was to set off for at first light), Cyril Kinsella returned to the library and softly closed the door behind him. In his hand was a rusted coffee can, the location and purport of which he had learned but two days earlier from the now-cold lips of the departed himself. Placing it gingerly atop the desk, he lit the small oil lamp and, walking to the sideboard, poured an inch of whiskey into a glass, which he carried to one of the high-backed armchairs beside the fire. There he sat for upward of half an hour, the smoke from his cigarettes hanging in a low, level mass above his head, before at last he stirred and, returning to the sideboard, wiped the glass dry with his handkerchief and carefully replaced it inside. Finally he turned, walked once more to the desk, lowered himself into the tall leather chair behind it, and twisted the lid from the can.

The contents were meager: a small cloth Bull Durham bag and a neatly folded sheet of yellow paper. Lifting out the bag, Kinsella felt the rustle and clink of money, paper and coin. He glanced inside to confirm this fact, then laid the bag aside and unfolded the scrap of paper. It was written in a neat feminine hand, one he did not recognize—Tabby Weepup himself not having numbered writing among his many accomplishments. This is what it said:

24 sep 1951

I am Tabby R. Weepup, sitsun of United States & Nevada. Wen I di I want Mistr Kinsella put me long sid Misis Kinsellas gardin pleas if he liks to do this. I don ned no box jus mi cloths black sut and wach windet up tit. Wen I am dug in go tel mi neec Misis Maria Bear Goshute Indian reservatun at the winmil Willard Canyun I hav did. Thank you.

Tabby R. Weepup. X

It was shortly after noon the next day that Tabby R. Weepup, citizen of the United States and Nevada, was laid to his final rest beside the garden plot. Cyril Kinsella presided, although he spoke no eulogy as such and indeed never once looked down as the resplendently attired corpse, gold watchchain glinting in the sun, was lowered below on a rough wooden plank. It was he, however, who uttered the only words of farewell—a simple "Good-bye Tabby," no more—then cast the first spadeful of earth into the deep, steep-sided grave. At last, the mound completed, he turned without another word and, motioning to Booker, preceded him to the house. The cowboys lingered a moment, then dispersed uncertainly in the direction of the bunkhouse—leaving only John Siloa, who had arrived with Lonnie but a few minutes earlier, to stand alone beside the grave. At length, however, he too moved away and, passing through the yard, walked to the waiting truck.

When a quarter hour later Booker Goodman emerged from the great house, there was no one else in sight. He walked quickly to the barn, backed out the blue Model A, and drove out the lane toward the highway, then headed resolutely south. When he returned six hours later, headlights like luminous antennae probing the night before him, he was able to report his mission fully accomplished.

Two days later, quite early in the afternoon, Cyril Kinsella was seated at his desk, a stack of neglected paperwork before him, when he heard the rumble of a vehicle coming up the lane. It did not seem by the sound of it to be one of his own, but for some days now he had been expecting to hear from Harignordoquy, who often passed this way on his way to Creighton, where he was apparently well looked after by his brother's widow. Knowing his Basque friend's penchant for unannounced action—and suspecting he would be curious by now to know how his rams were working out—Kinsella rose smiling from his desk and moved toward the window, fully expecting to behold there the fairly new white Cadillac always used for these sentimental voyages.

What met his eyes, however—and indeed his ears had begun to question long before it actually rounded the corner—was surely not a Cadillac of any age. It was not in fact a car at all but a truck—a filthy and dilapidated flatbed of uncertain vintage. On the otherwise empty bed, firmly tied down with a rope, were two ragged suitcases and a large parcel wrapped in brown paper. As for the occupants of the cab, it was impossible to tell just who he or they might be, the closed windows being utterly opaque with mud and caked dust. Yet as Cyril Kinsella looked out from behind the immaculate window of his library, the fingers of one hand slowly stroking the tip of his chin, he quite suddenly and inexplicably experienced a fleeting, vagrant sense of . . . vulnerability.

Turning quickly, he walked through the parlor to the front door and, drawing it open, descended the little-used front stairs.

The driver of the truck had alighted now and, standing beside it, banged the dust from his worn black hat on the seat of his trousers. He was an Indian, seemingly of late middle age, greasy black hair hanging limply over his collar. Seeing the master's approach, he quite suddenly broke into a broad, open smile, thereby exhibiting a set of incredibly rotten teeth, and began to walk around the front of the truck, extending a hand of greeting as he came.

Kinsella, however, whose dark brow suggested he had little intention of allowing the matter to proceed much further, ignored the gesture entirely and moved directly to the passenger side of the vehicle. From here he could see that two more occupants remained inside, sitting motionless beside one another on the seat, but the coating of grime forbade any identification beyond that.

"Pleased to know you," the Indian was saying, apparently proof against the malevolent glance which now, very briefly, lingered upon him. "Wash Bear, that's me."

Kinsella, upon hearing the name, again turned to examine the face of his audacious caller, this time a bit more carefully. Deeply scarred by acne, the murky, red-rimmed eyes deep-set but wide apart, the carious smile still enduring, it was the face of a snake oil merchant about to close a sale.

"Tabby's cousin," the man continued, apparently determined to establish his credentials without the inconvenience of interrogation.

Kinsella had not yet spoken—although by the look of him that lack was soon to be remedied by an invitation to depart. For now, though, he turned once again from his importunate visitor and, reaching out, grasped the dusty handle of the passenger side door and drew it creakily open.

The occupants were two Indian women—one old and rather plump, her hair done up in a neat gray bun at the nape of her neck, and the other quite young, not much over twenty by the look of her. The older woman looked out at Kinsella with calm, unsmiling black eyes, as though measuring him for a suit. The other, however, did not look out at him at all, instead regarding the backs of her folded brown hands with curiously concentrated scrutiny.

"Maria Bear," Kinsella said simply.

The old woman, still watching him carefully, gravely nodded.

"Well, what do you want? You have the money. There was nothing else except his watch, and . . . well, my man told you what became of that."

The old woman, her eyes unblinking, regarded him with an eerie, almost supernatural placidity. He continued to have the impression that he was being measured, appraised, assessed for value. It was not a sensation to which he was accustomed, certainly not one he enjoyed, and his thin lips had begun to form a less modulated inquiry when suddenly, unexpectedly, she spoke.

"Tabby tol' me to come." The voice was low, calm, matter-of-fact, as though announcing something wholly self-evident. There was only the slightest trace of accent.

"To come? But I told you there was nothing else. Nothing!"

Again the woman fell silent. This time, however, her expression had altered to one of perplexity, like a teacher with a backward scholar she knew to be capable of better work. Kinsella was again on the point of raising his voice, feeling the blood rising, when all at once the younger woman lifted her face toward him.

"This is my mother," she said sharply, the voice high and clear like a scolding child.

Her face was quite pretty, with the fine, narrow features he associated with the more northerly tribes. Now that she had finished speaking—for already it was apparent she would say no more—her dark, round eyes blazed out one last angry glance at him, then suddenly grew cloudy with confusion as their gaze descended once more to her hands, which only now began to relax from the small fists they had become.

Kinsella, momentarily disarmed, stood silent as the older woman reached out her own, square-fingered hand and patted the girl on the thigh—speaking as she did so some soft, swishing words in their language. Then, his balance somewhat recovered, he glared impatiently at the iron gray of her hair until, after a moment, Maria looked back toward him.

"This is Consuela," she said softly. "My daughter." Her expression, wistful and proud at once, made it clear that there would be no further explanation.

Kinsella nodded, assenting, and after a moment Maria went on, her voice seeming to strive for patience.

"Tabby said when he was gone I should come help you, do what he did. He said you would need someone, someone who knew how . . ."

The man, Wash Bear, who to this point had observed a prudent silence in the background, now saw what he thought was an appropriate moment to intervene. "Maria knows about everything. She cooks, she sews. And scrubbing? Why that woman scrubs like nobody you ever . . ."

Kinsella, wheeling about, silenced him with a glance. Yet when he turned back to Maria, snorting once as he did so, his expression had softened, reflecting a confused mixture of sympathy, fatigue, and mute incomprehension.

"Come in, won't you, and have some coffee?" he said.

Cyril Kinsella's long legs were unsteady beneath him as he mounted the front stairs and, reaching the porch, turned to watch the small, ragged delegation ascending in his wake. He sensed significance in all this, a significance which, for all his inability to identify it, he was utterly powerless to ignore, much less avert. And yet he found in himself none of that old urge to take command, to resolve by domination and abruptness. In its place, as he turned to swing open the great oaken front door and motion them inside, was only a calm curiosity, a placid, fateful foreboding.

And so perhaps it should have come as no great surprise when nearly two hours later, just as the shadows of evening were beginning to lengthen down the slopes of the western mountains, the short, dark figure of Wash Bear was seen (by old Carl Withers, specifically, who had been watching all these proceedings with ever-mounting astonishment) emerging through the same front door, descending the same little-used front stairs,

retrieving the two battered suitcases and the paper-wrapped
parcel from the bed of the truck, and hulking up the stairs to
disappear once more inside. Here, however, there might perhaps
have been a justified moment of uncertainty—until, that is, the
same dark, slightly paunchy figure was seen to appear again in
the doorway, quite alone and empty-handed, and, descending
for the last time, climb behind the wheel of his venerable truck,
encourage it into halting progress, and disappear down the lane.

The interview, at least in its early stages, had shown little
promise of such a result. Once within the rosy stone walls of his
stronghold, Kinsella had seemed to recover his balance markedly—until soon even the redoubtable Maria Bear had begun
to sense the strength of his resolution. "We have no amenities
for women here, you must see that, nowhere you . . . you and
your daughter might be comfortable. I am grateful to Tabby,
don't misunderstand me, but it just would not work out." Until
at last the old woman had begun to grow weary. It was clearly
hopeless, not to be.

She had just been at the point of announcing her, their, departure when all at once there came the sound of a large vehicle
moving up the lane, then stopping, turning, backing, and retreating once again. More out of simple curiosity than anything
else, she decided to wait yet a moment. Leaning back in her
chair, she had once more raised the fine china cup to her lips
when she saw out the window, just passing before it, a small,
golden-haired figure carrying a blue lunch pail. The braids,
Maria Bear noted, were rather badly done.

Deirdre, although she seemed to accept the fact of Tabby's
death with a stoic grace, had not yet managed to accommodate
her conduct to his absence. At this time of day especially, when
the school bus deposited her at the head of the lane, something within her continued to expect the old Indian to meet
her at the kitchen door and, taking her lunch pail, place before her the warm milk and bread and honey that were always

ready—then to settle into the chair across from her and, his old hands busily shelling peas or peeling potatoes, prime her with soft questions until she was fully launched, chattering into his receptive silence. Today, as on the two days preceding, the realization had not fully struck her until she reached the kitchen door and, passing inside, found the room quite empty—worse than empty, really, for now where Tabby had been there was only his palpable absence. Again, as before, she had wandered distractedly about the kitchen for a few moments before at last, with a heavy sigh, she deposited her blue lunch pail on the sinkboard and passed into the hallway.

This day, however, was not quite like those others. Rather than the broad, breathless shoal of silence that had greeted her before, today there were voices, certainly voices, echoing up the hallway from the front parlor. Remembering the strange, shabby truck parked outside, she moved slowly toward the sound, passing her hand along the smooth wainscoting as she went.

One voice, of course, she instantly knew—that harsh, low-pitched rasp, her father's—but the other, providing those short, compact replies to his insistent questions, she did not. It was low and calm, soothing in a way that somehow seemed familiar to her, although she was sure she had never heard this voice before. Even more astonishing, the voice was female. She stood listening for a moment, trying to place that soft resonance, that way of drawing in the breath before speaking, until at last, overcome by curiosity, she went to the doorway and looked in.

They did not see her at once, and she had a moment to examine them, one by one. Seated in one corner, on the blue velvet chair that always remained there, a dark Indian man gazed mournfully out the window, his crooked hands holding an empty cup and saucer as if they were a bird in a nest. The old woman who had been speaking, seated on the couch across from her father, had a look of puzzled weariness about her eyes now as she listened to yet another question, offered yet another futile explanation. Neither of these two, however, were awarded more than a brief glance, for almost immediately Deirdre's gaze fixed upon the third figure, who, seated beside the old one on the couch, had now turned and was looking toward the doorway.

If Cyril Kinsella would later have great difficulty, when he had the opportunity to reflect on it, in expressing even to himself the quality of that first look which Consuela Bear had bestowed on him, his daughter would experience no similar incapacity, for the gazes she and the daughter of Maria Bear now exchanged were equivalent—each the complex yet utterly focused regard of a child assessing an unknown contemporary. The fact that one of them, golden-haired and blue-eyed, was a few days shy of six years old while the other, her brown-black eyes set wide apart beneath neatly trimmed, blue-black bangs, was at least fifteen years older—this meager fact was wholly lost in the subtle yet innocent interplay of their glances.

Kinsella, noticing Consuela's changed expression, quickly turned in his chair.

"Well, there you are," he said simply. His drawn, craggy features seemed at last to relax, reflecting immense relief. He had heard the bus come up, and although he would be the last to admit it, had for several minutes been anticipating this appearance, from which something within him seemed to expect respite, if not blessed rescue. "Come on in," he continued immediately, brightly, as he stood up. "These are Tabby's people, come to visit."

Deirdre continued to stand quite still.

"Well, come on in," Kinsella repeated. "You needn't be shy."

At last, seeing the growing importunity of her father's expression, she stepped slowly into the room.

"This is Deirdre," Kinsella was saying. "She is just home from school."

The little girl dutifully advanced to her father's side, where, feeling his hand on her shoulder, she heard him speak the names, then recite the relationship of each to Tabby. Her soft blue eyes, however, acknowledged neither the man nor the old woman, remaining fixed on the figure beside her on the couch. A broad silence descended as Kinsella, overtaken by a mounting uneasiness, glanced helplessly from one face of complex innocence to the other. Then, like the sudden chime of a bell, there came the high, slightly nasal voice of the young woman.

"I went to school too," Consuela said brightly, directing her words wholly toward Deirdre. "Not today, though," she added, her tone altering to one of vague regret.

"Where?" Deirdre responded immediately. "I go to Mrs. Warden's class."

"No . . ." came the thoughtful reply. "Not that class; I don't think so." She seemed puzzled, confused, as she turned to her mother for assistance. Maria Bear, softly taking her hand, nodded no. "It was another class," the old woman said.

"Another class," Consuela announced decisively, looking from Wash Bear to Kinsella, then back to her tiny blonde interlocutor. Her dark eyes shone with vindication.

Kinsella looked stunned. He had, it seemed, expected assistance of a somewhat different character from his daughter. Now, his face slack with weariness, he watched while Deirdre moved from her place beside him to the couch, where, her small hand coming to rest on Consuela's dark forearm, she was soon lost in whispered conversation.

A few moments passed, the only sound that of this sibilant, animated interchange, before he seemed to come to himself a bit. There was a stubborn, dogged note in his voice—as though he had determined to overwhelm the inexplicable with solid, adult concerns—when he again turned to the old woman.

"Maybe you can tell me," he resumed, resolutely straightening in his chair. "Tabby never wanted to say just where he lived . . . before he came here. I figured that was his business, maybe he was in trouble or something, but now that he's gone . . . Was it with you; on the reservation, I mean?"

At first it was as though she had not heard. For all her apparent imperturbability to this point, she seemed deeply affected

by Deirdre's reaction. Now, as the two girls—for such they
truly were, whatever the difference in chronological age—avidly
whispered beside her, she seemed absorbed in some distant
memory, her gaze fixed on the far wall. All at once, however,
she appeared to revive, almost to start, as the question settled
in upon her. Then, quite suddenly, her gaze had returned to
Kinsella's face, as if searching there for some sign.

And now, just as suddenly, she had begun to speak—not in
the clipped, clear fashion with which she had met his previous
inquiries but in a tone almost conversational, her voice assuming
more strongly than ever the strange singsong quality that had
distinguished Tabby's speech.

The answer, if such it could be called, had begun at least
on a responsive note. Yes, she said, he had lived with her—
with them—until her husband, who "liked to drink," had died.
Then yes, for three more years he had lived there, until some
difficulty, some disagreement with tribal authorities had caused
him to leave . . . At this point, however, her reply had begun to
wander—for suddenly it was not of Tabby but of the girl that
she was speaking, her birth, her childhood, the difficulties of
her upbringing. "Because I was all alone then, you see, jus' me
and . . . this little girl." But then, by means of some transition
that Kinsella, at least at this point, could not begin to follow, her
course had returned to Tabby, this time to his young manhood,
or what she knew of it, for apparently there had been more than
twenty years between them.

From time to time, Kinsella noticed, the old woman would
glance warily to his left, toward the blue velvet chair in the
corner behind him where the Indian man—her late husband's
half-brother it now appeared—sat stiffly against the wall.

Until at last, after what must have been at least ten minutes—ten minutes during which Deirdre and Consuela only
once ceased their whispering, and then only for a moment as the
Indian girl, with a sly, conspiratorial smile, produced a handful
of lemon drops from her pocket—until at last it seemed that she

was about to conclude. As Kinsella watched her, sensing now a note of agitation, anxiety in her voice, the words had begun to trail off, grouping themselves into disjointed phrases rather than sentences, then finally ceased altogether in a sort of embarrassed silence as her gaze slipped downward to her folded hands.

Sensing that the moment for leave-taking was approaching, Kinsella had begun to rise to his feet when all at once the old woman drew herself up on the couch and, glancing once more toward the figure in the corner behind him, loosed a sudden, urgent rush of words.

"I never saw him again after he left. We never wrote. There was only that one letter a week ago—my aunt in Creighton made it for him. Only that one letter, telling me to come when . . ." Her dark, powerful hand moved stealthily to rest on Consuela's arm.

"He never knew . . ."

Kinsella, a sense of something very much like panic suddenly upon him, had turned his gaze toward the two still-whispering figures at the far end of the couch when from behind him, over his left shoulder, there came a sudden rustling, then the sound of breaking china. Turning in his chair, he saw the man on his feet, the shattered pieces of the cup and saucer on the floor, the red-rimmed eyes darkly glistening as, in a flood, the Indian words burst from him. But almost at the same instant the old woman had also begun to speak, very quickly, her strange, sibilant words sharp with attack. And then it was over, as abruptly as it had begun. Wash Bear, the sting of reproof printed across his pitted, dark face, sank back in his chair and was still.

"My brother-in-law says we must go now," Maria Bear said. "If you will tell the price, we pay for the cup." Slowly she reached out and took her daughter's hand, then rose to her feet. The young woman's eyes were frightened, confused, as she began to get up.

"But can't she stay and play, Poppa? Just a little while?" There was a note of outrage in Deirdre's small voice as she looked over at Kinsella, who remained rooted to his chair. He, his mind awash, could only shake his head—less, it seemed, in negation than in mute incomprehension.

"But why not?" the little girl insisted. "She only just came."

Slowly Kinsella raised his head, the hollow, ashen eyes at last coming to rest on the immobile features of Maria Bear. She, however, did not immediately return his glance; her own, fixed on the figure behind him, seemed weighted with an abject helplessness as she said, turning at last to face him:

"It is quite . . . safe."

"Of course," Kinsella murmured, as if to himself. Then, turning with a smile toward his daughter: "Of course."

The three adults remained quite still, utterly silent—Maria Bear on her feet, the two men crumpled in their chairs—while Consuela, her face now glowing with pleasure, rose from the couch and, with a last quick glance toward her mother, followed the little girl through the doorway and down the hall.

Kinsella listened in silence to the hollow sound of their twin footsteps mounting the stairs. Then, with a heavy sigh, he too rose to his feet.

"You should bring in your things," he said softly, and crossed to the window.

2

"We have no amenities for women here"—so Kinsella had put it, and indeed in many ways it had become so. This was not to say, of course, that the basic facilities did not in some form remain, the same luxuries and comforts that two different women had already, albeit briefly, enjoyed. True, a good number of the rooms were no longer used now (indeed several, to tell the truth, never had been), and most of the better linens and china and glassware had long since been packed away, but everything,

everything was here, from the silver napkin rings and Waterford crystal to the big Steinway, all in quiet material readiness for any feminine eventuality that might come to pass.

And yet there was something about the place now that seemed to preclude any such occurrence, as though some protective field had grown up about it since the last mistress's departure. It was, after all, six years now since Margaret Kinsella had lived and died here, and even so her tenure had extended over no more than twenty months. Beyond, behind, before her stretched a period of sixteen years, long, weary years of solitary building and brooding, and behind that was only . . . Abigail. Twenty months and a week, then, twenty months and a week—out of all the twenty-four years this house had loomed up here on the sage flat.

Until at last, during these past few years, it seemed that what was once mere fact had finally and irrevocably hardened into principle. It was as though the entire sex—at least the adult manifestations of it—had been banned by solemn edict, permitting nothing more threatening to enter than the Vargas girls tacked up on the bunkhouse walls. So, then, it had become, and so, one thought, it ever would be. So one had thought.

In one sense, of course, the miraculous change so suddenly come to pass was not so radical as it might first have seemed. Maria, in many ways simply the female edition of her . . . uncle, had certainly not come upon the scene like a new wife, trailing scented frocks and issuing veiled decrees all about her. On the contrary, her insertion into the normal and existing routine had seemed almost effortless—so much so, in fact, that it was sometimes difficult to avoid suspicions of some kind of supernatural coaching. She knew, seemed always to have known, just what to do.

She, they, lived, as Tabby had lived, in the little one-room cabin behind the house, in the shade of the sighing poplars. Very few changes were made. An additional bed, for which there certainly was adequate room, was politely but firmly refused;

they had slept together in a narrow bed of this kind since Consuela's birth, and there was no reason to change that now. The
rough cedar-plank floor, worn smooth near the threshold and
bed and stove by a quarter century of gentle footfalls, remained
wholly bare—as did the single lightbulb, which, innocent of
any kind of shade or decoration, continued to hang mournfully
down from the rafter above the stove. As it turned out, however, the brown paper package had contained several curtains
of coarse blue linen, which were promptly put up in place of
the tattered, smoke-stained chintz rags that hung there, the last
sorry relic of Margaret Kinsella's parturient handiwork. These,
along with a faded purple doily which came to grace the top of
the pine dresser, turned out to be the only conspicuous evidence
of changed occupancy.

As for Tabby's household duties, Maria had assumed them
with a skill and efficiency that made even her brother-in-law's
high recommendation seem modest. Her cooking was equally
good, if not better, and included some additional dishes which,
as soon as the sense of unfamiliarity was overcome, were quickly
assimilated into the regular menu. The cleaning tasks as well
were done almost from the outset to Kinsella's complete satisfaction—often with an unprompted attendance to detail that was
little short of uncanny. Small, idiosyncratic matters—the place-
ment of ashtrays at meals, the arrangement of items on a bedside
table, the way towels were hung and folded—were mastered as
if by instinct, with a single reminder at most.

Until soon it was as though she had always been there, her
predecessor no more than a prior incarnation, his decease no
more than the occasion for a change of bodily form—the vague,
toothlessly smiling visage of Tabby Weepup become gravely
watchful, darkly inscrutable; the halo of white, close-cropped
hair given way to a severe, steel-gray bun, drawn tightly to the
back of the head; the sparse, frail physique suddenly broadened,
solidified, mysteriously augmented in substance. And finally, as
the weeks passed into months, even the sense of alteration began

to dissolve, then fell away. Tabby Weepup, fully assimilated into Maria Bear, slippered soundlessly from table to stove, stove to table—and never had been other than what he had become.

All such pretty fictions to one side, however, there was one aspect of the daily routine that could never be quite the same for Maria Bear as it had been for Tabby. For the fact was that Tabby had had but one child in his charge—one pair of braids to be done each morning, one small body to bathe and clothe, one tiny spirit to entertain and educate—whereas Maria Bear had two, the second body being simply somewhat larger and differently formed than the first. It was difficult to say just why this should have been so; surely the girl Consuela, who for all her other failings peeled potatoes with a sharp knife, ironed linen like a chambermaid, and rode a horse like the very wind, was fully capable of learning to bathe and dress herself as well. But the plain fact—doubtless because Maria, for reasons sufficient to herself, had *made* it a fact—was that the tasks of each morning involved, and quite prominently, the bathing and dressing and grooming of two.

It was perhaps fortunate in this respect—at least from the standpoint of Maria's time—that her two charges, from the moment of their first meeting, had treated one another more or less as sisters, with all the enduring trust and confidence that relationship can suggest. To the extent possible—which is to say at all times that Deirdre was not asleep or in school—they were utterly inseparable, playing and conversing and conspiring in precisely the same fashion as two girls of equal age. The fact that they were not of equal age—that the larger was in truth seventeen years the smaller's elder—seemed never to occur to them, just as all the apparent incongruities arising from that basic difference seemed never, or almost never, to catch their attention.

So it was that early each morning—after Maria had dressed Consuela in their cabin, brought her to the big house, led her softly up the stairs to wake and dress the little girl, then led the two back down the stairs to the kitchen—so it was that the two would sit quite contentedly side by side, their faces toward the softly purring woodstove, while the old woman brushed out and braided their hair, alternating the order between black and gold according to the day. Nor did either find it at all unusual or curious that Maria, declaring it time for the Wednesday or Saturday afternoon bath, should lead them both together to the third floor and, undressing them one by one, place them together in the large, claw-footed bathtub at the far end of the hall. If there were questions at first, Maria seemed to have the answers, and soon all attention had come to rest upon its proper object, which is to say the flotilla of small, brightly colored plastic boats which Maria kept in the cabinet.

It is difficult to say just what might have occurred if Cyril Kinsella, the stern master of all these persons and domains, had learned of activities such as these—most particularly the last described. As it happened, however, he noticed nothing more troubling in his daughter than an increased liking for sweets, a commodity the Indian girl seemed always to possess in abundance. Indeed, it is perhaps not too much to say that he, for all his usual powers of observation and penetration, had following their installation taken but little notice of his two new charges—and certainly suspected nothing of the strange female alliance fast growing up about his feet. To put the matter plainly, and by way of some defense, Cyril Kinsella, just at this moment, had other things—one in particular—on his mind.

It was now more than twenty-three years since that dry summer of 1931—twenty-three years of success and anguish, bright hope and gnawing despair—all of which, as he now thought back upon it, amounted to little more than an effort to somehow efface, cast back into nonbeing, those days and the five years before them. It was, of course, a lost endeavor, had been from the first, but if ever there had been a chance for progress, at least in achieving some more useful perspective, Abigail had made it her business to prevent it. All the same, it was curious that she should have succeeded so well.

For it should have been so simple to avoid. She had never even threatened to visit, never in all these years—and by now he had ceased to fear that she would do so. Perhaps in the beginning it had been mere haughtiness, simple outrage that kept her from it—even, perhaps, a nagging thought that she could not yet trust herself to act as she had determined to act—but now, he knew, it had become something else, something colder and more deliberate. She wanted him to remember her only as she was, had been—never to have that memory softened by seeing what she had become. And oh yes, she knew him well enough, more than well enough, to know that he himself would never come, never seek her out.

And so it had been only the letters, letters which, as Booker never ceased to remind him, he need not ever have received. Yes, Booker would have taken care of that, as he took care of so much—and having done so might have allowed the normal process, the beneficial anaesthetic of time, to at last begin to do its work. But no, it had been too late for that even then, for there had been nine years of them, nearly a hundred, he would guess, before Booker had ambled upon the scene. By then, by then . . . No, she had her claw in him, and now it would stay there to the end. The end.

Yes, she knew that, had always known it—and now it seemed the time had come to press it a little deeper, embed it a little more firmly.

Twenty-two he would be now, the boy—already a man by some measures. And already a brush with war. So young, even he had not been so young. And yes, too young, perhaps—for he himself at least had had the wit to stay away, to linger on a while until the stupidity and horror of it could begin to disperse into the renewed quotidian, the spectacle of individual people dusting themselves off and simply trying to get on with it, rebuilding what could be salvaged of their lives on the very soil that had swallowed so much of their blood. No, he could never have fled from it so soon, returning to the parades and waiting arms of those who could never begin to understand. As it was, even two years had hardly been enough, as a thousand years could never really be enough—and that cold October morning in 1921 when once again his foot had touched the New York shore had ever afterward remained in his memory as the coldest, darkest day of his life.

Yes, but then again, Seoul was certainly no Paris, Pusan hardly Naples or Marseilles . . . In any case he, the boy, had returned straightaway, unwilling, it seemed, to tarry a moment longer, eager to take up just where he had left off, as if none of that, from Inchon onward, had ever really happened. Or so she said, so she told it.

And yet that was not all she had said, all she told . . .

But no, nothing could come of this notion of hers. It simply could not be, that was all. The fact that the boy might be back now, that he might have begun to mutter now and then about coming to Nevada, that could be of no consequence at all—no more than had been her constant, faithful reporting over the years, the detailing of each setback and victory in that young life. No, nothing had changed, nothing ever would change. She knew that. The boy knew that. For it all had been decided, and very long ago.

And so yes, Cyril Kinsella may well have had some very good reasons—one in particular—for that uncharacteristic want of vigilance, that uncharacteristic neglect, at least insofar as Maria's innovations in domestic routine were concerned. Even so, however, there were certain more troubling aspects of this new arrangement that should certainly have come to his attention—not least of which was that certain vague indisposition that lately seemed to have arisen among the cowboys, the source for which became apparent each time the slim form of Maria Bear's daughter came into view. As it was, however, he was more than ever relying upon another who, in trying moments like these, had always served him as his eyes and ears—and where necessary his fist. Yes, after all there was Booker. There was Booker Goodman after all . . .

3

The bare lightbulb over the workbench seemed to flicker briefly as he applied the last bit of glue and secured the clamps. Quickly he glanced at his watch, then began to put things away. Only when everything was in its place, the bridle laid out carefully to dry on the now-clean surface, did he reach up to the softly playing radio, click it off, and turn away. Moving to a narrow doorway to the right of the bench, he turned the knob and went inside, leaving the door ajar behind him.

It was a square, rather dark room, with but a single narrow window, high up against the rafters over the sink. Against the facing wall was his bed—a narrow, iron affair identical to those in the bunkhouse, the blanket drawn tight enough to satisfy the most fastidious of sergeants. Above, on a narrow, freshly painted shelf, were a few magazines and newspapers, a tattered Gideon Bible, an assortment of various other objects— the carved wooden head of an Indian chief in full headdress, a cracked crockery vase full of pencils, a large ball of undyed wool yarn, a pair of long-roweled Spanish spurs, and a small framed photograph, quite faded, of a young black woman holding a dog. At the foot of the bed, near the opposite corner, was a second doorway leading outside.

Moving to his left, Booker went to the sink and washed his hands, then opened the little refrigerator and, after gazing inside for a moment, took out a pair of eggs. These he put into a small pot, then returned to the sink for water. Turning the tap, waiting for the eggs to be covered, he looked up into the old, chipped shaving mirror attached to the wall. The weary expression uncertainly reflected back at him seemed to utterly arrest his attention—until at last, the water overflowing the pot, he closed the tap. For a moment he continued looking, peering into the face of the image as though he failed to recognize it. Then, turning quickly away, he put the pot on one of the burners of the old gas hotplate, not yet turning it on, and walked slowly to his bed. There, slipping off his boots, he sat motionless for several minutes, his eyes directed vacantly toward the far corner, where a tattered oilskin raincoat, draped over two wooden pegs, made an empty scarecrow against the wall.

It had become more difficult for him now, with Tabby gone. The old Indian, for all his mulish habits, had been a great comfort to Kinsella, like a pinching but familiar old pair of slippers—although Kinsella himself would have been the last to confess it—and however efficient Maria had proved to be, however effortless had seemed her assumption of Tabby's physical duties, the comforting patina of long use and reliance was still missing. The difference showed itself in many ways, of which the most conspicuous was a heightened irritability in the old man, an impatience that dwarfed all that had come before. More to the point, and although Tabby—so far as Booker knew—had never been called upon to share his explicitly interlocutory duties (in part, perhaps, because the old Indian would never have sat still for it, walking out in mid-sentence as he was wont to when the conversation began to weary him), the absence of the old Indian had seemed to increase the master's needs in this regard. It was as though all these years the two of them, Kinsella and Tabby, had carried on some kind of silent conversation between them, a conversation which he now was forced to articulate into Booker's well-seasoned ear.

Yes, it was becoming very, very difficult, maybe too difficult for him. He had never thought he would find himself admitting to such a possibility—that something Kinsella asked of him he might not be able to provide—but perhaps, after all, it was so, was fast becoming so. For now, compounding everything, was that other . . . circumstance as well.

The sound of shouts and laughter, coming from the direction of the big house, passed along outside, just beyond the wall of his room, seemed to fade away, then burst like a bright wave into the barn. He sat for a moment listening, the echo of their chatter filling the great, high space to the distant roof beams, before at last he drew on his boots and walked out into the shop, carefully pulling his door closed behind him. Then, crossing to the threshold, he stood for a moment looking out across the vast, rough-planked floor of the barn.

It had been unseasonably warm these past few days, a late Indian summer in seeming honor of the departed Tabby Wee-pup. Even now, with evening beginning to fall, there was a strange heaviness in the air, a sultry vestige of the long summer just past. The last rays of the sun, pushing feebly through the yawning main door to his left, seemed to gather a momentary strength from the motes of suspended dust through which they passed, then guttered out exhausted on the hay-strewn floor. Before him and to his right, filling the far wall and entire rear of the structure, three great seven-tiered structures of new-baled hay loomed darkly, like ships passing in the dusk. The air was heavy with the pungent, almost acrid smell of it, the odor of the fields still too concentrated by confinement to yield the sweet fragrance that would come later. Nearer to hand, at the feet of the fresh stacks, the remainder of last year's crop lay bright and golden, the further bales in low stacks, the nearer in tumbled disarray.

A thin, tiger-striped barn cat, crossing toward the main doorway, looked haughtily back at him a moment, then continued on its way.

They were nowhere to be seen, but still he could hear the sound of their voices—the high, eager chime of Deirdre, the only slightly lower tone of the Indian girl—echoing against the high, raftered roof. At last, his curiosity getting the better of him, he descended the single step and set out slowly in the direction of the main door.

He had not walked twenty paces, no more than fifty feet, when the chattering abruptly ceased. He drew up listening, and after a minute or so had passed in silence heard it—the soft giggling he had by that time long expected.

It came from quite nearby, and yet just where, just how, was very difficult to say. He at first remained quite still, expecting at any moment to see them rushing out upon him from among the tumbled, golden bales, but when several more minutes passed, the only sound the same soft giggling as before, he at last grew weary of the game.

"Come on out," he said. "It's almost time for Deirdre's supper. And mine."

Again nothing beyond another round of delighted snuffling.

"Okay, then. I'm going for a walk. Don't be late for supper." Setting out again, he strode briskly toward the wide doorway. He was just passing through it when the sound he next expected— or one of them—came rushing up behind him.

"You would never have found us," Deirdre said, pulling on the pocket of his trousers. "Why didn't you look?"

He turned, lowering his glance to confront the haughty, petulant expression directed up at him.

"Well, if I never would have found you . . ."

"But you should have *looked!*" she cried, her foot stamping on the dusty floor.

"Okay," Booker relented. "I'll look now—but not for long. Your father's going to be waiting."

"He's not waiting. He's sick again."

"Sick or not he's waiting, missy, don't you bother yourself about that. But okay, for just a minute. She's still hiding, isn't she?"

"Not hiding, but you still can't find her," the little girl said enigmatically as they headed back into the now-darkening barn. "Besides, you left your light on."

She was certainly right about that. From the open doorway of the shop the dim incandescent glow shone out, making antic patterns on the hay-littered floor before it.

"Go get it for me, will you, missy?" he said, reaching down to pat her gently on the back. "This shouldn't take long."

As the little girl set off he angled to his left among the fallen bales—just where he thought the giggling had come from before. This time, however, there was only silence, or so he thought at first. As he stood there looking about him, however, Deirdre apparently having found something to detain her, he was sure after a moment he could hear the soft, even sound of breathing. She was very near, then, but still he could see nothing. The tumbled bales were all about his feet, but there was nothing—certainly not the dark, crouching form that he expected—behind any of them. Beyond, though still quite nearby, was a broad four-tiered stack of last year's hay, and beyond that only the dark, pungent towers at the rear. He was about to turn away, concluding that Deirdre's supper and his own should now take precedence, when all at once he felt his glance drawn back—to the gleam of an eye. Sensing herself discovered, its owner began to laugh—a lower, somewhat different laugh—then pushed down the upended bale behind which she had been sitting.

"You're smart," she said. "You found my house."

It was indeed a house, or as near to one as could be fashioned from last year's hay. The bale she had pushed down, serving as a kind of door, loosely filled the opening into a low chamber, about waist-high, of eight or ten bales' volume, perhaps six feet square in all. At the darkened rear of it, having drawn back from her place of observation, sat Consuela, legs curled up beneath her, dark eyes gleaming like a cornered animal. Here and there, littering the floor, were a few crumpled candy wrappers, an old magazine, and an empty Coke bottle or two.

"Did you make this?" he said at last.

"Yep," she answered, remaining in her place. "All by myself."

"What do you do here?"

For a moment there was only silence. "I just come here, that's all," the voice said at last. Another brief silence, then: "None of your business."

"Maybe," he said. "Who knows about it?"

There was no answer.

"Your mother, does she know?"

"Ha! She's the one I hide from."

"Deirdre, then. Only Deirdre?"

"None of your beeswax, you old Booker." And again, softly, she began to laugh. "None of your damn beeswax."

There was a sudden rustling in the hay behind him as the little girl, out of breath, ran up.

"Ah," she bawled. "You found her."

"Never mind that," Booker said, an odd note of irritation in his voice now. "You just get off home now. Where the heck you been?"

"None of your beeswax," Deirdre said, stepping back a pace. Then, as he moved toward her, she set off quickly toward the door, turning as she reached the opening.

"But I saw your dirty magazine," the small voice shot back at him. Disappearing around the corner, she ran off toward the house.

He stood looking at the yawning doorway, its frame now filled with a soft, rosy light, until he heard the same low laughter, softer this time, beginning at his back.

"Now you get out of there," he said sharply. The dark form seemed to draw backward, then slowly, slowly gathered itself and began to inch forward on hands and knees.

He watched in silence as she materialized in the opening, the dark eyes looking out at him with a mixture of fear, wariness, . . . and something else he could not, in that moment, have identified. Slowly, deliberately, she rose to her knees, then to her feet, brushing a bit of hay from her shirt front as she did so. Booker found himself watching her hand, the long, slim fingers striking softly against the fabric—until all at once that other, vague expression had become a smile. Abruptly, almost violently, he turned away.

"Get along," he said. "My supper's waiting."

He watched as she carefully replaced the hay-bale door, then turned to pass before him, eyes downcast, and make her way slowly toward the entrance. For a moment he stood in silence, looking after her, then he too set out.

At the doorway they drew even and she stopped. She did not look over at him, nor he at her—the two simply standing there in silence, framed in the darkened opening, for what must have been a full minute. Above their heads, swooping and veering through the cool evening air, the nighthawks were already at their work; far off to the north, beyond the tightly fenced hayfields, rose a trailing cloud of dust.

"Antelopes," she said at last, her voice with a soft, hoarse note to it.

He nodded. "There's been a bunch up that way the last few weeks."

"I love them," she said. "They're my friends."

He glanced quickly over at her, noted the firm set of her jaw. "Your friends?"

"Yes," she said, at last looking up at him. The glance was sharp, challenging, but soon, as it began to soften, she turned away again. "I used to watch them, how they run. Sometimes, when they'd go along beside the car, I used to look in their big eyes. They know me. They taught me how to run."

Booker, silent, watched the faint trail of dust until at last it was gone. He moved to go, then suddenly turned back to face her. The dark eyes looking up at him were soft, unblinking, but there remained that certain light of wild, animal fear in them that never seemed wholly absent—never, that is, unless she was alone with Deirdre. He reached out his hand to touch her, then drew back.

"Booker," she said all at once. "Booker, please don't tell my mother. Please."

The dark eyes, glistening, were stricken with alarm.

"Your mother . . . ?"

"'Bout my house. You won't tell her, will you?"

The big man looked down at her gravely.

"No," he said at last. "I won't tell her. I won't tell anybody."

The smile was radiant, open.

"Oh, Booker," she said, suddenly reaching out to squeeze his arm, enfolding it in both of hers. Feeling her breasts against him, he slowly drew away.

"And you won't hurt it? You won't kick it down?"

"No," he said, more grave than before. "I won't hurt it."

Again she seized his arm, again the soft pressure. This time, however, he did not pull away—until at last, releasing him, she stood back, looking brightly up into his face.

"Oh, Booker," she said softly. "Booker, you're so good."

He continued looking down at her for a moment, then turned to go. "My supper," he said weakly as he stepped back into the barn.

But again she had him by the arm, drawing him back into the great doorway, then a step outside. "And I won't tell on you neither, Booker. You'll see. And I'll tell Deirdre too, she won't say nothing. You'll see." She seemed slightly out of breath, her bare, slender arms rising and falling gently as she spoke.

His face must have reflected his incomprehension.

"Your dirty magazine!" she whispered knowingly, conspiratorially tugging on his arm. "Nobody's gonna know nothing!"

He walked with her to the corner of the barn and stopped. Looking past her upturned face he could see the lights of the bunkhouse in the dusk—then the door opening as another came out to join the two or three already smoking on the porch. He could not distinguish who it was, but he could see the faces turned toward him. Toward them.

"So just don't you worry," Consuela said. "Don't worry 'bout that for even a minute."

"I won't," Booker said weakly. "No, I sure won't."

"But you go on now," he added after a moment. "Your mama'll be starting to wonder."

"Okay." She turned, stopped, and gazed at the bunkhouse lights for a moment before she added, half turning, "I'll run. I'll run so fast they won't even see me . . . those pigs." She spat in the dust at her feet. "Just like an antelope, you'll see!"

And then she was gone, skirts flying wildly out behind her, strong brown legs pumping, pushing, as she dashed along the length of the barn, swept past the porch of the bunkhouse, and then at last was swallowed by the growing darkness. He stood in silence for several minutes, only vaguely aware of the blur of pale faces now reflected back toward him, before at last he turned, walked slowly back through the great high doorway, and disappeared inside.

CHAPTER 5

1

The early lights of the little city flickered white and gold in the distance, like a fairyland just coming to life after a long and sleepy afternoon.

They had left behind the company mill town now, the two blackened smokestacks of the smelter looming like sooty fingers above their heads, and they moved out again through the dry, flat sage country to the south. The evening air was mild and clear, unseasonably warm for this season; the dusting of snow remaining on the hillsides to the east seemed strangely out of place. And yet in just two weeks it would be Christmas.

At their backs, in the bed of the pickup, the Lindsay brothers had started to sing—the pint picked up in the mill town already beginning to do its work. They listened in silence for several minutes, Booker seeming to hum softly along as he peered down the long, straight roadway before them, until all at once there came a violent banging on the roof of the cab.

"Come on boys, not so glum! There's wine and women just around the bend!" The florid face of Nat Lindsay leered grinning in at John's window, the smell of cheap whiskey already strong on his breath.

"You won't be in any shape for either one if you keep nipping at that bottle," Booker, smiling, shouted over at him.

Nat Lindsay's cheeks brightened one tone deeper as he gave a loud guffaw. "Fat chance, big fella. Drive on!" The face withdrew. Again, briefly, the banging on the roof. The song resumed, softer than before.

Booker smiled into the growing night. Up ahead the lights drew nearer, as if pulled toward them on a carpet.

"They're happy," John said, folding his hands in his lap.

"Too happy too soon," Booker said. "On the way home they'll be laid out back there like two sacks of wheat."

They were approaching the outskirts now. Up ahead, the barrier at the railroad crossing was lowered, lights flashing, and they drew up behind three or four waiting cars. Off to the west the headlight of a locomotive swept slowly around the bend, then moved toward them.

"It's a steamer," Booker said. "Most of 'em are gone now." John watched in silence as the big black engine drew nearer, the brass dome atop its boiler gleaming in the crossing lights, then lumbered past, bell clanging, and down the line. The low ore cars, piled high with a grayish rock, clattered over the crossing one by one. Nat Lindsay began to bang on the roof.

"What's this fucking delay?" he shouted, addressing the train itself. "Don't you know we're on an urgent mission?"

Booker stuck his head out the window. "Better hold it down, little buddy. They'll have you cooling off in a cell before you ever get there." Nat muttered something and went back to join his brother, who leaned against the tailgate, his face beaming, the bottle clutched like a dead chicken in his hand.

There were many ore cars, each moving past with a clatter identical to the last. John looked beyond them into the city. In the distance, at the far end of town, he could see the glowing bulk of a big hotel, at least three stories by the look of it; in between lay a softly glittering pathway of lights. He felt a tremor of anxiety and excitement as the last ore car rumbled over the crossing, then a dilapidated green caboose, and the barrier at last began to lift.

They moved slowly up the street, toward the main part of town. This seemed a residential section—low, well-kept houses on square, orderly blocks. There was a sense that it was a later addition, its relatively flat terrain in marked contrast with what lay ahead; still, the houses were by no means new. Down the hill to the right, barely visible in the deepening dusk, were the sheds and shops of the train yard, dominated by a substantial sandstone building which must have been the main station. Beyond the tracks were only the sage flats, the outline of low mountains to the north.

Now the street bent off again around a high, flat bluff— the dim shapes of monuments and markers identifying it as the cemetery. It had a peaceful, open air about it, low clumps of cedars among the stones, and John found his eyes lingering upon it as they passed. A dim vision of other places, the crowded, walled churchyards of his youth, flickered briefly across his consciousness—but then the street had turned once more and the bright lights of the town were just before him.

Booker slowed and came to a stop. To their left, on a dark, tree-studded eminence, loomed a high sandstone structure topped by a copper dome, the courthouse; at the far end of the street, its way prepared on either side by the neon of small clubs, the hotel squatted like a well-fed bullfrog in his pond.

Booker stuck his head out the window. "Where to, boys? Want to grab a little something to eat?"

"Naw," Nat Lindsay bawled, the toes of his boots pointing upward as he lay back against the tailgate. "We'll work up an appetite first."

"The Shamrock, then?"

"The very place, my man. And not a moment's delay!"

They continued on down the main street, past the hotel—its long bar and gaming tables gleaming brightly through the windows—then turned off to the right. Ahead, not two blocks away, loomed the dark shapes of the hills. Just short of them, however, Booker turned again, this time to the left, and headed down a pitted, dimly lit street. At the far end of it, a block or two distant, were four low buildings, two on either side, their eaves and doorways dimly lit with faded red and green neon. Beyond them, again, were only the low hills, and the dark mouth of the canyon behind.

Night had fallen, dark and soft as velvet. The stars were small and bright, like pinpricks in the fabric.

"Do you want to get out now with them?" Booker asked, pulling in at the first place on the left. "I've got an errand to run, and then I think I'll grab something to eat first."

Inside, visible through the open doorway, a lanky, bespectacled man sat at the bar, a young, dark-haired girl in a high-necked white satin dress close beside him. As the truck drew up the two looked out, then returned to their conversation.

"Could I jus' come 'long with you?" John said. The Lindsay brothers thumped to the ground.

"Why sure," Booker answered, regarding him with a kind, careful smile.

Nat Lindsay's face again appeared in the window, this time from ground level. Behind him lingered his brother Carroll, looking sidelong through the open doorway.

"John's going to take a little run with me first, something for the boss. Be back in an hour or so."

"Done," Nat Lindsay said. He ambled down the little incline, his brother close behind.

When the two were safely inside—the girl in white satin nodding as they passed, then glancing briefly, with a little smile, out at the truck—Booker backed out and headed slowly back down the dark street the way they had come. When they reached the street leading down, however, they did not turn; instead they continued straight ahead, weaving among the potholes as they went. Soon there were trees along both sides—fruit trees by the look of them but all naked now—and small, modest houses, most with lights visible inside, and three blocks further on two churches, the second massive in gray chiseled stone. Booker went on another block, past houses of the same kind, before at last he slowed and stopped, this time turning off the engine.

It was a tiny, dimly lit house on the left, the sage and cedar hillside rising directly up behind it. Set back just a bit further than the rest, perhaps twenty feet, it had a faintly patrician air—if such could be claimed of something so small and simple, and in such a setting. The picket fence was newly painted, and on each of the two front windows a long windowbox waited for the spring. In the yard was a small, well-tended weeping willow, now bare of leaves, and beyond that a modest plot for flowers.

"Come on," Booker said, and reached across to open John's door. "Someone for you to meet."

They passed through the gate and ascended the gravel walk. There was no lawn, but the weeds appeared to have been kept down, and the narrow, rock-lined path leading to the flower garden was utterly clear of them. Booker mounted the two steps to the porch; then, motioning John to follow, he knocked lightly on the curtained glass pane of the door. On the porch was a weathered wicker couch with faded canvas cushions, on one of which curled a sleeping cat. There was a watering can, a broom, a pair of gardening gloves.

Soft footsteps echoed from within, and a light came on behind the door. A small, mottled hand appeared, drawing aside the curtain; then, a small, mottled face. As the expression of inquiry dissolved into a smile, the curtain fell back into place. There was the clattering of locks as the door drew open, revealing a tiny, birdlike woman—abundant, iron-gray hair pulled back over her ears in a loose bun. Her eyes were dark and very large, almost too large it seemed for the small, weathered face.

The smile remaining in place, she looked Booker up and down—
then reached forward to touch his broad black hand.

"Well come in, you splendid giant. It's cold out on the porch."

It was only then, as she spoke the words, that she seemed to
realize that John was there. "Why, you have a friend with you!"
she said, squinting a bit to make him out in the half-light. Her
voice was low and very smooth, as though she had once been a
singer. There was just a trace of accent.

Booker smiled and stepped aside. "Yes ma'am," he said, taking
John by the arm. "This is John Siloa, who works with me at the
ranch. John, Miss Suzanne Devereaux."

John came forward, feeling her dark eyes upon him, and
took off his hat. "Ma'am." Then, slowly, he extended his hand,
which in that moment became something awkward and gro-
tesque. The old woman, smiling, reached out, took his index
and middle fingers, and looked him up and down—just as she
had Booker. Her touch was cool and very smooth, like polished
wood.

"Yes, you're a nice-looking fellow too," she said—"though not
quite like this great black god here." She glanced quickly, slyly,
at Booker, then back to John, now looking straight into his eyes.
"You know," she said, "this is the first time he's ever brought
anyone. He must like you."

"Ma'am." It was an expression of vague assent.

For another moment she was silent, considering him. Then:
"Well come inside then, both of you. There's a fresh pot of coffee
on the stove."

They followed her through the doorway, she pausing to fasten
the locks once more, then down a short hallway to the kitchen.
It was surprisingly large, doubtless the largest room in the
house. There was ample room for the table and six chairs, a big
Spark stove, a refrigerator, and along the rear wall, with a view
to the beetling hillside beyond, a long wooden sinkboard half
covered with potted plants. There was even a small bookcase, in
which John noticed two or three foreign books among the others.
Around two of the walls, high up, extended a wooden dishrail,

on which the three or four decorated china plates seemed all but overcome by an array of books, folded linens, plants, sewing implements, and faded, largely unframed photographs. The paint looked fairly new, a bright eggshell white.

The old woman, Suzanne, busied herself with the coffee. Booker, walking to the sinkboard at the rear, looked out at the dark hillside, over which a narrow moon had just begun to rise. John simply stood near the doorway, his hat clutched in his hand.

"It's been a long time, Booker," the woman said, not bothering to turn toward him. "I was beginning to think you had deserted me. You've deserted women before, I suppose."

"Never you, dear Suzanne. That could never happen."

Booker, smiling, turned away from the window, watching as she laid the cups and saucers out on the table. They were very delicate, John noticed, very fine; for the second time, as if in anticipation, his hands felt like hams dangling from his wrists.

"Yes, you devil, and I suppose you've said that a few times before too." Suzanne smiled and motioned them to the table. "Well come on then, sit down both of you," she said, nodding in John's direction as she turned to get the coffee.

They had been seated for several minutes, the woman adding a plate of small cakes and a bowl of fruit to the table before at last she sat down. "Well, John," she said, settling lightly in her chair, "let's talk about you. I'm sick of this faithless Othello."

"Ma'am?" He sat up straight in his chair.

"Well, for a start, where are you from?"

Suddenly, from deep in his chest, Booker began to laugh. "Can't you tell? He's from France!"

"You be quiet. He can talk for himself." A coquettish frown, as much as her words, brought the big man to order.

"Well, where are you from?" she said to him in French.

John felt the blood rush to his face. "The Basque country," he said, vaguely surprised to hear his own voice in this language.

"I thought so," she said. It was not a French like his own; it was much more fluid and smooth, spoken further forward in the mouth. Although he would not say so, he knew where she came from too.

"You have a lot of countrymen hereabouts."

"Yes, I think so."

"Think so?" The old woman raised her eyebrows in mock surprise. "It doesn't sound like you have much to do with them. Don't you go to those big picnics of theirs, the hotel downtown . . . ?"

"*Non, madame.*"

Suzanne looked curiously at him, then bestowed a warm, almost motherly glance. "I understand," she said at last. "I'm just the same. There are two big French families in town, one from Paris. They don't like me. I don't like them. We nod on the street, we pass, that's all. They're very good Catholics, of course."

Booker, the grin of a successful matchmaker spread across his face, at last seemed to have heard a word he recognized. "*Catholiques,*" he repeated, leaning hard on the final syllable. "Is she off on those poor folks again?" Booker said archly, his eyes twinkling with mischief.

There was a flash of exasperation in her voice as she turned, glaring, to face him. "No more than they deserve," she snapped. "My church, at least, knows how to forgive."

Booker, sensing that he had overstepped his bounds, looked out the window. For a moment there was silence—then only the rustle of her dress as she reached over to refill their cups.

"Well, how is the old man, your . . . Mr. Kinsella?" she said softly, settling back in her chair.

Booker sighed, whether in relief or resignation it was difficult to say. "Okay, I guess." Folding his hands before him, he looked down at the ridged yellow thumbnails.

"Doesn't sound okay to me," Suzanne said. She lifted a cookie to her mouth, bit the edge, and softly laid it on her saucer.

"Not okay, then, I guess," the big man said, raising his eyes to hers.

"That woman again?"

"Yeah. But now it's the boy too, some talk about him coming."

Suzanne, frowning, pursed her lips. "Hardly a boy now, I'd guess. How old was he then, when he went over there I mean?"

"Nineteen, twenty maybe. I don't know."

"I do," she said. "He'd be twenty-two now. Twenty-two— and a war already behind him." With a long sigh she got up and went to the sink. There was the sound of running water, then the squeak of a faucet closing.

"He must be in a perfect fury," she said to the window.

"Yes'm."

The old woman turned, drying her hands on a towel, and returned to the table.

"He brings all this on himself, you know. But of course he brings everything on himself. It's his way, his passion, his *métier*." She drew up, sighing, and turned to John. "Do you know about this business?"

"Some."

"Some." Again she sighed, deeper than before, and looked away.

"This needn't have been, you know. If he wasn't such a blind, selfish, stubborn . . ." Another sigh, then she went on. "I could have saved him from it all. I'd have had her running for cover in a minute, and she knows it. And he would at last have agreed to it, I know it. I know it. But then, after . . . Oh God, if only I had never sent him!" Abruptly she raised her hands, covering her face. The mottled spots about her knuckles seemed to take on a darker hue.

"I've never told you all of it," she said, looking up at Booker. "Not even you."

"No ma'am," he said softly.

"Well, tonight, tonight . . ." She seemed on the point of crying, then abruptly righted herself. "Tonight I'll tell you . . . both. All of it."

The old woman's voice when she resumed was clear and calm, even eager—as though she anticipated some long-deferred relief. John, watching her, felt privileged, yet at the same time somehow fearful and uncertain—whether for her or for himself he could not have said. He found his glance wandering to her hands, which as she spoke were softly folded, one atop the other on the table. They must once have been very beautiful, he thought. Even now, their backs marred by the marks of age, they retained the shape, the grace and delicacy of youth. That narrow palm, those slender, pointed fingers—they seemed to have touched so many things.

The tale she told began more than twenty years before, when that first wife, she of the letters, had only lately vanished into the night—and with her the invisible burden she had already begun to bear. Kinsella was alone, walled up in the great stone castle he had built for her, and this old woman, Suzanne, not much past forty then, had just moved into this little house. They had known one another for a number of years, under circumstances which did not appear in the telling, and she had done her best to comfort him, to blunt his bitterness insofar as she was able. They met several times, in Salt Lake City and elsewhere, and it had seemed at first that a certain understanding was taking shape. She, for her part, was willing; he, for his, somewhat less so. And yet never had he offered outright opposition, never the kind of resistance that might have caused her to abandon hope, and so she had persisted, struggling to bridge the gulf of rage and disappointment that seemed always to lie between them. Until in the end, it seemed, that gulf had begun to widen rather than contract. Unable to move him, helpless to convince him that all he feared, all the complications he foresaw, could be overcome, she had watched in stunned silence as the understanding, what there had been of it, at last faded and died away.

Still she had remained loyal to him, ready at his slightest whim to meet him when and where he wished. She was his friend, his comforter, his confessor, as she had always been— but nothing more now, nothing more. And so matters had continued for several years—he ever more resigned to his castle and cowboys, his solitary fate, she refusing to give up the last spark of hope. They corresponded as they always had; they continued to meet from time to time. They settled into their lives.

It had been the merest whim on her part to send him. In the fall of 1945 this was, almost fifteen years since he had been alone. The years, which should at last have applied the balm of forgetfulness, or at least of forgiving, seemed instead to have hardened him, tempering his ingrown rage like a sword. Until at last she had been reduced to pity—to simply doing what she could to ease his pain. There were certain things she could still provide, had always known how to provide when that was his need, but she longed for something to truly divert him, to deflect his attention into some new pursuit or project which might revive his spirit, even cause it to take on some new direction. She resorted to small, sometimes capricious schemes, even to sending him on errands for her. And yes, this had been an errand, nothing more.

She had read of the event in the newspaper, the *Denver Post.* There were not many in Creighton—other than the mining people, of course—who read the *Denver Post,* but she had her reasons. Suzanne's younger brother, who had emigrated with her after the war, the first war, lived in Denver with his large family. He was a baker and had had great success—now owning a large baking company in the city. They did not get on, he and Suzanne, and had not spoken or corresponded for more than twenty-five years. Still, his affairs and activities often made their way into the Denver paper, and Suzanne, in spite of everything, liked to keep informed.

"It would be just the thing for you," she had said to him. "Something to take your mind off yourself for a while. You'll like Henri, you have much in common. And besides, you owe me a favor. Or two."

And so in the end he had gone. His mission: to buy and personally deliver her gift. Henri's youngest and prettiest daughter, his favorite, had just been married, and Suzanne was determined, this time, to be counted. As for complications that might arise, she had told him nothing. Why should she? He was told what to buy, where to buy it, provided with the address and some telephone numbers—and that was all.

"He still could be quite charming then, you see—your . . . Kinsella. His hair was still quite black, just a little gray here and there, and he hadn't forgotten all he ever knew. If Henri proved a problem, well . . . he could handle it, I knew it. And if there were dues for me to pay when he returned . . . well, what of it?" The old woman sighed and, reaching up, pushed back a drooping strand of iron-gray hair. When she looked up, her eyes seemed to have darkened, the bruised underside of a heavy cloud.

"It seemed almost a joke to me. On Henri, on him . . . on all of them. Perhaps I was angry. Yes, thinking of it now . . . I was angry, at all of them. But a joke?" Again she sighed and, drawing a handkerchief from her pocket, softly blew her nose.

One thing she had been quite right about—that he and her brother would get on. Henri, indeed, seemed delighted to see him, and, though little disposed to any change in their relations, eager for news of his long-lost sister. The years and his successes seemed to have softened him, sweetened him. He had invited Kinsella to join a dinner party at his home the very next evening. And Kinsella had gone. Also one of the party was Henri's eldest daughter Margaret, who two years before had lost her husband to a sniper's bullet on the beaches of southern Sicily . . . .

"And Deirdre, the little girl, how is she?" They had finished the coffee now, and Suzanne, her eyes still a bit cloudy, had gotten up to rinse out the cups. "She must be big now, seven last October. A big girl."

"Getting bigger all the time—and just as spoiled as ever," Booker said. His eyes were troubled as he looked over toward her, an old, weary back stooped over the sink.

"Oh, he would do that. It can't be good for her, you know, without a mother. I suppose he does the best he can."

"I s'pose."

Her face, reflected in the glass, seemed turned to stone.

"But such a strange name," she went on after a moment, still looking out the window. Her voice was low, meditative, as though she were talking only to herself. "Terrible too, that name. He told me once . . . why he chose it. Something about an Irish princess, something about a curse. I don't know, something terrible. 'Too much beauty for good luck,' he would say. 'Too much beauty for good luck.' An awful thing to do to a child, an innocent child . . . but he was so angry, angry with God."

There was a long, weary sigh as, very slowly, she turned back to face them once again. "And is she? Beautiful, I mean. The child."

"She's quite pretty, I suppose—blonde hair, blue eyes." Booker hesitated a moment before he added: "Looks a lot like her mother."

"A lot like her mother," Suzanne repeated, her face now utterly, eerily calm. "But then, you understand, I never saw her mother."

Wiping her hands on the front of her apron, she turned and hung it neatly on the peg.

They were standing in the kitchen doorway, about to go. The telling done, she had seemed to revive, and now, as they bade their good-byes, she was again the person who had greeted them at the door.

"Keep an eye on this big fellow, John," she said, reaching up to squeeze Booker's broad forearm. "When he comes into view, the girls are hard to manage. There may be attempts to kidnap him. Who can say just what might happen?"

"I'll watch him," John said, smiling.

"Yes," she said, "you watch him." She seemed to hesitate a moment; then, very slowly, she lowered her hand to her side.

"And what I said before," she continued after a moment, now looking gravely at them both—"what I said before, please don't misunderstand. I get along quite well, and perhaps it has all been for the best. All of it. Yes, I get along quite nicely. I have my house, my church"—a darting glance at Booker—"my church, which he will make fun of. I enjoy going there. I even rather believe it. But he will have his fun." Again she paused, sweeping a hair from her brow, before she reached up and, with a sly smile, again squeezed Booker's arm.

"And so you watch him, John. Don't let him out of your sight."

"Yes ma'am."

They walked toward the front door, pausing while Suzanne again fiddled with the locks. When she turned again to face them, Booker slipped a plain, unsealed envelope into her hand. She reached out to take it calmly, resolutely, as though this were a ritual often observed by them before.

"Yes," she said, "he is very generous, your Mr. Kinsella. He has always been . . . very generous."

" 'Bye," Booker said. "Until the next time." Bending down, he kissed her gently on the forehead.

"Good-bye," she whispered back. She smiled at John. "*Et au revoir.*"

The bright track of a single tear gleamed briefly, then disappeared behind the closing door.

2

They sat alone in the small back dining room, each with a large steak and a bottle of beer. Through the open doorway leading to the main lobby and casino came the low, earnest hubbub of gaming, the soft clink of glassware at the bar. Occasionally there was the squawk of a buzzer, occasionally a shout of delight or disappointment, but the underlying murmur, heedless, went steadily, implacably on.

The plump blonde waitress, her gray starched uniform whispering as she moved, seemed to know Booker very well. She had gone now but still looked in at them from time to time, stopping briefly in the doorway before again disappearing into the larger room.

John, although all too familiar with the doubtful comforts of those glorified rooming houses known as Basque hotels, had never been inside an establishment anything like this. On their way here, following in Booker's ample footsteps through the big, crowded hall, he had gazed about him like a greedy child, his eyes lingering in wonder on the long, polished wood bar, the green felt surfaces of the card tables, the glitter of the whirling roulette wheel, the ornate crap table presided over by a tuxedoed, mustachioed croupier—but most of all on the people, young and old, in every mode of dress, but all with the same abstracted but vaguely nervous gleam in their eyes. It was fantastic, unreal, like something from a picture book of Monte Carlo. Even the lowly slot machines, standing in shining rows against the walls, seemed utterly exotic to him, as though the jaded women who slumped before them, cigarettes dangling from their wrinkled lips, might at any moment, by some incredible stroke of luck, some unimaginable jackpot, be transformed into virginal young princesses and swept off into the night.

Booker seemed ravenously hungry, engulfing his food with an animal fervor which, for him at least, was strangely out of character. Long before John was finished the big man had laid aside his knife and fork and, washing down the last two slices of bread with what remained of his beer, sat gazing vacantly toward a far corner of the empty room. John sensed a deep unease, a preoccupation, as though the conversation with the old woman had reopened some long-forgotten wound. There was much that he, John, had not quite followed in what was said, and much of the rest he had found difficult to believe, but even he had felt the urgency in her tale, the yearning to be understood, even forgiven—and the enormous effort it had cost her to bring it all into the light. And yet he had expected that Booker, who seemed to know her so very well, would have taken it a little more in stride. Perhaps then there was something more—

some inner dissonance which the old woman's tale had simply brought into focus. He did not, could not, know. Slowly, methodically finishing his meal, John looked up from time to time, but always the vacant stare remained, drawn over those chiseled ebony features like a fitted mask.

At last, when he too had laid down his knife and fork, it seemed the time had come to speak.

"Have you known her a long time?" he asked, his voice ringing hollow in his ears. "The lady, I mean."

The big man's eyes swam into focus with a soft, vaguely baffled smile. For a moment he seemed not to have understood, but then: "Suzanne? No, not so very long. Five years, maybe—sometime in forty-nine, I think, when he started to send me to her. Right after . . . after Deirdre was born."

"But him, Mr. Kinsella—he's known her a long time, then?"

"Long and long," Booker said softly. "Almost from . . . the beginning."

John picked up his bottle of beer, feeling the tingle of the last swallow in his throat. Over in the doorway the blonde waitress looked in, then made her way toward them. For a big woman, she was very light on her feet, gliding like a dancer as she moved across the room.

"All done, boys?"

Her face was quite pretty, or once had been. The pale, deep-set eyes looked down at them calmly, with an openness that was vaguely unsettling.

"No more for me, Betty," Booker said. "Jus' coffee."

"How 'bout you, John? 'Nother beer? Or there's some hot apple pie, just out of the oven."

Feeling the blood rise to his face, he could only shake his head. "No, just coffee," he stammered at last, incredulous that she had remembered his name.

"Two coffees it is"—and she swept away, floating with that smooth, sibilant stride toward the doorway.

After she had returned and again withdrawn into the main room, Booker suddenly seemed revived, in the mood to talk.

"He used to work for her, you know. The boss."

"Work for her? Mr. Kinsella . . . for Suzanne?"

"Yep. Twenty-five, thirty years ago, I guess."

"But what . . . ?"

Booker smiled, tolerance and amusement struggling together in his eyes. "Is it that tough to guess? The kind of business she might have been in?"

"Well, no," John said at last. "I s'pose not." He knew what he thought, but he did not want to say it.

For a long moment Booker looked at him, the smile gradually fading until it was gone. His eyes seemed to grow cloudy as he said: "She had a place up near the mines, in a little burg name of Runcietown—mostly gone now. The Daisy, it was called—and she was Daisy. Or Black-eyed Susan, as Kinsella liked to say."

"Black-eyed . . . daisy?"

"It's a flower."

"Oh," John said uncertainly and looked away. The waitress briefly glanced in, then disappeared once more.

"He was—what do you say? The man of the house."

"The man."

"Yes," Booker said. "Kinsella."

"Kinsella," John repeated dully, wooden with disbelief. All at once there was a distant ringing in his ears. He wanted to leave now, pushing back against the table with his palms, but Booker, slumped in his chair, seemed determined to go on.

"Yep. Long, long time ago. Before he built the big house, before Tabby, before . . . everything. Black-eyed Susan."

John did not answer. He could not, and besides there was no need. The big black foreman, eyes dull and lifeless, lips moving with an automatic, uninflected urgency, seemed powerless now to stop.

"The old man would never admit it, but all the same I think

he knows. Somewhere, down deep, he knows. He should have taken her, that Black-eyed Susan. He should have been content with her, black eyes and all. Black eyes . . . and all."

There was a brief, empty silence, no more than it took for Booker to swallow, then clear his throat.

"Let's go," John said, glancing hurriedly toward the doorway. Again the waitress was there, watching them—or rather, watching Booker. Meeting John's glance, she quickly turned and was gone.

Booker, looking down at the backs of his broad black hands, seemed not to have heard.

"What do you think, John? Have you ever had a woman?"

"Ha-had?" John stammered, looking away.

"No. Lived with one, I mean. Ate out of the same pot, worried about the same bills. You know."

"No," John said quietly. "Nothing like that."

"I thought so. You've been like me, like all of us. But have you ever wondered—how it might be?"

"Sometimes," John murmured. He moved uneasily in his chair.

"Sometimes," Booker repeated dully, his eyes growing cloudy once again. "Sometimes."

Then, all at once, the waitress was there, looming like a great gray iceberg out of the fog. Extending a fleshy white hand, she laid the check in the precise center of the table, then reached up to the little tray she carried. "Jimmy says hello," she said, placing a double shot of whiskey before each of them.

Booker, starting, looked up. For a moment, his eyes gradually becoming clearer, he said nothing. Then, very quietly: "Dear Jimmy." He lifted the whiskey. "May he live forever," he said and tossed it down. John looked down at his own glass for a moment before, abruptly, he did the same. When he opened his smarting eyes the waitress was looking down at him, a cool, even smile on her painted lips.

"We're off, Betty," Booker said, laying a large bill on the check. Pushing back his chair with a loud scrape, he rose to his feet, then stood smiling down at them. His dark, smooth cheeks gleamed like polished teak in the lamplight.

"Nice to meet you, John," said the waitress and held out the plump white hand. "Come back again." Again feeling the blood come to his face, John took the hand for the briefest of instants, then let it drop as he got up.

"And there's no need to bring this guy at all," she said, with an arch, sly smile for Booker.

"Now don't start in on my help," Booker said and gently slapped her on the rump.

"Ow!" she pouted. "You go get lost." And she began to clear the table.

They passed again through the main room, the dapper croupier watching through narrowed eyes as Booker led him toward the bar. Jimmy the bartender, fat and red-faced, took John's hand in a firm, damp grip, then offered them both another drink.

"No thanks, Jimmy, we're on our way," said Booker, nodding up the hill.

"Have to keep alert for that kind of business," Jimmy said, and waved them smiling out the door.

Outside the night air was clear and cool, the soft wind moving up above. A thin crescent moon, pushing above the dark line of hills, thrust one bright horn into the sky.

"Might as well walk," Booker said softly. They crossed to the corner and headed up the hill.

3

At the far end of the bar, one foot resting on the low rung of a stool, the girl in white satin was deep in conversation with a pale, red-haired older woman. Hearing footfalls in the doorway, they both looked up together; together, their faces bloomed into smiles.

"Evening, ladies," Booker said. His gold eyetooth gleamed like a nugget in the light.

Over in the far corner, seated alone on a low couch, a big, heavyset Mexican peered up from his newspaper. Exchanging a somber nod with Booker, he watched through narrowed eyes as the tall black figure, uncertainly followed by his smaller companion, proceeded down the length of the bar. Then, his features utterly without emotion, he returned his attention to the newspaper.

"Booker!" the red-haired woman cried. "It's about time you showed up! Those two damn drunken cowboys of yours weren't much comfort for lonely girls, you know."

"No, I don't expect so," Booker said, slipping his arm about her well-upholstered waist. "How ya been?"

"Wasting away, pining for you only." Her pale, dimpled cheeks, rouge-bright, swelled with pleasure as he bent to plant a kiss on her neck.

"You black devil," she crooned, playfully pushing him away.

"You know Doris," she added, affecting the straightening of her draped, coppery dress. The girl in white satin smiled, more demurely this time.

"Yes indeed, but my good friend John doesn't," Booker said, turning to glance at the slight figure in his shadow. "John, Doris. And this is Edna Sharp, boss lady last time I checked."

"Not that you check very damn often," Edna said.

John stepped forward, shyly nodding first to one, then the other.

"And so what did you do with my wandering cowboys?" Booker said. "I don't s'pose they're still around."

"Long gone," Edna said. "Said you'd know where to find 'em."

Booker smiled. "Only three places left to look, I guess they meant. But they're right, I'll find 'em sooner or later. Don't expect they'll be moving too fast by now."

"Not likely," Edna said—"at least not judging from the speed they were moving when they left here." She looked over toward the big Mexican, who slowly put down his paper and, with a slight limp, began to make his way behind the bar.

"What're you drinking?" Edna asked when at last he had arrived there.

"Just beer for me," Booker said, turning toward John.

"How 'bout a little pink sham-pain instead?" Edna said. "Got a case in just today."

"No, not for me," Booker said. "John'll have a touch, though."

"No . . . ," John began to protest, but Edna had already nodded to the Mexican, who bent to take a bottle from the cooler, then awkwardly began to disengage the cork.

"I insist," Edna said, silencing him with a wave. "It's a rule, for our new guests."

"Since when," Booker smiled.

"You be quiet," Edna said, just as the cork popped. She turned again to John. "You and Doris just take this over in the corner and get better acquainted."

The girl in white satin produced a little tray, took up the bottle and glasses, bestowed an inviting smile, and led the way to the low couch against the wall. John, his quizzical glance at Booker met only by a raised eyebrow, dutifully followed where he was led.

"New guy?" Edna said when the two were safely seated on the couch.

"Yup. Boss decided he just had to have some sheep, and John's the man. Good fellow."

"Basco, by the look of him."

"Yes ma'am, but a good one."

"I s'pose there's a few of those too. Doesn't look likely to break the place up, anyway. Might even wash his feet by the looks of him—which would be a treat. Now your cowboys, on the other hand . . ."

" 'Least I left the other two at home," Booker said, lifting the frosty bottle to his lips.

"Thank heaven for small favors," Edna said, then peered toward the long corridor to the rear. Down the length of it, swinging faintly in the light breeze, a row of six paper Chinese lanterns, one before each curtained doorway, cast a ruddy glow upon the darkness.

"No hurry," Booker said. "Have a drink why don't you."

"She shouldn't be long," Edna said. "But yeah, maybe I will. It's been a long night, and plenty more of it to come."

Patting the bar before her, she stirred the big Mexican from his lethargy. He dropped two ice cubes into a glass, added half a shot of tequila, and filled it up with orange juice.

"How's the foot, Manny?" Booker said. "You seem to be walking better."

" 'Lot better," the Mexican said. "Cast's been off more'n a week now."

"They ever catch that guy, the one that stomped it?"

"Not that I know of," Manny said. "Tell you one thing, though."

"What's that?" Booker said, looking down the hallway.

"If he puts his face in here again he'll leave with *two* broke feet 'stead of one."

"Among other things," Booker said.

" 'Mong other things."

There was the flutter of a curtain at the back. A tall, broad-hipped woman, an Oriental dressing gown wrapped loosely about her, appeared in the incarnadine glow of the hallway and, moving her head to avoid the lanterns, began to walk toward them.

"Well, look what the coyotes drug in," she said, emerging into the light. Her voice was low and husky, her smile an equal mix of pleasure and amusement. The mass of strawberry blonde hair loosely pinned atop her head seemed ever on the point of falling.

"'Lo, Mary Kate," Booker said quietly, watching her approach. "Long time."

The woman did not answer, stopping at the end of the bar. "Manny," she said. "Whiskey and seven." Only then did she turn to face him—a cool, contemplative glance. "Long time," she said at last. "How'ya been?"

"Okay. You?"

"Okay," the woman said. Manny put the drink on the bar before her. "You going to be around a while tonight?"

"A while," Booker said.

Again she did not answer. Putting the drink on a little tray, she turned back down the darkened hall.

Over in the corner, seated close beside him on the couch, the girl in white satin was refilling John's glass.

"I think she wants to say good-bye," Edna said. "She's off to Reno end of next week."

"Oh." He was silent a moment before he added: "What's she got there?"

"More money, change of scenery, the usual. Can hardly blame her, I guess. She's good enough to have what she wants. Anyway, what she really wants is out. I can always tell."

Booker, silent, took a long swallow of beer.

Suddenly there was the sound of raised voices down at the end of the hall. A short, broad-shouldered young man, fancy hat pulled low on his head, backed out of one of the rooms, beneath one of the Chinese lanterns, cursing as he came. There was a tearing sound, the curtain coming down, as Edna shot a quick glance toward Manny, then disappeared down the hallway.

"Don't waste your fuckin' breath, lady. You can fuckin' keep your fuckin' two-bit whores."

Manny had reached the end of the bar now, but there he stopped, waiting. Edna's voice, talking fast, echoed for a moment in the darkness—then a sudden thump, the sound of falling, and the young man, red-faced and out of breath, emerged alone into the room. "Manny!" came Edna's muffled voice from the darkness behind just as the big Mexican reached out and grabbed the man hard by the forearm. The other turned violently, as though he had been stung, and hit Manny flush on the right eye. The big man stumbled but seemed about to right himself when all at once the cowboy grabbed a chair from behind and broke it heavily over his shoulders. Manny crumpled behind the bar. "Fuckin' spick!" the young man shouted, turning as he did to sweep a whiskey bottle and six glasses to the floor. It was just at that moment, however, that Booker reached him. One hand on the front of his shirt, the other on the big polished buckle of his belt, he lifted him until their eyes met, which is to say about a foot and a half in the air, and slammed him once, very hard, against the doorjamb, then let him slide to the floor like a limp rag doll.

"You'll be wanting to settle up some accounts before you leave," Booker said.

Edna, looking disheveled but otherwise unhurt, came to the end of the hallway. Behind her, through one of the curtains, the face of a young girl looked out, her eyes bright with tears. Then two more of the curtains parted—Mary Kate and another older woman, then two dazed-looking men.

"Little bastard," Edna said, looking down at the crumpled but still conscious figure in the doorway. Stepping lightly over him, she went to Manny, who was groaning behind the bar.

"Oh shit," she said, looking down. "You son of a bitch," she said to the cowboy. Returning to where he lay, she kicked him once, hard, in the stomach before she again stepped over him and disappeared down the hallway. "Okay, it's all over," she was saying. "Come on, Sam, you just got here. It's all over. Emily, take care of him. George, hold on now. There'll be a free round of drinks coming down in just a minute. That's better. Just relax and have a good time. It's all over."

"I was just now leaving," a man's voice said.

"Well, stay for one drink anyway," Edna said. "Mary Kate . . ."

"No, I've got to get going. I promised . . ."

A stocky, white-faced miner appeared at the end of the hallway, gingerly stepped over the now-stirring young man, and walked hurriedly, without a word or nod, across the room. "That drink'll be waiting for you next time," Edna called from the darkened hallway, but the man had already disappeared out the door.

The cowboy, with a faint, distant moan, had drawn himself up on one elbow now; leaning against the doorjamb, he looked blearily out across the littered floor. Booker, bending down, gently raised him to his feet and, supporting him by the armpits, helped him to the couch in the corner. John and the young girl, on their feet now beside it, stood looking down as the young man settled among the brightly flowered cushions.

Manny too was on his feet now, his hands unsteadily gripping the back of the bar. Edna, close beside him, was ineffectually daubing with a bar rag at a ragged gouge in his cheek. "Here, let me," Mary Kate said, emerging in Levi's and a rumpled shirt through the hall doorway. Shouldering the older woman aside, she withdrew a first-aid kit from beneath the bar. "You take care of Mr. Wonderful," she said, with a brusque nod in the direction of the couch.

"You bet I will," said Edna, her face as red as her hair as she wheeled about and swept across the room, her victim wincing at her approach.

Later, when the impetuous young cowboy, a hundred dollars lighter, had at last been suffered to beat his meek retreat into the night; when Manny the long-suffering, his swarthy cheek adorned with a neat, snow-white bandage, had resumed his duties behind the bar; when the distraught young apprentice, one Esmeralda Hutchison by name, had been adequately comforted and assured by her new employer that the complaints lodged against her sprang more from the perversity of her client's appetites than from any grave failing on her own part and, being so comforted and assured, had been given the remainder of the evening off, with pay, as a token of her employer's continued confidence; when the last splinters of glass and wood, the last drops of whiskey and blood, had been swept or mopped up from the floor; when the versatile Mary Kate, having followed her demonstration of nursing skill with an equally impressive performance on the mop, had gone to exchange the shirt and Levi's for a more customary working costume; when even Edna, encouraged to think that this matter, at least, could be considered at an end, had withdrawn to a dressing room for the purpose of repairing her public image against what the evening still might hold in store; and when John Siloa and the girl in white satin, at last persuaded that the complimentary bottle of champagne might be better finished in the reflected glow of a Chinese lantern, had retired to one of the small rooms down the hall—only then did it occur to Booker Goodman that he might just do with a breath of fresh air.

The moon was fully up now, hanging low on the horizon. The nearby hilltops, bulking directly behind the two low, neon-bedecked buildings opposite, were bathed in a dim, brittle light. Here and there the call of a night bird could be heard. The gentle wind sighed through the nearby cedars, moaned in the canyon beyond. Down the highway threading through it, from the direction of the mines, came the lights of a single car. For a moment he watched, following the sweep of the twin beams as they moved through the turns. Then, however, they disappeared from sight, and he again looked up at the moon, wondering how long it would remain before, tiring of the Creighton sky, it once more slipped below the line of hills.

There was a troubling of shadows in the doorway behind him, then a single figure moving, stopping at his side. It was Mary Kate, a plain woolen range coat thrown over her shoulders; beneath it, visible through the open front, the peach-colored cocktail dress was cunningly gathered at the sides to show off abundant, softly freckled breasts.

For several minutes neither spoke, both equally engrossed, it seemed, in the doomed progress of the moon.

"Edna says you're going," Booker said at last, his eyes still searching the sky.

"Yeah, I think so."

"Reno, she said."

"Mmmm."

She seemed pensive, disinclined to talk, and again a ringing silence fell between them. Perhaps a minute passed before Booker finally spoke.

"You got something lined up?"

"No. I'll find something though. I worked there before, two years ago I guess. Still know some people. Anyway . . ."

"Anyway, you've had enough here."

" 'Bout it," she said. "Nice vacation, though."

Booker, looking directly at her for the first time, caught the last trace of a smile. With a listless movement of her hand, she swept a drooping strand of hair from her forehead.

"Well, there's plenty of other things you could do, you know. You're not stupid; you know how to get along with people and such."

Again the silence descended, a dark, heavy curtain between them. Booker, looking away, traced the line of the horizon with his eyes. Again the night bird called, a single plaintive note. A woman's high laugh echoed from across the street as a door swung briefly open. Down the street to the right, moving uncertainly toward them, the dim, splayed beams of a pickup truck cut through the darkness, bouncing off the houses on either side as the driver tried, sometimes successfully, to avoid the potholes.

"You could be some kind of secretary," Booker said.

Again there was a shout from across the street, then the sound of breaking glass. He sensed a sudden movement as she gathered the coat about her neck. Looking down, he saw that her eyes were fixed on the approaching lights.

"There's plenty of things you could do."

"Why don't you shut up?" Mary Kate said.

The front door across the way abruptly swung open and two Indians, propelled by someone from inside, stumbled out and came to rest against the side of an old, battered car. The door slammed heavily behind them. After a moment one of them, the drunker by the look of him, went to the driver's side and got in. The other, dully waiting until the driver had backed out, fumbled with the door handle a moment before he too climbed inside. The car slowly ground away, met the approaching truck at the intersection, then turned to the right and disappeared down the hill.

"Now, Mary Kate," Booker ventured at last, and lightly touched her arm.

"Just save your breath," she said, turning as if to go. "I've got some business on the way."

The truck, slowing only briefly to look at the other three places, turned into the drive and stopped.

"Just stay a minute," he said, catching her arm more firmly. She made as if to draw away, then stopped and was still.

The two doors of the pickup truck swung open together, and three men came out. One, the tallest, was a thin young Indian, a long scar across one cheek. The other two, older, had the look of ranch hands, their faded, pearl-buttoned shirts riding up over their bellies.

"Well, well," said one of them, "if it ain't my good gal Mary." He walked over and stopped, looking Booker up and down as he came.

"This your friend, Mary?" the man said after a moment. He was quite drunk, but fairly adept at hiding the fact.

"Yes," she said.

Accepting the answer cheerfully, the man again looked Booker up and down, then held out his hand. "Len Winters," he said.

"Pleased to meet you," Booker said, but did not move. Blinking his eyes twice, the man turned aside, then followed the others through the door.

Again they were silent for several minutes, Booker's hand still resting on the arm of her coat. At last, drawing away, she turned and looked straight up into his face. Her smile was soft, relaxed, open.

"Come on," she said, taking his hand. "This is no way to say good-bye." Drawing him meekly after, she led the way back inside.

4

They drove along in silence. Behind them, in the bed of the truck, the two Lindsay brothers lay arm in arm upon their backs, the toes of their boots jutting upward against the tarpaulin. From time to time there came the sound of coughing as Carroll, who seemed to have weathered the evening a bit worse than his brother, tried in his sleep to clear the sour taste of vomit from his throat, but for the most part they were silent and utterly still, their identical faces wearing identical openmouthed expressions of utter peace, bodies rising and falling in eerie unison beneath the canvas as the truck passed over the occasional irregularity in the long, straight highway. They were, as Booker had predicted, just like two sacks of wheat.

The moon was down now, and the stars were strewn over the blackened sky like diamond dust. First light was still two hours away, and the dark line of the mountains was barely visible against the sky, and yet John found himself thinking of the sheep, how they would soon begin their stirring, their morning restlessness. They had never faced the dawn without him, and he hoped they would not this morning. It would be close, even with Booker delivering him out there as he had promised. Too close. And all at once he wondered why he had come at all.

It seemed a long time since he had been with a woman. He tried to remember the last—could it be almost a year? Yes, almost. That night outside Ogden, just before they left for the desert; it had been that big Mexican. Fat as a pig, she was, with great folds of flesh about her waist, but all the same she had been a happy woman, always laughing and making a good time. Harignordoquy himself had been with them that night and brought her over. "Here's the girl for you, Joanes—cure you of your moping and bad temper." Then in English to the girl: "Dolores, can you cure him of his moping and bad temper?" "Oh yes I can," she had said—"oh yes sir you bet I can." And she had started laughing. Even later, when they were about it, she had been laughing and squealing, laughing and squealing all the time. Then afterward, just as they were leaving: "Whenever you are moping, or feel in bad temper . . ."—and she had started up again.

Up ahead the distant gleam of headlights, too far yet to be resolved into two beams, bore toward them through the darkness. It was amazing how far one could see here—so far that headlights first showed as a single far-off spark against the night, as if the very distance itself conspired against plurality. So it must be with the stars, he thought. Each pinprick in the dark sky was perhaps really a group, a cluster, a galaxy. There was no end to it, no limit. And as the skies grew larger, a man grew smaller, more alone. Until he was gone. Even Booker, he thought, who picked up full-grown men and banged them against doorjambs, was only a lonely speck of dust in the night.

He looked over toward his friend, dark features dimly glowing in the light of the dashboard. He had been unusually sober and silent on the way back, had uttered not a single word from the moment when, parked outside the Green Lantern, he had deposited the last of his comatose charges in the bed of the truck and tucked the tarpaulin about them. "Sleep tight, little buddies," he had said, and then there had been no more. Not that long silences were anything new between them—often, especially during these last few months, their meetings had been made up of little else. Now, however, the silence seemed even more intense, as though all the events of the evening had conspired to compound something that had been there, festering, for a long time. It had gone beyond Kinsella now, he sensed—or at least Kinsella had become no more than a part of it. Something new, something more profound and complex, had settled in—some deeper sadness, some . . . longing.

"Good-bye, Booker," the woman had said as they were leaving, just that. "Good-bye, Mary Kate, and good luck." The soft bitterness of her smile, the heavy weariness of his step as they passed outside. And before that the old woman . . . Suzanne. The gleam of that single tear, the soft, weathered cheek, the closing door. And yes, even before that . . .

He had insisted on riding in. In the more than two months since coming down from the mountain the big gray had begun to get a bit fat and fractious; and besides, he needed to be shoed before Christmas, when at last it would be time to set off for the winter range. And so they had come, winding south through the low hills, then over the ridge to the north of the hayfield and down along the creek—the same way that he and Kinsella had come, he on this very horse, on that first afternoon—long ago, it seemed. Now the field was dry stubble, the birches and willows starkly naked beside the stream, but still the jackrabbits peered out at him, their coats already showing the dusting of white that signaled the imminence of winter. And then suddenly, after all those months, that first glimpse of the house, looming up like a great anchored ship as he drew near, evoking that same troubling mix of awe and outrage . . .

But no, it was not that, not even that, which now, as they drove along in silence, came to linger in his mind. It was rather the dark, wary face, the grave yet questioning glance that had rested upon him, watching his approach—then quickly withdrew behind the corner of the barn. For that had been all: the dark face, the still silence of her watching . . . and then nothing.

He had seen no more, but it was enough to begin to understand.

The approaching headlights, twinned now, had drawn nearer. As he watched they disappeared for an instant behind a low place in the road, then rose up brightly to linger for a moment over their heads before descending to meet them. Simultaneously, as if in response to a common signal, Booker and the other driver dipped their lights—and then they passed. It was an empty cattle truck, moving very fast. John turned to look, watching as the brace of red lights at the rear briefly illumined the sleeping brothers, then receded down the long, straight highway over which they had come. As he turned again to face forward John found himself thinking of the girl in the white satin dress.

She had been very nice, very warm and patient with him. And she had known just what to do. "Don't worry," she had said, "it's often that way after a long time. You ought to come to see me more often." Until at last it was all right, more than all right. "Once you remember, you really remember, don't you?" she had said afterward. She was happy, all soft smiles. "Yes, you must come to see me much more often." How strange it was, he thought—that one so young could know so much, be so clever. Perhaps there were some who were born for it. He had heard it said that a really good whore likes her work. Yes, perhaps it was so. And suddenly he imagined her now, at that moment, the smooth, narrow back moving gently, yet urgently, beneath the long hands of that thin, intense young Indian who had been waiting, the one with that long welt of scar, like a whip cut across his cheek . . .

"Have a good time tonight?"

For a moment he did not know where the voice had come from, so long had he been listening to his own. Then, the realization settling over him, he looked over to his left—the dark features, as before, faintly illumined in the dashboard lights.

"Yeah, fine," he said, shifting in his seat.

"Nice girl, that Doris. High class."

"I s'pose so. She was nice to me, anyway."

"Hasn't been there too long—but knows what she's doing I guess. Edna likes her."

John did not answer. It was not something he wanted to talk about just then. And yet he knew that Booker would pursue it—use it to say whatever else was really on his mind.

"All the same it's kind of a shame, you know. Girl like that, young, pretty . . . still innocent in a way. Girl like that still has a chance. Later, when it's turned to habit . . ."

John looked away, out the side window. The dark clumps of sage, vaguely shadowed in the wake of the headlights, moved like silent watchmen through the night. He sensed already where Booker was headed—was a bit surprised, in fact, that he had come to the point so soon.

"Someone her age, your age . . . There are all kinds of possibilities then, chances that won't always be there. Later on . . . There are other things to do, you know, besides following sheep or going to bed with whoever . . ."

John, still looking out at the passing sagebrush, heard the big man sigh, then settle deeper into his seat.

"You should get out, John. Get out while you still can."

Slowly, reluctantly, he turned again to face the windshield, the gently dipping beams of light.

"I don' know what you're talking about," he said softly, gazing at his own image in the windshield.

"I'm talking about getting out. Going to a town, learning to do something."

"This is all I know," John said. "It's what I do."

"Doesn't have to be, though. You're smart enough, you could learn. I've seen plenty of others—fixing cars, building houses, anything. Successful people now, respected." For a moment Booker was silent, then again there was a long sigh.

"Kinsella, you know, will eat you up—after he's done with me."

John again looked to his left. Booker's coal-black face, still bathed in the greenish light of the dashboard, had taken on an eerie, unreal color, deep in the hidden recesses of the spectrum.

"He talks about you, you know—in a way he doesn't talk about the others. He likes you . . . too much."

For a moment John was silent, knowing the while that it was fruitless to resist.

"I . . . I like him too, I think," he said at last, very softly. "I'd like to know him better."

Again Booker sighed, this time deeper and more resignedly than before. Now, at last, he had no more to say. And there was silence once again.

Minutes later, the dark shape of the mailbox loomed up on the right.

"Well, here we are," Booker said. "I'll go up and dump 'em off first, then take you on back."

The emptiness of his tone was still ringing in John's ears as, slowing, they turned up the lane and headed east, their headlights probing angrily across the sage-littered flat.

CHAPTER 6

1

The light from the single lamp lay in a warm, bright puddle on the surface of the desk. At the edge of it, just where the darkness would no longer yield, a half-full glass of whiskey had gathered up a single amber spark, softened only slightly by the dim red glow from the fireplace beyond. Nothing stirred, nothing sighed, for a long time—until all at once, from among the shadows trooped behind, there came a harsh cough, the rustling of fabric, and a sudden spurt of flame. Then it too, the flame, was gone, leaving only the crimson coal of a cigarette in the dark.

A few moments passed, marked only by a brief effulgence of the ember, then a long, weary exhalation of breath, before again the shadows stirred, this time gathering themselves into a hand, a single piece of paper held lightly between its fingers, which now intruded into the pool of light. The paper settled on the surface and the hand moved slowly away, reentering the darkest shadows as the face of Cyril Kinsella, like the very face of God, materialized from the void above and hovered, peering down.

It was the tenth time he had been over it, this latest one, although Booker had brought it only that afternoon. Not that it was so very different from the others, really—at least not from the two or three that had arrived since the boy's return. By now, in fact, he had almost accustomed himself to that too—the talk of uniforms and medals and citations, even the muted threats themselves.

It was sometimes almost funny to him, the devices and pretexts she employed—as if she supposed her point somehow sharpened by being awkwardly hidden. "Now, after all that he has gone through, it is no wonder that he should begin to think more of where he came from, who was his true author." He had become so used to her way of thinking by now, her way of working out an idea, that it had in a sense become a part of his own. So that this latest gambit—for really it was nothing more than that: the boy had other fish to fry now, just as he had himself, thirty-five years before—even this latest one had a certain familiar resonance about it.

He wondered whether they had begun to look like one another now as well, as old couples so often did—as an old man and his old dog so often . . .

For a moment the loud, sharp knocking seemed only a scrap of memory, a vagrant product of his musings. Then, however, it came again, more urgently this time. "What is it?" he heard himself growling as he abruptly started for the door, the letter still in his hand. As he passed around the desk he heard the glass of whiskey fall and shatter on the floor. He stopped but did not look back. Stooping to one knee, he carefully laid the letter on the coals of the dying fire. He watched it flame up, then proceeded toward the door.

"It's me—Carl," came the muffled answer. "I know it's late, but . . ."

"Well, come on in, for hell sake," he muttered. "It's not locked."

He had almost reached it when the door swung open. Old Carl Withers, his white hair tousled with sleep. Behind him in the shadows, the dark, solid form of Maria, and close beside her another, softly weeping. Even before the old cowboy had stepped aside, urging them forward into the half-light, he knew it could only be Consuela.

There was an indescribable expression—the mixture of terror and savage defiance of a badger caught in a trap—on the dark features of the Indian girl as she allowed herself to be drawn forward. Her right cheek, scarred with a broad, dirty abrasion, was already beginning to turn blue, and the blood from a deep cut, only recently congealed, made a red, shiny welt beneath her eye. There was bleeding from the scalp as well, apparently from some hair that had been pulled out over one ear. Looking at the bits of hay and twigs that still remained there, the torn dress clutched together over her breast with one hand, Cyril Kinsella could not avoid the thought that he had been caught up in a cliché.

"What happened?" he heard his voice say, reinforcing the impression. Somehow he did not really expect to hear that she had fallen from the hayloft.

There was no answer—none, that is, until Carl Withers at last broke the glaring silence. "I'd just got up to take a leak," he began, "and then there was this racket from the barn. Hollering, screaming, I dunno. I was still half asleep. But I went out on the porch."

"Come on, damn it!" His voice, strangely strident, seemed to come from far away. "*What happened?*"

"Hold your goddamn horses," Carl Withers said. "I'm telling it as fast as I can."

It was not the first time Carl Withers had spoken to him that way. Now, as before, the shock of it left him strangely refreshed. "Okay," he said quietly.

"Anyway, as soon as I got out there here she comes, running like hell out of the barn, then past me like a shot, that dress half off her. When she got to the cabin, well, I just pulled on my pants and went down there. Maria was there with her. Then I thought you'd better know."

"Who's around?"

"Just Lonnie and Darnell. Rest of 'em gone to town with Book."

"Where are they?"

"Damned if I know."

"Was it them?" he said, turning on the girl.

She glared savagely back, as though focusing her rage upon him. Then, with a sudden jerk of her head, she spat once on the floor—then once again. He could feel his muscles tensing, beginning to move toward her, when all at once she turned away, clinging to Maria's breast. Then, as the tears began, he could feel the old woman's eyes upon him, forbidding him.

It was at that moment that the sound of Booker's pickup was heard coming up the lane, then passing toward the bunkhouse.

"Tell him I need him," Kinsella said softly. And Carl Withers vanished out the door.

2

"Come on," Booker said. "I know where they'll be."

They moved out across the worn planks of the barn floor, John hanging a few steps behind. It was dark, but not so dark as it might have been, the light from the shop casting eerie shadows against the raftered vault above. Outside in the corral he heard a horse whinny, then another, then all was still again, the only sound that of their passing feet.

He did not want to be here. The image of Booker's face—the face that had met him as the big man emerged from the house, then in a few hoarse words had told it—that face still lingered in his mind. Yes, he thought, there was only one reason for him to be along now. The hard yet half-pleading look in those eyes had told it all too plainly. And yet he knew that it was hopeless, that he could do nothing. If Booker really undertook what his eyes announced he might, so feared he might, there was no way that he, alone, could prevent it. And yet he knew it was that, just that, which was expected of him—to prevent it.

Indeed, the big man seemed to have no doubt where he was headed. He, John, had thought at first that the tackroom or the shop, perhaps even that little room he lived in, would be the first stop, if only to . . . get something. But never once did Booker turn or even glance in that direction, instead striding straight toward the rear as if drawn there, the tall, heavy-shouldered form swinging slightly from side to side as he proceeded. He had seen that walk, that particular way of moving, only once before—earlier that same evening, in fact, when Booker had passed down the bar to intercept the young cowboy. There was something almost joyful about it, as though the body performing it anticipated some long-deferred exercise of its true function and purpose—and yet a certain wistfulness as well, the wistfulness of some deeply felt regret.

Ahead and to their left the dark, pungent structures of new hay beetled over them, dwarfing even Booker beneath their towering bulk. Yet they seemed in no sense the destination— like eager spectators, rather, looking on with silent, watchful menace as events unfolded before them.

But now he, they, seemed to have reached the place. Threading through a litter of fallen bales, Booker moved straight toward a low stack of last year's hay, then suddenly drew up.

"So," he said softly, looking into a jumble of shadows.

At first he, John, could see nothing, but as he moved forward, as his eyes began to probe the darkness, there indeed seemed to be two forms, one lying across the other, in a sort of recess there in the hay.

"I guess it's them," John said, repressing the desire to bolt. "Looks like it's them."

Booker had not yet moved. Now standing behind, his dim shadow cast over John's shoulder, he seemed to be waiting for something—or for something to pass. John turned, peering up into the dark face, then abruptly looked away.

Yes, it was still there—that look.

But then it had begun, the big form brushing past him, moving toward the opening, just as he himself reached out, feeling the tensed muscles of that broad arm under his fingers.

"Wait," he said. "Jus' wait and let me . . ."

And then he seemed to be falling, spinning. He crashed over a bale of hay and down, his face now against the planks of the floor. He was raising his head, getting back to his feet, when he heard the first cry, then another.

"That's good," he later remembered thinking. "If there were no sound, or only that certain grunting . . ."

And then, indeed, they had emerged, the two of them flying out of the dark opening like rag dolls, crashing crazily into some low bales before they fell to the floor. But Darnell, his trousers still half off, was already talking, the drink-slurred words welling out of him like vomit even before, with a convulsive movement, he began to raise himself up.

"C'mon Book, jus' a l'il fun. You had a l'il fun di'njew—well, same as us, same as us. Buhsides she was askin' for it, you know that yourself, jus' askin'. Dumb P-p-p . . . Pocanhonis . . . canhonis . . ."

Then there were no more no words, just a kind of muffled whimper, as Booker jerked the fleshy, white-buttocked body to its feet, then began to raise it, to lift it high, high—and he, John, his mind seeming to watch his own body even as he began to move toward them, was upon them, seizing Darnell by one naked leg. Then he himself was being lifted, both of them together, and his mind had begun the task of preparing for it, the crashing impact that would surely come—when all at once it had stopped, the soaring, the lifting, and he had felt himself being let down, almost gently, to the floor.

"Okay," Booker said, allowing Darnell to slump down once

more. "Okay." He sat down heavily on a bale, his great black hands folded as if in prayer between his knees.

Lonnie Wilson, who had said nothing, peered up over the top of a broken bale. His face was pale, his eyes wide with terror and incomprehension. He was very still.

"It's the best way," John said. "You said the boss wanted . . ."

Booker nodded, his hands still folded between his knees, his eyes cast down to the floor.

"C'mon," John said, looking over at Lonnie. The young man warily got up, then began to brush the hay off his clothes.

"C'mon." Darnell, his eyes muddy with terror and drink, seemed about to say something in reply—but then he too began to get up, drawing on his trousers as he raised himself from the floor.

"C'mon." For a moment Booker remained quite still, as if he had not heard. Then, very slowly, he looked up. His eyes seemed calm, almost happy—as though a burden had all at once been lifted from him.

"You betcha," Booker said, a quiet smile on his lips, as slowly he rose to his feet.

As they passed through the yard, Lonnie and Darnell shuffling along in front, they could see the lights from the kitchen and, hovering near the stove, the somber, solid form of Maria Bear. John could hear Darnell muttering, half to himself, and realized that this, the muttering, must have been going on for a long time when Lonnie, who had been ahead by a few steps, suddenly stopped and wheeled about.

"Oh shut up, you sack of shit!" he spat. Darnell, falling silent, did not reply. They mounted the stairs and went in at the back door.

"They're still in the liberry," Maria said to Booker, glancing coldly but without emotion at the others. "Here, take this to her." Lifting down a cup, she filled it with hot milk from the stove. "I'll wait here," she said, and turned her back again.

"I better wait too," John said. "Or maybe I'll jus' be getting on back. I got the horse."

"You come on," Booker said. "I want you along. Then I'll take you, like I said before."

They walked down the long hallway, John bringing up the rear. He had never been beyond the kitchen before, and the dark splendor of these rooms, or what he could see of them in the dim light, was both sobering and a bit frightening to him. There was what seemed the dining room—a gleam of silver candlesticks, a heavy table and some chairs—then another long hallway off to the left, then the carved railing of a stairway heading up, and just as they were turning into one the lefthand doorways he glanced into the little room just opposite, across the hall, where a pair of low French divans could be seen against the wall. Then, however, they had passed into a large sitting room, upholstered chairs and couches and a big, covered piano by the window—but again they passed through quickly, Booker stopping at a heavy, closed door on the far side. There was a knock, a word from inside, and they went in.

The Indian girl, a heavy woolen blanket about her shoulders, had been in one of the two chairs before the hearth, where a bright fire was now burning. Now, as they filed in, John saw her rise to her feet and, gathering the blanket tightly about her, hurry to the far side of the room, where she stopped near the corner of a large desk. There, turning, she fixed a sullen glance upon the group, seeming to recognize no distinction at all among them.

Kinsella, however, standing beside a table near the window, had already focused his attention, the ice-blue eyes narrowing with contempt as Booker, the cup of milk in his hand, herded them before him. He did not speak at once, simply looked them up and down as Booker took the milk to the girl, then went to stand facing the fire.

There was a long, heavy silence, the only sounds that of Darnell's heavy breathing and the soft roar of the fire. When at last it was broken, after several minutes, it was not Kinsella who spoke.

"Well, talk at least," Darnell muttered. "Get it over with, damn it, if . . ."

"Shut up," Kinsella said. And again the silence descended.

"Where'd you find 'em?" Kinsella said at last.

"In the barn, just where I thought," Booker said quietly, still looking down into the fire.

Again there was silence for a moment, only the sound of the fire, the labored breathing, until . . .

"In my *house*, my *house!*"

The voice was high, strident, at once a shout of outrage, a moan of anguish, and a bitter shriek of dismay: the cry of a female eagle returning to her plundered nest. John, who had remained by the door, glanced quickly at the girl—but not quickly enough to see the beginning of her swift movement. Cup in hand, she was already halfway across the room when he saw her. Then it, the cup, had seemed to spring from her, spreading its steaming contents over Darnell's face and shirt, the side of Lonnie Wilson's trousers, and the dark maroon of Kinsella's rug.

And now Darnell was howling, body twisting to one side. Through his fleshy fingers, raised to his face, the milk seemed to flow like honey.

"Get Maria!" Kinsella thundered—and John, turning, was running down the hall. A few moments later he had returned, the old Indian woman preceding him with some wet towels and a bowl of ice. As he came though the doorway he could still hear Darnell's howls, and above them the thunder of Kinsella's voice, as if it had never stopped.

"Get her the hell out of here, damn it!" he bellowed at the old woman. "I don't want to look at her!"

Maria, ignoring him utterly, moved straight toward the figure writhing by the fire, then began to pry at Darnell's fingers. "Take away your hands," John heard her murmur, the voice gentle as a breath of wind. "I've got something . . ."

Her blanket once more drawn tight about her, the Indian girl now huddled in the far doorway, behind a corner of the big desk. Her eyes, fixed on the flushed face of the old man, were the eyes of a bobcat in the dark.

"Book!" Kinsella howled—but already the tall figure was moving, in two strides reaching her side. Then, saying something in a low voice that John could not hear, he opened the far door and, with a quick, sharp glance over his shoulder—first at Kinsella, then at John—led her quietly out.

Afterward, when he was back among his sheep—yes, and long, long after that as well, John sometimes found himself thinking back upon that glance, remembering. Written there, it seemed, had been an augury of all that was to come.

Kinsella seemed instantly calmed. Moving to Maria's side, he took two towels from her and, handing one to Lonnie Wilson, began daubing at the rug with the other. For a brief moment John, uniquely disengaged, simply stood and watched; events had passed him by. But then, as the awkwardness of this position settled in upon him, he hurriedly set off across the room.

"Here, sir, I can do that."

Kinsella looked quickly up at him, then across into his face as John settled to one knee on the rug beside him. There was a sudden strange intentness in the old man's gaze, a momentary failure of recognition, it almost seemed—but then, almost immediately, it was beginning to fade, the hard blue glance softening, softening, into an expression of consent, but somehow too, or so it seemed, something more than consent. And then it was gone. Kinsella, still silent, made as if to rise. John reached over, guided him upward, and fell to work.

"Thanks, son," he heard the old man say, the words coming from above. John looked up with a smile—but already Kinsella was moving, rather urgently, away. "Aw, baby . . ."

Deirdre stood in the doorway, one hand gripping the front of her nightgown, a small fist of flannel. Her face, puffy with sleep, wore a vague expression, wonder and disapproval at once.

"All this racket," the old man was saying, but then he had turned again, this time toward the Indian woman.

"That's enough coddling for him," Kinsella snapped. "Take her back on up."

Orson Darnell, still softly whimpering, held the ice-filled towel to his cheek, his eyes mournfully following as Maria crossed the room. In a moment she and the little girl were gone. The desolate little moans went on for a moment, then abruptly ceased. Booker had reappeared in the far doorway, his dark form filling it to the transom.

But now another, higher voice was speaking, the muffled words tumbling one upon the other. "It's not like we jumped her, you know. If she tells you that, well . . . not like she didn't ask for it. Wasn't our idea, the candy and such. One time I gave her something, okay, a Snickers or something, I dunno, one time, and after that she just wou'nt let up. Meet me here, meet me there . . . and what are we supposed to do, her always swinging everything around and all? You seen her yourself, Mister Kinsella. You seen her, all the time. So tonight she says meet me there, in that place of hers she's dug out in the hay. So okay, we bring what she wants, candy bars, lik-rish, all that kind of shit—and maybe a little something for ourselfs too, you know. A little party, you know, she didn't seem to mind. Well . . ."

John, still kneeling on the rug, looked up—but not at Lonnie, never once at him as the words went on, one piling upon the other. For Kinsella was by that time in motion, his stooped, wiry form sweeping across the room with astonishing agility, then striking—hitting Lonnie once in the pit of the stomach, then again, as he bent, in back of one ear. Falling, Lonnie seemed to look up, his eyes widened with disbelief just as the toe of Kinsella's boot buried itself in his groin. He crashed to the floor, then began to vomit.

The old man, breathing heavily now, turned away, as if the writhing figure at his feet had ceased to exist. For he, the old man, was now glaring toward Booker, who still had not moved from the doorway.

"I want you," Kinsella began, but then it seemed he could not go on. For a moment he stood quite still, ignoring the strangled sounds at his back; he seemed to be trembling a bit, his face flushed with effort as he struggled to catch his breath. Then at last, the words coming slowly, deliberately: "I want you to pack up these two pieces of shit and everything they own . . ." Again he stopped, then again pressed on. "Right now, I'm talking about—down to the highway and *dump* 'em. Understand? I want 'em *gone!*"

Booker, immobile in the doorway, showed no trace of emotion as he said: "Shall I pay 'em?"

Kinsella sighed. "Hell yes pay 'em, and a hundred for Christmas each. Now get 'em *out* of here!"

With a laconic, easy movement the big man crossed the room to where Lonnie Wilson lay and, taking him under an armpit, raised him to his feet. The retching had subsided now, replaced by a dry, hollow coughing as Booker, rather gently it seemed, half-carried, half-led him across the room.

"Keep him off the rugs, for God's sake," Kinsella muttered as he turned away. Heavily, his face now drained white, the old man sank into one of the chairs by the fire. Darnell, who had already begun to move, was close behind the others, the towel still held to his cheek as they passed out through the doorway.

And then only John remained, still kneeling on the rug as before, the damp, milky towel still clutched in his hand. Slowly, as if not wishing to be noticed, he rose to his feet and started toward the door. He had almost reached it when he stopped, turning. "I'll be going too," he said.

With what seemed enormous effort the old man turned to look at him. For an instant there was that same strange intentness in his eyes, but then it faded and was gone. He turned away again, looking into the lowering fire.

"Yes, go on," Kinsella said weakly.

There was a pause, a weary sigh, before he added: "And send Maria. Tell her . . . tell her right away."

He stood on the back porch and watched the coming dawn. There was a chill in the air now, the smell of a change in the weather. Far off to the north the dark flanks of Molly Peak lay shrouded in shadow, while behind, above the topmost ridge, the gray had begun to soften into the palest yellow, brushing the backs of a band of cirrus clouds stringing off to the east. It would not be long before the wind rose, pressing gently against the trees until the earth was warmed, or as warmed as it would be. Yes, there was a definite chill in the air now, the smell of a change in the weather.

From inside the kitchen came the sound of running water, Maria filling the bucket she would take in with her. He turned to the window to watch her, the deliberate, implacable movements of that broad, powerful back as she passed from the sink to the mop closet, then back again. Over in the corner, huddled on the floor near the stove, the girl sat enveloped in her blanket, knees drawn up to her chin like a child. Indeed she seemed a child now, at this moment, her eyes vaguely following her mother as the old woman passed through the doorway and down the hall. Still, it was easy to see the rest of it too—now, as he regarded her unawares.

He abruptly turned from the window, glanced up once more at the awakening ridge, then descended the low stair and started across the yard. The gray, half-frozen grass crunched gently beneath his feet as he reached the battered gate, then pulled it open and passed through. Up ahead, at the front of the bunkhouse, he could see the outline of Booker's truck backed up to the porch, shadowed figures moving through the light of the doorway and back again. A tall form, Booker's no doubt, emerged from the barn with two saddles, approached the bed of the truck, and heaved them atop the heap. "Well, that's it," he heard Booker say. He stopped, remaining in the shadows at the corner of the barn until he heard the sound of the engine, then watched as they pulled out and headed down the lane. When he could no longer see the truck's lights he went inside, retrieved his saddle, and passed through to the corral, whistling for his horse.

3

"You'll live," Booker said. "Here's your money."

Darnell, ruffled through it, then stuffed the envelope into his pocket. "Damn fucking little for five years in hell."

Booker said nothing. He lifted the last box, full of dirty laundry, down to the shoulder.

Darnell, scowling, sat down on his saddle, the gravel crunching beneath.

"Just shut your stupid face for once, okay?" Delivered of this, Lonnie Wilson blew his nose.

A big, square-nosed cattle truck appeared over the rise and moved toward them, heading north.

"Sure you don't want to go up that way?" Booker said.

"To what?" Darnell muttered.

"Suit yourself."

They watched as the truck approached, moving fast, then roared on by. The driver, a young Mexican, looked curiously out at them as he passed; he did not wave.

"What'dya think you're looking at, fuckin' spick?" Darnell shouted after him. He kicked at the gravel shoulder with the toe of his boot. "Shit," he muttered, and slumped lower on the saddle.

"Well, boys, it's been nice," Booker said. He swung into the cab. "Take care of yourselves."

"Yeah, swell," Darnell muttered. Booker turned away, reaching for the ignition key.

"You jes' get on back to yo' massah."

Booker stiffened against the seat.

"Jesus Christ," he heard Lonnie Wilson whisper, then all was silence—the only sound the chilly wind moaning across the flat.

For a moment he sat very still, eyes closed, left hand tight on the door handle. Then slowly, slowly he raised his right hand to his face, pressing thumb and forefinger against his eyeballs for several seconds before drawing the palm slowly, slowly down across his chin.

Reaching down, he turned the key, heard the engine come to life, and headed back up the lane.

Carl Withers was on the porch of the bunkhouse, rinsing out some things in a bucket. As Booker drove up, the old cowboy, looking tired, glanced briefly up at him, then returned to his work. Booker parked the truck beside the barn and walked over.

"He took off," Carl Withers said, wringing out a worn pair of long underwear. "Just saddled up and left."

"I told him to wait, I'd take him."

"He just had enough, maybe." The old man spread the underwear and a pair of socks to dry on the porch rail, then emptied the bucket beside the porch. He turned to go inside. "I've about had enough myself. Getting too old for this kind of stuff."

Booker continued down toward the big house. The wind had begun to die now, ruffling the tops of the poplars as it passed, but the thin sunlight had not yet softened the night's chill. As he passed through the gate and into the yard he felt a great weariness settling over him, a numbness in his very bones, but he knew that it was not yet time to catch his breath. No, not yet.

The broad form of Maria Bear, as if responding to a cue, emerged on the back porch, drawing her daughter behind her by one hand. Consuela was crying. The old woman stopped and took her arm, roughly shaking her as she said something in their language. Then the girl was silent, her eyes downcast, as they descended to the yard. Booker stopped and watched as they moved across the little bridge over the ditch and headed toward their cabin.

Maria seemed to have seen him, glancing once in his direction as they crossed the yard, but she continued walking, her jaw set, her hand tugging the girl behind, until they reached the cabin and disappeared inside.

For a moment Booker stood as he had been, quite still. Then, passing over the little bridge, he went to the door and quietly knocked. Almost immediately the door drew open, Maria's face framed in the opening. Behind her, slumped on the iron bed, Consuela had buried her face in the pillow.

"We have to go," Maria said, her face utterly without expression.

"Of course," Booker said. "No matter what it costs him."

Maria did not change her expression, nor did she reply.

"What did he say?"

"Lotta talk. We jus' have to go, that's all."

"What does he think he's going to do without you? Take care of Deirdre himself? Scrub his own floors?"

"Don' know. We jus' have to go again."

Booker felt his brow contracting. "Again?"

The old woman, impassive, nodded. "It's . . . a problem."

"You mean it's happened like this bef- . . . ?" He could not finish the word.

Slowly, sadly, Maria nodded, then began to close the door.

"I'll talk to him," Booker said, and quickly turned away.

There was a humming, a desperate burning in his brain as, with long, urgent strides, he moved across the yard and mounted the porch. The door was still ajar; he jerked it open, half hearing it bang against the wall as he passed through. In the kitchen, perched on the stool by the stove, was Deirdre, still in her nightdress and slippers.

"What are you doing up?" he said. "It's not time yet."

"I heard some noise again," she said. "Where's Maria? I'm hungry."

"She'll be a little while. It's not quite time yet."

"But I heard her. When I was sleeping I heard her. Why isn't she here?"

"Just a dream, maybe. Anyway, it's not time yet. You go up and climb in again. Then in a little while she'll come and wake you, just like always."

Deirdre smiled. "Okay," she said, hopping to the floor. "But not too long, okay?"

"Not too long," Booker said. "But get along now. Good girl."

He watched her shuffle through the doorway, then followed her down the hallway to the staircase. She had mounted several stairs when suddenly she turned, looking with a curious intentness down at him.

" 'Bye, Booker," she said gravely.

"G'bye, sweetheart." There was a moment's silence before he added, very quietly: "Now get along." She turned and went up the stairs.

The door to the library was open. Kinsella, slumped in one of the big blue chairs by the hearth, was looking dully into the dying coals. His cheeks were pale, his eyes sunk deep beneath the grizzled thicket of his brows. He did not look up, did not move, as Booker entered and, passing beside him, sank down in the other chair.

"You're making a mistake," Booker said.

For a moment Kinsella did not reply. Reaching into his shirt pocket he pulled out a single cigarette and a match. Then, leaning over, he held the head of the match to a coal. With a sudden violence it burst into flame.

"Wouldn't be the first time," the old man said, bringing the flame to him. He lit the cigarette and threw the match back in the fire.

"Sure wouldn't," Booker said.

Kinsella coughed, but said nothing.

Booker shifted in his chair. "But it might be the worst."

"I doubt it," Kinsella muttered.

"You gonna take care of yourself, then? Deirdre too?"

"Maybe. Or I'll find somebody else. I can't have her around, that's all. That's it."

"You don't mean Maria."

Kinsella sighed, blowing a cloud of smoke upward.

"No, I don't mean Maria," he said bitterly.

"But suppose the girl could be . . . ?"

"Don't waste your breath. I went over all that with her, up and down. There's no one left to take her, no one she'd stay with, anyway."

Booker closed his eyes for a moment, listening to the soft breathing of the fire. Then, pulling his knees toward him, he got slowly to his feet.

He had never really looked at the picture before, this one over the hearth. Dark and somber, its colors dulled and deepened by a quarter century's smoke, it had become to him a part of the wall, no more distinct from it than the jumble of dark-spined books heaped on the mantle below. But now, in the light of early morning, this particular early morning, it seemed aglow, the heretofore invisible figures speaking out to him with the clearest of human voices. There were three, three men, emerging from the darkness behind. To the left, in the background, a bearded ancient looked sadly, but with a certain air of vindication, at the figure in the foreground, while on the right a haughty, turbaned king looked on as well; the gold of his crown and chain glowed warmly in the light. The one they both regarded stood before them, withdrawing from their presence. Richly turbaned like the king, his robe a warm, rusty orange, he bore his hand pressed hard against his heart. The eyes, downcast, were the eyes of the condemned, his face, no longer young, the face of one departing to his fate.

With an abrupt movement of his head, Booker looked away.

"*I'll* take her," he said. "If she'll go with me."

For a moment Kinsella was still, rigidly still. Then, very slowly, he turned his face from the fire, then upward, looking for the first time. Booker had turned again toward the picture, gazing deep into the exile's face.

"You're going to leave me, then," Kinsella said softly.

Booker nodded but did not look down.

Kinsella, with a violent movement of his head, spat into the fire.

Again Booker nodded, seemingly to the painted figure before his eyes. "It's time to go," he said. "Past time."

"Maybe. You owe me nothing." The voice was bitter, yet hoarse with grief.

Now, at last, Booker could no longer look away. "We both know that's not true," he said softly, meeting the pale, tired eyes he knew so well. "But it's not something I can pay back. Not anymore."

"I'll pay *you*, then. Twice what I pay you now. Just forget all this shit, will you? Go to Denver, see your people for a few weeks, bring me back somebody to do the cooking . . ."

The words, at last taking stock of themselves, trailed off into silence.

"No," Booker said. There was no bitterness in the smile, only a weary sadness. "But thanks. This is what I'm going to do now. I want to be on my own."

"Well for God's sake, then, *do* that!" Now the old man too was on his feet, his pale eyes blazing into the dark face above him. "Find yourself some little place, I'll even front you the money . . . but with this half-wit Goshute chippy, for hell sake? Come on!" Trembling now, Kinsella gripped the high back of the chair for an instant, then seemed to buckle. Booker, taking his elbow, gently lowered him to the seat once more.

"I'd like to buy the truck," Booker said after a moment. "I'll pay what it's worth."

"God, I don't believe this!" the old man bellowed, his hands tight on the arms of the chair. "You great black fool!"

Booker, his hands resting atop the blue velvet back, was silent, listening as the sound died away.

"I'll pay what it's worth," he repeated quietly.

For what seemed several minutes they remained just as they were, immobile and silent as figures in a frieze. Then, at last, there was the sound of a bird outside, clear and bright, and as though growing out of it a voice, Kinsella's, speaking softly, almost at ease.

"In the second lefthand drawer of my desk there's a wooden box. Bring it to me, if you will."

Taking his hands from the back of the chair, Booker crossed the room. In a moment he was back, handing it down.

Kinsella opened the box and found the paper he wanted. Then, closing it again, he reached into his pocket and withdrew a pen. He signed his name, then handed up the paper.

"I'd like to pay," Booker said. "I'd take it as a favor."

Again there was a brief silence, then Kinsella's voice, deep and calm as before.

"Get out of here."

Booker straightened. Then, after a moment's hesitation, he bent again, extending his hand.

"Get out of here," Kinsella said, unmoving. "And close the door behind you."

Booker raised up, withdrawing his hand, and walked slowly to the door. With a long sigh he drew it closed, then started down the hall.

Outside, across the yard, Maria and Consuela were hanging out some bedding. He breathed in once, deeply, and started walking toward them.

4

John slumped at his little table, absently daubing at the last yellow of the eggs with a piece of stale bread. There was a bit of coffee left as well; he drained the remaining wine from his cup and refilled it from the pot on the stove. Then, tossing the piece of bread into his mouth, he slowly got up to tend to the dishes.

He was very tired, but it could have been much worse. They had been scattered, of course, by the time he got to them—having had to stop off here first for the dogs and the other horse—but not nearly so badly as he had feared. Within an hour he had located the last bunch, far up a blind canyon, and by eleven he had them together and happy and was on his way back. Yes, he thought, it could have been worse, much worse.

There would be plenty of time for a nap now. He wanted to check on them again in the afternoon, just to be sure they had calmed down, but there were a few hours to kill before then. And yet somehow he did not feel sleepy. Too much had happened, too many thoughts seemed to be jangling together in his mind. Even if he had managed to fall asleep, he knew there would be no rest in it. No, to that kind of sleep he preferred none at all.

Putting away the dishes, he again sat down at his table, then reached up to his bookshelf for *The Spirit of St. Louis.* He had made considerable progress by now, very considerable indeed. The first test flight a success, all was being readied for the trip back to St. Louis. A hundred twenty-six pages copied—before too long he would need a new ledger.

Yes, he had made great progress; he had every right to be proud. Indeed, he seemed to have passed a kind of milestone—when exactly he could not have said, but recently; that he knew. The challenge of the words, the task and joy of wresting meaning from their mute surfaces, suddenly had ceased to be the whole of it. All at once the account itself, the story, had begun to draw him along—so that sometimes he would go nearly half a page now before running aground on a word he did not know. And sometimes even that did not defeat him, for he knew so many now that often—not always, by any means, but often—he could guess the meaning of the word and go on. Still, however, he remained careful, deliberate about it. No matter how far he found himself going ahead, always he forced himself back to where he had begun, copying out each sentence, word by word, in the tall, yellowed pages of his ledger; and always, still always, the words he did not know came to appear, with their increasingly less awkward definitions, in the pages at the rear.

He was quite a fellow, this Lindbergh, there could be no doubt of that. It was difficult even to imagine that kind of vision, that kind of energy and resolve and stubborn insistence upon success. He seemed not to know what it was to doubt; the notion of failure, although always a possibility, had no real meaning for him. Yes, quite a fellow—and yet there was something about him that John found troubling. Often, peering down at that photograph on the back of the dust jacket, he searched for the answer in that youthful, dauntless face, but always it eluded him, lay just beyond his reach. That look of haughty solitude, that indomitable stare . . . yes, it troubled him, and more and more these days, it seemed. Sometimes, after looking at it, he too felt very much alone.

Slowly he opened the book. The sentence he had last finished was before him, the next after it ready to begin. For several minutes he looked down at it, willing himself to speak or write. Then, with a snap, he closed the book, got to his feet, and quickly went outside.

It was almost an hour later when, again astride the big gray, he reached the ridge above the hayfield. The sun stood high in the sky, but a wash of thin clouds had covered it since midmorning; it was growing colder by the minute. Off to the northeast, near the base of some low hills, dust from a band of wild horses, returning to the cedar groves after a late feeding, rose gently in the clear air. He watched until he could no longer see the dust, then started down.

Perhaps, he thought, he would not wait until Christmas after all. Suddenly he was impatient to go—to head north with his ripening thousand into the desert, where they could be truly alone. He had had enough of company for now, even—or perhaps especially—of Booker. Yes, after this, today, it would be time to get ready to go. This, today . . .

He was, he thought, prepared—as prepared as he could be. Glancing back into the saddlebags, he again made the inventory. On the left the folded trench shovel, its handle protruding from under the flap, and with it the kerosene lantern and flashlight. On the right, neatly coiled and packed, the ladder. For almost three months now he had had it, his ladder, ever since . . . that time. He had almost forgotten about it, stuffed there in the bottom of his chest. Almost, until today.

, Yes, he had been on the mountain then, in the heat of the summer. He remembered planning it out, then setting to work, sitting in the shade of the wagon tying the knots as the dogs, perplexed, gazed out at him from beneath. It was not much of a ladder, really—three lariats tied together with a loop every two feet or so—but it had been the best that he could think of. It would have to do.

Absently, he reached back for his canteen. His mouth, he had noticed, was very dry. He could not get enough to drink. Glancing down, he watched the easy movement of his wineskin against the saddle. Then, looking away, he raised the canteen and drank. He knew he was afraid.

Soon they had reached the bottom and were moving toward the upper corner of the hayfield, the big horse moving briskly, impatient now that they were headed toward it, the creek on their left. It was a strange thing about this horse. Six years it had been now, more than six years since those days when she had come here with him, leaving him to browse as she read her book beside the spring—and yet the horse remembered, seemed incapable of forgetting. Whenever they passed this way it was the same—the peevishness, the fidgety stubbornness. Yesterday afternoon—could it have been just yesterday?—yes, yesterday it had been the same.

But today one thing was different. Reaching the little bridge, then crossing over, he allowed the horse to pass the trail heading south along the creek and continued upward, toward the tall cottonwoods. They were almost leafless now, their branches a lonely filigree against the hillside, and as he drew nearer— passing now the place where he had left the sheep then, then the little meadow, then finally up toward the low saddle— they seemed strangely vulnerable, tentative, like naked patients awaiting the arrival of the doctor. He looked away, up to the hillside—and then he was over the top and heading down.

The spring was full, just as before, just as always. That, at least, never changed. Drawing up beside it, the horse now willing, gratified, content, he looked down into the rolling, up-welling waters only briefly before, lifting the wineskin from the pommel and draping it over one shoulder, he dismounted. A moment later, burdened with his implements, he started up the hillside.

It was as steep as he remembered, but the heat and haste of that other time were blessedly absent today, and the ascent seemed easier by half. Other things were missing as well—the little yellow-throated lizards peering down from the rocks, for one, and for another . . . the bats. The lizards, he supposed, would already be half asleep, curled together in their winter dens. And the bats? Perhaps, perhaps. He knew nothing of bats.

No, he had no intention of hurrying today. He had two hours, at least that—and besides, he was determined to be careful, to try nothing that he could not easily do. There would be plenty of time for the rest—if there was anything to it at all. Yes, he thought, perhaps it would be nothing, nothing at all.

Scrambling up the final pitch, he at last came to the opening.

For a moment he simply stood there, stiffly looking down. The sound of his breath was heavy, hoarse; his heart was beating on the surface of his eardrums. It was about as he remembered it though, a bit larger perhaps. Still, it was far too narrow, far too tight. He stood a moment more, listening, waiting. Then, with a sigh, he raised the heavy coil of rope from his shoulders and put it off to one side, the lantern and flashlight beside it. And he began.

Even with the shovel, even though it could also be made into a kind of pick, the blade at right angles from the handle—even so it was very difficult. Several times he found himself striking at a stone with all his force, bending the tip of the heavy blade in the process. At last there was enough room to put his arm in all the way with the flashlight; he bent down, feeling the breeze—a bit warmer than before, it seemed—in his face. But the daylight made it impossible to see inside, and he went on digging, now using his fingernails sometimes as well. He could hear the hollow rattle of stones as they fell inside, the emptiness of falling, the sound of striking. There was one sound, though, that seemed to be missing—that soft, urgent fluttering of wings which had lately come to visit him in his dreams. No, it was not there—at least not so that he could hear it. Aside from his own labored, desperate sounds, aside from the rattle of the stones— and occasionally now the soft whine of the wind in the naked limbs of the cottonwoods as well—aside from these there was nothing, nothing at all.

And then it was done. He gathered up the rope ladder, carefully uncoiled it, and secured one end to a crooked little cedar trunk nearby. Then, loop by loop, he fed it in—until all at once it swung freely, side to side. Quickly feeding in the rest, he rose to his feet.

He had thought that now, above all now, he would be very much afraid. The opening finished, the ladder waiting, the lights ready at hand—yes, he had expected that hesitation and terror, if they were to come at all, would come at just this moment. And yet there was no trace of those feelings. Instead all was haste, impatience, an eagerness like none he had ever felt before. Reaching into his shirt for the battered old beret he had resurrected from his trunk, stuffing the flashlight deep behind his belt, snatching up the lantern and lighting it with trembling hands, he backed crabwise into the opening and, finding the first loop with the toe of his boot, took another step backward, found the next—and lowered himself into the void.

His first impression, aside from the uneasiness of dangling in space, was of sudden suffocation. Not that there was any lack of air or circulation—the breeze at the opening had been ample assurance of that—but here, inside, there was an oppressive mustiness, even a hint of decay, that the breeze had carried no hint of. He could think of nothing to compare with it—nothing, that is, until the long-dead memory of his uncle's earth-walled cellar, the smell and sound of rats scuttling by in the dark, came unwillingly to his mind. Reaching down for the bandanna knotted about his neck, he drew it well up over his nose, then slowly extended the lantern out to one side. But there was nothing, nothing he could see at least, to account for it—only the dark, dry rocks looming above him and to one side. Whatever it was—the rotting corpse of an animal, the stench of some subterranean pool—whatever, it lay below in the darkness. Groping for the next loop in the rope, he continued down.

He had expected silence, but nothing quite like this. There was a kind of hollowness about it, a beyond-silence like a vacuum, and yet as he proceeded, one loop after the other, he became aware of what in fact did seem to be sounds, yet sounds that somehow did nothing to attenuate, in fact even seemed to heighten, the all-enfolding hush. One was a kind of high squeaking, occasional and sharp, something like a small mouse might make. But yes, he had heard that sound before—yes, on that first afternoon, overlaid against the soft fluttering in the darkness. It was the bats—somewhere. Again he held out the lantern, looking, but there was nothing, nothing at all.

The other sound, from far below, he also knew, or thought so. It was the echo of dripping water.

The rocky walls seemed to have receded from him now. He knew, of course, that they remained, somewhere outside the globe of dim yellow light, but their sudden absence was unsettling, more than unsettling. Now, for the first time, he seemed utterly suspended and alone, like a spider hanging from a strand of web. Longingly he looked up toward the opening, hardly more than a spot of light now. And he began to tremble.

Clutching the rope, leaning his weight full against it, he waited until the worst had passed. Then, reaching down to his side, he brought up the wineskin, carefully unscrewed the top, and directed the thin red stream against the back of his mouth. In a moment it was better. Remaining very still, his chest pressed hard against the rope, he waited until his breathing had slowed. Then, with a long sigh, he capped the wineskin and went on.

He had not forgotten the flashlight. Now, once again, he felt its reassuring rigidity behind his belt. Yet he had promised himself that he would not use it, not until he reached the bottom—if he reached the bottom. If he were to drop it . . . No, he would not use it, not even now, not yet.

There was, after all, a limit to how far he could go. Forty-two loops, a little over a hundred feet, yes; but that was all. Counting each loop as he descended—twenty-six now, twenty-seven, twenty-eight—a part of him always had that final loop in mind, eager to reach it so that he could at last begin the ascent, the climb toward that distant, ever-receding spot of light that opened to the sky.

Yes, he thought, there he would use the flashlight, there at the forty-second loop. If he should happen to drop it then, listening as it fell and struck, then rattled to pieces against the rocks or whatever lay there below, below—well what of that? All that would remain was the climb, and the ever-growing patch of blue which would lure him upward. Yes, it would be time to

look then, time at last to see what he could of this great cavity
before at last bidding it good-bye. For it would be good-bye, he
was sure of that now. Once all this was done, once he again
stood in the light of the sun, he would trouble this darkness no
more.

Thirty-two, thirty-three . . . Yes, he thought, the smell, the
stink of the place, if nothing else, would be more than enough
to keep him away. More than enough. He had hoped that it
might weaken, or at least he might become somewhat more accustomed to it as he descended, but the opposite seemed to be
occurring. With each step, each loop, it had become more pronounced—until now it seemed on the point of overpowering
him. Again the image of the spider flashed through his mind—
but with it this time came the image of a cloud of gas engulfing
it, causing it to drop . . .

For that, really, was more and more what it was coming
to resemble, some kind of gas, ammonia perhaps—like a heap
of moldy, rotting rags. He could not imagine it growing any
stronger, and yet . . . Thirty-five, thirty-six—he found himself
yearning for that forty-second loop, longing to feel the pressure
of it on the ball of his foot.

It was just at that moment, gazing idly down into the darkness as his foot groped for the next loop, that he saw it. A gray,
granular surface some ten feet below him—it could have been
the surface of the moon. Easing his weight into the new foothold, he swung the lantern about him in a wide, lazy arc. Yes,
it was a floor, or something like a floor. Before him it seemed to
stretch a considerable distance, far beyond the reach of the lantern. Behind and to the rear, however, perhaps fifty feet away,
a dry slope of stony rubble rose upward from it toward a wall—
in the base which seemed to be a kind of low opening or portal,
perhaps four feet across. Beyond the portal . . . no, the light was
far too dim.

And suddenly he could not move quickly enough. Sliding
down the rope, missing first one loop, then another, he caught

himself on the next to last—noting with a strange satisfaction
that the last, the forty-second, lay lightly on the floor below.
Oddly, the surface seemed vaguely scarred, disturbed where
the loop had moved, to and fro, during his descent. Flexing his
knee, he leaned closer, then probed downward with the toe of
his boot. At last, feeling it beneath him, he slowly began to
transfer his weight—then abruptly withdrew his foot. Below
him, neatly pressed an inch into the surface, was the outline of
his boot, its edges brightly viscous with a kind of gray, faintly
moving slime.

But he was not about to be dissuaded now—no, not so easily.
At the same time he was not sure just how long he could remain
there, the awful fumes rising up to meet him. It was time for a
decision. He felt he had already made it.

Again he stretched the tip of his boot downward. Touching
upon the surface, feeling a slight surge as it yielded, he pressed
harder. Still it yielded, until it was about to reach his ankle, but
then . . . solid rock. At last he looked down at his boot; then,
with a soft, sucking sound, he withdrew it once again. There
was a sudden tightness in his throat, a suggestion of gagging,
as he straightened up, his full weight again on the penultimate
loop, and reached for the wineskin at his side.

It was only moments later when, his equanimity restored, he
reached down for the flashlight stuck behind his belt. Switching it on, he directed the beam directly upward—and saw what
he now expected to see. Some forty feet above him, covering
the underside of a vast rock shelf like a furry blanket, were the
bats—or some of them. There were thousands that he could
see, thousands, tens of thousands more perhaps that he could
not. Most were still and silent, sleeping, but now that the light
played over them the few that he had heard while descending
were joined by others, still only a few, fluttering about under the
shelf while voicing those same high, urgent cries. He lowered
the light, briefly playing it over the stony slope behind him
and the dark opening beyond, before at last he switched it off.

Then stepping down, he lowered himself again into the granular slime, felt until he reached the rock surface beneath it, and removed his other foot from the loop. A moment later, the end of the rope gripped in one hand, he was moving, slogging toward the rock-strewn slope.

He had not thought it possible, but the smell of the stuff seemed to have intensified, as though in some kind of unconscious outrage at his tread. In a sense, of course, it *was* alive, for the bats' excrement, centuries upon centuries of it perhaps, was only a part of it, although by far the greatest part. With it, however, seeming to form a living whole with it, were the other creatures—cockroaches, crickets, beetles, millipedes— the whole incredible crawling profusion which had first come to feed upon the bodies of fallen bats, then upon themselves, until a kind of eternal organic stew was born. It was strange, he thought, wading toward the portal and higher, drier ground— strange that now, embarked upon, over, through it, he had lost all sense of revulsion, yes, even in spite of the stench, as though familiarity had brought with it a kind of acceptance, an understanding. It was really not so different from the rest of life; there was nothing much to be gained from thinking about it very much.

Then at last he was there. Climbing out, upward toward the dark portal, he paused on the dry, stony slope a moment to secure the end of the rope ladder, wedging it tightly between two rocks. Then, as he scraped what he could of the stuff from his boots against an outcropping, he lowered the lantern and again reached for the flashlight at his belt.

It was a massive space, perhaps seventy feet across from where he stood—great shadowy shapes of dry rock overhanging and intersecting above into the ever-narrowing chimney through which he had descended. And yet it appeared that even now he was not really at what could be called the bottom, the floor if there was one, for ahead and off to the right, across the gray expanse that now bore his footprints, it seemed to drop off again,

leading down. Picking up a loose rock he threw it that way,
then listened. There was a long, hollow clattering, gradually
receding—then, far off, what seemed to be . . . a splash.

But no, he would not go that way today—perhaps he never
would. It was not a pleasant place to be, really. Again he looked
out at his footprints, the faintly moving iridescence about the
edges. The rest of it would just be more of the same, more
shelves and bats and stink and muck. Besides, it was time to
go; a quick glance down at his watch only confirmed what he
already knew. It would be all he needed now to have the sheep
getting nervous on him. Enough of that for one day. Yes, and
enough of this.

There was one thing, however, that he *did* want to do—one
sound he wanted to follow to its source. Behind him, through
the portal, he could again hear the occasional dripping of water,
but now much clearer, much nearer than before. It would take
only a moment . . . and then, taking up the rope, he would
swing out and be on his way.

Leaving the lantern behind now, he turned and continued
up to the opening. It was quite small, really, yet not so small
that he had to get down on all fours. Bending over, sometimes
squatting as he moved, he made his way down a rubble-strewn
tunnel. The water, by the sound of it, was very close now, but
bends, sometimes abrupt turns made it impossible to shine the
light more than a yard or two before him. Perhaps, he thought,
it was simply some effect of echo that made it seem so near; the
tunnel might go on for some distance, really, further than he
was prepared to go. Another turn, then, two at most . . .

All at once the passage opened out. He straightened, then
stopped. A high, vaulted room, its broad floor bejeweled with a
hundred shallow, stone-rimmed pools. Above, hanging in mossy
beards from the lime-encrusted ceiling, a thousand thousand
spikes and spears and fringes of damp, translucent stone; below,
among the pools, great capstans and mushrooms and peaked hills
of damp, translucent stone; beyond, and beyond, and beyond,

littering the walls and crevices like the graffiti of the blessed or the damned, parachutes and draperies, shields and angels' wings of damp, translucent stone. John Siloa stood very still, the beam of his flashlight moving quietly, reverently among them. Then, swallowing once, he turned to go, retreating down the stony passage like a thief.

It was almost dark when he returned, coat buttoned close against the bite of the wind. He picketed the horse and fed the dogs before he went inside, thinking all the while of a fire. The note was on the table.

We came to say good-bye. Consuela's with me, we'll be OK. I'll tell you the rest sometime. Your turn now.

Booker

He crumpled the paper into a ball and opened the stove, dropping it inside.

PART TWO

···

1964

CHAPTER 1

1

When the second spring began to fail, Cyril Kinsella looked upon it as a malicious act of spite.

Not that the word *God* ever crossed his mind, of course—not with a capital G in any case. If ever he had even vaguely entertained the notion of a single divine, abiding presence—at least one with the attributes claimed for it by Christian believers—all that had been swept away in the flames and cries of the Great War. No, he had long ago decided, a God who could permit the things he had seen and heard and witnessed was, if not a clear self-contradiction, a God he could only despise. Like Ivan Karamazov before him, Cyril Kinsella had respectfully returned his ticket.

And yet he saw nothing inconsistent in viewing this grave matter, this affair of the spring, as he did. Whatever his views on these "greater" questions, he had never for a moment doubted the existence of something, some vast, brooding intelligence afoot in the earth. Yes, as Satan had put it when asked where he had been—"going to and fro in the earth," and "walking up and down in it." And so it was, so it was. And it was this something which now had come to visit this, even this, upon him. But no, not as a matter of Fate, Justice, Punishment; none of these had any part in it—for this being, if such it was, would never stoop to the merely vindictive. This was the work of a Humorist—a whim, a joke, a nonchalant amusement to pass the heavy hours, eternity . . .

The murder of the president late last year had struck him in much the same way. Surely that young fellow, for all his good points, had plenty to atone for—not only in his own transgressions and assorted stupidities but in those of his whole wicked family before him. But the thing that brought him down was really something else. Call it hubris, call it evil, call it what you will—the fact was that the Great Humorist was again at his work, whiling away the time on a hot November afternoon.

"Like flies to wanton boys . . ."

They had been standing there for some time now, at the edge of the faintly troubled pool that was all that remained, there beneath the two great, sighing cottonwoods. Neither had spoken until now—neither he nor the thin, dark man at his side—but now the other looked up at him, eyes full of questioning.

"Sir?"

"What's wrong?" The old man, his shoulders stooped now as he looked down, seemed impatient.

"You said something. Flies, I don't know."

"Yes," Kinsella said, looking up the hillside toward the stone marker. "Yes, maybe I did. Nothing though, forget it. Let's go."

They turned and walked down the nearly dry creekbed to the little bridge, where they had left the truck.

It was the spring of 1964, almost ten years now since John Siloa had come to Phoenix Ranch. Much, very much, had changed. The days of cowboys' laughter in the bunkhouse, herds of sleek, white-faced cattle roaming the hills and flats, Tabby

Weepup and Booker Goodman and all the rest—those days had long since become mere scraps of memory, no more real to John's present mind than the soft green Pyrenees, the whitewashed villages of his youth. And yet no less real for all that. Just as the voices of that far country, the country that was home, would sometimes emerge to trouble him through the mists of sleep, so the broad, tall shape of Booker's back, walking from the campfire toward his faithful orange pickup, would all too often be there to remind him of those days before. John regretted nothing, but he did not easily forget.

The cowboys had been first to go—although to establish some real precedence between that and the selling off of the cattle would have been a futile exercise. Carl Withers, a few days before Christmas, decided it was time to take up his sister's long-standing invitation to live with her in town, and three weeks later the Lindsay brothers, mysteriously come into a substantial amount of cash or credit or both, announced that they were leaving too, their offer on that Reese River ranch they always talked of having been accepted. By that time the Denver cattle broker had come and gone, and the seemingly endless procession of trucks was under way. Delaying his departure for the winter range, John fully expected to be next, and when a Harignordoquy truck turned up one morning, loaded horse-trailer rattling behind, he was not at all surprised. It was a herder he knew quite well, in fact, a partner from former years, but the curt note the man brought with him said nothing about John's leaving. He was to bring the horses back to the ranch—and move into Booker's quarters. And so he had, leaving the dogs—yes, so he had. Met only by Maria, sharing the noonday meal with her alone in the empty kitchen, he had tended to the home stock and waited. Mercifully the weather held, and on the twenty-ninth of January the last of the trucks, filled to the limit with Kinsella's fat cattle, had rolled away to the north. Two days later, beginning at midnight, the first big storm of the season had settled in about them, and for the next three weeks, without a single day's respite, the snow had fallen in a way that beggared legend.

John never saw his sheep again—or, for that matter, his dogs. A week after the storm had broken, or at least had petered out into flurries as it waited to welcome its successor, he had come in one evening from feeding the horses to see the sheepcamp, hooked up to one of Harignordoquy's trucks, being backed into the barn. Knocking the snow off his coat, he had walked to the big house then, rapping on the door of the library for the first time in his life.

"I expect you'll be wanting me to go back with them," he had said when the old man, clearly less than pleased at being disturbed, had sharply told him to speak his mind. "I thought I'd better come 'round to draw my pay."

"It's here if you want it," Kinsella had said. "But I'd just as soon you stayed."

"Stayed? But what for?"

"We'll figure that out later. Somebody's got to take care of the stock. Just think about it. Sleep on it. I'll take you on over tomorrow if you're really set on going."

"Okay," John had said, not knowing what else to say.

"And shut the door behind you, damn it."

To the people of the ranches across the valley, huddled about their crackling, blackened stoves, the doings at Phoenix Ranch that winter—the winter of 1955—had come as a curious and delightful shock. There were many still among them who had witnessed all that had gone before, from that day more than twenty-six years earlier when Kinsella, his hair still black as a raven's wing, had first appeared with his team and wagon and began to raise his cabin beside the creek. The younger members of this group, some of them still under forty, were of the same generation who in those distant days had eagerly scanned the springtime horizon for the first appearance of the bright blue Model A, then stood by awestruck as the great stone house rose out of the sagebrush and into the sky—but the weight of years and responsibility had given them a slightly different point of view. If Big Bob Fisk (as the boy of the somnambulant horse was known these days) still seemed able to derive some pleasure from the telling—even going so far sometimes as to bring out the still shiny Indian head nickel that Kinsella had given him (and one to Orson Pratt as well) when they had helped carry the stove pieces inside—it was a pleasure long since leavened with hard reality. The fact was that Kinsella, however fabulous he might have seemed to their eager young eyes, had managed to take the best for himself while they across the valley made do—had always made do—on what was left. This at least was a subject on which he and his aged father-in-law could agree.

"Snooty bastard," old Ira Murchison would say, sucking on his teeth by way of punctuation. "Give me Uncle Billy every time. He might knock you down, but he'd always give his hand to help you up again. That damn Kincaid, he don't even know we're here."

Recently, since the death of his wife of sixty years, Ira had again taken to calling Kinsella by that other name.

"Now, Dad," Wanda would say, looking up from the book she was reading to the boy. "Don't get all het up over that again. You know what the doctor said about your pressures."

"Let him alone," Big Bob would tell his wife. "After ninety-one years he's entitled to speak his mind."

But now it seemed it was beginning to unravel—not old Ira's mind, that is (although there were a few dissenting voices on that as well), but that oppressive operation across the valley. It made no sense, of course, letting the hands go and selling off all the stock just when it would fetch next to nothing, but by now they were accustomed to having what Kinsella did make no sense, at least at first. However that might turn out, the plain fact was that all that acreage was going to be empty now, just as it had been when he had come. And whatever else you might say about Kinsella, no one had ever accused him of being less than fair when he had ground to lease. At last, it seemed, they were going to have a little room.

The most curious part of all, however, was the part about the Basco. For he, it seemed, had stayed, even though those fancy sheep of his had been sold off as well, taken off again to where both they and he had come from, so they had heard. Yes, it was anybody's guess what Kinsella was up to now.

Ira Murchison, of course, had his own personal theory.

"The nigger, as I see it, must have found him out—and that's one thing Kincaid wouldn't take to. Whatever you say about niggers, some of 'em make damn fine hands—and that one was plenty smart too, ran that place tight as leather. As for this Basco, if he's like any Basco I ever knew, he's just too dumb to know the difference. Besides, he'll be moving on too come spring, just you wait and see."

"Okay, Dad, but don't wake little Eddie. I just got him to sleep."

"Yep, it's all coming apart for Kincaid now, all coming to pieces."

"Maybe so, but here's your milk ready now. You know what the doctor said about your nap."

But when spring at last had come, the snow standing heaped to the bunkhouse eaves until mid-April, John Siloa was still there—although Ira Murchison, sad to relate, was not. There had been little actual work to do, aside from caring for the four remaining horses and a few cows, but he had long since become accustomed to idle winters and put the time remaining to good use—moving confidently onward from *The Spirit of St. Louis* to the pile of Zane Grey westerns the Lindsay brothers had left behind. Then, late that month, Levi Mondragon had appeared as always, although John half expected to see him depart the next day. But nothing of the sort had come to pass; the battered trailer took its usual place beneath the still-naked poplars, and within a week the two of them had begun to work together, first cleaning the barn and restacking the small amount of hay Kinsella had not sold off during the winter, then turning to the machinery, cleaning and greasing and repairing until all was ready. John had been an attentive student, and when that first season ended, the barn once more full to the eaves, the hired crew sent happily on their way, he felt that he already had a good grasp of what there was to know. All of which proved fortunate indeed, for when the twentieth day of September came 'round again—the battered trailer once more ready for its journey— it had become apparent that Levi Mondragon was leaving for the last time. The gentle Mexican, apparently further gentled by a stroke of financial good fortune not unlike the Lindsays', had not protested—and his departure, marked by a fine and vi- nous dinner together in the trailer, had borne considerably more resemblance to a celebration than to a wake.

"Now, perhaps," Levi Mondragon had said in parting—"per- haps you will truly come to taste the apples of Taos. When the hay is in next year . . . it really is not far. I will make you a great *fiesta*."

And so it was that when the cold winds of November came again, sweeping the last stubborn leaves from the poplars, the outlines of John Siloa's new life had been firmly, surely drawn. The people of Phoenix Ranch, where that life was fated to un- fold, now numbered only four, and so they would remain, it seemed, for all eternity. And so in fact they had remained for nearly a decade now—ten long years which yawned between them and the days of Booker Goodman.

It was curious, John thought, that in all the days in all the years that had come and gone since then, not one had passed without his thoughts returning, if only for a fraction of a mo- ment, to the big black foreman he had loved. And yet never, not once in all those days and years, had he felt the slightest impulse to learn what had since become of him. It would have been easy enough, he supposed, a few well-placed inquiries in town, but really, to be honest, he had no interest. For it was the man who once had been, not the man he might somewhere have become, who now frequented John's thoughts—who never really had ceased to frequent them since that mid-December afternoon, almost ten long years ago now, when he had returned to the sheepcamp to find the note placed neatly and precisely at the center of his little pull-down table. "Your turn now," the note had said, and so it was, had been, and yes, seemed ever would be. His turn.

Over the years—since Levi Mondragon's final departure, that is—John's basic responsibilities had changed but little. There were always the horses and a few head of cows to look after, and now and then a little work on the fences or with the Indians who came to cut firewood in the hills, but always his major focus had remained the hayfields. He usually worked alone—except when the summer crew was there, of course—and in time had come to know a good deal about machinery, both how to run it and how to keep it running. Occasionally, especially in the beginning, there had been teachers—an obliging blacksmith in town, a Basque truck mechanic at the mine, a few others—but as the years had passed he more and more relied upon his own instincts, refining what seemed to work and abandoning what did not. In the same way, but in this case with the aid of a book discovered in a long-shut drawer, he had learned to repair harnesses and other tack—to the point that now he felt his work compared with Booker's best. And then, of course, there were the endless errands, not only the normal sort of trips to town for groceries and supplies, banking and payments, shipments and repairs, but also, and even more often it seemed, that other sort, those particular and always urgent assignments that Kinsella never seemed to run out of—everything from delivering messages and documents, often to people John had never before known existed, to sending wires and dispatches to strange and distant places and searching through dusty records at the copper-domed courthouse on the hill. There were many in Creighton—not to mention many of those watchful souls across the valley—who when they spoke of him never used his name; to them he was simply "Kinsella's man."

Yes, Booker had known, foreseen it all. And yet, John wondered, had he really sensed just how far it would go? And those in town and elsewhere, those who applied that convenient epithet, had they the smallest notion of the extent to which he was, in fact and in practice, Kinsella's man?

They had begun almost at once, the "summonses," as Booker had called them. At first, in spite of all the forewarning those long conversations on the mountain had provided, he really had had no notion what to expect. And so he had presented himself simply as one ready to receive orders, commands, injunctions. And indeed there had been some given then, at least at first, the old man seeming to sense his confusion and dismay. But gradually, little by little, all that had passed away—gradually, as the true purpose, the meaning of these nocturnal meetings became clear. For they were almost always at night, when the wine of dinner had given way to the more potent spirits of the darkness. And almost always they ended in the same way—a slow, ineluctable descent into unconsciousness. Then John would at last get to his feet and, crossing to the desk, stub out the still-burning cigarette in the ashtray before he turned to go, softly closing the door behind him.

The true purpose? The meaning? It was difficult to know just how to put it. For it was not as though his own function there were simply that of a listener, a silent, sympathetic receptacle into which the old man's thoughts, as they took shape with the telling, were poured. No, for he too was required to speak, to participate, at least until the hour grew very late. Empty and banal as they might have seemed—and surely they all too often seemed so to him—John's own contributions were for all that essential, indispensable to the process. For there was something in the old man that struggled against isolation, refused to submit to that aspect of himself which, as the years passed, seemed ever more bent upon enclosing him in some narrow inner space, where his own thoughts would ceaselessly reverberate about him as if he were the clapper of a bell. He needed another, a chosen interlocutor, to draw him out of that space, to keep it from closing in—to save him. He had needed Booker Goodman. Now he needed John.

Kinsella never asked him about himself—or only very rarely. Only when such a contribution might have some bearing on the theme, give some purchase for further development, only then might the old man elicit some brief explanation. Almost always these inquiries touched upon the war—not his, Kinsella's, war but John's own, when as a boy his village had been occupied by German troops. Here again, however, the old man never seemed in search of mere anecdote for its own sake, but only as it might shed light on or add a dimension to something already troubling his mind. When he questioned John about the war— asking him, for instance, to tell again how fleeing Jews were smuggled, under the Germans' very noses, across the mountains into Spain—it was only because he had again been brooding over one of his favorite themes.

"Is there a way, John," the old man might ask when the tale had again been told—"a way to resist evil without becoming part of it?"

"Well, I guess stand up to it, or walk around it maybe, the other way."

Then, after a long pause, the old man gazing out the window into the night: "Yes, that's it I suppose. Just walk around it. But when you took these Jews, for instance . . ."

But if John's own past, John's own life, was only rarely the subject of discussion, the same could not be said of Kinsella's. Especially when the hour grew late, when whiskey and tobacco had begun to take their inevitable toll, especially then the old man's mind seemed doomed to dwell on what had been. Rarely was there any shape, any order to it, and events of long ago might weave in and out among happenings of yesterday or a year before, but the result was a kind of antic tapestry which, to John's eyes and ears at least, had a sobering, awful beauty about it. At the same time, however, there was all too often that mounting sense of unease, then dread, as the stripping away went on, the relentless process of self-exposure that never seemed complete enough to content the speaker. John, captivated as he was, felt at the same time a kind of responsibility—as though in some way he had failed in allowing it to begin—and all too often when the night was done, the cigarette safely extinguished in the ashtray, it was with a vague sense of remorse in his heart that he drew the door closed behind him, passed through the silent house, and headed across the yard to his room, Booker's room, in the dark, lofty barn.

But yes, this matter of the second spring had become a cause for real concern. True, it was by no means a question of survival, for even if it dried up completely there always remained the other, the first spring as it was called—that rocky cleft just east of the house where its very stones had been quarried. This little outlet, although subject to periods of waxing and waning, had even in the driest years provided more than enough water to take care of the needs of the house itself, and this spring of 1964, after a series of very good winters, it was fuller than anyone ever remembered it being. All of which was very fortunate, for if matters continued as they were, it would soon become necessary to draw from the little reservoir below it to save even some of the hay. John, expecting the worst, had already begun to lay the piping he would need, and a big new pump was already on the way.

That was the strangest part about it, the part most difficult to understand. The second spring, unlike all the others in the neighborhood, had never been subject to the yearly fluctuations in flow that were the normal lot of springs. Wet years and dry, regardless of the season, it had always been the same, bubbling merrily up out of the earth as though of its own sweet will. If there was one thing that could be relied upon always and without exception, it was, had been, the second spring. But now, it seemed, it had begun to fail.

None of which, of course, had escaped the notice of the people across the valley. It was difficult to say just how the knowledge had come their way, but bad news travels fast when it's someone else's. They knew—and they rejoiced. Even Bob Fisk, who, if anyone, had a kind of divided loyalty in the affair, made little secret of his satisfaction. For he was nearing fifty, an age of taking stock, and he had for several years now assumed his father-in-law's dusty mantle of reproach.

"About time, I'd say," he was heard to confide one day to old Wilbur Tipton, who still at seventy-three was to be found beneath his green eyeshade at the Murray station. "More than time. All those years we watched him, him with his fancy hay-fields and fat cows while we made do on dust and guts—it's all coming home to roost now. Let him sit in his castle and rot."

"Well," Mr. Tipton said, sucking on his snow-white mustache—"I don't know about rotting, but it won't hurt him to chew on the other end of the stick for a while."

"Damn right," Big Bob said, and turned to go outside. "Won't do him no harm at all."

2

. . . *because when you're young and full of spunk there's always something in you that wants to play with the grownups, to show them not only that you can play but can beat them sometimes too. That's how it was with me, anyway. I was champing at the bit, raring to have at them—and soon enough I was playing at the same table and beating them too, more often than they damn well liked. I loved it. I ate it up. For the first time since before the war, maybe a long time before that, I felt alive, Lazarus risen.*

That was a big part of it, the war—even then I knew it. It had put me in a kind of rage, a slow-burning fury that even now has never really left me. It was so unnecessary, so futile and pointless—oh God, I still can't bear to think of it, and yet I never cease to. It follows me around day and night, pointing its dirty finger . . . And so when I got back, even after those two years afterward rattling around over there, trying to shake it off . . . until at last I knew it was no use—when I got back, wanting to make some kind of beginning in spite of it, the only thing I could think of was to do what I'd rather vaguely studied to do before. I'd never really thought I was cut out for it. I'd hated law school, just went through the motions because there was nothing else, nothing, that really seemed worth doing. But then here I was back again, and amongst the other junk in my bottom drawer was a Harvard law degree. And so I just went to it—and before long I found that I could play, really play, and beat them more often than they liked. A damn sight more often than they were willing to admit.

Until at last a few years later there came the day—and a fine New York autumn day it was, the leaves all a-riot in the park, a cloud of steam on every breath—the day that Blickendorf, old Dan Blickendorf himself, struggled up the three flights to my dark little office and, breathing hard, settled himself deep in my one leather chair. He was inevitable, I suppose, he or someone like him. If he hadn't come along I would have had to invent him.

But you're not drinking, John. How about a drop more? Come on, I didn't mean it literally really, about the drop—drink up. Well, suit yourself, you do have a long day tomorrow. As for me, well . . . You're very kind. You've always been very kind.

Yes, Blickendorf. He was made for me really, and I for him—and yet even then I wondered why. For the more I thought about it, the more I came to know him, the more it seemed that he stood for everything that had inspired and nurtured and sustained it. That filthy war. All wars. Greed, vanity, guile, cruelty—all of it. And yet there I was, longing to do his dirty little business, work the deals that only someone like me, as I had become, could work. I couldn't figure it out—and yet there it was. A pact with the devil. No, I couldn't understand then. It was only much later that I read Goethe . . .

Have you ever wondered why it is, John, why we so often choose what is poison to us and turn away from what'll do us good? No? A pity. But you ought to think about it—in relation to your own life I mean. I've had it happen often, often—most particularly on one occasion I can think of. But then you'll hear all about that too. Be patient. And could you bring that box of matches over from the shelf? Obliged.

In any case I signed on with him—and went at it with a will. I kept my little office open, somewhere to keep the books, but from then on there was only one client. And he was more, far more, than enough. From that point on, it seemed, my life was spent in trains and telegraph offices and shabby boardrooms in jerkwater towns the likes of which I never knew existed. For I came west.

It was a miracle to me, a holy revelation—like nothing I had ever dreamed of. I still remember that first morning out of Chicago, waking up into a murderous hangover. Out the window the broad, open plains speeding by—the space, the endless space . . .

I had read of it in books, I suppose, but to see it, be actually moving through it . . . I was stunned, dumbfounded—and yes, in a way . . . humbled. It was a strange, confusing feeling, for by then I had begun to think that that emotion was one I had long since left behind. I could feign it, of course, masterfully, but to actually feel it? And yet here it was, no mistake. Humbled, and not even by a man. By a land, a country. I thought about it, brooded over it, as the wide expanses rolled by, as the dim shape of the mountains began to loom on the horizon. For alongside this new sensation, embedded in it, was the fact that it was here, nowhere else, that I was to do my . . . Blickendorf's dark business. For this was where it increasingly was now, his business. To him the West, this country, had nothing humbling, nothing remotely holy about it. It was his oyster, and he meant to eat it whole. With my assistance. Very well, I at last decided, so it shall be. And then the train rolled into Denver.

There was something intoxicating about them, those first few years, something that went to my head like fine old cognac. It was a great time, just then, for a young man to be trying his wings, on the loose. For I was still young then, at least in years—and very much on the loose. My only law—not counting, of course, the kind I used as a tool, a lever and a hammer, to make my way—was Blickendorf himself, and he was very far away. There was the occasional trip back, of course, far too many of them to suit me, and the more than occasional meeting in some dingy office or hotel room or train station with one or the other of his minions, mining engineers mostly; but aside from that there was only the clicking of the telegraph, and that was something I quickly learned to ignore. Gracefully, you understand, with a certain fine sense of discretion and style. All he really wanted, after all, was results, and results were what I gave him—in spades.

I'm sure you've noticed how that can be. Give 'em what they really want, they'll shut up about the rest. Don't you agree? Well, you should give it some thought, you've lived a little, after all. But no matter . . . could I trouble you again? Yes, this glass seems to have a hole in it. And have another touch yourself; it's not that late. Well, as you like, you know best. But just where was I? Oh yes. Right. I see you've been listening.

Yes, I'll have to say I was pretty good at it—getting what he wanted, what I wanted. But just what might that have been, what I wanted? Good question. Although you didn't just up and ask it I know that's what you were thinking. I wanted . . . many things, I suppose—but all of them really amounted to the same. Power might be one name for it, although that too is a little off the mark. Because I didn't really want to control things, even to have people fear me. Something like that might have happened, you understand, but it wasn't really what I was after . . . for myself. No, it was something a little different, a feeling more like . . . potency. You're smiling, but never mind—because that was it, really, the feeling that once I set my mind to do something, there was nothing, nothing that could stand in my way until it was done. Across the board it was the same— for it was not only the deals, it was everything. Especially it was the women.

That surprises you? I don't wonder. I don't seem that sort, do I? But now is now, then was then. And then . . .

After a while it became part of almost every job, every . . . arrange-

ment. There always seemed to be a woman—a daughter, a sister, a restless wife—and I always got to meet them too, for before we got down to business there was always that bit of socializing, a dinner maybe, an afternoon tea, something. I knew the purpose, of course, what the old men had in mind. Setting a proper tone, they might have called it, observing the civilized amenities of business; but really, as we all knew, they just wanted to size me up, get some idea just who they'd be dealing with the next day—or days, or weeks. Which was all fine with me, for while the old man was sizing me up I was doing a bit of sizing up myself.

But wait, I don't want to leave the wrong impression. Many times, quite often in fact, it went no further than that. Different reasons, I guess, it was hard to tell. But once I set my mind on one . . . Sometimes it would take awhile, longer than the actual business, but there was always a reason for coming back, always some papers still to be signed, and in the end I had my way. But then, that was my private religion, wasn't it? To have my way.

You seem a bit restless, John. Yes, I understand, this is all rather tedious, I admit it. But sometimes it gives me a strange kind of pleasure, thinking about those days, even though what was to come, continues to come, lurks behind them like a shadow . . . I had an uncle once, long ago now, who was in a wheelchair, crumpled up like a rag doll. He'd been thrown from a horse, one of those jumpers I think, years before. He still could talk though, sort of talk, and I used to go see him sometimes in the afternoon; it wasn't far. I still remember the heat of that house; he always kept it very warm. I remember the flies caught under the curtains, buzzing against the window. I remember . . . what was I saying? Oh yes, my uncle. In his wheelchair. Yes . . . Well yes, what he talked about, liked to tell me about those afternoons, was how he loved to ride a really spirited horse, bend it to his will. That's just how he used to put it too—bend it to my will. Until the day one bent him. But he never mentioned that . . .

But then that's neither here nor there, as my sainted mother used to say. Neither here nor there. What's here is here and what's there is there. And that's neither . . .

3

He stood in the shade watching, beneath the wide eave of the barn, as the gleaming yellow Chevrolet moved slowly up the lane. At last it reached the house and, turning about, came to a gentle stop. A tall young man, the driver, got out and walked around to the other side, where he opened the door and stood holding it as the passenger, a slim blonde girl in a light blue dress, emerged. They spoke for a moment, a chime of laughter rose, and then, without touching, they parted. The girl, passing through the yard toward the rear of the house, stopped to wave, and then the bright yellow Chevrolet retreated down the lane.

It was half an hour later when he saw the girl, dressed now in Levi's and riding boots, emerge on the back porch of the house and, slamming the screen door, begin to walk quickly toward the barn. He watched her come, as he always watched her, each swift movement of her long legs announcing the intensity of her anger.

"I'll get your saddle," he said as she approached. She, her mouth set hard, did not reply but turned into the tackroom. He followed, watching as she snatched her bridle from the peg and swept outside, into the corral. He stood for a moment before the saddle, a soft, troubled look about his dark eyes, before at last he lifted it down and went out. She was already standing beside her little black-legged buckskin, the catch rope loose about its neck. He drew near, then stood in silence as she slipped on the bridle. When she was done he came forward and, with a low "huh," lifted the saddle and began with the cinch.

"Why does he have to hate Eddie?"

The voice, sharp and sudden, startled the horse. Patting it on the flank, soothing with his voice, he at last made it stand, then went on with his work.

"Well, why does he? I'm talking to you!"

Again the little mare stiffened, but then grew still. He finished with the cinch, again stroking the smooth tan flank before he turned. Her blue eyes, bright and hard as stones, met his with a jolt, but he, like the horse, was still.

"He doesn't hate anybody," he said softly, evenly. "He doesn't even know who your Eddie is. When will you get some sense?"

Her glance flared up. "He's not *my Eddie*. Besides, what if he is?" She paused a moment, the fire ebbing into petulance. "Anyway you sound just like him. I'm always wrong."

"Sometimes you don't show good sense," he said.

"Good sense! What good sense then, Mister Know-It-All?" She stamped her boot in the dust.

"The good sense not to have some young fella bring you home in his shiny new car. You know your father."

"Don't I ever! And you sound just like him, hanging around him so much! What's wrong with the bus?" she mimicked, making an ugly face. "I was late, that's all, and he was coming home. There's nothing wrong with it—he just lives across the valley."

"I know where he lives," John said quietly. Then, after a moment: "But that's not quite the point."

"What *is* the point then, if you please? I'd really like to know." Her sarcasm had an awkward, exaggerated quality about it, as though she were still experimenting with technique.

"You know," he said. "You just want to hear me say it again."

"Well say it, then!" she cried. "Say it!"

Again the horse stirred, stamping its rear hooves from side to side. John made it stand.

"Okay, if you like. Your father is an old man, over seventy by anybody's counting, and you're all he's got left, or so he figures. He's sensitive about things he maybe oughtn't to be, but that's how he is. That's all." He smiled.

"Satisfied?" he said mildly, looking straight into her face.

She did not answer. With a toss of her head she drew the horse to her, away from him, and with a quick, smooth movement leapt on. Startled, it began to wheel, stamping, but soon she had it moving in high, nervous steps toward the gate. John was already there.

"Can I ask you a question?" he said as she passed through, eyes averted, head held high. Outside the gate she stopped, turning to face him.

"Where'd he get that fancy new car anyway?"

"Bah, shows what you know," she spat derisively. "That's no new car—it's a fifty-eight, a fifty-eight *Impala*. He just keeps it nice."

"I see," John said thoughtfully. "Impala." He scratched his head and smiled. "But a nice car anyway. Where'd he get it?"

"Well his dad didn't buy it for him, if that's what you want to know."

"No," John said. "I don't suppose he would."

"He works, that's how. He works hard, and I don't mean just for his father." Abruptly the sarcasm was gone, replaced now by an earnest, almost plaintive tone.

Looking up at her, he waited.

"He's got a job after school, a regular job at the hardware. He likes to work. He wants to *be* something, not kick around on that ranch all his life."

Slowly he lowered his eyes. Then, after a moment: "Okay. Just curious."

He waited for her to move away, his gaze on the square toe of her boot. At last, when she did not, he looked up again, meeting her cool blue eyes.

"Where'll you be?" he said quietly. " 'Case he asks."

"Up the creek," she said with a little smile as, slowly this time, she turned the horse and moved off.

He stood watching until she had disappeared into the cedars, beyond the first bend of the road. Then, picking up the catch rope, he walked slowly back inside.

4

My nerves are bad tonight, John. Stay with me a while. I'll be better after we've talked.

Yes, thank you. Just a bit. That's good, not too much. I know all about this stuff, you see. It calms you down, all right, evens you out, but then next morning it takes its revenge. Nervous as a cat, and the only thing that'll take the edge off is . . . Oh yes, my boy, I know all about it, chapter and verse. Might as well leave the bottle though.

I was just going through a few of these old clippings. That always seems to do it, set me off. But if you'll just stay here with me a while . . .

Kind of you. I can't say how much . . . But then maybe you've heard all this before. I just can't remember sometimes what we've talked about and what we haven't. But no matter. There's always that little detail that might have slipped through the cracks, that little something that might have made it real if I'd remembered. Not that you can ever get it really right, how it was, but sometimes . . . just a little closer to what . . .

And maybe I haven't really talked about her that much. Shied away maybe. Because she was the beginning, if you look at it a certain way. Without her, that night, all the rest would never . . .

But I must have said something about the dance—oh excuse me, the ball, that's what they called it, the grand ball, if you please!

Are you sure? I can hardly believe it. The word? Ball, you mean, grand ball? Well maybe so, you might not have come across it. En français . . . bal, I think, something like that. Same thing, anyway. Not too common a word, really, at least not out this way. That's what made it so funny at the time I guess, at least to me. Because this grand ball was held in the schoolhouse, or the high school maybe it was, I'm not all that sure.

The hotel? No, that wasn't much more than a few foundation stones back then, but they, or their wives at least, were bound and determined, and so . . . Yes, must have been the high school. Anyway there was a little orchestra brought in from somewhere, along with a dozen cases of champagne, caviar and oysters and such like, and we all arrived there in splendor, tuxedoed and begowned as though we were at the Waldorf—and we had our grand ball. Yes sir, so we did.

Would you mind fetching me those matches from the shelf?

Obliged. For the life of me, I don't know what I do with matches . . .

Can't say she was the first one—a wife, I mean. Those other times though, well it was just one who happened to be about, whose husband spent just a bit too much time at the office or the mine. Now and then I had the feeling that somebody'd been there before me— once or twice even that this was considered a part of the business, an incentive to be reasonable. Reasonable . . . Yes, but this time, with her, it was different. Different.

Sometimes, John—do you ever feel this way?—sometimes now, these past few years especially, it's as though I've become a hall of mirrors. Strange way to put it I guess, but that's just how it feels. The minute I start to do something, say something, anything—write a simple letter, tell Maria about dinner, talk to Deirdre, even to you here—anything, there always seems to be a part of me left out, watching me do it. But that's not the worst of it, for part of that left-out part is left out too, watching me watching, judging me watch- ing me do, then watching me judging, another part. And another. Can you imagine such nonsense? No, I thought not—but no matter, maybe it's enough just to know; how it can be, I mean. And yet that's still not all of it, you see. If there were some kind of a progression, something that could be predicted, counted on, well that would be one thing. But no, it's not like that—because it all seems to be hap- pening at once, and yet no, not all at once. Like . . . like an engine, maybe, with an intermittent short. Sometimes one cylinder will hit, then right away another, then that one and a different one, then three of them, then all six, then two again . . . But no, that's not right either. Because I don't want all six to go at once. I want just one, any one, without the others. A good, solid contact. So the current can flow. Yes, nowadays it seems there's just one thing that can make the current flow . . .

No? Just a touch? Well, suit yourself.

And so where was I? Before the mirrors, I mean. Forget the mirrors, they don't mean anything . . .

Oh yes. That was it. And thank you.

No, there were no mirrors then. The current flowed clean, strong, and swift down the wire. When the switch was thrown. And that night, oh yes, the switch was thrown.

It puzzles me that I could have been so different then, so sure of myself. Now . . .

She wasn't what I'd call pretty to look at, although I think a lot of others might have said so. Once, maybe . . . but she must have been near forty by then, not that it showed, really. Ash blonde, tall, even a little on the gawky side—but there was a certain kind of energy about her, a kind of openness that you don't see that often. She'd look right at you when you talked, no matter who you were, those calm, gray-blue eyes taking it all in, and then she'd smile that smile, soft and . . . confiding. Confiding. And yet there was nothing flirtatious about it, nothing you would have mistaken for an invitation. Because if there was one thing that set her apart, made her different from all those others, the ones before, it was the way she had of letting you know that she was his, part of a team almost. It was the same feeling you get sometimes from a preacher's wife, like she's doing her part while he does his. Know what I mean?

No, perhaps not. Not likely that you might have encountered that many. But maybe you get the idea. Anyway there was that feeling, part of the team . . . But it's a shame you haven't met a few preachers' wives.

Because then you'd understand the next part too. There's something about a woman like that that makes her more . . . interesting to a certain kind of man. And it's not just the forbidden fruit I'm talking about, the urge to take what's out of bounds. It's something else, a kind of curiosity to know how much of that stance, that teamwork face they put on so firmly, is real, based on . . . love and devotion, say—and how much is only a sense of duty, a felt obligation to carry through on what she signed up for. Yes, it makes you curious. Sometimes it makes you so curious you want to find out . . .

I don't know why, but I had the feeling as they came in that night that they'd been arguing. Something about the way he stood with her, the way she smiled, something. In any case the moment she could she was off and away, bustling about in that awkward way she had, arranging things just right—because she was the one in charge, of course. I watched her out of the corner of my eye for a while, half-listening to the business chatter going on around me, all for my benefit no doubt, before at last, seeing her struggling to move an urn, I detached myself and went over. It was at that moment, I remember—seeing her with the silver urn, the mauve silk of her dress reflected in it, the flash of anger and frustration, a momentary betrayal, in those always calm gray-blue eyes—yes, that was the moment . . . that I decided.

There was nothing really strange or foppish about it, my going over. I'd been a guest at their house for four days, and would be for three more. Nothing could be more natural than my going to help—but when I arrived, took the urn from her, she knew from my eyes that I had seen, comprehended, what had been in hers. Her only word was a gracious thank you, her soft smile, careful and alert, again firmly in place—but an understanding had passed between us. Nothing more was made of it just then, although we danced together more than once—charming but careful, hostess and guest—but later that evening, when the famous grand ball at the high school had at last run its lugubrious course, when Reston had not yet returned from the mine office . . . Later that night. Or morning. Later . . .

Damn this cough. No secret what brings it on, of course, but damn it anyway. Water? Yes, okay, but come right back. I'm not done yet. Nowhere near done.

Oh yes. Thanks. Kind of you. Just resting, I was. But yes, that's better.

And don't go thinking I've forgotten. Where I was, I mean. My mind may have run ahead a little but . . . I put in a bookmark. You know about those, being a scholar and all.

Yes. Well, afterward—and there was just that once, you understand, no more—anyway, I stayed on just like before, meeting with our people and his and being squired all about the countryside to look at machines and visit sites in which I had absolutely no interest, though they, of course, thought I was just enthralled. Certain way I had . . . She, for her part, seemed withdrawn and distant—stunned, you might even say. We never spoke of it. There was no need. But occasionally at dinner I'd meet her eyes, those wonderful calm eyes. There was never any bitterness in them really, certainly nothing that might have been mistaken for rage or spite, but something was there that had not been there before, something . . .

She spent most of the time in her room, I think, but there were other things for her to do as well. For on the Thursday, I think it was, the day before I left, the two daughters were to arrive from Europe, where they had been traveling with a Boston aunt. And so there were things to do—times when I'd meet those eyes more often than I otherwise might have. That time in the kitchen, when I'd gone in to ask for a cup of tea. Then on the stairs . . .

I'm all right. Just a kind of nod. Maybe if I just rest here a minute . . .

The day they came. Yes, the same day I'd . . . sprung Blickendorf's trapdoor under his feet. It was done, over, time for me to go—but then here they came, on the evening train. He, ever the gentleman, the soul of chivalry, asking me to tag along. The aunt, little Marcella rustling down . . . and then Abigail.

I'd won, taken it all—and yet, there on the platform . . . I'd lost it all. Pity . . .

But what do you think of this boy of hers, John? This kid from across the valley.

Fisk, you say? Bah! Might as well be Murchison, all from the same trashy nest. Looks like one of 'em, all right. Spitting image.

Maybe so, but I don't trust him. Don't trust any of 'em. Anybody who'd drive a goddamn Chivvie . . .

5

He moved up the creekside trail, the tall cream-tailed sorrel stepping briskly beneath him. It was hot and dry, for early June at least, and the branches of the cedars alongside were already coated with a light, powdery dust. Occasionally, through a break in the trees to his left, beyond the creekbed, he could catch a glimpse of the hayfield—or what once had been. For already they had had to choose which portions would be irrigated and which would not, and this stretch, sadly, had been left to wither in the sun.

He had not come this way for a long time—since last fall, in fact. In the winter he took a slightly different route, at least when there was snow, and this spring, aside from that brief visit with Kinsella in April, he had been too busy with the new pumping system to come at all. Now, however, all that was finished, and he hoped to have a little more time.

Yes, he was happy to get away, if only for an afternoon. Kinsella's moods had been very dark of late—as dark, perhaps, as ever he had seen them since those first days, when the enormity of Booker's desertion, heightened by the real or imagined imminence of a visit from that long-scorned son, had combined to so undo him. In the years since then, as both of these, the rage and the fear, had seemed to recede together—the first through a kind of imperceptible healing, the second as the threat just seemed to fade away—the old man had seemed to mellow a bit, increasingly turning his attention to the spectacle of his daughter's soft unfolding. There had been lavish clothes and gifts, teachers and tutors of all descriptions, and above all a vast amount of personal attention and concern. This is not to say that the late-night meetings had become any less frequent, only that their subject matter had changed somewhat, gradually shifting from that haunted obsession with the letters to other, more hopeful matters. And yet now, these last few months, all that seemed to have changed. Again the letters, and the memories summoned up by them, had crowded to the center of the stage—but were joined there now by something entirely, utterly new, which occasionally brought forth a summons even in mid-afternoon. Kinsella, it seemed, had at last begun to notice that Deirdre was no longer a child.

Today, however, the old man had undertaken one of his increasingly rare trips to town, backing the Model A out of its

garage just after lunch. It was a matter of consulting his lawyer, Kinsella had gravely explained, and John's presence would
not be required. Mysterious as this announcement seemed—for
Kinsella's business with Mr. Lehigh had always before been dis-
charged by telephone or through John himself—he had secretly
rejoiced at the news, and by the time the ancient blue car was
out of sight, chuckling merrily off down the lane, he had already
gathered up his saddle and headed for the corral.

He reached the end of the hayfield and, continuing on beside
the creekbed, arrived at the little meadow where they had found
Tabby. He often thought of that last visit, almost ten years ago
now, when Kinsella had brought the old man to the camp—
and sometimes he took out the little cross Tabby had entrusted
to him, silver and coral stones, from its folded handkerchief at
the bottom of his drawer. He had told no one about it—no, not
even Booker in those days before, and certainly not Kinsella.
It was his secret, his alone, and over the years its meaning for
him had changed in a way he never could have anticipated. He
wondered, all too often now he wondered, whether when the
time came to give it up he would really be able to do so. He
supposed he would—for it was, after all, a solemn obligation, a
trust—but the thought of letting it go, and just at that particular moment, was one he had increasing difficulty accepting. In
a sense, he thought, he would need it all the more.

Driving these thoughts from his mind, he urged the sorrel up
the narrow trail to the rise. It had never ceased to surprise him
that other horses—those, that is, that had come after the big
gray he had called Azkar—failed to approach this rise with the
same enthusiasm. He remembered the day the big horse had
died—kneeling beside it in the barn as those last rattling breaths
came one upon the other, then shuddered into silence. It was
the only horse he had ever named, and even then it had been less
a name than a description—strong, powerful, vigorous. And so
Azkar had been, even on that dark November day—until the
end. He remembered thinking at that moment that a link, like

the big horse's heart, had broken—the link between him and
. . . someone he had never known.

He drew up at the top, immediately half regretting that he
had done so. Mentally prepared as he thought he was, still the
sight of the spring was like a blow to the stomach. Somehow he
had imagined it might be better than this, even that the first
signs of revival might be appearing. At least, he had thought, it
could not be much worse than when they had come up in April.
But no. The broad, shallow basin was almost dry now, only two
small pockets of water remaining. Of these only one seemed to
remain active at all; the other lay slick and flat off to one side.
Mounds of dried and drying watercress lay everywhere, clouds
of flies upon them—and overlaying all, like a frothy white mold,
was the seed-laden cotton from the two great trees above. It was
a scene of death, a battlefield the morning after.

Wresting his eyes from the sight, he looked up into the
branches of the two cottonwoods, the catkins bursting now.
They, at least, seemed no worse for it—not yet. Their roots were
deep. Their hearts were strong. And perhaps they felt some
greater loyalty as well, as sentinels. He glanced across to the
other side of the dying spring, where the roots of the larger tree
cradled that little depression in the earth, and the unmarked
marble shaft, piled about with down now, that rose from it.
Then quickly he turned away and dismounted, tying the horse
before he started upward.

In the nearly ten years since he had come upon it, the cave
had yielded but few of its secrets to him. Still he had returned
often, as often as he could manage. He had told Kinsella about
it, of course, but aside from one perfunctory visit the old man
had stayed away, although he offered no serious opposition to
John's coming himself when there was time. And so over the
years it had become a place to which he always came alone.

Perhaps it was this very lack of a companion which had pre-
vented him from exploring the place. He had been down to the
first level many times, of course—albeit now with the assis-

tance of a proper chain-link ladder he had purchased from one of the mines—and the features of that ornate little chamber off to one side had become as familiar to him as those of his own room, but the levels below remained as they had been, an utter mystery. He knew just where he would like to begin if there were someone to go with him. Yes, each time he went down he glanced over that way—where the floor of the bat chamber seemed drawn into that rocky chute—and often he repeated the experiment of that first day, tossing a stone down, then waiting for the distant splash. But no, there was no one to help him, no one at all.

Reaching the top of the rock-lined trail he had made on the hillside, he emerged on a small flat area. There, set a little back in the hillside, was a rusty steel door. He put down his little rucksack, drew back the bolt, and pulled it open, revealing a low, rocky chamber about eight feet deep with a wooden bench along one wall and an assortment of ropes, lanterns, and tools along the other. He picked up the rucksack and laid it on the bench, then continued to the back of the chamber where the end of the ladder was secured. A moment later he had disappeared from sight.

Almost an hour had passed when he reappeared, the beam of his miner's headlamp preceding him up the shaft. He removed the lamp and hung it on a wooden peg, at the same time taking a battered tin cup from the peg beside it. Then he went to the bench and, sitting near the open doorway, raised the rucksack to his knees and took out a small parcel wrapped in white butcher paper, a can of sardines, a filled pint Mason jar, and a small vacuum bottle. Carefully unwrapping the parcel, he flattened the butcher paper on the bench beside him and laid the bread and cheese upon it. Then he opened the sardines, poured half the jar of wine into his cup, and began to eat.

He could not have said just why, but these little solitary meals here had become one of his greatest pleasures. In fact, given the practical limitations on his explorations below, they were a large part of his reason for coming at all. Summer and winter, in sun and snow, there was something about them that at once reminded him of those simpler days with the sheep and inspired him with new thoughts and plans for the future. Here on his bench, sitting in his own wood-framed doorway, things always seemed clearer, simpler than they did below—just as they had, so long ago now, up on the mountain. Perhaps, he thought, it was simply that he was up so high, with the world spread out at his feet—for it was remarkable how much could be seen from here. From the ranch buildings and big house far off to the southwest, to the ragged line of peaks across the valley, to the broad, arid flats off to the north, all was laid out before him like a great, glowing map. There was a great calmness about it all, something that seemed to supersede all human concerns. Here, more than anywhere, he felt at peace.

He ate slowly, in the fashion he had learned as a boy—left hand grasping the bread and cheese, right thumb working against the upturned blade to pare off a piece of both together, then raise them to his mouth. He had learned to eat otherwise as well, carefully watching others when he had the chance, but only the old way seemed right here—as indeed it did in his own room in the barn.

He wondered if he could ever be truly different from the way he had been, the way he was. Yes, there were the occasional refinements—such as learning to eat with a proper knife and fork, napkin spread across his knees—but at bottom he sensed that he could never really change. It was troubling, to feel that there were limits, immovable limits, beyond which he could never pass, things that lay forever beyond him, above him. To take the most obvious example, he certainly could never be Kinsella, or anyone like him. There was a fundamental difference between them that no amount of money or property or education, assuming he had those, could hope to change. Such a thing as that took more than a lifetime. It was a matter of generations, generations upon generations—until a new kind of person at last emerged. In the meantime it would be folly to aspire to such things, Kinsella and all he stood for, all that was his . . . Yes, in the meantime it was enough to serve.

He reached beneath the bench, pulling out a little oil heater that was there. He had brought it here for warmth during one of his winter visits, but it had come to serve other purposes as well. Lighting it, he finished the last of the sardines and put the tin, a bit of oil remaining in it, atop the flat surface. In a few minutes it was done. Impaling the last scrap of bread on the tip of his knife, he lifted the tin and carefully poured the warm oil over it. A few drops fell to the earthen floor as he lifted the morsel to his mouth, then followed it with the last swallow of red wine.

Content, he leaned back against the wall of the chamber and looked out over the scene. Sundown was still two hours off, but already the sun had begun its dying fall. He would be sorry to miss the moment, the kiss of brightness against the ridge of western crags, but by then he would have to be on his way, ready for whatever Kinsella might have in store. Thinking this, he looked off to the south, expecting at any moment to see the glint of blue as the Model A turned off the highway and headed up the lane. There was nothing, however; at least not at first. He opened his vacuum bottle and poured the coffee, hot and sweet, into the tin cup. Yes, he thought, the old man must have found something else to do.

It was just then that he saw a single car, far off to the south, moving his way. He watched it carefully, his nostrils filled with the hot, exotic aroma rising from his cup, until he was satisfied that it had passed the lane and was continuing on, heading north. At that he looked away, his gaze idly lingering on the outline of peaks across the valley. How often he had spent the late afternoons on the mountain studying this very scene, rejoicing in the deep blue color of the sky where it joined that ragged silhouette, watching the slow, steady acceleration of the sun as it began its nightly plunge! It had truly been one of his greatest pleasures—and yet always, he remembered, there had been a twinge of pain as well, knowing that another day of that warm, carefree summer was about to pass away . . .

He lowered his eyes to the line of highway once more, resolving to get up and leave when the northbound car finally passed out of his sight. It was now almost directly before him, directly between him and the mountains to the west. It moved slowly, languidly—its motion somehow resonating with the bright yellow color the sun reflected from its sides.

He put the cup down on the bench and watched, his eyes narrowing as he sought to be sure. Then he was sure. After a few minutes the car slowed, then turned off to the right, up the rough road leading to the place he had used for breeding . . . that year. Within a few hundred yards, however, it came to a stop, then pulled into a little turnoff sheltered from the highway. It had remained there for ten minutes, its bright yellow top gleaming in the sun, when he gathered up his rucksack— dropping the butcher paper, the empty sardine tin, the Mason jar, and the vacuum bottle inside—and went to the back wall to hang up his cup. It had remained there for fifteen minutes when he pulled the steel door closed behind him, pushed home the bolt, and headed down the trail. The cream-tailed sorrel, looking curiously up at him, whinnied softly, then once more dropped its muzzle into the bank of tender grass.

6

Late? Well yes, a little, I suppose. Went to see a lady I used to . . . but of course, you know her. I went to see Suzanne.

Well I'd hardly go that far, to say never. I drop by every now and again. We've got a lot in common, besides our age, that is. We understand one another better maybe than . . . We've got a lot in common.

Oh yes, a long time. An eternity. Ever since . . .

Yes, might as well. Just bring it on over here. You've taken a bit for yourself? Enough to keep you? Good. Yes, that's fine. Just leave it.

She doesn't change much, not like me. Still a fine-looking woman in her way—although if you'd seen her then . . .

Make up a little fire for me, would you? I feel a bit of a chill tonight. Yes, go on ahead, Maria should have filled it. But don't be long. I'll be right here.

Good. Much better. I like a fire now and then, don't you? Even in summer. Thaws the bones . . .

Yes, she was quite a woman, Suzanne, the woman for me, I suppose, all said and done. But then, when we first began to . . . know one another, well, I had other things on my mind. And afterward . . . sometimes things just work out some other way. That was a long time ago.

Other things on my mind—one way to put it, I suppose. Actually there was only one thing on my mind, that was enough . . .

I'm going to ask you a personal question, John, do you mind? Very kind, and forgive my prying; I don't mean it badly. But tell me this, have you ever been totally . . . overcome by a woman?

I see you're confused; with good reason, I suppose. It isn't the sort of question that really can be . . .

No, not love—although I suppose there's some of that too, whatever love might be. But what I'm getting at is something else. It's as though you've been emptied out of whatever was there before and filled up only with her, to the remotest corners of your being. Everything else, what you had thought, what you had been—it's gone.

No? Well, I congratulate you. Let us hope . . .

Because that's the way it was then, you see . . . with her. From the moment I first saw her, heard her voice, saw her move, until . . . I still remember the way I felt, walking down the train platform with them, back to the car. It was a kind of numbness, but with every nerve ending alive—to feel the ache. It was a disaster. It was my disaster.

I left the next day—one day too late. To be in the same house, and then her mother there, and then her father . . . No, I couldn't get out fast enough. I fled.

It was futile, of course. It wasn't the sort of thing you flee from, get free of. You can go wherever you like, but it comes right along— occupying you like an army, all your provinces . . . But anyway I left. Denver, I think it was, then somewhere in Montana, then . . . until one day I'd had enough. I went back to New York. There was a kind of meeting, hard words. He cursed me. I left.

This is all so hard to say. And yet I think I need to say it, get it out again where I can see it. You don't mind too much, do you? You've listened to my blathering long enough, God knows, all these years, but . . . Another drop? Sure? Well, suit yourself.

I knew what I had to do. Otherwise . . . it was eating me up, killing me. I knew what I had to do. Later that same afternoon, his curses still ringing in my ears, I was on the Century heading west.

It was a few years since I'd been to San Francisco, but nothing much seemed changed. It was evening, the lights of Market Street glittering in the fog. I took a cab up to the Palace and got a room, then walked over to Hoffman's for an early dinner. By ten I was back in my room, just me and a bottle of old Scotch. But even that was not enough to kill the taste of dread, flat and metallic, at the back of my mouth. It was clear enough in my mind, what I had to do the next day—but I hadn't the smallest notion how I was ever going to bring myself to do it.

And yet the next day came, and somehow, somehow I did . . . do it. I remember the morning, a morning such as they only make in San Francisco. Cool, translucent, Mediterranean sunlight filtering down through the last wispy traces of fog, the air fresh and bracing, full of promise . . . And as I walked down New Montgomery and crossed Market I all at once felt buoyed, heartened by the morning. The taste of dread was still there, like an old worn-out penny on my tongue, but somehow the air, the light, had softened it, altered it, even to the point of fatalism. Yes, I remember thinking for the briefest of moments, yes, what will be will be. At least it will be over and done, put behind me. But only for the briefest of moments, for even as I made my way through the morning crowds up Montgomery, I knew all that was a lie, self-deception of the worst kind. And yet I kept on, down California, the bell of the cable car rattling like thunder in my head, down to Battery, then left . . .

It was a small, unpretentious suite of offices, nothing fancy, really, but the comfortable smell and patina of long use and occupancy was everywhere. Yes, he was there and would see me, even came to the door to usher me in. The soul of honor. The soul of grace. Always.

Still, there are certain things even he . . . But no, she hadn't told him, hadn't . . . confessed; I knew it from the first moment. I remember the small, silent easing of the muscles at the back of my neck, the small, silent sense that yes, perhaps . . . There was, after all, no need for anyone but us, she and I, to know, and in time perhaps . . . Yes, I remember thinking at that moment, perhaps I had underestimated her after all.

And so, that moment passed, that barrier breached, I stumbled on . . . with all the rest. I remember that look of cool incredulity that gradually took possession of his fine features as I began to tell it. He had expected something else, a business proposition perhaps—something that he, being Reston, would not be too hasty in rejecting; no, not even after all that had gone between us. Now, with Blickendorf no longer a factor . . . And yes, I remember thinking, perhaps that might have been the better way to go about it. But by then I had already begun, plunged into it, driven by the need to put this, at least, out in the open—spread out in the fresh, cool San Francisco air. And then at last I was done.

I remember the silence that followed, the buzzing of a fly, the honk of horns rising from the street—and then his voice, calm and soft. "I suppose such things do happen—but still, having seen her only that once . . . And she is quite young. But yes, I suppose such things do happen."

You see I still remember the words, each one as it came in order. And then, after another long silence, stroking that well-shaved chin as he looked out the window . . . "But as long as you're in town, perhaps you'll join us for dinner this evening. Juanita I know would be pleased, you had such good times together. She has not been feeling well of late, not quite herself." Then, after another little pause: "And the girls too, of course."

Would be pleased. Pleased . . . Not quite herself. And the girls too, of course . . .

Evening came. And I came. Nod from the grave butler at the door, up the long, polished staircase. And they all were there, waiting. He rising to his feet; they, all three, ranged like dolls along a single brocaded couch. How nice to see you again, and how nice, how nice. So nice.

I had tried to imagine what they would look like, how they would seem after . . . was it only two months? Yes, just that, and another week. Abigail I remembered only too well, from the cool, haughty eyes to that softly ironic line at the corner of her mouth, the smooth, dark chestnut hair mounded atop her head, a single curl escaping at the neck. Her neck. My hands began to tremble, and I looked away . . . Little Marcella, already seeming less so, sensed my discomfort and smiled.

But her mother, her mother—all seemed changed. What, I remember asking myself—what had it cost her to be here, to appear like this? It was only later that I knew . . . He had told her, of course, of my purpose, perhaps even my pain. I longed to speak to her alone, if only for a moment . . .

I wouldn't have known her if we had met on the street. Her hair, ash blonde, seemed more ashen than blonde now, and there were lines on her neck and face and forehead that makeup could not quite hide. But most of all it was the eyes, those calm, gray-blue eyes that had haunted my dreams. Now, where immense tranquility had been there was only a kind of emptiness, and then from time to time a certain furtive desperation—it isn't easy to describe it. Yes, she looked at me—would not avert her gaze. But there was nothing there. I felt she didn't really see me, had convinced herself not to see me.

And yet she spoke, even laughed—the laugh of a preacher's wife. We ate, we talked, the conversation seemed almost bright. Marcella's recent engagement, Abigail's new job in New York . . . That soft chestnut curl at the back of her neck . . . Oh yes she knew, and she was pleased—although from time to time there was that hasty, worried glance toward the chair where her mother sat . . .

Then at last it was time to go . . . and we were standing together downstairs at the door—he and she at first, the girls as he called them having demurely excused themselves for the evening. And then the ring of the telephone, the butler coming to tell him. And his words: "You understand these nuisances, of course—but do call again before you have to go. Juanita, my dear, if you will . . ."—and off down the hall.

And so . . . I sought her eyes, but now, for the first time, she would not look at me, would not speak. She drew open the door, holding it . . . and I went out. But then, standing on the porch, I turned . . . and she was still there, watching. But now, suddenly, the eyes were those I had remembered, encountered in my dreams—the same calm, even, gray-blue gaze that had watched me as I rose from her bed . . . that night.

I said, mouthed, a single breathless word: "Please."

Wordless, unmoving, with utter, eerie calm, she gazed into my face—then shut the door . . .

The note was on my breakfast tray the next morning. "An hour after your departure last night, my wife sadly took her own life. She left a note, providing reasons. Please do me the great kindness of neither writing nor calling again."

Leave me now, John. I thought I wanted to talk but . . . tomorrow perhaps. Yes, I'll be fine here, just leave it there. You go on along.

What? Oh yes. Don't slam it, though—but then you never do.

Yes. Good night. Good night.

CHAPTER 2

1

They sat alone at the heavy table, she in the smaller carved chair at his right hand. Before them, atop two tall silver candlesticks, the flames shuddered in an imperceptible draft, casting uneasy shadows against the coffered ceiling. The serving dishes spread about on the table, like the plates from which they ate, were fine English china, and the tall crystal glasses before them—hers filled with water, his dark red wine—gleamed in the flickering half-light.

They ate in silence, the silver of their knives and forks clicking like indolent crickets against the surface of their plates. There was, however, no trace of tension or anxiety in the air—certainly nothing that might have been mistaken for hostility or spite. This was a silence which, if not exactly companionable, at least was rooted in long, mutually comfortable habit. Or so it seemed.

The broad form of Maria Bear, chestnut-dark behind the star-

tling white of her apron, suddenly filled the doorway. She did
not break the silence as her dark eyes moved among the plates
and dishes spread out on the table. The old man reached forward to take one, a few dark strands of spinach clinging to its
sides, and held it up.

"Just a bit more," he murmured. "Then coffee."

"Do you want some dessert?" the old woman said to the girl.
"There's still a l'il of that rhubarb pie."

"No," Deirdre said softly, looking up. "But put it in my lunch
tomorrow, will you?—before John gets to it."

Taking the dish from Kinsella, the old woman turned and was
gone. In a moment she had returned, the refilled spinach dish
in her hand.

"Just a little, I said, not a whole . . ."

Ignoring the reproof, Maria moved to his side, then spooned a
small amount onto his plate. Leaving the serving dish and spoon
beside him, she gathered up two of the others, both empty, and
went out the door.

Kinsella snorted—then lifted the decanter to refill his glass.

"I don't know how you can eat that stuff," Deirdre said.
"Looks like old rotten lettuce and tastes worse."

"All you know," the old man said, then deposited a large fork-
ful into his mouth. "If you ate a bit of this now and then you'd
be able to whip some sense into that little bangtail of yours."

"She's got all the sense she needs—we get along just fine."

Again Kinsella snorted. "Little devil," he said. "Needs to be
taken out and . . ."

"Oh Daddy, please don't get on that again!"

"Just like someone else," he said. "Would never listen."

"Daddy, please!" Something in her tone, however, suggested
that she rather enjoyed the comparison—with the mother she
had never known.

Maria again appeared in the doorway, a laden silver tray held
out before her. She moved to the table and set out the coffee

and cups, then cream and sugar, and finally a single apple on
a pewter plate. Then, her hands moving like swift dark animals across the surface of the table, she gathered the remaining
dishes onto the tray, excepting only the decanter and Kinsella's
glass, and placed the apple directly before him, beside it a small
silver knife. A moment later she was gone, the whispering of
her slippered feet receding toward the kitchen.

It was only after the sound had died away that Kinsella poured
the coffee.

"I have something to discuss with you," he said.

She, looking down into the steaming dark liquid in the cup before her, slowly raised her head. The expression on her face was
complex; curiosity, amusement, and concern were all there—
but along with them was something else: determination, anticipation, even a kind of relief. Her blue eyes sparkled in the
light.

"Yes," she said softly.

He looked down at the apple on the plate before him. Its
green, red-flecked skin was covered with gleaming droplets of
dew. Slowly, uncertainly, he reached for the little knife and,
taking it up, laid the point against the skin.

"I've been thinking a good deal about your future," he said.
"Especially your education."

"My education?" Her smile was wary, but curious all the
same.

"Yes," he said. "There's really not much for you here. Certainly nothing remotely resembling what you deserve. With your
talents and background, your family heritage . . ."

His voice trailed off into silence. Laying his forefinger atop
the knife blade, he pushed gently down upon the apple. With a
soft, succulent pop the point passed through the skin.

She had looked away now, her gaze fixed once more on the
coffee before her. She reached out for the sugar bowl, filled half
the spoon, and listened to the soft hiss of the sugar striking the

surface of the coffee. Then, after adding a little cream, she at last looked up again, watching as he meticulously divided the apple into small, white-sided wedges.

"I'd like you to have something better, more . . . appropriate," Kinsella said.

"But this is what we have here," she said. "Besides, I'm only sixteen, you know. There'll be time."

"Seventeen this fall," he said, spearing one of the wedges on the point of the knife. "Certainly old enough to begin thinking."

She raised the cup to her lips, taking a small, breathy sip— then quickly put it down again.

"Thinking of what?" she said, a flash of impatience in her voice. "Next year I'll graduate, and then . . ."

"And then?" Kinsella said. He thrust the wedge of apple into his mouth, then reached for the glass of wine.

"I don't know," she said sulkily. "Go to college maybe. Get married. I don't know. What the other girls do."

For a moment the old man did not reply, instead regarding the surface of the wine as though it held some secret. Then, slowly, he put down the glass and looked over at her. Her head remained bowed, bright hair like a burnished helmet.

"I have a proposal," he said. Then, seeing that she was about to reply: "I've had Lehigh make some discreet inquiries for me, and it seems it might be possible for you, this coming fall, to enter a good women's college in the East. Smith, Bennington, Mount Holyoke, Bryn Mawr—the kind of place that . . ."

"I don't quite get it," she interrupted. "I mean I don't get it at all." Her voice was sharp, urgent, the note of impatience returning once again. "You keep me, have always kept me, so close here—almost afraid, it seems, to let me out of your sight. It hasn't always been easy for me, especially this last year, but at least I thought I was beginning to understand a little better. About you and Mother. About a lot of things. But now . . . now you want to send me off to the East alone. At sixteen; all right, seventeen. I don't get it, Daddy. Besides, I don't want to go. Not that far. Not yet."

The old man seemed chastened, taken aback. For a time he did not look up; his wiry eyebrows knitted a frown as he again peered down at the shimmering surface of the wine. She watched him carefully, as though at once afraid of him and of herself.

At last he looked up, meeting her level gaze. "I know," he said, the low, rough voice resonating in the darkness. "I know. But I want . . . I've wanted the best for you, only the best. You know what you are to me."

"Yes, Daddy," she said softly. "I know."

"And I'm afraid sometimes that . . . No, it's more than fear, it's like a kind of terror sometimes—that by keeping you here, afraid to let you go, forcing you to live in this godforsaken place, that I've been doomed to . . . that I'll make you, let you become—what did you say just now? about the other girls?—that you'll settle for being one of those . . . other girls. And this place will have captured you, as it has captured me."

Again he was silent, again she watched him for a moment before she said, very softly: "Would that really be so bad?"

Abruptly he looked up, his eyes dark with grief. "Yes!" he said, almost shouted, his voice not far from a sob. "Yes!"

For a moment neither spoke, his sudden violence stunning them both into reflection. At last, with a kind of relief, both raised their faces at the same moment to see Maria again standing in the doorway.

"More coffee?" she said. The dark eyes, moving from one face to the other, seemed vaguely troubled.

"No," Kinsella said, "I don't think so. You go on along."

"I've left something out for John, when he gets back."

"He probably won't come in," the old man said, "but that's fine. You go on along now."

Slowly, with a last glance into both their faces, the old woman turned and was gone. There was a feeling of respite, a vague sense of truce in their silence as the whispering footsteps receded, then a moment later the back door opened and thumped shut.

Kinsella drained his glass, returned it softly to the table. He picked up a slice of apple and, raising it to his mouth, sucked reflectively on one corner.

"Where's John?" Deirdre said.

"Town," the old man said, his mind clearly elsewhere. "I had a list of things for him."

Again the silence fell, heavy as a cloak. Yet it was clear that this moment would not pass off so easily. It was Deirdre who spoke first.

"I'd maybe like to go to college, Daddy—although those places seem awfully far away. I'd thought of Boulder, somewhere in California maybe. But why next year? In another year, when I would normally graduate . . . well, maybe I'd think differently. If you say those other places are . . ."

She hesitated a moment, her gaze on the candle flame, before she added: "But anyway, I'd come back here. You know I would."

"Why should you?" he snapped. "I won't be around that much longer, and this place, without water—because that's what's happening, you see, that's what it's coming to—this place will just dry up and blow away." Quickly, with a savage movement of his hand, he refilled his glass, drinking half of it off before he put it down again.

"But this is my place too," she said. "No matter what becomes of it. I was born in this house, brought up here, the people here are the people I know. In a few years this dry spell will be over for us and . . . I'd like to get married someday Daddy, to come back to this place and take care of you and . . . Really, isn't that what you want too? This is our place, after all, whatever you say about it."

She paused for a moment, again looking into the shuddering

flame, before she went on, her voice softer, more careful now. "But next fall, Daddy. That's too soon. My friends here, my life here—it's too soon."

When she looked back toward him she found his eyes, dark and narrowed, staring into her face.

"You mean your *friend*, don't you?" His voice was hard, the sudden anger barely contained within it.

She did not look away, but behind her eyes there was terror and determination at once, a sober recognition that the moment had arrived. For an instant she seemed to be measuring, considering her response, but already the words had begun to come.

"All right. I mean my *friend*. Other things too but . . . yes. Does that bother you?" The last sentence, heavy with sarcasm, lay like a snarling animal on the table between them.

And he was on his feet, his hand trembling as he swept up the glass and dashed it into the empty fireplace. "Bother me? Damn right it bothers me. Oh I know well enough what's in your little mind. Finish school, then off to some junior college for a year to make it seem you tried, then a quick trip to the altar before you start making little Murchisons! No, by hell, it's not going to happen! Come September, might as well make up your mind to it—come September you'll be at Bennington or Bryn Mawr, or wherever else they'll have you. And in the meantime your young Murchison, or whatever his name is, is going to have nothing to do with you. I'll see to that damn quick!"

"I won't go," she said softly. "You can't make me go." Her eyes were dark with anger, bright with fear. She had overheard him speaking like this to others, but to her . . . One thought suddenly possessed her: she would not cry. No matter what, she would not cry.

"You can't make me go," she said. "Besides," she added, "his name is Fisk."

"Fisk! Murchison! What's the difference? Damn saddle tramps, that's all! And as for whether you'll go or not go, you may have a few things to learn, young lady, about that. In the meantime . . ."

The sound of the back door opening, then closing with a bang, brought a breathless silence in its wake. They had both heard the approach of the truck, but neither had thought to mark it. Now, motionless, they listened to the footsteps coming down the hall, then watched the narrow figure materialize in the doorway.

"I didn't think you'd still be eating," John said. "I'll come back." He looked quickly from one to the other, then turned to go. The footsteps had retreated halfway down the hallway when all at once, drawing himself erect, Kinsella bellowed after him.

"Come back here, damn it! There's something I want you to hear!"

The footsteps ceased, then softly drew near once more. The face reappearing in the doorway was pale and tense.

"There he is!" Kinsella shouted, turning once more on the girl. "Take a good, long look. If you're going to marry anyone from this godforsaken country, that's who it'll be!"

With a violent movement, the old man lurched to the doorway and, pushing John aside, stumbled down the hall toward the library.

John and Deirdre, motionless, faced one another across the table until once more the old man's voice was heard. "Murchison! I have a few choice things to say to you!" There was a brief silence. "All right, Fisk then. Now listen, and listen good." Then the slamming of a door—and again all was silence.

"I'm sorry," John said. "I didn't . . ."

Stopping in midsentence, he stood aside as the girl rose from the table, crossed to the doorway, and suddenly broke into a run. He listened until she had reached the top of the stairs; then, her urgent footsteps still ringing in his ears, he walked slowly down the hall, through the empty kitchen, and out into the night.

2

Oh she'll get over it. It's for her own good. Down deep I think she already knows that, not that she'd admit it now, of course. But she'll come around—there's more than a month left. She'll go. It's all set.

Haven't I told you? Up in Vermont, place called Bennington. Just the place for her, I think. Nice country, quality people. Just the place.

Anyway, looks like the boy has finally got some sense—or at least had some whipped into him, which is the same thing. Haven't seen him all summer. Have you?

Oh that's it. Elko, you say? Didn't know Murchison had any people up there. But just as well. Does she get letters?

That'll pass too. After a while back there . . . with new friends, a new perspective. It'll pass, you'll see.

I know. I know. Do you think it's been easy? Or that I've liked doing it? But it had to be done, that's all. You see that. In the end she'll realize, and then she'll thank me. When she's a little older she'll know . . . just how hard it was for me. But it had to be done. You see that.

Yes, it'll take a while I guess—but in the end . . .

Oh that? Don't let it bother you. It was a way to make a point, that's all. Perhaps it did put you in a bit of an awkward . . . wasn't fair to you. But never mind, just forget it. She has by now I'm sure.

Even Suzanne agrees with me, you know—that it's the right thing, I mean. At least did when I saw her. Does that surprise you?

Well, she does.

No, I'm okay, but take a bit more for yourself. I'm tapering off. Trying to. Expect I'll catch up again before long. Seems to be the way it goes.

How was she the other day? Suzanne, I mean.

Good. Not getting any younger, you know. Older than me by a few years, if you can believe that. But she's okay, you say.

Good.

Last time I saw her—almost two months now I guess it is—she had a kind of a cough. Nothing much to it, I suppose, but I didn't like to hear it. She was always the tough one, you know. But even the tough ones . . . eventually.

You talk French to her, I guess. I did too, back then, but now . . . Well, I never see her that much.

Anyway, she said I was doing the right thing. That ought to be worth something at least. Something.

Strange thing about that. That I still ask her for advice I mean. But it's always been that way. When she talks, I've always listened. Except when it really counted . . .

Forty years, think of that. Because in another year or so that's what it'll be. Hard to imagine. Forty years . . .

December, it was. Nineteen hundred and twenty-six. And cold as hell.

Curious, when you stop to think about it—that I came running back to the same place. Then again, maybe not so curious after all. The criminal, they say, always returns to the scene. But of all the other places I could have gone . . .

Top me up a little, would you, John? Just thinking about it . . . those days . . . has given me a chill. Or maybe just the shakes. Yes, that's fine. Good.

Oh, you might as well. Save you getting up again . . .

Strange thing—but no one knew me. I remember that morning in the train station when it hit me—that no one, not a soul, seemed to recognize me. I walked through the town like an invisible man, a ghost. I had died, then come back. But no one knew me.

I remember smiling to myself. It was a gift.

But then why should they? The elegant chap who had passed through before, spent a few glittering days among them—stealing their companies, seducing their women, entertaining the crowd— that gay, charming fellow was now no more. This drunk in ragged clothes, the dark, heavy beard plastered across his ugly face . . . this boor who quarreled with the porter over his shabby suitcase, surely this had to be someone else, someone nobody knew—or wanted to. And so it was. Someone else.

There'd been time enough to work a change. A week in Oakland down by the waterfront, two in a Wobbly hobotown outside Portland, another two hiding out in Cheyenne—oh yes, time enough.

I walked through town and on up the canyon a little way—until one of the mine trains came along and I hitched a ride . . .

Runcietown. Don't suppose there's much left up there today, but then . . . Bootleg joints on every corner, dance halls, girls, and gambling—everything to keep a tired miner broke and happy, the rim of the big pit looming over it like a watchful mother. Yes sir, a right lively place, Runcietown . . . in those days.

But that afternoon it wasn't too lively, at least not yet. It was just too damn cold, and the sun too damn bright. It had snowed the day before, then cleared off cold as hell, and as I crunched up the street, that beat-up suitcase under my arm, the brightness seemed like to split my brain in two. I remember the dark shanties in the snow, rocks sticking up beside them. An old orange tabby crossing the street, shying a rock at him just out of spite—the clatter of it hitting the fence. The cat dived under a porch and was gone. I found a backstreet rooming house and flopped.

When I woke up it was dark. I could hear the tinkling of a piano somewhere. I put on my coat and hat and walked downstairs, then out to the main street. There was a fight heating up on the corner, dagos and Greeks, something, but I walked around it and down the street. Hadn't gone half a block when I saw her there on the porch, all bundled up in a rocking chair. The glow of her cigarette as she watched me go by. I stopped, asked where I could get some dinner. She said to come on inside . . .

We got on from the beginning. Not what you would have expected, the kind of temper I was in. She was straight ahead and to the point. I liked that. She let you know who was the boss, case you were inclined to be forgetful. I liked that too. I liked everything about her, and she put up with me. More than put up with me. It was enough for the moment. I needed a place to be then, a place to hide. She was that place, simple as that.

Oh yes, she was the boss, no mistake, but as time went on there were certain things she mostly left to me. The bar, the kitchen help sometimes. And trouble. That was my department.

It was the part I liked best. I had to have someone besides myself to take things out on. Her, sometimes—although she had ways of putting a stop to that. Some drunken Croat or dago though, to crack him a few good ones before I chucked him out headfirst in the snow, well that was just the ticket. And the girls too, although she handled them mostly. Sometimes . . . I don't like to think too much about that part.

We did a good business. Not only miners either but all kinds— cowboys from every damn place you can name, millhands, an occasional sheepherder or two . . . usually two. The girls used to laugh about that, that they were afraid to come in by themselves. No offense, you understand. And then all those others that used to come up from town, plenty I could name for you now. Now and again there was even somebody from the company—somebody I remembered from before. At first when one would come in I tried to lie low, keep out of the way, but then once or twice there was no help for it. After a while I began to get kind of a kick out of it—pouring them a drink, suggesting a girl. Not that I really blamed them—I'd met a good number of their wives, too—but something about it always tickled me half to death. Sometimes I'd just have to go out back, I couldn't stand it.

I longed for one of them to get out of line, just once. No luck there, though. Perfect gentlemen, thank you very much. And so they'd go on their sainted way, back to wifey and warm bed.

Does all this shock you?

I thought not. You're not so easily shocked. And maybe you've heard something about it before. Maybe even from her.

No, you say? You're right, not the sort of thing she'd . . . Proud, haughty as an eagle, that woman.

She's had to put up with a lot from me. Back then . . . and later.

Plenty. More than anybody needs. I've tried to make it up, what I could, but . . .

She knew from the first, of course, that there was something wrong—something I just couldn't seem to get worked out. I tried to tell her about it once or twice, but it was no good; I just couldn't put it so she'd understand. It was . . . too hard. And so we just kept on, this silent thing between us. We did the best we could.

Strange, but the fact of . . . what she did never bothered me that much. Because I did like her, much as I've ever liked anybody, really. If only liking was enough . . . Not that I particularly enjoyed it when somebody felt flush enough to ask for her, but that didn't happen all that much, not at five times the price—and when it did I always seemed to find something to do down the street. Afterward there was sometimes a little coolness maybe, but that soon passed away and we were fine again. In a way we were fine. In other ways the fact that we were fine . . . wasn't so fine itself.

Oh yes, she knew there was something wrong—something she just couldn't get at. She made the best of it. We made the best of it, the best we could . . .

Once, I remember, we went on a picnic up the canyon, just the two of us. Not the usual thing, of course, and I can't for the life of me remember the occasion. But I do remember the day, every minute. Early summer it was, the sweetest afternoon you could imagine. Little flowers everywhere, the creek full up to the banks. We left the horses in a little meadow and went up along the creek with the blanket and basket. There was a little warm pocket in the sun. We laid out the food—some cheese, a pâté she had made special, bread, a little champagne. We laughed. I remember the sound of the creek, the soft smell of the grass, the warmth of the sun, her eyes on me watching as she took down her hair, pulling out the pins, one by one . . .

Yes, a fine-looking woman, and sweet as they make them when she had a mind to be. She had a mind to be that afternoon, and it was nearly dark when we went down again.

I remember the moon, a clipped fingernail over the tops of the dark

buildings. I remember the clear, cold sound of a dog barking some-
where, the smell of cooking in the air. I remember the feel of her cool
little hand as she reached up to touch my cheek by the stable door.
    I remember too damn much sometimes.

3

The days of early September were clear and cool, the nights
bright and cloudless and shoaled with stars. Summer, with its
heavy afternoons and sudden, violent cloudbursts, was all at
once no more; the chill of November, the snows of winter,
seemed too far off to think of. It was a moment to savor, abducted
from time.

    To John Siloa, the onetime shepherd of Molly Peak, it was also
a moment for taking stock. These last days and weeks had lain
full-length upon him. He felt sapped by them—in his spirit, in
his self-conception and resolve, in the very sinews of his body.
He had stopped his English reading, something that never, since
that long-ago summer on the mountain, had been allowed to
happen. And at night he had begun to dream—vivid, inviting
dreams of home.

    The nocturnal sessions with Kinsella were by no means all
of it, although there could be no doubt that the old man had of
late become much more demanding. Especially since the business of Deirdre's schooling had arisen there were few evenings,
very few indeed, that he did not spend at least a good part of in
the dark library—and many mornings, very many indeed, when
even the alarm clock he had finally forced himself to buy, the
first he had ever owned, seemed powerless to wake him. But
there had always been occasional periods like this, times when
the old man seemed almost desperate for his company, and he
knew that this one too, like all the others, would ultimately
wane to the level of frequency he had come to regard as normal.
Now as before, he thought, he should have been able to steel
himself to the task. If it were not for those other things . . .

It had taken him a long time to admit—if only to himself—just how he felt about Deirdre. There had always been feelings that he could not quite understand—yes, even at the beginning, when she was a child of six or seven—but he had found it easy, or at least possible, to justify them by a sense of wonder. She was, after all, so very different from anyone to whom his limited experience had exposed him that he was in a way dazzled, as when one is suddenly wakened by a bright light in the dark. And so he had been able to explain it all away, or almost all—until these last few years. Then, beginning with her twelfth or thirteenth year, it had begun to grow more difficult. Feelings imperfectly expressed, imperfectly conceived, began little by little to draw into focus—and he was ashamed. For a time then he had drawn away, avoided contact with her as a repentant drinker avoids bad company—although even in those days he had not been able to restrain himself from lingering near the house when the soft strains of the piano echoed in the still afternoon air. There were times then, when she was just beginning high school, that he caught her regarding him curiously, with a deeply puzzled look in her soft blue eyes, but even these glances had not deterred him. He had looked away and to his business, Kinsella's business. But then that too had changed.

It was hard to know just when it had begun, this drift toward a kind of . . . understanding. She, for her part, seemed quite prepared for it—as though something in her young spirit had been patiently, indulgently waiting for him to pass through an awkward phase. And indeed it had begun to melt away, that dark, protective time. Her glances grew less anxious, his reactions less abrupt, and gradually a kind of wary truce had intervened. Still from time to time he felt ashamed, but less so out of fear for his own feelings. He was ashamed because he sensed that she had always known his mind, and because he felt that he had been a fool.

Yes, and for over a year now it had seemed better, more reasonable and . . . appropriate. A kind of comfortable reliance, a vague camaraderie one might even call it, had seemed to grow up between them—as between elder brother and young sister. Her father's moods, familiar as she was with them by now, often left her bewildered and angry, and increasingly now it was to John rather than Maria that she turned when this occurred. Not that there was ever anything like an outright request for counsel. Indeed, more often than not the matter took the shape of an attack—for he, after all, had increasingly become the master's alter ego—and yet his responses, always soft, yet firm and reasoned all the same, seemed somehow to satisfy her. There were frequent smiles, an occasional joke. Yes, everything had seemed much better, more in perspective.

But then, these past three months, that too had begun to change, to slip away. Not that there was any outward change in their relations—the smiles were still there, the soft jokes—but it had all become much harder for him to sustain. He had found the old, unbrotherly thoughts returning—and along with them a new feeling, one he had never experienced before. Nevertheless he knew it, recognized it well enough. John Siloa was jealous.

To know that it was absurd, all this, was no help at all. He was more than twenty years older than she—more than twice her age now. And that, of course, was by no means all. For she was who she was, and he . . . who he was. It was hopeless and impossible; it was absurd. And yet that did not prevent it from being.

And then, as if all this were not enough, there was the matter of the second spring. It had been completely gone for over a month now, the creekbed a dry wash, the spring an empty cup. The hay, what there was of it, was already in, a pitiful stack barely filling one corner of the barn, and Kinsella had announced that the following year, saving some miraculous intervention, they would not bother with it at all.

Yes, it had been a difficult summer—and the fall promised no better. Now and then he found himself thinking of Levi Mondragon and his invitation. Almost nine years had passed since then, but he knew the gentle Mexican would still remember, would welcome him eagerly if he came. The apples of Taos . . . But no, something within him knew that he would not go—no, not even if Kinsella would permit it, not even for a month. He knew that he would stay, as he had always stayed.

Sometimes he wished—for the first time in ten long years he truly wished—that he knew the whereabouts of Booker Goodman.

It had been the first really chilly afternoon, a sharp, blustery wind out of the northeast. There were a few clouds, long, clotted cirrus rising like vapor trails above the eastern ridges, and the first faint smell of autumn was in the air. On the hillsides the brilliant yellow of the blooming rabbitbrush foretold the turning of the leaves, and Molly Peak, dark and massive against the deep blue of the sky, seemed crouched in anticipation, yearning for winter.

He had been working in the hayfield for several hours, getting the sprinklers ready for the long, cold season to come. It was an eerie feeling, knowing that this task, by now so familiar, might before long be taken from him. He and the sprinklers, he and the machines, all becoming obsolete at once. The second spring, their common master, was dying, dying, dead.

He wondered just what he would do then, when the hay and the machines were no longer there to fill his days. There would be no real reason for Kinsella to keep him about then, no reason for him to stay. Perhaps, he thought, one of the other ranches might have something for him; he had, after all, learned to make himself quite useful, and in spite of everything was on good terms with most of the neighbors. If not—well, there would always be the sheep, somewhere. And yet even as he pondered these dark considerations—sometimes even going so far as to admit, if only for the briefest of moments, the thought of going home—even then he never really doubted, if that was the right word. No, Kinsella would never ask him to go, not even then.

He would stay, as he had always stayed. Even then.

He could see the little black-legged buckskin almost as soon as it left the ranch buildings. He had watched it moving up the creekside trail for almost fifteen minutes now, returning briefly to his work when it disappeared behind a screen of cedars. He knew just how long it would be before it reappeared, and he was always waiting, his eyes on the precise spot where it would emerge. Now, however, as it drew nearer, he turned his attention more fully to his work, or at least so it seemed. Only when horse and rider dropped out of sight, descending to the dry creekbed to make the crossing, did he look up, watching until they shouldered up over the near bank and started toward him. Then, leaving the spanner on a wheel of the sprinkler, he turned and walked to the truck, opened the near door, and took out the large silver thermos.

"Coffee?" he said when she had drawn up before him. "I have plenty."

"No. Just a little water if you have it."

Again he opened the door of the truck, taking out a green gallon wine jug and a tin cup. When he had filled the cup he held it up to her.

"I'll get down," she said, patting the horse's neck as she dismounted, then started toward him. Her eyes were dark, shadowed. He saw for the first time that she had been crying.

She took the cup from him and leaned back against the fender, looking vaguely up toward the summit of the mountain. He filled his own cup from the thermos bottle, moving it to the center of the hood, then turned to face her.

"He's gone," she said suddenly. "Eddie's gone."

"Gone? Well, he's been gone—in Elko, wasn't it?"

"No," she said darkly. "Not in Elko. He's really gone now— as if he never was."

"As if . . . Tell me," he said quietly.

"He's joined the army."

"Joined the . . . ?"

"The army. Enlisted. Gone."

He sighed, looking up toward the mountain. But he said nothing.

"In a month or two . . . ," she began, then stopped, reaching up to wipe her eyes with the back of her hand. A moment passed before she finished. "In a month or two he'll be . . . over there. He said . . . said that's where he wants to go."

Again John did not answer, but now he lowered his head. There was a sudden gust of cold wind; the buckskin, snorting, stamped its black-stockinged feet in the dust. John, putting down his cup on the fender, walked over to it, stroking the broad, smooth neck with his hand.

"It's so *stupid!*" Deirdre cried suddenly. "*Stupid!*"

The horse shuddered but was still.

"Maybe . . . ," John began weakly. "Maybe he just thought that's what he had to do."

She glared across at him for a moment but did not speak. Then her eyes began to fill with tears.

"Come and sit inside," he said, walking to her. "It's cold out here." Gingerly he touched her shoulder, then guided her toward the door. They were almost there, his hand reaching for the handle, when suddenly she turned, wrenching away from him.

"I don't *want* to sit inside!" she said, almost shouting, into his face.

"Well," he said weakly. "Well then just . . ."

"Just what, you . . . you stupid Basco!"

She stopped. He watched the color drain from her face—was still watching as she started toward him, reached him.

"Oh John," she sobbed, her cheek pressing hard against his chest.

Hands hanging limply, emptily at his sides, he could think of nothing to say, nothing to do. Perhaps a minute passed, perhaps two, the girl clinging to the worn flannel of his shirt, the gusty wind shouting all about them, before at last, as if at a loss, he slowly raised one great hand and passed it awkwardly across her back, just as moments before he had stroked her horse's neck.

In a moment the sobbing slackened, then suddenly was no more. She drew away, looking strangely up into his face, then turned and walked to the horse.

"I think I'll go," she said at last. "To that school back East, I mean. I want to get away from here."

"It would be good," John said softly. "A change."

He watched in silence as she slowly raised her foot to the stirrup, then lifted herself to the saddle. She did not look at him again until, turning the horse, she made to go.

"G'bye, John," she said softly, her eyes looking straight into his face. "And I'm sorry."

He stood weakly, watching her go, until she and the little horse had disappeared over the rim of the creekbed. Then, raising his hands from his sides, he stood looking down at the dark, callused palms until they, the horse and girl, again appeared, mounted the bank on the far side, and set off briskly up the trail.

He knew where she was headed—even as it was now. With weary, leaden steps he walked to the sprinkler and went back to his work.

4

Where were you this afternoon? I was out looking.

It's all right. Nothing important. Besides, the ride did me good. I'd been wanting to take that pony of hers out anyway, give it a bit of exercise. Not too bad a horse really, catches on quick enough after a few licks.

Oh, nowhere in particular. Once I saw you weren't up in the field I just kept on, up the mountain a ways, round about. Have to do it more often—keep the little bangtail honest. Might have it whipped into some kind of shape by the time she gets back for Christmas, who knows.

Fine, just fine. I called her yesterday, as a matter of fact. Seemed content, interested, full of plans. I knew she'd like it—remember what I said? Anyway, she's fine; busy with her studies and now this presidential campaign, passing out literature and such.

Can't you guess? The slick old Texan, of course. She says that Goldwater reminds her of Hitler. A lot she knows about Hitler . . . Oh, and she said to be sure and say hello.

I really can't understand what you see in that place, though. Mines are bad enough, but a filthy hole like that . . .

No, thanks all the same. Not my cup of tea. I'll stay on top of the earth as long as I can.

Don't bother your mind about it—I know there's not much to do now, and if that's where your fancy lies . . . But maybe it'd be a good idea to tell Maria when you go. Just so we'll know where to go look for the body.

Oh, nothing really. Another letter . . . but you know that. Whenever they come . . . well, you know that too. You'd think that after almost thirty years I'd be a little better . . .

Still not sixty, imagine that. Younger than Marlene Dietrich. Just as pretty too, I expect, even now—and yet she busies herself writing letters to someone she's not seen for . . . what is it now, thirty-three?—thirty-three years, then, someone who's never answered a single one of them and damn sure never will. Someone she hated enough to . . .

But then that's the hardest part, isn't it?—knowing whether she ever really hated me, even then. Now . . . well, it's different, that's all. It's passed beyond all that, like something gone through a furnace and come out the other side. Shriveled, hardened—in a way the same, but in a way . . . something else too. In a way I suppose it's become a kind of marriage after all. What could not be before, appearing now, long after—deformed, shriveled, hardened, but still . . . a kind of marriage. An insoluble, mutually indispensable knot. A . . . gall knot.

Yes, might as well. Top it up good, my boy, I feel a long night coming on. Don't worry, I'll let you go after a bit. I know you're busy. Or bored. No matter. After just a bit . . .

*How she ever managed to find me—it's puzzled me all these years.
She'd never say, of course, even when I asked her—something coy
like, "Well, I have a sixth sense," something . . . I was so convinced,
so certain that no one had recognized me, but there you have it; somebody, somebody must have. Somebody she knew, who would write to
her. Because she did . . . find me. That day in August.*

*I was out back, helping in the kitchen, up to my elbows in a bucket
of potatoes. It was hot, I remember. Blazing. Flies everywhere . . .*

*Had an uncle once who used to say, telling about a particularly
warm day, that it was so hot the flies all died. Wasn't as hot as that,
I guess, because they were everywhere . . .*

*Somebody, Mazie I think, came back to tell me. Lady to see you.
Pretty, young. I remember saying to her—Mazie wasn't too smart—
I remember saying, "Mazie, it's Missy she wants, not me." "No.
You. I asked if she wanted Missy. It's you she wants."*

*She was sitting, hands folded, in the corner by the window, look-
ing calmly out—Suzanne in the far doorway watching her, eyes like a
she-eagle guarding her nest. Suzanne didn't know her, but she knew
enough, I think, just the way she was. Those she-eagle eyes turning
up then to meet me, stop me. I stood in the hall doorway, looking
dumbly from one to the other—my shirt and forehead still soaking
with sweat, wiping my hands on a towel. Then, with a quick, furious
motion, before a word was said, Suzanne had turned and was gone.
I could hear the sound of her footsteps, small and sharp, as she went
up the stairs. Then the slamming of a door, and it was quiet. Too
damn quiet. Even the flies were quiet.*

*She looked up then, smiling. It was not a kind or a happy smile,
but there was nothing outwardly cruel about it either. It was a . . .
secret smile.*

I asked her what she wanted, still standing there in the doorway.

*Her face was all innocence. "Why, I just wanted to see you, that's
all. To know how you were."*

*"Well, you see me," I told her. I wasn't exactly accommodating. If
there was nothing else, I told her, I'd just be getting on back to work.*

She made a face then, not hurt, exactly, but . . . kind of thought-

ful. And then she turned away, looking out the window. That dark curl at the back of her neck . . .

I was about to go, leave her there to her own business while I tended to mine, when all the sudden she was looking back at me, those cool, haughty eyes kind of clouded now. It was an expression I'd never seen there before. An expression I'd never expected to see.

"Don't go," she said. Just like that. Taking a handkerchief out of her pocket, she made as if to raise it to her face, then stopped, twisting it on her lap between the net fingers of her gloves. "I . . . anticipated this," she said then. I remember those very words, the way she said them. And then that little speech.

Oh yes, she'd half expected me to act like that, she said. Because what else could I think except that she'd come just to gloat, see me in my wallow? But it was a little different, the way she put it. The Prodigal Son, she called me. The Prodigal in his pigsty, yes, that was it. And I had a perfect right to feel that way about her coming, she said, but I was wrong. She asked if she could tell me why.

I didn't budge. No, not yet. I remember what I said—and just the way I said it, hard and mean. "Go ahead," I told her—"but briefly, if you don't mind. I have things to do."

I remember her voice, the sudden stillness then, the hush that came over it. "Very well," she said. "I'll try to be brief. But please, I beg you—please sit down."

The . . . pleading in those haughty, lovely eyes. "Please . . . sit . . . down."

Oh yes—and thank you. Getting a little sloppy in my old age, I guess. But this stuff does raise hell with the finish, you're right. This desk—all the way from London, did you know that?

Well it is. Was. Along with . . . Forget it. No call to get into all that.

Okay. Perfect. Go on now, sit down.

Just what she said, only "please" . . .

And so I did . . . sit down, on the couch right by the door. And she began it.

I can't really remember the words then, what they were—but the sound, the sudden . . . rush of them still rings in my ears. Like pigeons in a belfry, alarmed, anxious, wanting to fly. Pigeons . . . I remember a few here and there, the actual words, and I remember the . . . drift, but mostly it's only the rush, the sound of it. The pigeons.

She had agonized over it, she said, for all those nine long months— over how, if she found me, she would be able to say it. All of the nine, she insisted on that, I remember, insisted that even as she stood beside her mother's grave the thought had been there, gnawing at her guilty soul. Or some such. And then she did find me, God knows just how, and knew that it would be even harder because I would think . . . just what I thought.

And then she started to cry.

The rest, there's no way I can tell it. Half an hour we must have sat there, she in her chair by the window, I on my couch by the door—her soft voice talking, telling, while I sat like a stone. The infernal heat, the hum of flies . . . Yes, and even when it was done, she rising to go, still I didn't move, just watching until her gloved hand had touched the knob.

At last, however, I managed to speak, somehow open my mouth. Was there an address in New York?

I've never quite forgotten her smile . . . just then. It often comes to me even now, in the drowsy heat of an afternoon, the dark early hours before the dawn. I can see it just as it was. Soft, happy, modest . . . and something else besides. Just a flicker maybe, the merest hint— but yet so clear all the same. "I've won," it said, says. "I've won."

I stood at the window watching as she walked down the street— to where the open car that had brought her was drawn up at the curb. Beyond, over the high rim of the pit, a big hawk was making wide, lazy circles in the sky. Grabbing a newspaper from the table, I killed six flies against the window before she had reached the car, then turned back toward the kitchen before it could begin to move away . . .

5

For a time they rode side by side, the breath of the two horses billowing out before them. Soon, however, long before they had reached the meadow clearing, the little buckskin had dropped back to follow, the drifts on either side mounting almost to its belly. Ahead, the sorrel made the going, sometimes keeping to the high ground of the bank, sometimes descending briefly to the dry creekbed below, where the snow lay in mounds like crystalline islands among the willows.

The previous night's storm, although not particularly heavy, had added its burden to that of two others the week before, and already the snow lay deeper on the ground than John had ever seen it at this time of year. This was a February prospect, not one to be expected the day before Christmas, and yet it was pleasant to have it so. In spite of himself—and all the Christmases he had now spent alone, with the sheep and without them—he had never completely put aside his childhood affection for this season, and even the lightest dusting of snow on the ground now had a strangely exhilarating effect on him. Always the thought of one particular Christmas long ago, the jagged spires of the mountain ridge across their narrow valley rising up frosty white into the morning sky, was never far from his mind. And now, today, it seemed much the same—for far off to their left, across this wider valley, the teeth of the western mountains bit with the same icy urgency into this vaster, paler sky.

They stopped at the clearing to rest the horses. The coppery trunks of the water birches glowed against the snow.

"I wonder how much longer they'll be here," John said. "I'll hate to see them go. The willows . . . well, they're tougher."

The girl, who had been looking beyond, at the tall, naked shapes of the two cottonwoods rising over the ridge, turned a quizzical face to him.

"The birches," John said. "They can't last much longer now."

"Why not?" she said. "With all this snow . . ."

"Takes more than snow."

"Oh," she said. Extending her gloved hand, she brushed the white crystals from the shoulders and neck of her horse, then turned in the saddle to clear its rump and haunches as far as she could reach. The smooth, tawny luster was gone now, dulled by the beginnings of a shaggy winter coat. Tiny droplets of ice clung to the horse's cheeks, in the coarse hairs beneath the chin.

"She doesn't like this much snow," Deirdre said, patting the neck again. "A bit of a softie, I guess." She leaned forward to gaze into an impassive brown eye. "Are you spoiled, Brooksie? Just a little maybe?"

"Maybe," John said, nudging the sorrel, and started up the hillside. She watched for a moment, her eyes on the powerful chestnut haunches of the bigger horse, then turned to follow.

At the top of the saddle they drew up again, looking down at the dry, almost snow-free depression that had once been the great spring. Here and there, on slightly elevated fingers extending down into the bowl, small clumps of hardy grass had sprung up bravely, rooted in the humus of the watercress before it. There would be flowers as well, John reflected gravely. For this next year, at least, there would be flowers.

Neither of them spoke, and within a few minutes they were headed down, the horses breasting the high drifts like ships at sea until at last, sprouting hoary legs, they emerged beside the bowl.

"We can leave them here," John said. "The trail up looks pretty clear."

They dismounted, tying the horses where they could reach the clumps of grass, and started up the rock-lined trail, John slinging the rucksack over his shoulder. There was indeed little snow here, the steepness of the way forbidding it, and before long they had arrived at the little flat area. The steel door, newly painted a pale blue, gleamed against the snow.

"When did you do all this?" she gasped, straining to catch her breath. "The path, the door—all this?"

"The last few years," John said softly.

"But why didn't I notice anything? I used to come up here all the time—at least when there was the spring."

"Maybe you had other things on your mind," he said, smiling. "Besides, there wasn't much to notice—just little by little."

"And of course you wouldn't tell me," she said. The smile was pouting, vaguely reproachful, and coquettish all at once. "Or bring me."

"I didn't think you'd be interested. You had other things . . ." For a moment his eyes lingered on the gentle rise and fall of her shoulders—then, abruptly, he turned away. "The door," he said, fumbling with the opening of the rucksack, "is just last year. The rest . . . well, little by little."

There was no answer. Finally solving the rucksack, John withdrew the old GI trench shovel from it, fixed the blade, and began clearing the snow from around the bottom of the door. Not until he was finished did he turn again, folding the shovel as before.

She was standing with her back to him, looking out at the snowy scene.

"I didn't notice when we came before—how pretty it is up here," she murmured. "Of course I was just a kid," she added after a moment. "Remember? The time I came with Daddy?"

"Yes. A long time ago."

Seven years it had been, in fact. They had come together, she and Kinsella, one fall afternoon while he was working on the trail. He had gone down to meet them beside the spring, then slowly led them up. He remembered Kinsella's face, the suspicious, vaguely offended expression that gathered about his eyebrows as he peered, sniffing, down into the dark hole. He remembered Deirdre too, eleven then, casting pebbles down, listening for the clatter, the thump. Then, when it came, her smile.

"But it's really magnificent isn't it, especially today." She glanced briefly back toward him, her face bright with the cold, beaming—then turned again.

"See how small they look, our buildings. Even the barn, the house. Like toys on a white carpet."

Dutifully he looked, his gaze following the thin column of gray smoke from the rear chimney until it was lost in the pale winter sky.

"And even beyond it, way out . . . something."

"Chokecherry," John said.

"Chokecherry—my, that far. And then on up the other side, all the little ranches. That would be Dunlop, I guess. And then Farley, and Grenville, and Sanguenetti, and . . ." She was silent for a moment, then turned back to face him. Her eyes had grown dark, sky blue to cobalt in a moment.

"Let's go inside," she said. "Can we?"

By way of answer he turned away, pulling back the bolt. After a long tug, the door scraped open across the snow.

She stood in silence, looking in.

"Are you surprised?" he asked after a moment.

"Yes," she said softly, almost in a whisper. "Amazed."

"It took a while," he said, "but it's nice now. Sitting on the bench. Looking out."

"But how did you make . . . this, out of that little hole? Where I threw the rocks down."

He smiled, looking up the hillside. "No, it's still there, up in those rocks. The bats still come and go just like before. I just made a drift, tunneled in from here, below it—until I hit the passage." He lowered his eyes, glancing over at her. "I wanted . . . a place to be," he said.

"Like your sheepcamp," she said softly.

"Yes, maybe. Like my sheepcamp."

Again she was silent, vacantly staring inside.

"Do you want to go in?" he said at last.

"Oh yes," she said, as if awakened. "Oh yes." She followed him through the low doorway.

"There's a heater too if you want it," he said, reaching under the bench to show her.

Again she did not reply, simply gazing about the little chamber with a look of wonder. Her face was smooth and bright, her eyes softened to azure. He stood by awkwardly, not quite knowing what to do with his hands.

"I've never quite forgiven you, you know," she said at last.

"Forgiven . . . ?"

"For not taking me with you, to live in the sheepcamp. That summer . . ."

Now it was he who did not answer.

"It was our house. We worked hard on it, made it together. I was devastated. Sometimes even now . . . just yesterday, in fact, when you were out feeding the horses . . . sometimes I go out to look at it there in the barn. I go in, sit at the table, climb up to the bed. It's silly, I guess, but I do it all the same."

Still he did not know what to say—might never have known if she had not rescued him.

"Why do you keep it around, anyway?" she said. "After all these years."

"I don't know," he said. "I just do. Besides, it's not mine really."

"It's yours," she said smiling, insisting. "Why?"

"Maybe I might need it again someday," he said at last, very softly.

Her smile was self-satisfied, vindicated, as she turned away, walking toward the rear. "Show me your cave," she said.

Her eagerness to come here, her insistence that he bring her, had taken him rather by surprise. She had never expressed any great interest in it before; indeed, after that first visit years ago she had never mentioned the cave again—and although she must have known that he still came now and then, never was there any suggestion that he bring her. This time, however, it had seemed one of the first things on her mind—as though she had been thinking of little else back there at her college in Vermont. She had arrived only the day before yesterday, after all, and there would be plenty of time after Christmas—but no, today, she had insisted.

"And you say we can go right in now, right inside?" she had asked that first night, coming out to see him after dinner.

"Yes, and it's quite safe, but . . ."

"It's settled, then. Tomorrow I have to go into town with Daddy, but the day after, Christmas Eve—it's settled."

"If you like. If your father doesn't . . ."

"Don't worry about my father."

He had warned her about the smell. Although much improved over what it had been before—most of the bats having decamped by now to join their brethren lower down in the cave—it was still quite unpleasant, and he had worried a good deal about it. As they descended the steel ladder, however, she made no complaints, and by the time they arrived at the bottom, and the little wooden platform he had made there to stand on, his concern had disappeared.

"It's wonderful," she whispered, casting the beam of her flashlight about. "And you say there's more, further down."

"Yes," he said. "Watch." Digging in his pocket for the stone he had brought along, he tossed it across the granular floor of the chamber to the rocky opening on the far side. "And listen."

He watched her face in the light of the headlamp as the long clattering came, then receded—then the distant splash. Her eyes glowed with wonder.

"It's . . . it's *water* down there!"

"Uh-huh."

"What's it like? Have you been?" Her voice trembled with excitement.

"No, not yet."

"Not yet—but why not?" she keened, tugging his sleeve.

"It's a long way, and dangerous. Too much for someone alone. Besides," he added after a moment, "there's plenty to do up here."

"But how can you *stand* it? Just knowing it's all down there."

"There'll be time," John said.

"But . . ." Her eyes glistened in the light.

"Next summer, maybe . . . if I'm still here."

"If you're . . . But why wait? I've got more than a week yet. We can get what we need and . . . we'll just go down, you and me! I can't wait!"

"You'll have to," he said. "It's not the sort of thing where you just get a rope and a flashlight and go. You have to be set up right, ready for trouble—preferably with someone who's done that sort of thing before. Anyway, at this season, with the snow and all—if there was trouble . . ." His words died away, strangled by the disappointment in her face.

"By summer, though," he began again. "By the time you're back I might be able . . . At least to find out what's needed. Then, if there was someone . . ."

The gloom seemed to lift slightly. "I suppose," she said at last. "And then, of course, that would give me time . . . I mean so I could find out about it too. I'm sure there are people I could ask. And maybe certain things would be easier to get in the East." She seemed placated, satisfied. "Then when I come back in June . . ."

"Yes. That would be better."

She smiled, a hint of forgiveness.

"Well, what else is there here? You said there was a room . . ."

"Do you hear that little dripping?"

"Yes," she said eagerly, as if she had not noticed it before. "Yes, I do."

"Well, come and see."

They proceeded down the little boardwalk he had made over to the rocky incline, then climbed to the low portal.

"You have to crawl," he said. "It's not far, but there's no other way, for now. Here, you take the headlamp. I'll be right behind."

She fitted it to her head, handing him the flashlight, and, bending down, went in.

"It's louder now!" he heard her cry. "The dripping is much closer!"

"Just keep on," he said, following her into the passage.

She did not speak again, and soon, fired by curiosity, she had opened a good distance between them. When next he saw her she had already emerged. Standing in the chamber, by the edge of a stone-rimmed pool, she swept the beam of the headlamp from one thing to the next, as if not knowing quite where to settle. Her face, seen in the reflected light, was a picture of rapture—like a saint beholding the Light.

She did not speak, nor did he. The only sound was the dripping water, troubling the mirrored surface of the pools.

Perhaps ten minutes passed before she turned and, with a brief smile, knelt again to enter the passage. He waited a moment before following, passing the light of his flashlight about the room as though greeting old friends. Then he too dropped to his knees and started back.

Afterward, seated on the bench by the open doorway, the heater warming her feet, the whitened prospect laid out placidly in the sun—afterward she seemed calm, yet strangely gay. She said nothing about what she had seen below, but he knew she had been impressed, even moved. There had been that look about her eyes, a look he had seen there only once or twice before—once at the birth of a calf, once . . . long before that, he didn't quite remember when. Now, as he took out the food he had brought, arranging the parcels on the bench beside her, she smiled briefly down on his efforts, then out again upon the snowy scene.

"This truly is a fine place," she said at last. "Not just here, where we are, but all of it—all that." Raising her mittened hand, she made a vague gesture outward, then lowered it again to her lap. "I never thought I would miss it, really . . . back there. But I have. I've missed it terribly."

He didn't know how, what to answer. "Well," he said after a moment, "it'll always be here for you." As soon as the words were out he regretted having said them, knew they sounded stupid and awkward.

"Do you think so?" she said, still looking out. "I wonder sometimes, really. Not that it won't be here, of course. Something will be here, no matter what. But *for me?* I wonder sometimes."

"Why shouldn't it be for you?" he offered lamely, ruing the fact that he, in his weakness, had actually begun this.

"I don't know. Something about Daddy. Something about me. I don't know."

"Mmmm." Praying that he might be released by making himself useful, he began to unwrap the parcels beside her. It was not his usual meal. In place of the sardines there was a small chicken Maria had cooked for him; in place of the common cheese, some *brebis* he kept for special times. The wine too was better, a Christmas bottle from town. And bread, of course, and coffee.

"Ever since Booker, in fact, something hasn't been quite the same between us. Maybe it was Consuela too, I don't know. Ever since Booker, anyway."

"Booker. That's a long time. Ten years."

"I know. I was just a little girl. But all the same . . ."

He was silent, fearing speech.

"Do you ever miss Booker?"

"Sometimes. I think about him, anyway."

"I know I do. And Consuela. It was the worst thing Daddy's ever done. Absolutely the worst. Even Eddie . . ." She stopped a moment, sucking on her lower lip. "Even Eddie."

Again he did not, could not, answer.

"Here," he said at last. "I've brought plates and glasses too, first class." Reaching into the rucksack he drew out two enameled tin plates and two jelly glasses, held them up, and put them down on the bench. Only then did he dare to look up into her face. She was looking down at him, a soft smile on her lips.

"I'm sorry," she said. "Let's have our feast."

More than an hour had gone by when, gathering up what remained, they rose to go. It was just past three o'clock, but already the sun had spent its warmth and started its descent. There were almost two hours of winter riding ahead; it would be dark and cold when they arrived.

She helped him with the door, straining beside him to push it closed across the snow. The meal, the empty talk of school and horses and eastern weather, seemed to have restored her spirits, resurrected the lost gaiety. She seemed refreshed, renewed, even now as she looked out across the valley to the ranches on the far side, fixing her eye on . . . just one.

"Next time I come," she said, turning away to face him— "next June it'll just swing open, creaking a little on its big hinges. Then we'll see about our cave. Just the two of us—until we find the water!"

He was still looking at her, wordless, when suddenly she reached over and kissed him on the cheek.

"Good John," she said beaming as, shouldering the rucksack, she set off down the snowy trail.

6

So there you are. And about time too. Did you get her off all right?

Good. And the car—no problems?

Good.

Beats hell out of me why she wanted to take that old bucket anyway, all the way to Salt Lake and in this weather—or why she wanted to fly at all, for that matter. Damn contraptions. I've hated 'em ever since the war . . . God help me, don't get into that.

But everything's okay, you say. She'll call from Boston. When did it leave? Anytime now, then. Good. I'll wait up.

You'll be wanting something to eat. Maria's still out there, isn't she? Suit yourself then. A drink, though. You will have a drink.

That's better. Yes, sit down. No, I'm okay for now. We'll wait together, you and I.

It was a good week, wouldn't you say? She seemed happy, content with her school—all around okay. We had some good times, good talks, she and I, better than for quite a while. Course I was on my best behavior—you must've noticed that. But anyway she liked being here, I could tell. She'd forgotten how fine it can be, in spite of everything. She'd forgotten a lot. You and Maria too. I caught them once or twice giggling in the kitchen, just the two of them like when she was little. And then that ride you two took up to that cave of yours— she wouldn't stop talking about it, all full of plans now.

Probably'll come to nothing, but it did my old heart good, I can tell you. I like to see her happy. Someday maybe, when she's got herself educated and had a sniff of the world . . . But for now she's in the right place; she knows it.

Things do tend to work out, you know—tough as it seems sometimes . . . Anyway—salut!

Maybe this should be champagne, though. There's something else to celebrate, you know.

No, you don't know. Anyway, celebrate *may not be quite the word. Old Jack'll have to do.*

Mmmm, yes. You're a smart one. I was just going to let you bring both days' mail up when you got back, but then yesterday I had a feeling and went down myself. There it was, all alone atop the newspapers—as though the postman made a special trip. I knew something was up. It was too soon—not time yet for the next.

Reston's dead, that's all.

Oh, eighty-two or three, I'd guess. More than I ever hope to see . . .

No, come to think of it, can't say I really want to celebrate—but drink up all the same. Santé!

You know, I'll almost miss him. Because in a way he provided the counterweight, the balance for the whole thing, the glue that held it all together. He died cursing me, of course—nice of her to report that little touch—but somehow that doesn't matter anymore either. Now that he's gone . . . well, things fall apart, as the poet said. They've already started to fall apart.

Yes, in spite of everything—there's no way I can blame him, really. No way at all. He was just being . . . what he had to be. We, all of us, were simply being . . . what we had to be.

What else could he have done, really? And yet, that last curse notwithstanding, I can't believe that any of it, anything he did, was the product of spite. No, I don't think he had a truly vindictive bone in his body. It was that sense of honor, of what was . . . appropriate to the circumstances, that drove him. Honor demands the prevention of what shouldn't be allowed to occur, simple as that. Simple as that . . .

But now he's dead, and . . . things fall apart.

And what else could he have done, really—what else would honor have allowed—other than what he did? Once he knew. Once he knew . . .

At first it was only the letters. Funny thing, just like now—the letters. Except then . . . mine was first. And then one from her. And I answered. That's different, for sure. Yet something, I'll never know quite what, kept me there with Suzanne, doing . . . all the things. Two, three months—until at last the winter began coming on. And then at last it was enough. Suzanne knew. I knew. It was enough. And by Christmas I was back in New York—for good now, or so I thought.

Twenty-eight that would be. No, twenty-seven. Winter of twenty-seven . . .

Do me this, will you John? I expect Maria'll be gone by now, but see if there's a bit of coffee left on the stove. She usually leaves some for me. If I keep on with this stuff too much longer, well, you understand, when she gets around to calling . . .

Ah, I thought there might be some. Little for yourself too, I see. Good idea. Get a handle. Good. Thanks. And where was I?

Ah. Just so. Twenty-seven. Just so.

Funny, I can't seem to recall all that much about it, that time. I got a little place not far from hers, spent days in the park, the library—anything to kill the time until evening. And even then I didn't always see her. She had her own life, her own place, her own job. But she had me too. Oh my, how she had me.

You needn't believe this—why should you?—except that I'm saying it and maybe that's enough: I never touched her . . . that way. Never once, in—what was it, three years? Not a single time until . . .

But maybe it's not that hard to believe after all. When you think of what had gone before. Not so hard at all. I just made up my mind, that's all, and stuck with it—even when I began to think that she might be . . . Anyway, I stuck with it. This was going to be different. This was going to be right.

I spent a lot of time thinking about that: how to make it right. I remember long walks in the park, rolling it about in my brain. And then it was September, the leaves turning—and all at once one day I knew. That night when I told her she didn't seem to believe at first, but then, before the dinner was done . . . She agreed, even seemed excited. I left the next day.

What the devil's keeping that girl? She's got to have arrived in Boston by now—but then maybe she wanted to wait until she got out to her friend's, in Newton, I think she said. I do wish she'd get a move on, though. Have a little mercy on her old father out in the snowy sagebrush.

Anyway, damn it, pour me another drop, will you? I've had enough of this sludge for now. Just a touch, mind you. To keep my voice clear. Good.

I wish I could bring it back intact, in a whole piece, the . . . illumination that led me back here. Those endless rambles in Central Park, afternoons in the library or museum or wherever my feet took me, dinners with her in some little candlelit bistro, long walks home that always ended at her door, no further—how all that yielded up the answer, that particular answer, is something far beyond me now. Part of it, of course, was that in spite of everything I simply missed the place. Once you've been out here, under these skies, watched the clouds marching toward the mountains, felt the wind on your cheek as it moves across the flat . . . once you've sniffed this air the sage just kind of gets in your head. Got in my head, anyway. Even now, no matter how I curse it sometimes . . . Even now.

And then—why deny it?—there was a kind of attractive perversity about the notion too. Same thing that had brought me back before, I suppose. The very place that had been the scene of so much I would have liked to forget . . . the very place. A kind of delicious penance, then. Or something like that. Something . . .

But the main thing, maybe, if there was a main thing, was a kind of slippery feeling that I could establish myself here. Make of myself what I wanted, in my own way. My own way.

I had a little money. Some would say a lot. I hadn't done Blickendorf's thieving for free, you know—and then there were a few other little investments along the way. It was enough, especially the way I wanted to do it. I spent a month looking, found this piece of ground . . . and that was it. Stayed just long enough to put up a little cabin—you know the one, still down there on the creekbank. Packed up. And Christmas in New York.

Or almost. Because she had promised to come back to San Francisco for that week, Marcella and the brand-new Cleveland husband joining her on the way. Needless to say, I wouldn't be along. I was still . . . invisible. But there were a few days before she had to go.

Even now, after all that has come after, the thought of those days, those few frosty days in December, has a way of warming me to the soles of my shoes. She was off from work, and every morning I called for her at ten. There were long breakfasts at the Waldorf, long, bright walks in the park, long dinners of champagne and candlelight, soft smiles and laughter. And through it all I always seem to hear my own voice . . . telling just how it was going to be. Describing the place, this place—the mountains, the springs, the creek, the air, all of it—

and telling, showing, even drawing just how the house would sit, how it would be. I remember her face, watching me—the look of quiet amusement overcome, little by little, by a kind of curious wonder as gradually, gradually, she too began to believe. Or seemed to.

And then she was gone, leaving me to my daydreams—but already by then I'd begun it: the books, the architects, the endless fussing over materials, exposure, all the rest. When she came back she seemed a bit preoccupied, less inclined to talk about it, anxious to get back to work, perhaps—but then so was I, and before two months had passed I was in Denver, then Salt Lake, finding the builder, ordering materials, getting ready. Mad. Utterly mad.

I'd give a lot to know just what was in her head then, when it all really began. My head . . . well, didn't I say I was mad? Possessed. And every day it seemed to get worse. That first spring—arriving in late March, Tegelvik and the Indians close behind—it all seemed a dream, a whirlwind, my brain sucked up in it. When I thought of her it was a part of that dream, until gradually she became a kind of vague ideal, always lingering, abiding there at the margin of my thoughts. Dulcinea.

Oh, never mind. Not important, really. But freshen me up a bit, will you? Obliged. Looks like she's not going to call at all, damn her. I'll have her hide.

I loved watching that man work—Tegelvik. Even the way he was with the Indians, although far as I know he'd never had a thing to do with them before then. He seemed to know the stones—not just how they were, how each would be when it was cut, but in a different kind of way, as though each time he cut one he both apologized to it, for taking it from the place it was born and up to then was meant to be, and somehow . . . ennobled it as well, anointed it by the choosing. The Indians knew it too, watched him like he was a kind of god—but then he began to teach them, and they learned. Swedish fellow . . .

But by then, when they began to cut the stones themselves and he started in below—by then I was gone again, first to Salt Lake and Denver for more ordering, more talking, then at last on back to New York. It was late June.

It was curious, the way she had changed. The fears that even then had begun to nibble at the corners of my dream—fears that she might have begun to "come to her senses," as the saying goes—all that seemed foolish now. For all at once, from the moment she met me at the station, she seemed eager to talk about it, to share each little detail and nuance of the thing—indeed, she wanted to talk of little else. There had been letters from her, of course, expressions of interest, even enthusiasm, but this was different. It had taken her over, the idea of it. Yes, the idea of it . . .

I have thought it all through. Again and again. Until now, thirty-five years later, I think I finally begin to understand.

Was she ever in love with me, I wonder? Maybe . . . that day in Runcietown. Maybe later. But even so, by the time that summer came 'round—that hot, humid New York summer of twenty-nine—she had already begun to fall out of love with me . . . and in love with the idea of me.

A difficult distinction? Maybe so. But there it was. And in the battle between me and what she'd made of me—I was bound to lose. Bound to.

Damn, will that girl never call? Must be—what is it, one o'clock there? It's not as if it's all that much trouble, you know, just to call, say she's all right. Once they're gone, no thought about . . . Damn her.

Hm. And so twenty-nine. Oh yes, it was hot, but it was bound to get hotter—once October arrived. Can't say I really saw it coming, what happened, although there may have been some still, small voice of good sense behind my madness after all. For I was all cashed out by then, everything in T-bills and solid banks, waiting for the bills and invoices that had already begun to come. And I escaped. Scot-free.

Reston unfortunately wasn't quite so lucky, nor was Marcella's young rubber baron, and when she came back from the obligatory Christmas voyage there were tales of woe to tell. Later, of course, it was all right—even the rubber baron was eventually able to put things back together—but right then it all looked pretty bleak. She was worried.

"It isn't fair," I remember her saying. "That they should have suffer so while we . . ."

I can't recall the rest. It was the "we" that struck me, the first time she had used it quite like that. And then, the next evening over dinner: "I just had to tell her. Everything was so sad and . . . I just had to tell her about us." Us, fancy that.

Because, yes, she had told Marcella, the two of them weeping on each other's necks in her old room. Oh my, quite a scene.

But by then my mind was already elsewhere—about twenty-five hundred miles west, in fact. The winter was starting to break already, Tegelvik had written from Salt Lake. We hoped for an early start. And by mid-March I was gone.

It was more than ten months before I saw her again. I thought of her every day, in that way I had of thinking of her . . . wrote once a week or so—but it was this house, this pile of stones and lumber, that really had me in its grip then.

Still, maybe. But no matter.

Anyway, there were the walls to finish, the beams and rafters going in as we went, then the floors and rough-out, the roof, and so on. And then the snow came. Early. But we were ready, the materials all inside, the stove set up and going. We stayed until almost February, Tegelvik and me, working nights half the time—but when we left it was done. Empty, but done. Done.

You look a little worse for wear. Time to turn in? It's okay, I'll stay on a bit longer. Never can tell, something might have happened. I'll tell her you got back safe and sound, that you were bushed. If she wants to say hello—well, there'll be another time. She'll understand.

No? Feeling okay? Sure? Well, in that case let's have another. Or a few others.

What? Ah, no matter. Suit yourself. Suit yourself . . .

It was mid-February before I got back there. Daffodils pushing up through the snow in Central Park, the tough winter birds expecting southern visitors. Spring was on the way—but the news was grim.

She hadn't wanted to write, she said. It was something best told face to face. And so she told it—the trip home with Marcella, their *decision that he deserved to know, be given at least a chance to grant his blessing; the conviction that in spite of everything he would at last consent, at least try to understand . . .*

It was a wasted hope, of course, doomed from the first. For they didn't really know him—as I knew him.

The heavy, heavy obligations of honor.

"I hardly recognized him," she told me. "His face seemed to change right before my eyes. 'No, this cannot be,' he kept on saying, again and again and again. 'No, this cannot be.'"

Of course.

"I don't know what to do," she finally said.

"Tell me when you decide," I said, and went back to my place.

That next month, at least the first part, I can't remember all that much about. The joints, the booze, the sleaze, the tears and beers and rages—oh yes, all of that and more besides. Only one night in jail, I think, though there might have been more. But then one morning all that seemed over. I remember looking out the window and there was a bird on the branch—kind of yellow, a spring bird. I thought of the willows reddening along the creek, the buds beginning to swell. And I knew it was time. In the pile of unopened mail on the table was a letter from Tegelvik, wondering about the barn. I threw on some clothes and went down to the telegraph office. Yes, I said, get on with it, anytime you can. More later.

More later.

I remember walking back to the flat, drawing the air deep, deep into my lungs. Yes, by God, I was going to keep on with it—with Dulcinea or without her. And then going up the stairs to the landing, hearing the phone begin to ring inside.

That night at the restaurant, even now I catch my breath just thinking how she looked. It was not that she was more beautiful— there was never much difference in that, not to my eyes; only . . . modalities of beauty. No, it was something else, a certain quiet sureness about her. Yes, she said, she had decided. Yes, and it was yes— if I would still have her.

If I would still have her. Indeed.

All that evening, I remember, I could hardly put in a word. She wanted so to tell it, say it so I would understand. I sat quiet, transfixed, as it all poured from her, those cool, once-haughty eyes now glowing with determination. It had been agony, she said—the night I had left her, the days and nights that came after. She knew her responsibilities, she said—oh my how she went on about that!—to her father, to her mother's memory, to her family, yes even to her sister, who now, it seemed, having witnessed his reaction, regretted her initial support. She had to look all that "full in the face," she insisted—as though that would somehow protect her, a kind of armor. Strange notion . . . But I was in no mood to argue, quibble over fine points. I had won the main event, it seemed. I had beaten him again. Yes, so it seemed.

That night, when we left the restaurant, we both knew I wouldn't stop at her door.

A week later I was gone again, heading for Salt Lake and a meeting with Tegelvik before he left. I'd rented a little warehouse where everything was to come, and already a good deal of the fine stuff, the furniture and such, had started to arrive. Much to do, and a steady stream of letters to New York. All seemed on course—steady as you go. By the middle of June I was out here again, and it all had started to arrive. And two weeks later I was gone again, this time to meet her. Steady as you go, sailor. And on to Guadalaja- . . .

Well I'll be damned. Hand it over, will you, before it wakes up all the jackrabbits.

Yes. Honey? Thought you'd forgotten us. But why the hell . . . ? Oh. Thought you might, was just telling John. And then a big supper too? Oh. That's nice. Good people. But you must be tired. Yeh, I'll bet. Well, get some rest. Nothing much has changed out here since this morning. What? Yes, he's here. What? Speak up—connection's not too good. Yes, okay, I'll tell him. He's smiling that cunning smile, you know the one. Yes, well okay, get some rest and have a good trip. No, I'm okay, maybe a little cold coming on, that's all. Yes. Okay. And call me when you get there. Okay. Bye, babe. Yes. Bye.

Didn't do too bad, did I? Considering. Another drop or two? I know, I know. Suit yourself. Somebody's got to behave.

Like a big load off me, though, I'll tell you . . .

And a word for you too, my boy. Beats hell out of me. Something about June . . . Oh yes. See you in June, and then . . . something else. Water, that's it. Find the water. See you in June, we'll find the water. Make any sense? Good. Greek to me.

You don't have to run off now, just because she . . .

Oh I know, I know—things to do, things to do. Well, I've got things to do too. Doing 'em right now. Believe I'll just keep on doing 'em a while. Anyway, g'night.

Not so fast, though. Here, something for the mail tomorrow.

Yeah, that's her all right. Don't make that face.

You thought, you thought—well sometimes different things happen. Sometimes.

That letter wasn't all about Reston, you know. Goes merrily on from there. Now that he's gone she wants . . . Just take up where . . . Very touching. Shed a tear.

What? I told her to go to hell, that's what.

PART THREE
•••
1965

CHAPTER 1

1

On the twenty-fourth day of May, the year 1965, a tall, dark-haired man stepped from the train in Creighton and, lowering a worn leather suitcase to the platform, stood a moment to look about him. It was a warm, clear afternoon, the lilacs beside the little station aglow with early blossoms, and he was seen to breathe in deeply once or twice before, taking in the modest buildings of the place with a glance, he walked the short distance to the hotel and disappeared inside.

Like those on the station platform before them, the handful of onlookers in the lobby that morning were not slow to notice the tall man, who now stood leaning against the counter in earnest conversation with Chick Rafanelli, the day manager. He was young, yet not so young as to give an impression of unsureness or lack of experience in the world; anyone who saw him there, overheard a few of his quiet, confident tones as he conversed with Rafanelli that morning, would have been quick to dispel any such notion as that. The day manager, whom many considered singularly ill-fitted for his not insignificant position, seemed but little inclined to assist in providing whatever it was that was sought of him and was making himself as disagreeable as possible to that end—but the tall young man seemed to take but little notice of Rafanelli's manners, and in the end it was he who carried the day.

"It's a long way," someone overheard Chick say. "And nothing when you get out there. What's your business with him anyway?"

This is the way that Chick Rafanelli was famous for treating his prospective guests, not to mention most of his actual ones.

The young man's answer, couched in low, pleasant tones, was unfortunately lost from hearing.

"You'd be wasting your time," Chick was heard to asseverate, taking on that brusque, know-it-all way of his. "Unless he's been expecting you a week, he'll just shut the door in your face. Without a by-your-leave or a fare-thee-well. Thing to do, young fella, is this. I got a nice room, third floor looking on the park, and after you've settled in, a little drink and something to eat maybe, why then you can just give him a call, simple as that. And if he'll see you, well tomorrow morning we'll work something out. If I was you."

It was at this point or soon after that someone saw a neatly folded twenty-dollar bill disappear beneath the blotter, and a few minutes later, after a brief phone call, Chick Rafanelli was leading the young man across the lobby and outside.

"If you'll just step this way, sir," he mewed, gathering up the leather suitcase.

To those who witnessed this odious little performance, then lingered long enough to see the young man seated in the car, driven by Chick's brother-in-law, that soon appeared beside the curb, the memory of that brief visit remained vivid for some time. And it certainly wasn't Chick Rafanelli's idea of small-town hospitality that anyone, at least anyone who knew him, would have remembered. No, it was the tall young man, who had made a kind of impression.

Mabel Lafferty, the head chambermaid, summed it up for many. "I've been reading *Photoplay* for going on thirty years now, never missed a single issue, and I've never seen anybody that good looking. Clark Gable, Cary Grant, whoever you like . . ."

2

They drew up on the bluff, then sat quietly looking down at the creekbed as the horses blew beneath them. Neither's face showed any expression—neither the worn, deeply lined features of the old man nor his own—but their very silence seemed to speak a shared regret.

At last it was Kinsella who gave it words, some words at least. "I've had the wind taken out of my sails a few times, John, felt a few hard cracks on the head, but this"—and he jerked his head, gesturing below—"this grieves me more than anything ever has, I think. Grieves and . . . outrages me all at once. It's like the blood's been drained out of me, of us. And yet we're both still here, me and . . . that. Bone dry, the both of us."

John sighed for want of anything to say.

"If only there were some meaning to it. Some reason. But there's nothing. Only silence. The rubbing of husks in the wind. And now and then that snicker in the dark."

The little buckskin, having caught its breath, began to fidget, stamping its hooves in the powdery earth.

"Calm down, damn you," Kinsella growled, then struck it across the nose with the ends of the reins. The horse jumped and shuddered, then was still.

"Doesn't leave much to do around here," John said after a moment. The tall, cream-tailed sorrel stood quietly, looking into the distance. "With just that little patch of hay now . . ."

"I know," the old man said. "Even that's not half worth doing—more trouble than it's . . ."

Again the buckskin seemed to grow impatient. "Huh!" the old man grunted, jerking the reins. Then: "Oh hell, let's go."

They descended the bluff and crossed the dry streambed, the coyote willows on the far side just leafing out now. Scrambling up the other bank, they stopped to pass through a makeshift gate in the fence, then set off side by side to the south, across the old hayfield.

Off to the northeast, massed above the ridges of the mountain and the pass further north, dark, glowering clouds moved down upon them. The south wind, picking up a bit now, raised low dust devils out on the flat.

"With the little we need we could just as soon buy it," Kinsella said after several minutes. "The hay, I mean—still thinking about that. Just not worth the hassle maybe."

"Maybe not," John said, wary of pursuing the matter. They continued on in silence.

Although only a year had passed, the long-pampered hayfield was already well on its way, on the brink of surrendering itself back to the land. Little stands of sage and rabbitbrush were everywhere, and the earth was already beginning to take on the rock-and-powder look of dry rangeland. Yes, John thought, it would soon be gone, as if it had never been.

Before long they had reached the far side, where the land stretching out before them had never been other than it was. They turned to follow the track along the fenceline, heading west, for half a mile or so before they found what they had come for.

"There it is," John said. "Just beyond the third post."

A part of the fence had been pushed down, by the weather or cattle or both, it was hard to say. But it was enough to let them through—John had chased out a dozen the day before. Kinsella, told of it, had said: "Not quite yet, not so fast. They'll get it soon enough, but for now, a little while longer, it's still a hayfield, damn it."

John dismounted, taking from behind the saddle the bundle of wire and tools he had brought along. While the old man watched atop the buckskin, he quickly made a temporary repair, resetting and bracing the three fallen posts until they stood upright.

"Should be okay," he said, returning to the horses. "For a few days, at least."

"I'll call him tonight," Kinsella muttered. "Tell him to get his ass out here." The old man seemed to smile. "Or his asses out of here," he said.

They continued along the fenceline for some distance, looking for other breaks, until they reached the far end. There they turned north again, went out through the big gate, then started over the low wooden bridge. Here Kinsella drew up again. Standing in the stirrups, he peered intently for a moment into the dry, rocky channel below—as if preparing to put it a question. Soon, however, the little buckskin had grown restive, its rear hooves thumping loudly on the timbers. The old man again seemed about to strike it, but then, with a weary look, allowed it to cross over—the sorrel following placidly behind.

"What's the use," Kinsella muttered, and turned down the trail toward home.

It was not until they were in sight of the barn, the rising wind now directly in their faces, that the old man spoke again.

"You know, that's the second time you've said that—not much to do here. You getting antsy?"

"No," John said. "I'm fine. It's just that I feel a little useless sometimes, and now, if you're thinking of just buying the hay . . . It just seems—well, you don't really need me . . ."

"Why don't you let me decide that?" Kinsella said darkly. "I need you plenty, even if you didn't do a damn thing. You do more than you think."

"Okay," John said. "Okay."

They rode in silence for a few minutes before Kinsella said: "Besides, maybe it's more than just me now."

John felt a shudder pass up his backbone as he turned in the saddle, looking into the old man's face. Kinsella, however, did not turn; his wiry eyebrows were drawn low as he gazed steadily ahead.

"Good a time as any to talk about it," Kinsella said at last. "Might as well."

Again there was silence, or only the sound of the wind and the creak of saddle leather—until suddenly, from somewhere in the cedars, came the hollow rapping of a flicker.

"I'd like you to stay on here in a kind of different way, with a different kind of . . . understanding maybe," Kinsella said at last. "I know I've kidded you a little about this, and I'm sorry, I guess. And Deirdre, well, she doesn't really know her own mind yet. But she will—a little time maybe, but she will. I think I already know how you feel about things. And don't make that face. I know." The old man coughed, clearing his throat. John was silent, still—unbelieving of what seemed to be unfolding before him.

"She's all I have, all I need—and when I go it's hers, all this, everything. Once I thought, well, she'll just let it go, sell it for what she can get and go on with her life somewhere else. Fair enough. I've had my time, much as I'd like her to be here after me. And now with the creek and all . . . And so really that's what I thought I wanted too, for her to just sell it off when the time came—at least if the only other option was for her marry one of these local . . . No, I'd rather have it gone.

"But these last few months I've begun to see things a little differently. Maybe that's not the only other option after all. Maybe there's somebody I could trust—with her, this place. And maybe, just maybe she's begun to feel something like that too. Not something she'd 'fess up to just yet, but . . . something. When I talk to her she always asks about you, you know." At last the great weathered head turned toward him, the pale eyes intent upon his face.

"Well, what do you think?"

Holding down the brim of his hat against the wind, John was silent for a moment before he said: "I'm getting close to forty, sir."

"So what? She's getting close to twenty. Her mother . . . well, let's just say there was a good deal more than twenty between us. What do you think?"

"I . . . I don't know. If someday she . . . well, I don't know. I hadn't really thought about it." The words seemed barbed, catching in his throat.

But now Kinsella, still looking at him, had begun to smile. "Well, while you're thinking it over," he said slowly, "let's consider we have a sort of tentative arrangement, shall we?" They had reached the gate of the corral. "And when we get these horses put up let's seal it with a little drink."

"Yes sir," John said, smiling too now, and began to draw open the gate.

They were walking back together, side by side, when Maria, her skirts flapping in the wind, appeared on the back porch and, slamming the screen door behind her, set off quickly toward them across the yard.

"Wonder what's got into her," the old man muttered, hurrying his step. "Never seen her move that fast."

She met them outside the picket fence.

"Thought you'd better know quick," she panted, struggling for breath.

"Know what, damn it?"

"You got somebody waiting—in the liberry. Man. Young. Wouldn' go away. I tried to tell him, but he jus' wouldn' go away."

"Wouldn't go away? Well, for hell sakes who does he think he is?"

The old woman pursed her lips and looked away, out toward the leafing row of poplars beyond the barn.

"Says he's your son," she said.

3

"Come along," Kinsella said. "No reason you shouldn't be in on this too."

"Well, I was going to get . . ."

"Come on."

They passed through the kitchen and went down the dark hallway, then into the sitting room on the left, John passing his hand over the dark lid of the piano as they continued through. The door at the far side was open, and beyond it, slumped in one of the two big chairs by the hearth, was a long-legged, dark-haired man. Hearing their approach, he sat up, turned to face the doorway. Then, as they came in, he slowly rose to his feet. He was tall, very slim, with pale, deep-set hazel eyes.

Kinsella stopped short, still six feet away. John, wishing he were elsewhere, moved gingerly off to one side.

For a long moment the two stood facing one another, neither speaking a word. The elder, so resolute before this moment, now seemed almost stunned, at a loss—even a bit confused. The younger, about John's own age it seemed, simply looked intently, his pale eyes dwelling upon the worn, haggard face before him. He did not smile.

No, John thought, there could be no doubt of it.

At last it was the younger man who spoke, extending his hand. "Hello," he said, the voice soft as a chamois glove.

The old man, ignoring the hand, still had not moved, nor had his expression changed. Now, however, there seemed to be something stirring within his breast—and words came.

"What put it in your mind to come here?" The deep, harsh voice seemed cracked, ragged, as though he had been crying.

"I wanted to see you, that's all," the other said. "It seemed to be the time."

"The time," Kinsella muttered and, walking stiffly past the still outstretched hand, went to the sideboard near his desk.

"Drink?" he said, after he had poured his own.

"Not just now, thank you, but if you happened to have a glass of water . . ."

The old man, scowling, looked over toward John, then nodded toward the kitchen. John, as though awakened, moved quickly toward the door and down the hall.

"Well?" Maria said archly as he stood at the sink.

"They're talking."

"I didn't mean that."

"It's him. No question about it."

The old Indian pursed her lips and looked away. Turning off the tap, he hurried down the hall.

They had not changed position in his absence—except that the younger man had now lowered his hand to his side. John, crossing to him, held out the glass of water. For an instant their eyes met. The young man smiled, his pale, almost milky eyes like smooth river agates set out to dry.

"Martin Kinsella," he said softly, again extending his hand. John, feeling the old man's glance hard upon him, hesitated a moment, then reached out to take it.

"John Siloa," he said.

"My foreman," the old man barked from the corner— altogether too loudly it seemed.

John nodded, returning the smile, and went to his place by the table.

"Drink, John?"

"Well no, I was just thinking I'd better . . ."

"*Drink?*"

Now he looked, meeting the old man's eyes. There was an expression in them he had never seen before—as though the answer to this question were of vital, indispensable importance.

"Yes, well maybe just a drop, then."

Sadly he watched the old man pouring, the slight tremor in the hand. Then, walking over, he reached out and took the glass. The expression, much changed now, was one of satisfaction, vindication almost, as Kinsella raised his own glass in salute.

"To the future!"

"The future," John whispered, then turned and walked back to his place by the window.

"Well, I guess you've seen me now." The old man, with renewed confidence it seemed, had turned now toward the other—toward Martin. "How do I look? About what you expected?"

"Yes. A little older maybe, but otherwise . . ."

"I'm old, if anything."

Martin seemed to smile. Lifting the glass of water to his lips, he took a small, silent sip.

"But otherwise, yes. I'd heard a lot, of course."

"Oh my, I'll bet you have," Kinsella said acidly.

"Yes, quite a bit, over the years." Again Martin smiled—a gentle, one might even have said tolerant smile.

"But even so you have the name now. I thought your name was . . . Worthington was it?"

"Whittington—you know, like Dick and his cat. But only a little while. After the divorce . . . I've really always had 'the name,' as you say—at least in my own mind."

"In your own mind," Kinsella repeated, his glance suddenly wary. "And your mother's."

"Yes sir, I suppose that too." Again, always, the voice was soft, comforting—as though the speaker had some deeper understanding of the situation.

Kinsella coughed and turned away, pouring a little more into his glass. He seemed shaken, disarmed by the simplicity of the response. John, looking over at him, felt a sudden impulse to go to him, take his hand. But he did nothing. After a moment the old man, at last leaving the sideboard, shuffled to his big chair behind the desk and sat down.

"And what do you do, exactly—for a living?" Kinsella said at last.

"I thought you knew. You seem to know . . . everything else."

"Not everything," Kinsella said darkly. "Not that."

"I was a priest." The words were quiet, final—with a vague suggestion of regret.

Again the old man was silent, studying his glass. More than a minute passed before he looked up, his eyes softer, almost misty now.

"No," he said. "I didn't know that. She didn't . . ." Again he looked down, studying the backs of his hands, before he added: "You mean a real priest? A Catholic priest?"

Martin smiled sadly. "No, not . . . a real priest. I was an Episcopal priest. Anglican."

"I see," the old man said after a moment. "But you're not . . . any longer? A priest, I mean."

"No, I'm not. Now . . . I'm not anything."

For a moment Kinsella seemed about to repeat the words, tolling them in that way he had. But nothing came. He was silent, utterly still, his gaze resting more lightly now on the younger man—or so it seemed.

A minute passed before he spoke. "Sit down, why don't you," he said at last. "Just haul those big chairs over, the two of you. I want to see you both."

John's and Martin's eyes met for an instant before the taller man turned and, lifting the chair in which he had been sitting, carried it easily to a place before the desk.

"I'll just take . . . ," John began, lifting the smaller chair by the window in which he normally sat.

"No!" Kinsella growled. "The other, the big one. You heard me. Go on."

Dutifully John walked to the remaining chair and, lifting it with some effort, moved it to a place beside the other. Then, retrieving his drink from the table, he gingerly lowered himself onto the soft blue velvet cushion.

"Yes, that's better," Kinsella said smiling. "Much better." He lit a cigarette and settled back, looking from one big chair to the other.

"And you were saying you were a priest."

"Yes, sir. I was."

"And just how did that come about?"

There was a moment of hesitation before the answer came.

"When I came back from the war—Korea, that is—I was just twenty-one. Things I'd seen maybe, things I'd . . . things I'd done, things I'd started to think—well anyway when I got back it seemed that's what I wanted to do. I'd never thought of it before . . . but then it seemed clear, that's what I wanted to do. There's a seminary in Berkeley and . . . well, that's how it happened. Generally."

"Amazing," Kinsella muttered, studying the palms of his hands.

"Sir?"

The old man looked up, his gaze seeming clouded once more. "Nothing," he said. "Nothing at all." Again there was a pause; then he went on.

"But you're not a priest anymore, you say. You're . . . not anything."

"That's right," Martin said very quietly.

"And how exactly did *that* come about?"

There was a moment of silence, then another brief sip of water, before the answer came at last.

"I'm not quite sure. One morning when I woke up it just didn't seem to make sense anymore. I tried, kept on with it for a while, talked to people, but . . ." Again he raised the glass and took a sip, then offered a wan, apologetic smile.

"Sorry," he said. "Not very exciting, I'm afraid."

The old man seemed perplexed. "Hm," he muttered, but nothing more.

Martin, however, seemed to have no need for prompting.

"Since then," he went on, "I've rather knocked about, wondering what should come next. I'll probably get into some kind of teaching eventually, counseling, something in that line, but for now nothing seems to appeal to me, really. I decided I just needed some time to think things over, get in touch with myself." Again there was that same soft, vulnerable smile. "And so I came."

Kinsella had seemed in a kind of reverie through all this last, but now, as the silence descended once more, he seemed to come to himself.

"John, another little touch, will you?" he said, holding out his glass.

Rising with some difficulty out of the blue velvet chair, John took the glass to the sideboard and began to refill it.

"That's fine. Yourself?"

"No, I'm good, and besides, you two . . ."

Kinsella, with a hard, level gaze upward at him, took the glass. "Sit down," he said quietly, and looked away.

Outside, the wind had begun to whip up in earnest now, and out the window John could see the shadows of dark clouds passing overhead. He had smelled the rain coming this afternoon; now, soon, it would be here. It was good, they needed it, but he wondered what else this night would bring.

"There's nothing for you here, you know," Kinsella said suddenly. His voice was deep and harsh, resolute. "That's all been settled."

Martin, slouching in his chair, suddenly sat up now, looking startled.

"But I only wanted . . ."

"That's okay, what you wanted—but that's not what's going to happen. Your mother made a choice once, a long time ago. I didn't like it, but I accepted it, was prepared to live with it, was going about living with it. Then, five years down the road, when she's of a mind to marry somebody else, she writes to tell me about you. She thought that changed something, I guess. Looks like you thought so too. But you're both dead wrong. For a minute when I saw you . . . well, let's forget that. The whole thing is settled, finished, done. Has been for a long, long time. And nothing anybody can do . . ." Kinsella raised his glass, taking a long, slow swallow.

"John'll take you back."

"But I don't quite . . ." For the first time the young man seemed flustered, at a loss for words. "I mean . . . I'm not my mother, whatever went on between you. I'm . . . for God's sake I'm your son!"

"I won't argue about that," Kinsella said slowly. "Matter of fact I won't argue about anything. Far as I'm concerned, you don't exist."

Suddenly, as if at a signal, a tattoo of raindrops rattled the panes of the windows. John, in spite of himself, glanced over his shoulder. The clouds had spread all the way across the valley now, except for one bright, sunny patch of blue atop the highest ridge. But that too, even as he watched, was closing, choked by the billowing darkness all around.

Martin, slumped in the high-backed chair, seemed stunned. His cheeks had taken on a pale, almost chalky hue, and the droop of his head had a hopeless, desperate look about it. Then all at once, as John sat watching, something seemed to gather itself within the tall, slouching form, as though all the energy remaining had come to be concentrated in a single, luminous spark.

"You can't say that," Martin said.

"I've said it. And I mean it." The old man, looking over the desk at him, seemed made of stone.

"But I *do* exist. You made me exist. You don't really doubt that, even you. And I'm not just something in Mother's letters now. I'm here, right in front of you. If you wanted . . . if you wanted you could reach out and touch me. To turn away now, to close your eyes . . . why, that's simply a lie."

He paused, taking in a deep breath. "If you do this . . . you become a lie."

Kinsella, glaring over at him through dark, hooded eyes, did not move. Nor, for a long moment, did he speak. It was as if he were waiting for something more, wanting it all to be said.

Outside there was another sudden sharp splattering on the window; then, the preliminaries done, the storm descended in earnest, the rain-laden wind raking the sides of the great house with greedy claws.

"I have no difficulty with that, young man," Kinsella began at last. "None of us has any difficulty with that. That's simply called living." The old man sighed, a deep, hopeless sigh, as he lifted the glass to his lips once more. Then, seeming to gather all his forces, he started to get up.

"And now, John, if you'll be so kind as to escort this gentleman . . ."

He had begun to move again toward the sideboard, reaching out toward the tall bottle remaining there, when his foot seemed to catch on something beneath, perhaps just the corner of the rug. But then he was down, fallen between the sideboard and the desk. There was a heavy, solid thump—then silence. The wind screamed at the window.

They were both on their feet now, moving together, side by side, toward him. But it was Martin who arrived first, and there was room for no more than one in the narrow space in which he had fallen. John stood back then, looking downward over the kneeling, dark-haired form until he heard the soft voice murmur: "Damn!" And now he saw the long, slim hand reach backward to a pocket, then draw out a large white handkerchief. John crowded forward just enough to see the handkerchief laid on the side of the old man's head, then begin to bloom with a widening crimson stain.

"Get some water," Martin said, not turning his head. "Ice, if you have it. And a towel or two."

John hurried down the hall, his mind strangely running backward to another time, years before, when he and Kinsella had encountered one another on that same floor.

Maria, hovering over the stove, turned to look as he came in. Stolid, impassive, she listened to what he had to say, provided what was asked for, and followed him back down the hall.

The old man, laid out flat on the rug now, head resting on Martin's neatly folded coat, seemed half a corpse. Yet the heavy, even sound of his breathing was audible as they came in—then a soft, weary moan. Martin knelt beside him, the now-bright handkerchief held to the side of the head. He turned as they came in, reaching for a towel.

"He'll be okay, I think," Martin said, handing up the wet handkerchief. "A nasty rap on the leg of the desk. There's a little corner on it, right near the bottom—caught him flush on the temple. He's coming around a little now, though."

Again there was a moan, softer now, and the eyes slowly began to open.

"Better now?" Martin was saying. "You'll be okay. Hold still, though—little cut on your head." Slowly, Martin drew the towel away. The bleeding had almost stopped.

"Not very big really, but kind of deep—and just in the right place." Again he turned, looking up at them. "Just put those things down here for now. The other towel too. Do you have some antiseptic? And maybe some gauze and adhesive tape—or just a big Band-Aid will probably do."

John, leaning down over Martin's shoulder, looked into Kinsella's face. Behind him he could hear the swish of Maria's skirt as she turned to go. The eyes were fully open now, looking calmly, one would almost have said thoughtfully, upward into Martin's face. He did not seem at all inclined to speak.

"How do you feel? Okay?" Martin asked, holding a cube of ice to the wound.

"Okay," Kinsella said—but nothing more.

"The lady's gone for some iodine and a bandage. After I put that on you can try to get up."

"Okay." The tone was soft, compliant, even submissive.

And now Maria had arrived. It was quickly done, and a moment later the old man, neatly bandaged, was seated on the rug, his back against the front of the desk.

And still he had not really spoken. The pale blue eyes simply looked about the room, searching out all the corners. But something, something seemed added to his expression now. It was difficult to say just what—a hint of perplexity, exasperation, pique. Something.

"Okay?" Martin said.

"Okay."

"Let's just try to stand up, then."

Slowly the old man, meekly accepting the hand at his elbow, got to his feet.

"Okay?"

"Okay."

At last, shaking off the hand, Kinsella walked to one of the small chairs by the window and sat down. Outside the wind was roaring, the rain hammering at the panes.

"Now," Kinsella said at last. "Where were we?"

Martin, standing by the dead fireplace, was smiling. "We were telling John to take me back to town," he said.

Kinsella's gaze was grave and even, utterly unamused, unmoved. But he did not answer at once. There would have been a moment of utter, empty silence—if it were not for the shrieking of the wind outside. At last the old man cleared his throat, then turned to look toward the open sitting room door.

"No weather for that. Tomorrow's soon enough."

And then, very slowly, he turned toward Maria, who still stood near the sideboard, the pot of water and bloodstained towels in her dark, strong hand.

"There'll be three of us for supper," he said.

Again he paused, seeming to study the wind.

"And fix the boy a room."

4

The morning was crisp and clear, the smell of wet sage on the air. There was not a cloud to be seen now, and the oncoming day announced itself in a pale yellow glow above the eastern ridge. A soft predawn breeze had arisen; he felt its cool breath on his face as he struggled to advance the wheelbarrow through the soggy, manure-laden earth, the four horses tracking him like inept, overeager sleuths.

He stopped beside the first manger, forking out half his load. Deirdre's buckskin and the bay, claiming this as their own, immediately began to eat, while the tall sorrel, nudging at his back with its muzzle, insisted that he move on, and only when he had filled the other did this rough pursuit abate. Stepping back, the sorrel and Kinsella's black having utterly forgotten him now, he laid his fork in the bottom of the empty barrow and again looked up at the brightening sky.

It really had been quite surprising, the violence of the storm last night. Spring had arrived early this year, the days warming up already, and although they had expected a bit of rain last evening, the notion of a cloudburst like that had been far from anyone's mind. Almost an inch must have fallen, perhaps more—and all in the space of those three hours. For when he had at last come out on the back porch, the long, talk-laden dinner finally at an end, it had all been over—the sky clear and calm, a symphony of stars.

It was always a chancy business, predicting the old man's actions, but after last night he sincerely doubted that he would be taking Martin to town that morning—or any other morning soon. There had been a bit of stiffness at first, of course, but a good part of that seemed as much due to his own presence there as to Martin's—for in all his years here it had never before been suggested, not even for a moment, that he himself might draw a chair up to that forbidding table. And yet there they had sat, the three of them—amidst the flickering candles and the wine, Maria passing to and fro like a silent, impassive ghost, as if nothing at all out of the ordinary were taking place.

And yes, almost from the first moment it had become clear to him that Kinsella had made up his mind, and in a way he would never have dreamed possible before. There was a bit of the gruff manner at first, of course, a few opening questions meant to be awkward or disconcerting, but the old man's heart was no longer in it, and soon the horn was rounded, the crisis passed. Yes, the boy would stay, at least for a time. He was sure of it, as sure as anyone could be.

It was strange, John thought, that he persisted in calling him "the boy," if only in his own mind now. The mathematics was clear enough: Martin must be thirty-three, only six years younger than he—hardly a boy. But Kinsella, after all, had never called him anything else, nor had Booker or Suzanne. He had always been "the boy," only that—and indeed, before yesterday John had never even heard his name. It would take a while, then, getting used to it.

But yes, it had been a good evening, a good result—from that point of view. Boy or not, Martin knew many things. Most of all he knew how to talk, to say what he wanted to say in the right way. And he had much to say, much to tell—as did . . . his father.

Yes, once that first awkwardness was past, the two of them had clearly gotten on, moving from one theme to the next with a kind of mutual understanding and common feeling that John could only marvel at. Not that he himself had remained wholly silent—although his words, weighed next to theirs, would not have amounted to much, for often the things they spoke of were utterly beyond him. But there had also been questions, things the boy wanted to know about him. They spoke of France, the Basques, the war—and then he and Kinsella, their wars as well. But only briefly, obliquely, that—for each, once begun, seemed anxious to pass on to other things. And so they had, until the clock in the hall had long ceased to strike the big numbers.

When at last he had been able to get away, leaving them before the fire with new-replenished snifters of cognac glowing in their hands, they seemed utterly at ease with one another, as though their separation had been a month or a year rather than a lifetime. And as he drew the door closed behind him there had come a sound he could not remember having heard before; he was halfway through the darkened kitchen before he realized that it was Kinsella's laugh.

The sun had breached the sky now, rising over the dark southern flank of Molly Peak like a bright, slow-moving balloon. He gazed up at it for a moment, his eyes tracing the contours of the mountain with a sudden inexplicable pang of longing. Then he turned away, gripped the handles, and pushed the empty barrow back toward the barn.

It was perhaps two hours later when, having finished the morning chores and started some work in the shop, he returned to his little room to make his mid-morning meal. It had not changed much, this room, in the more than ten years he had lived here—nor indeed had it changed much since the days before, when its tenant had been Booker Goodman. The narrow iron bed, the old chest of drawers at its foot, these remained just where they had been, against the far wall. The shelf above, its paint sadly peeling now, bore other objects—the faded New Testament he had brought with him from France, a badly focused photograph of the steeple of his village church, two or three old sheep bells, a wooden spinning bob—but the difference in effect, if indeed there was one, could hardly be noticed. The only significant change in the whole room, really, was the addition of a small, oilcloth-covered table in the corner, just to one side of the wooden pegs from which the coats hung, and a low steel bookcase to its left. Here he had set up a lamp, and a coffee cup of sharpened pencils bristled at one corner of the table, but otherwise its checkered surface was completely clear. The same could not be said, however, of the bookcase, which was crammed and heaped with a disarray of books and papers and magazines in all stages of faded glory. Tacked to the wall above it, just at the level of the table, was the yellowed dust jacket photograph of Lindbergh and his airplane, obscured at one corner by a battered wineskin hanging from a nail.

John's morning appetites had also changed but little since his days on the mountain—and all the days before. Going to the little refrigerator beside the outside door, he took out a large, cold baked potato, two brown eggs, and a length of chorizo sausage. From a tin beneath the old gas hotplate came a few cloves of garlic, from another a chunk of sheep cheese, and from yet another half a red pepper. Ten minutes later, the coffee perking on the gas ring behind him, he had just drawn his chair up to the little table when there came a soft, insistent rapping at the door. Taking a sip from his glass, he returned it softly to the table and went to the door.

"Hi," Martin said, his angular face bathed in warm sunlight. "Dad said you'd be here."

John stepped back from the door, motioning him inside.

"Lord, it smells good in here. Do you eat like this every day?"

"Just about," John said. "It's what I'm used to."

"I'm surprised you're not fat as a pig," Martin said. "And wine too, at this hour?"

"It's what I'm used to," John repeated, smiling. "Since I was a boy."

"Well, I'm amazed you can get anywhere near it—considering what we put away last night. 'Course maybe you got off a little easier, leaving when you did."

"There were things to do. The chickens get hungry all the same."

"I suppose so," Martin said, looking over toward the steaming plate on the table. "But don't let me bother you. Eat it while it's hot. Maria's cooking something up for us." Gingerly, he sat down on the bed.

"Coffee?" John asked.

"Love it," Martin said, looking about the room.

John took the cup to him, then filled one for himself and returned to the table.

"Quite a hideout you got here," Martin said. His teeth, John noticed, were very white.

"Good thing, to get away. You know Dad a lot better than I do, goes without saying—but even after just last night—I mean the idea of staying in that big empty house with him day after day, I can see why you'd rather be out here. A little privacy. Even Maria has her own little place, I notice."

"Yes," John said. "We all have . . . our own places."

"Good. That's the best way."

Sitting sideways in the chair, John fiddled with his eggs.

"You're quite a reader too, I see," Martin said, nodding toward the choked bookshelf. "I've heard about that."

"Heard about it?"

"From Dad, last night. After you left. Up on the mountain, teaching yourself, all that. He thinks a lot of you, you know. Respects you. Trusts you too—and that counts for a lot these days."

"I s'pose so," John said, lifting a cool piece of potato to his mouth. "We get along."

Martin's face lit up, a sudden smile. "I guess I can see why, even after just . . . although there's a few rough spots, you'll have to admit. A diamond in the rough, as they say. Especially after you get to know him, I suppose. The way you've come to know him, I mean." He lifted the coffee to his lips, took a short, breathy sip. His eyes, looking over the rim, were noncommittal—but full on John's face.

"But in the beginning, I'll have to say—well, he can be tough. Forbidding, if you know what I mean. I swear if he hadn't just happened to fall down—you know, when he got that bump— well, if that hadn't happened I'll bet we really would have been driving back to town, you and me, rainstorm or not. Yep, that's what turned it around." Martin sighed. "Close call," he said.

"Close call."

"Anyway, that's all done," Martin resumed, taking another sip of coffee. "We're in pretty good shape now, I'll have to say, he and I, considering . . . everything. Pretty good shape."

"That's good," John said. "I'm glad."

"It's a start, anyway, after all this time. All this . . . stuff. You know what I mean."

"Yes," John said. "Some of it."

Martin was silent for a moment, looking down at the tops of his shoes. He seemed suddenly downcast, overcome with thoughts. Then, however, that seemed to pass and he looked up.

"But that's not what I came for, to talk about all that. There'll be plenty of time . . . No, I'm on a mission. A messenger from the throne."

Again, like a ray of sunlight emerging from behind a cloud, the bright smile had returned.

"Dad has this idea—that we should saddle up some horses and take a kind of tour of the place. Just the three of us. What do you think?"

"Can't do it," John said. Putting down his fork, he pushed back the chair. "I'll get the horses ready, though, while the two of you are having breakfast."

"Well I don't know," Martin scowled. "The old man seemed pretty set on it. And when he's set on something—well, you know better than I do."

"I'll tell him myself," John said, getting to his feet.

They walked side by side toward the big house, past the old bunkhouse. The corral fences steamed in the sun.

Kinsella was in the kitchen, hovering over Maria's shoulder. "We'll need a lunch too," he was saying as they came in.

"You'll get one," she said, brushing past him toward the refrigerator.

The old man turned to face them. "Ah, there you are. I guess you've already had breakfast, John, but I was thinking . . . well, I suppose he's already told you."

"Yes," John said. "But it'll have to be just the two of you. It's town day for me."

Kinsella made a face. "Well for hell sakes, what's wrong with tomorrow? We're not going to starve, are we?"

"Maybe," Maria muttered.

"Oh shut up," Kinsella snapped over his shoulder.

"Not just that," John said. "There's a couple of things at the station, that generator waiting at Charlie's, Suzanne . . ."

"All of which can damn well wait. This doesn't happen every day, you know, with Martin here and . . ."

"And something else too," John finished.

"What, damn it!"

"My tooth."

"Your . . . *what?*" Kinsella keened.

"My tooth."

"Well I'll be fried! Can't your goddamn tooth wait a day?"

"Appointment's today. Putting on the cap."

"Putting on the cap," Kinsella muttered, kicking the leg of the chair.

Maria took the long way around him, heading for the sink.

"Well, to bloody hell with you then," he said at last, slumping down on a chair. "We'll just go anyway, the two of us."

John turned to Martin. "Have you ridden much?" he said.

"Quite a bit really, but always English, I'm afraid."

"Give him my black," Kinsella muttered as John went out the door.

5

His jaw still numb with Novocaine, he pulled up behind the station and went inside. Grover the freight agent, his brow furrowed like a plowed field, was laboring over a crossword puzzle.

"Can I help?" John said.

The man looked up scowling. "Not unless you happen to know the Jewish months," he said.

"Sorry."

Grover got up from the crate, laying the newspaper carefully upon it. "What've we got today, John?" he said. "Besides the booze, I mean."

"Well, there'll be some of that, I guess, and then some pump parts. Maybe one other."

"One other," Grover muttered, heading toward the back.

Outside, across the main track, one of the old steam engines they used for switching now was backing up to the water tower. Beyond, beside the signalman's little hut, a row of early tulips glowed brightly in the sun. Far in the distance, out on the sage flats, an ore train labored northward toward the mill. There was no cloud in the sky, no breath of wind.

"There's plenty this time," Grover said, straining behind the handtruck. "I hope you didn't bring that little blue jalopy."

"No. I've got the truck this time."

"You'll need it," Grover said, lowering the two boxes. "Looks like he cleaned out the distillery." He turned and went back through the door.

John looked vaguely down at the wooden box lids, the familiar design traced upon them. Just where, he wondered, was Lynchburg—besides in Tennessee.

"Okay," Grover said as he returned. "One of these is wine I think, the other I guess is your parts. Heavy as hell, that's all I know. Your 'one other' is still to come." Again he turned to go.

In a moment he was back with a single box, carried under his arm. "Not much to this one. Somewhere in Pennsylvania. Caver's Cooperative, whatever that means." He scratched his head. "Did you order this? Addressed to you."

"No. Someone else did. But it's okay. I was . . . expecting it."

"Great. Saved me one big headache. Now just sign these up and I'll help you get them outside. Sure you don't know any Jewish months?"

He sat in the truck a long time, long after the agent had disappeared back inside. The numbness was fading from his jaw now, and he savored the sensation as it proceeded, like spring ice melting from a leaf. From time to time he looked up into the rearview mirror, admiring the bright gold bicuspid glinting in the light. Only once did he glance down at the unopened box on the seat beside him, and then he quickly looked away.

The little street was a glow of purple and pink and white, lilac and cherry blossoms high and low. Last night's storm had taken its toll, and the pavement was bright with the bodies of the fallen, but most of the stubborn little flowers had somehow managed to survive, and after a morning of warm sunlight all seemed well again. As he drove slowly up toward town, weaving among the tumbled blooms and the ever-present potholes, it seemed to him that the trees this year were the best he had ever seen.

He stopped before the house, turned off the engine, and sat for a few moments gazing absently at the small weeping willow, just leafing out now, behind the fence. Soon he noticed coming toward him, moving down the uneven sidewalk from the direction of town, an erect, white-haired old woman with a wicker basket on one arm. He watched her come, marveling as always at the vitality of her step, the straightness of her carriage, until she had reached the cross-street at the corner. Then, getting out, he set off to meet her, arriving just as she spryly stepped up on the curb.

"Well, you seem to know my movements," Suzanne said smiling, and took his arm.

"Not really. This was pure luck."

"Well you should, you know. Altar Guild on Wednesday, have you forgotten that already?"

"Yes," John said. "Appears so."

"Incorrigible boy," the old woman said, pursing her lips.

They continued in silence down the block, stopping at her gate. As he stooped to push it open, then stood aside for her, she suddenly looked up into his face. "I didn't really mean that, you know, what I said just now. You're always very good to me, better than anyone has ever been. God, in the end, has given me a son too."

He smiled sheepishly, then looked away as she passed. It was sometimes difficult for him, this occasional . . . frankness of hers, especially now that a touch of sentimentality, even mawkishness, was so often there as well. He much preferred the gentle mocking, her shadowed side.

With quick, small steps she mounted the stairs, then drew the key from her sweater pocket. It was not until she had opened the door that he stepped up as well and followed her inside.

In the more than ten years that he had known her now, Suzanne had hardly seemed to age. There were certain subtle physical changes, of course—the hair a little whiter, the voice a trifle weaker, and now lately that certain transparency he had begun to notice in her skin—but otherwise she seemed much as she always had been. The way she moved, the way she thought, the way she expressed herself, none of these had changed much, unless, of course, one were to count that penchant for sudden tenderness which the years seemed to have nurtured. John sometimes wondered if this might be the effect of too much religion.

And yet they got on well, as they always had—since that first cold winter evening so long ago.

"Terrible storm last night, wasn't it?" Suzanne, leaving her basket on the wooden sinkboard, was already washing out the coffeepot. "And the trees—all those lovely blossoms down on the street."

"Lots made it through though," John said vaguely, looking out the window.

They were speaking English now, as increasingly they had over the years. The French language had become for them a badge of recognition, a tool of memory, and very little else. Even the fact of their common heritage, or what Suzanne took for such, was something that rarely came up between them anymore. In that respect, then, this day was a clear exception.

"I thought of all those poor boys," she said. "Each blossom lying there on the street, so many already blackened by the tires of cars passing over—each one was like one of those boys, those children, who won't come back."

"Ma'am?"

She turned to face him, her great doe's eyes like dark pools on the surface of her face.

"The war, of course. Don't you ever think about the war, John—this . . . thing we've got ourselves into again?"

"Sometimes," he said. "Not like you do maybe."

She sighed, scrubbing the palms of her hands on her apron.

"Because in a way it's even more *our* war you know, yours and mine. We, after all, are French."

John swallowed hard, then looked down at the backs of his hands.

"It was just when you came, when Booker brought you to me—Dien Bien Phu. All our own boys then, ten thousand French children perishing like rats in that soggy, pestilent hell. And nothing changes. Nothing ever changes. Now, ten years later, it is our boys again—American this time, but we are, have become that too, you and I. More flowers, more blossoms to be blackened by the tires."

John looked up, yearning to add something—anything—to deflect her. "There is always war," he said softly. "We all have our wars. Just last night they, we were talking, Kinsella and . . . how each one . . ." His voice trailed off, realizing.

Suzanne, her dark eyes suddenly narrowed, looked straight at him. "They?" she whispered.

"Yes," he said quietly. "I was going to tell you anyway."

"And?" Her hard gaze seemed to press against his forehead.

"The boy—Martin's his name. He's here . . . since yesterday."

Slowly, mottled hands pressed hard against her thighs, she turned about. For a moment she remained perfectly still, leaning against the sinkboard, her eyes directed out the window at the sage and cedar hillside rising up behind the house. Then, as if awakening herself from slumber, she abruptly reached up to the cupboard for the can of coffee. A moment later, the pot settled over the flame, she took off her apron and hung it on the peg.

"*J'ai un peu d'anisette,*" she said. Her voice was soft and very calm. "I've had the same bottle for thirty years, in fact," she went on in French. "But only a centimeter or two is gone. Will you have a glass as well?"

He nodded gravely. "*Oui, si tu veux.*"

She disappeared out the door, toward the little front parlor. In a moment she had returned, a small, dusty bottle with a yellowed label in one hand. In the other, the stems cradled between her fingers, were two small crystal glasses, each of a different kind. Carefully, ceremoniously, she lowered them to the kitchen table, then put the bottle beside them. Retrieving a dish towel from the rack, she wiped the dust off the bottle, then pulled the cork and carefully poured a small amount of the clear, viscous liquid into each glass. Then, replacing the cork, she pushed one over to him.

"*Merci bien.*"

"*Je t'en prie.*"

They drank.

"Now," she said, resuming in English—"now tell me all about him."

The coffee had begun to perk.

They stood together at the front door. More than an hour had passed.

"And the girl," she said. "When does she come back?"

"About two weeks now," he said softly, almost wistfully.

"And so—assuming he stays, of course—he'll be here too, the . . . priest. The two of them."

"Yes."

"A first meeting."

He looked out the window, toward a mass of fallen blossoms near the curb. "Yes," he said.

She was silent for a moment, perfectly still. "Will you do me a favor when they're here?" she asked at last, looking steadily up into his face.

"Sure."

"Bring them to me, both together. You needn't tell them much about me."

He hesitated for a moment before he said: "I'll try."

"Yes," Suzanne said smiling. "Do try."

She watched him intently, a suggestion of puzzlement in her dark gaze, as he descended the stair, crossed the little yard, and closed the picket gate behind him.

CHAPTER 2

When the good people across the valley got wind of the fact that Phoenix Ranch was entertaining an actual visitor—then factored in the information that Big Bob Fisk, reporting the observations of his old friend and former classmate Mabel Lafferty, was able to supply—the long-idled engines of conjecture, though by now a little rusty, lurched once more into motion. Mabel having reckoned the young man's age as early thirties (and Mabel was known to have an eye for such things), those with a head for numbers had immediately set to work, their findings gaining quick endorsement among volunteers of a more historical bent. And soon the answer began to emerge; yes, it was all too clear. A man of the age in question—especially one with those various attributes, physical and otherwise, that Mabel had so avidly described . . . It was possible, even probable. Considering Kinsella's irascible and sedentary ways, it had all the earmarks of a fact.

Yes, this was a fascinating piece of news, no question about that—one which, precisely because of the dearth of actual, verifiable information about the newcomer, allowed the fullest play to their collective powers of curiosity and imagination. Distinguished, articulate, doubtless the beneficiary of a fine and costly education, there could be no doubt that he had led a favored life—but why, they asked themselves, had he stayed away so long? If Kinsella was in fact his father . . .

But if there were some in the valley who viewed this recent appearance with excitement, greeting it with no end of deliciously provocative questions, there were others who soon came to view it in a different light. Kinsella, who had everything— or everything but water at least—now had his son with him as well. And there were many in those days who could not claim as much, or at least could not count on claiming it for long. The draft had begun in solemn earnest.

"I find myself just looking over there sometimes," Bob Fisk confided to his wife one evening. "Just standing there, looking out. The big house, the barn . . . and now . . ." He did not finish the thought.

"I'll be outside," Bob said. "Think I could use a breath of air."

For Martin Kinsella, who had little suspicion of the strange celebrity he enjoyed here, such imputations of favor and privilege, if only he had heard them, would have brought forth the wryest of smiles. There was no denying the material benefits he had up to then enjoyed, but even so he might well have wondered whether the good people of the neighborhood, had they known all there was to know about him, would have found much there to envy. To his own eyes, his life had been lived in the still point at the center of a hurricane, while all about him whirled forces he could never begin, even had he so wished, to grasp or understand.

The first of these, his grandfather, had appeared to his infant eyes and ever afterward the very embodiment of God. And yet a strange, twisted God he had been, not only in his physical self, that shambles of rictus and flaccidity whose emergence had heralded his own birth, but in the old man's manner as well, his way of being. Was it mere rage, he wondered, which had made his grandfather what he was, had been, or was it something more as well, a bitter, impossible argument with that other, greater God he so unceasingly cited as authority for his own edicts? Martin did not know. Even at the end, when he had so wished to learn the answer, it had not come. The bitter old man, rigid in his silence, had mutely passed into darkness.

Yes, he thought, even his mother had never really known the answer. Their relationship, hers and her father's, had never been clear to him—no, not even later, after that other daddy and his starchy name had at last fled from the scene, when she had truly begun to confide in him. How he remembered those long afternoons in her big bedroom, the summer wind groaning against the window—her beautiful, still-smooth face bending low above him, soft, sea-green eyes gazing down, a falling lock of chestnut hair . . .

And yes, the telling, long and long. At first, of course, when he was only ten or so, there had been only bits and pieces, but as his questions came, as indeed in time they had, the answers gradually came as well, until at last, when he was seventeen or so, it had all been laid out in the sun. Or so it seemed.

He remembered asking her again one day the one question that never ceased to recur to him, but which until then had always been avoided, deflected, finessed.

"But why, then, after . . . coming to terms with all that, after going ahead in spite of it—why did you leave him like that, just walk away?"

Her face had seemed to tighten somewhat, then suddenly relaxed, as though reflecting a sudden, unanticipated decision. "I came to my senses," she said.

"But . . ."

"Your grandfather needed me then, and . . . I owed it to him."

"Then?"

"Yes, in his . . . sickness."

He still remembered her face then, the expression of dark resignation melting into a look of quiet, eager joy as she had leaned down toward him, then bent to kiss his mouth.

"Besides," she had said a little later—"besides, you hadn't come along just yet."

"And if I had?" he remembered asking. "Come along, I mean. Would that have made a difference?"

A soft, almost dreamy look had come into her eyes, those beautiful, deep, wise, malicious eyes. "Maybe. But I still have you both, you see . . . just as I want you. All to myself."

No, he had never really understood any of it—his grandfather's dark, inscrutable ways, generosity and bitter spite yoked side by side; his mother's blend of responsibility and passion, both nested in a kind of hard, unscrupulous cunning; and always looming in the distance the shadowed figure of his father, who so far as he knew had simply and mysteriously ceased to exist. For all this had been before . . . that afternoon last month.

Yes, when he thought back now upon his childhood, the days of growing up through one war before submerging himself in the next, it was always with a feeling of emptiness, of loss. There was something absent, as though it were not a real life, or part of a life, at all, but a sketchy story, like an ill-remembered movie one had not really liked. Oh, there were the obligatory signposts along the way—the schools, the acquaintances, the trips—but none of it seemed quite real. Reaching for it, trying to grasp it, his hand always came back empty. Or almost empty—for always there were his grandfather's rages, his mother's soft kisses.

And other kisses too, of course; yes, even then. There had always been the girls, then later the women. Always. Strange, but his mother had never opposed it; as he thought of it now, she seemed in a way to have encouraged it, fostered it, even brought it about. And she always wanted to know, to hear him tell it afterward—like a presiding hetaera reviewing the work of a novice. And yet for herself, after that Whittington debacle, no one. Never. Except himself, of course. Always himself.

No, it certainly had not been a "normal" youth, a "normal" growing up—but what, he wondered, really was? It was what he had known, as others had known other things. He should, he supposed, have been confused, disoriented by it—but in the end he was simply bored. And then, as if to save him, had come the war. His war.

And yet his memories of that too remained rather vague. For he had only been nineteen then, when it came. Why he had gone, what had inspired him to appear at that overheated little office one rainy afternoon—yes, he supposed it must have been another argument with Grandfather, for by then there had been so many, so very many.

The old man had never really forgiven him for insisting, upon the final exit of the lugubrious Dr. Whittington, that his name be returned to what it was, had been—and that resentment had increasingly found means of harsh expression as he moved into his teens. For by then—yes, already—the girls had begun to appear. He had no doubt that Grandfather never knew or even suspected his mother's part in it—or surely not all, not half—but even the simple fact had seemed to drive him wild. And so there had been words. And threats. And actions. Very tiresome, the whole thing, often inconvenient as well. Until at last he had had enough, and so had come that rainy afternoon, that ugly, steam-heated office. And he was gone.

The war, what he saw of it, had held little interest for him, but it was a different place to be. Seoul and Pusan, having welcomed warriors many times before, knew just how to do it. Even the lowliest quartermaster (himself, that is) had no difficulty on that particular score. The work itself, confined to drafty warehouses and wharves and depots, was of the dreariest kind, but it was something he could do without thinking, and even on the darkest, most discouraging days he had little difficulty convincing himself that it was preferable to a rain-filled foxhole. The people who had been in those foxholes—and he had seen many of them passing through, on their way out—even the haughtiest of them, not to mention the broken and deranged, had never succeeded in evoking the smallest trace of envy in his heart. In any case, there were so many evenings when one could forget one's doubts and misgivings, as it were.

But then, all at once, there was no more, and in the summer of 1954 he had come victoriously home.

He did remember, and this very clearly, how the notion of entering the Church had come to him. From his dear, beautiful mother, on another of those long afternoons—for they had soon resumed, of course, and yes, just as before.

"Why then don't you enter the priesthood, dear?" she had said. "It would please your grandfather so much, you know."

Yes, he recalled them very clearly, those words—and just the way she had said them. He had been lying on her bed, watching as she brushed out that still-marvelous chestnut hair at the little dressing table. He often helped her with it, brushing that hair—but today, that day, she had been alone at the table. And yes, he remembered her big eyes watching him in the mirror, that little smile.

"You might actually enjoy it," she had said. "You have some gift for scholarship, as I recall, and there are languages and history to be learned. There would be a few years of college first, of course; one or two, I don't know. But then afterward, when you are ordained, opportunities to meet new people. You've always been good with people. Yes, you might just like it—and as I say, your grandfather would be very, *very* pleased."

There was some truth in that, of course, and the idea of going back to school had not been entirely unsympathetic to him, but he certainly had no intention of letting her, at such a moment, get away with such a suggestion scot-free. And so he had said nothing—just watched in the mirror until her gaze, now gravely devoted to the stroking of that lovely shining hair, at last acknowledged the silence with the briefest glance. And she was doomed, she knew it, utterly. He had always been able to do this to her, and this time was not to be an exception. And soon it had come, that first shudder, in spite of all she could do to hold it back. No, she could not take her eyes away then—never had she been able to. And so the rest had followed—that first small giggle, then the next, then "Damn you!" as she, they, began to laugh.

And yet in the end he had done as she said, emerging a little more than five years later, to his grandfather's singular delight, in the stiffest of white collars. There had been little humor, however, little mockery remaining by then, for somewhere along the way, he knew not how, it had seemed to draw him up, then truly catch hold. There was something about it—perhaps as simple as the saying, day after day, of that bare general confession embedded in the Mass. "The remembrance of them is grievous unto us; the burden of them is intolerable." For yes, little by little they had become intolerable, his "manifold sins and wickedness"—and yes, at last he had sought, truly sought to lay that burden on those other, always-willing Shoulders.

His mother, strangely enough, seemed to welcome this metamorphosis, utterly unexpected as it had been. Their afternoons together, of course, were quite different now, but any regrets she may have had on that score were soon swallowed up in the idea of the thing. There was something about his standing before her as a priest, a living symbol of the ancient faith of her fathers, which was more wonderful to her eyes than anything she may have lost in the bargain.

"I shall be fifty-two this year," he remembered her saying wistfully during one of those transformed, platonic afternoons. "Fifty-two years is perhaps enough—to be as I have been." She had cried then, bitterly. Then, together, they had prayed.

As a fall from grace is itself a kind of death, it was somehow appropriate that his should have followed so hard upon an actual death—his grandfather's. He had been out of seminary for more than four years then, was assisting in a large parish north of the city. His work there, which included most of the pastoral responsibilities of the parish, had been widely appreciated, even noticed in high places, and there were already murmurs that he had been marked for bigger things, perhaps even a canonry at the cathedral. He had never quite understood his aptitude for that particular kind of work, but he suspected that it was the complexity of his own past life that made him so effective in addressing the needs of others—the damaged and confused, the weak and the dying. In any case he had enjoyed some success and fulfillment, and the future seemed to promise much more of the same.

In a certain sense, then, his visits to his grandfather—twice a week or more as the end approached—were not unlike countless other visits he had made. In so many other senses, however, they were utterly different. This, after all, was his own grandfather, and whatever his tyrannies and inconsistencies, certainly the dominant male presence in his life. Lacking anyone who could really be called a father, this old man was all he had. Not that that singular lack had ever been something he truly grieved over. No, on this point he was rather of the same mind as Sartre, who was convinced that the presence of a father, bestriding his back like a latter-day Anchises, would only have crushed him, suffocated his spirit. All the same, however, each particular situation had its own particular problems. Sartre's dead father had simply been a passing shadow, of small concern to anyone; his own was a mythic thunderhead, against whom his grandfather's tremulous fist was ever raised in malediction. And he himself, a drop from that cloud, had always shared the curse.

Even so he had tried to understand—meeting fury with patience when he could, with flight when he could not. Grandfather had his reasons—and by then he thought he knew most of them pretty well. At the same time, however, especially these last few years, he had become increasingly troubled by the old man's obduracy, his utter refusal to entertain any notion of forgiveness, even mere acceptance, in his heart. Still, he had kept silent, thinking it was hardly his place to raise the issue—but now, as it became increasingly apparent that the end was drawing near, he at last had determined to act. There had, after all, been other cases in his ministry, similar situations in which he had at least partially succeeded in bringing the previously unregenerate to that final moment with the peace of forgiveness in his soul. It was, he decided, his solemn and holy obligation to seek the same end for his grandfather.

And so he had tried, earnestly he had tried, using everything he had learned in his experience. How he remembered those long afternoons in that darkened bedroom, the old man's eyes like two blazing coals against the pillow. Subtlety, indirection, exhortation, he tried them all, always seeking for some flicker in those eyes, some sign that a different chord had at last begun to resonate behind them. But it had been all in vain. That bitter spirit, mute for almost a year by then, had passed to the other side intact, its enmity inviolate.

Perhaps no other outcome had been possible, who can say, but the fact of his failure in this, or what he considered as such, had weighed more heavily upon him than ever he might have anticipated. He had done his best, but his best had not been good enough—and something, it was difficult to say just what, had seemed to give way within him. Driving back after the funeral on that rainy December day, he had begun to doubt.

But no, that was not all. For there had come that other feeling too, the feeling that something had . . . dropped away. And all at once it was as if something within him that had been disabled, short-circuited, had stealthily clicked on again once more.

The following week, to the astonishment and wild delight of the parish secretary, he had clumsily seduced her in the sacristy, among the chasubles and robes.

His mother's reaction to her father's death had been quite different. If anything she seemed even graver, even more preoccupied than she had increasingly become over the past few years. Even his suggestions, by indirection to be sure, that his own convictions had begun to waver had little effect upon her. Her mind was elsewhere, far away.

"Perhaps you just need a vacation," he remembered her saying one afternoon, absently probing at the fish the waiter had brought. "You're overtired, I can tell."

And so, yes, he had taken a month's vacation, to the Bahamas. An unremitting orgy of delight. And he had returned, convinced now of the course he was going to take.

This time, however, there had indeed been a change in her. From the first moment, not five minutes after he had paid the airport cab, he had been able to see it clearly, acutely. And then that first half question, half command as she had led him by the hand to that little frilly parlor adjoining her bedroom. The sly look he had almost forgotten. "Now, my Martin, you must tell me all about it. Don't leave out a thing now—you know very well what I mean. I want to know it all, just how it was."

Yes, something had happened, there could be no doubt of that. Yet to this day he could not begin to say just what it was. All he knew was that they were again . . . as they had been.

The winding up of his affairs took some time, of course. But at last it was over, those lugubrious seances with well-meaning, understanding clerics, the tearful good-byes, the wringing of hands. At last, again, he was free—as he was meant to be.

It was good to get back again to the big house on Jackson Street. He had missed the city more than he knew, and now there seemed to be something added as well. He did not know quite how to put it—a kind of expectation in the air, perhaps, a feeling that something significant was afoot. Perhaps it was only that dirty war, but there was a vague restlessness, especially among the young people—an impatience with things as they were, had been. Those student demonstrations in Berkeley last fall had been the beginning, at least so far as his own awareness was concerned, and now . . . He sometimes went in the afternoon to that little district over by the park, along Haight Street; there, it seemed to him, he felt it strongest, this new thing—but really it was everywhere. New music, new ways of thinking about values, about drugs, about sex. You've had your way too long, they seemed to be saying, and where has it gotten us? Now we'll try our own way.

His mother did not approve. He had mentioned an experience the previous day, when he had joined some people under a tree in the park, his first taste of marijuana. "In the first place," she had said, "those people are dirty. I don't like that, all that greasy hair. Like animals, that's all. And then all those drugs, LST, whatever you call it. And I'll thank you just to keep them to yourself in future, those seamy little dope-fiend escapades of yours. You have no business getting mixed up in that sort of thing."

Even the other aspects of the matter, those that might have been expected to interest her, in this case did not. She had her standards, his mother, and all this just did not measure up. "It's the same thing," she had said. "Like animals coupling in the woods. Not my cup of tea, I'm afraid, thank you very much."

No, not her cup of tea. Nor, really, was it his. There had been a few encounters here and there, but on the whole he had found them unsatisfying. There was something too matter-of-fact about it, something assumed, foregone, an ethic he didn't quite understand. No, not really his cup of tea at all.

And yet the whole phenomenon, the whole "movement" as they called it, continued to interest, even fascinate him. Perhaps it was simply the assumption, the given, that they did not have to play by the same rules that had applied to the world for so long—the rules of power, influence, wealth. It was quite remarkable when you thought about it. It was something he wanted to watch unfold.

But his mother, it seemed, had other ideas, other plans for him just then . . .

It had been unseasonably hot in the city, that April day. They had been to the museum in the morning—not the one in the park, which she considered common, but the Legion of Honor, perched on that headland above the Golden Gate. She had always liked this place, had taken him here when he was but a child to see the French pictures she so loved. But even her two favorites, the Renoir and the Greuze, had not really held her that day. She seemed preoccupied—and of course she had never liked the heat. And so after a light lunch they had returned home, opening the windows on the promise of evening fog. Then, taking her tea, she had retired to her bedroom for a nap, asking him to come and wake her as she often did.

He remembered going out into the garden, reading the new Durrell in the chair beside the fishpond, under the plum tree. He remembered nodding off for an hour, awakened by the cold. The fog was in already, swirling about the eaves. He had gone in.

"Oh, so late," she had murmured when he came, sitting down on the bed beside her. "Look, it's almost five."

He had told her about nodding off.

"And cold too. Do go shut that window."

He had done so, then stood looking out, watching the fog move through the rooftops.

"Come here," she had said after a moment. "I want to talk to you." The sea-green eyes, softened with sleep . . .

"Stop that, now. I'm serious. I have something important to say. Sit down and behave."

Something important to say. And so she had.

"I've not been completely frank with you about your father."

For almost an hour then he had sat and listened, moving after a few minutes to the low chair beside the window. The low, droning sound of her voice telling it, the wind in the trees . . .

"And so you see he's been there all along. All these years. I couldn't tell you. And Father cooperated too, for his own reasons, I suppose. I was terrified, you see, that you'd go to him—and leave me alone. And so I couldn't. I didn't. I'm sorry. But now . . . it's different. I know I'll never lose you, not now. And so . . ."

She knew everything about him—all, it seemed, there was to know. For she had a friend, a schoolmate, who still wrote to her. A friend of forty years who knew, had always known, all there was to know.

"Do you despise me?" she had said at last, when it was done. He had only smiled, for they both knew that could not be so.

"Well, are you disappointed in me, then? What do you think about all this?"

"I think it's interesting," he had said, still smiling.

"Only that?"

"Only that. I'm sorry, Mother."

"Hah! Now *you're* sorry! Really, we're quite a pair."

"Yes, quite a pair."

He had watched then as she smoothed her comforter, those white, still-lovely hands stroking the cover. Her pale forehead gathered in thought.

"Well," she had said at last. "I think you should go anyway, just to see him, what he's like."

"Go . . . out there?"

"Of course," she had said then, her eyes suddenly flashing, alive. "It isn't as bad as all that, you know. It's quite nice, actually—mountains, horses to ride. You do like to ride—don't tell me you don't."

"All right," he had said, grinning impudently at her. "I won't."

"And anyway . . . I *order* you to go. You should see your father. It's only right."

"If you say so."

"Besides, it will be interesting, you'll see. And one thing more."

"Yes?"

"The daughter should soon be there, home from school. Edna says she's a lovely girl—quite pretty."

"You don't say."

"I *do* say."

"You do say."

"Yes—and so that's settled."

For a moment then she had closed her eyes, that lovely, re-markable face utterly calm now, speaking vast relief. He, keep-ing silent, had watched until the eyes, very slowly, reopened.

"Come over here beside me now, you saucy boy. I still feel a little chill."

CHAPTER 3

1

The pickup lurched up the rocky track, low gear grinding querulously between them. Boulders exposed by the winter littered the way, and when it was not possible to avoid them the old truck's frame groaned, a ship's timbers in heavy weather, as they passed slowly over.

"Do you think we'll make it?" Martin said. "Can't say I've ever been on a road quite like this before."

"Oh, we'll make it all right, one way or the other." John glanced over at the rigid figure, hands tensed on thighs. "You should have seen it when I came up the first time, end of April. I had to get out half a dozen times with the pick and shovel. And then a couple weeks ago, after that cloudburst when you came— only once or twice then. But there hasn't been that much since. Should be okay today."

"If you say so," Martin murmured, looking out the dust-streaked window.

They continued on in silence, the dusty sage on either side seeming to part before them. Now and then a lone jackrabbit, solemnly marking the languor of their progress, moved out to lope before them up the way, then skittered off into the brush. At last, creeping up through a stand of low, gnarled cedars, they reached the top. Just below them and to the right, behind its dam of earth, the little reservoir shimmered in the late afternoon sun. John stopped the truck and turned off the engine.

"That's it?" Martin said.

"That's it."

"And where's the spring, the one that feeds it?"

"There," John said pointing up the gentle slope—"beyond that jumble of boulders."

"Anything to see?"

"Not really—and we should be getting back."

Martin sighed, folding his hands on his lap. "Well, what do you think?" he said after a moment. "About what you expected?"

"About. A little lower than I'd hoped, maybe. It'll be okay though—for this year."

"I should hope so," Martin said. "Dad's really counting on it. The hay, I mean."

John turned to look at him—the smooth, well-shaped features, the mass of thick black hair, the pale eyes trained in seeming interest on the gleaming surface of the little pond. But he said nothing.

"Just what do you think of the old man lately?" Martin said after a moment, turning to face him. "Sure seems to have perked up. That trip to town last week to pick up her car, then going in again for her today. Other things too, drinking a little less maybe . . . I don't know—just seems . . . happier."

"It's you," John said.

Martin looked surprised, but he didn't protest. "Yes, maybe so. Could be."

"He's been thinking, stewing over you for thirty years, and now . . . he seems to like what he sees. No, I've never seen him like this before—and now with Deirdre coming . . ."

"I suppose you're right," Martin sighed. "Having both of us here and all."

"I'm right," John said.

Again they were silent for several minutes, John watching a hawk working the ridge.

"But what do *you* think about it?" Martin said at last. "All this change, upheaval."

"I like to see him happy," John said.

"Sure," Martin murmured, "but still . . ."

"And what do you think Deirdre will think?" he went on after a moment. "She knows about me now, I suppose."

John nodded.

"Well?"

"She'll like you," John said simply.

"I hope so," Martin said smiling. "I like her already."

They had talked about Deirdre before, he and Martin. Somehow it made him uncomfortable, though he couldn't really say why. Martin himself, he was sure, had a good deal to do with it, but even before he came John had begun to feel a strange fretfulness whenever he thought about her. Part of it, he knew, was simple anxiety, fear that now, coming back, she would see him as he really was. And then there were those new things she had begun to talk of now—things he knew nothing about and could not hope to understand. Kinsella often read him her letters, or parts of them, and this passion of hers for "civil rights" as she called it was simply confusing to him. Yes, he remembered Booker, but no one had had more rights than Booker. In any case he had a hard time understanding it all—what the fuss was about. But she understood—and Martin did too, as he had quickly learned. Martin understood.

"I think it's marvelous, don't you? And going down there at Easter—that took real guts. They're animals down there, those Bull Connors types. Lucky she made it back alive."

Yes, he knew she had changed. It was perfectly natural for a girl that age to change. And yet in spite of the changes there was still that one thing they shared, she and he. She continued to speak of it in her letters to Kinsella—and the packages had not stopped coming.

John looked at his watch—then, one last time, at the hawk on the ridge. "Well, better head back," he said. "Train was due at four, and they can't take more than two hours—even the way your father drives."

"Yes, isn't that something?" Martin laughed. His white teeth shone in the sun. "The other day when I went with him to Chokecherry in the Model A—thought we'd never get there."

John smiled and started the engine, then turned the truck about. Slowly they headed down.

The new white Mustang, washed and waxed the day before, stood gleaming beside the picket fence. Beyond, across the ragged yard, three figures stood together talking in the garden, a riot of daffodils about them.

"Train must have been early," Martin said.

John, nodding, parked beside the bunkhouse. Side by side they walked toward the house.

"Ah, there you both are," Kinsella said, looking up as they crossed the yard. "Where the hell have you been?"

"Reservoir," John said. "Didn't expect you this early."

"Didn't expect myself this early," Kinsella smiled. "She drove, of course, just to show me. It's her car, after all, but Lord, you'd think she was trying out for Indy or something."

"I'll start some coffee," Maria said. With a quick glance up at John, she passed through the little gate.

There was a brief, uneasy silence before Kinsella spoke. "Well," he said at last, "I guess some introductions are in order."

"Not really," Martin said. Taking a step forward, he held out his hand. Deirdre, hair drawn back over her ears, flushed slightly—then smiled shyly as she took it.

"Hello, sister," Martin said softly. "At last."

"Hello, brother." The words seemed whispered, like soft wind.

"Well," Kinsella said after a moment, "you'll get to know one another soon enough. How about John, honey? John's here too." Deirdre lowered her hand, glancing up at her father.

"Silly," she said pettishly. "I know John's here too." Stepping across to him, she grasped his arm tightly, then kissed him on the cheek.

"Hi, John," she said. "Are we all ready?"

"Ready," he murmured, feeling the blood rise to his face.

"Come on now," Kinsella said smiling. "Don't pick on him. Let's go have some coffee. But first—well never mind, I've got something else too. For the occasion."

"I'll bring in her bags," John said, turning.

"Like hell you will," Kinsella said. "Martin can do that later. Come on."

"Ever tried Dom Perignon?" the old man was saying to Martin as, Deirdre on his arm, he walked toward the house.

2

The morning sun was warm, unusually so for this time of year. As they parked the truck beside the little bridge they could see tall, dark thunderheads massing over the low hills to the northeast. There would be rain before the day was out.

"I'll take the big one," Martin said to him. "You lead the way."

"No," Deirdre said. "I want to go first—to get there, be up there all alone. Is that all right, John?" she asked, turning her eyes up to him.

"Sure," he said. "We'll just come along behind. But don't go down, not 'til we get there."

"Still worrying about me?" she said mockingly.

"Yes," he said. "I am."

Deirdre sniffed and tossed her head—long, bright hair shining in the sun. Then, turning, she started quickly up the trail.

Soon she was out of sight. The two men, tall packs weighing down their shoulders, moved slowly along beside the old creekbed.

"Do you want to lead?" Martin said after some distance.

"No," John said. "You'll see the way."

Soon, passing the narrow trail up to the ridge, they reached the little meadow clearing. The grass was already yellowed now, and the willows and birches along the empty creekbed, strewn with cotton from the two great trees beyond, seemed braced for a long, difficult season. Still, it was a logical place to stop and rest for a moment, leaning their packs against the tree trunks.

"May I ask you a question?" Martin said suddenly. "A little personal perhaps, but . . . well, you don't have to answer."

"Sure," John said warily. "Whatever you like."

"Well, I've been here almost a month now, and we've spent a good deal of time kicking about, you and me—on the horses, in the truck, you know. And yet this place, where we're going today, you've never even let on that it existed, not once. Why if Dee hadn't mentioned it the other day . . . Just seems a little odd, that's all."

"Maybe so," John said quietly. "I just hadn't thought about it."

Martin smiled—his patient, weary smile. "Okay. Maybe so. Just thought I'd ask. I don't want to horn in on anything, that's all."

"You're not," John said. "And since you seem to know something about this sort of thing . . ."

"Not that much, really," Martin said. "But anyway . . . let's go."

The lie lingering on his tongue, John straightened his pack and followed. Yes, it had been foolish of him, he supposed. It was inevitable from the first that Martin would find out—and yet he had not been able to help himself. The longer Martin stayed, the more he had felt things slipping away—until sometimes only this seemed left to him. And so he had guarded it, hedged it about in silence like a packrat hoarding a chip of mirror. But then, of course, the inevitable had occurred. Yes, a foolish performance, no doubt of that.

Yet perhaps he was to be forgiven—it had been so very difficult for him, this time, these days. Especially these last, dread-
ful days. How, he wondered, had he ever been able to persuade
himself that it could be otherwise—that he could sit at the elbow
of kings, even marry their only daughters? He was ashamed.

It was their talk that had made it clear to him—gradually, bit
by bit, brought him back to what he was. Oh yes, he had heard
plenty of high-flown talk before—the talk of Kinsella, creating
himself. But somehow that world, Kinsella's world, had seemed
a part of his own, something he could assimilate into his own
spirit. The world that now emerged, however—that took shape
out of this new talk—was entirely different, beyond him, alien.
How, he wondered, could Kinsella himself have come to know
it too? The newspapers, he supposed—but John too read the
newspapers now and then. No, it was something else. A recep-
tivity, a congruence. Something. Yes, even when they disagreed
among themselves—as so often they did, Kinsella digging in his
heels—even then there was a kind of agreement between them,
a common language he could not, would never be able to speak.

It was Martin, of course, who had brought all this about.
Without him they would be as they had been—he and Kinsella,
he and Deirdre. Or almost. For Deirdre too was somehow different. Could it be only six months since they had come here,
that snowy Christmas Eve? It seemed so much longer, especially
when he looked into her face. More beautiful than ever, he supposed—knew—but there was something else as well, a kind of
. . . worldly wisdom. And even beyond that there was something—a kind of hunger, maybe, he couldn't really say. He had
no way of understanding such things. No, he thought, he never
would. And so in the end, he knew not how, even Deirdre's
interest in this place had become a burden, a drop of acid on his
heart. This, at least, he had at last come to feel, should be his
own. And yet now it too was not.

They passed over the low saddle and headed down, the cup
of the spring now utterly empty, overgrown with down-covered
weeds. Deirdre was nowhere to be seen.

"That the old spring you two were talking about?"

John nodded, feeling a renewed surge of irritation.

"How long's it been that way?"

"Not long. Less than a year."

Martin smiled wanly. "Looks like it never was," he said. They started up the rock-lined trail.

The door was wide open, but she was not inside. John went quickly to the back of the chamber—but the steel chain-link ladder was still folded by the opening. He went back outside, where Martin was waiting.

"Quite a view from here," Martin said, shielding his eyes from the sun. "Did she go down?"

"No," John said. "I don't know where she is."

"I'm here," a cracked, hesitant voice said. Together they looked up.

About twenty feet up the hillside, among the rocks beside the old opening, Deirdre sat looking out across the valley.

"Are you all right?" John said. He could tell she had been crying.

"Yes," she said. "All right. You get set up. I'll be down . . . in a minute."

"Are you sure?" John asked.

"Yes, John, I'm quite sure," she said curtly, and turned away.

Stung, he returned inside. In a few moments Martin joined him, laying out the gear on the bench.

"Something wrong with her?" Martin said after a moment.

"I don't know," John replied. He did not look up. "Sometimes she . . . well, she'll be down soon." They went on emptying the packs, then began to make up the bundle to be lowered below.

"Not done yet?" Deirdre said brightly, appearing in the doorway. "What've you guys been doing?"

John looked up, but her eyes seemed directed beyond him, toward her . . . brother. It was difficult to say just what was in that glance—beyond the fact that it had emerged from tears, and that it was wholly new. A kind of resignation, perhaps, a kind of consent; he could not really say. But then, all at once, it was gone, replaced by a bright, open smile. Lowering his eyes he answered softly: "Just be a few minutes."

"Good," she said. "Let's get to it. Anything left for me to do?"

Soon the bundle—ropes, lights, ratchets, pitons, the small descending packs—was complete, and they took it to the opening. When it was safely resting on the platform below, they donned their headlamps and followed, hand over hand down the long chain-link ladder.

"There's a gorgeous chamber over there—lovely formations, dripping pools," Deirdre said, pointing with her headlamp toward the dark mouth. She turned to John. "Do we have time for him to see it?"

"Another day," Martin said. "I've seen a few things like that before, and there's no telling how long this is going to take." He pointed across the chamber. "Is that the opening, where we go?"

He had told them of two other cave descents he had made, along with a group of young people in his parish—"spelunkers," he called them.

"That's it," Deirdre said, the excitement beginning to show in her eyes. "Watch now—and listen." Reaching into her pocket, she took out a dark stone.

"You see," she said to John—"I brought my own this time."

She threw it across, into the opening. Together they listened to the long clatter . . . then the distant splash.

"Let's go," Martin said. "This could be interesting."

It was fortunate indeed that Kinsella had no knowledge of what they were doing. Given his feelings about the cave in general, and the nature of this project in particular, it had been necessary to conceal the scheme from him entirely, hoping for a day when he might be away. When the preceding night at supper he at last announced an intention to go into town alone, the decision had been made on the spot, even Maria not to be told until they were ready to set out. Now, following the others down the steep, rocky chute they had entered, John—knowing as he did so that other, more pressing concerns should have occupied his mind—unaccountably found himself again thinking of the old man.

Yes, he seemed very happy now, far happier than John had ever thought possible. This summer, his two children here together, had taken him utterly by surprise, and his reaction had perhaps been predictable. Still, the magnitude of the change had been difficult to adjust to. Those solitary nocturnal meetings, so long the very essence, the juice of their own being together, were wholly gone now, never even hinted at—displaced by other, more lively gatherings and discussions. He was always invited, of course—expected at supper, encouraged afterward—but he was always glad when he could gracefully excuse himself and return to his familiar room. It was all so very different, so foreign to him. And yet Kinsella was happy, blissfully happy. That, he had decided, must be enough to make it all worthwhile.

They had descended well over a hundred yards now, Martin confidently, boldly leading the way. It was by no means perpendicular, but the angle of descent was well over forty-five degrees, and the nylon support line, although not absolutely necessary at this point, was a welcome comfort as it slipped through his hands. Now and then he noticed other passages branching off— in one of them a suggestion of bat activity, in another a hint of gleaming limestone—but never did he stop any longer than it took to direct his light that way, perhaps probing about just a bit. Still he made a mental note—for other days. Yes, he thought, there would be other days—when Deirdre had returned to her school, when Martin at last grew weary of his rustic holiday. But for now there was only this—the dark, dry rocks looming overhead, the hard, scaly surface underfoot, and now and then the sound of a few muffled words beneath him.

They had moved ahead a good distance. Now and then he could see their lights, the fleeting illumination of rocks far below, but for the most part they stayed beyond him—leaving him quite alone. He found himself savoring the feeling, for a

moment imagining that only he was here, as it had been before
. . . as it was meant to be. Recognizing the thought, however,
he shook it off and resolved to move more quickly.

It seemed a good deal steeper here, but still he found no need
to use the line directly. Always there were footholds, always
somewhere for his hands. He liked the cool feel of the rock
under his fingers—more than that, sensed a kind of kinship
with it. Yes, he thought, they were in many ways the same, he
and the rock. He hurried on.

Perhaps fifteen minutes had passed before he stopped. Suddenly, from far below, he thought he heard a voice—then realized it was Deirdre, calling his name. He listened again, waiting—and yes, it came again, from far, far down in the darkness.

"John! John! Come quickly!"

He called an answer, then waited for the reply. None came—
and then he was moving, scrambling down over the jumble of
stones. He felt the blood pounding in his temples, the scrape of
rock upon his fingers as he slipped, then caught himself on a
crumbling ledge. And still the calling came.

"John! John! Oh hurry!" He set out again.

Until at last it seemed much nearer and he stopped. Yes, he
could see them below now, their lights, moving in wide sweeping arcs across the rocky walls of what seemed a larger space,
a chamber. He returned the call, then saw the lights, moving
together, sweep upward over the rocks toward him.

"Listen, John! Be very quiet and listen."

"Are you all right?"

"Yes, fine. Both of us. Now listen, just be quiet and listen!"

And at last he listened, holding his breath, still feeling the
thump of his heart behind his sweaty temples.

It was water, moving water.

And he listened, greedily he listened.

"Are you there?" he called. "I hear it."

"No, it's a little further yet. But hurry down now. We'll
wait—then we can all go on together."

"Yes!" he called eagerly—and "Together," he whispered to himself as, his heart swelling with sudden inspiration, sudden, unexpected belief, he started down again.

Afterward, as he lay in the dark, waiting, he tried to remember just how it had happened. A missed foothold, he supposed, but then he had been sliding, scraping down the face of a huge rock, the size of a boxcar it seemed, his fingernails splintering as he sought to catch himself, slow himself, and then . . . letting go. The fall had been a short one, no more than six feet surely— but then the feeling of his ankle being caught beneath him, the popping sound, the giving way. He had lain in the darkness breathing, his shattered headlamp somewhere, and listened to them coming, the pain swelling like an inkblot.

"What was the hurry?" Martin was saying. "He would have got here eventually, and now . . ."

"Oh shut up, will you?" Deirdre's voice said, and then they were there. Bringing him down to this cold, rocky floor.

"Oh John, why did you have to do this?" Deirdre was saying then. "We were going to go together, you and I, and now . . ." Together.

"Well, let's pack him up," Martin was saying then. "There's no way to get him the rest of the way now, not down that damned hole, and no way to get him back up even if we could. From here . . . well, I think I can make it with him. He can't weigh that much. But we'd better get started."

"But no," he was saying then, he himself. "You go on down, the two of you. You can tell me how it was. For me . . . there'll be another time."

"But John . . . ," Deirdre was saying.

"Go on. I'll be all right."

And in the end they had gone, hand over hand, lowering themselves into that dark void, their lights gradually fading as they descended. And then only darkness—and the sound of the moving water, far, far below.

Perhaps he slept. He had no way of knowing. After the first half hour or so it was difficult to be really certain whether he was awake or not. The ankle, no longer throbbing, had settled into a low, steady ache. The blanket they had wrapped around it seemed to help. And the flask of whiskey he had brought, that seemed to help as well. He lay back against the rocks, cradling his head in a niche that seemed made just for that. Yes, it was a great joy to be here, alone, benighted, even as he was— even as he thought of what they, below, were claiming as their own, even as he dreamed, thought, he knew not what, imagined should be his alone. Alone . . .

A distant murmur awakened, alerted him. The rising, intermittent glow of their lights, moving upward. He raised his head and listened, listened. There was the music of the water, moving, flowing, far away; then nearer, the crunch of their booted feet on the rocks; then, as they drew ever nearer, rising up to him, the faint but clear sound of their voices.

"Let's just not talk about it anymore, okay?" she was saying.

"Don't give me that stuff, not now. A little beyond that by now, aren't we? So why not just admit it, at least to yourself?"

"Just shut up now. We're not quite alone, you know."

"Not quite . . . What? Him, you mean?"

"Shut up."

He listened to his blood, the crunch of their boots on the rocks. He watched the rising light.

3

"Seems fine to me," the doctor said, rapping on the plaster with his knuckle. "Itches like hell, I know, but that can't be helped. Set up an appointment with Yvonne for—what is it now?"

"The eighth," John said.

"Around the eighth of August, then, okay? A month. Then we'll get that thing off you."

He went out into the lobby and spoke briefly with the nurse, then started down the dark staircase, one step at a time. The thumping echoed against the flyspecked walls.

The light reflected off the sidewalk was stunningly bright. He stood for a moment outside the doorway, allowing his eyes to adjust, before he stepped off the curb and started across the street. The little white car, parked under a soaring maple, looked cool and inviting.

They seemed to have been talking, but now, seeing his approach, they stopped. Martin, at the wheel, looked vaguely out at him; Deirdre seemed to have turned, to be looking up the green, shady hillside toward the courthouse on the hill.

"Well, Crip," Martin said with that sudden smile. "Are you going to make it?"

"He seemed to think so," John said, and passed around the back of the car.

By the time he reached the other side Deirdre had already slipped into the back, leaving the door open for him. He stepped inside, easing the cast up and in.

"Do you mind making a stop before we head back?" he said.

"No, I guess not," Martin said. "Forget something at the store?"

"No," he said. "There's somebody'd like to meet you."

"Me?" Martin said, raising his narrow eyebrows.

"Both of you. She'd like to meet you both. Old friend of your father's. Just take a minute."

He felt Deirdre looking at him, her glance cool on his cheek.

"Sure," Martin shrugged. "Okay with you, Dee?"

"Sure," he heard her say softly behind him.

"Well then, lead on, Macduff," Martin said, starting the engine.

They turned at the next corner and mounted the hill, the fluffy down from the cottonwoods like drifted snow against the fenceposts. The gray stone church loomed up in their way.

"To the right here," John said just as they reached it. They turned.

"Hey, was that an Episcopal church? I thought I saw the little sign as we went by."

"Yes," John said. "It is."

"Well I'll be. Last thing I expected to run into out here." They continued on down the street.

"About three blocks," John said. "I'll show you where."

They stopped beside the picket fence. Suzanne was in the garden, a big straw hat on her head. Recognizing neither the car nor the driver, she stood blinking in the sun.

"Wait here a second," John said, opening the door, and stumped down to the pavement.

"It's only me," he said, going to the fence.

"Yes, so it is," the old woman said. "But what's that thing on your leg?"

"Little accident," he said, smiling.

"And that shiny new car?"

"Deirdre's," he said. "Present from her father." Then, after a brief hesitation: "I brought them."

"Yes," she said softly. "So I see." She paused a moment, her hands trembling slightly, before she said: "Well, bring them in." Without looking again at the car, she started up the stairs.

After a few minutes they had begun to speak in French. Martin, who seemed to have spent a good deal of time there too, was quite fluent, and his accent was surprisingly good. Even Deirdre, with only her high school classes and a year in college, seemed determined to hold her own. And so they spoke in French.

John, sitting on a chair in the corner, the plastered ankle stretched out before him, had watched in silence. Martin, although having little idea and apparently less curiosity about just who this old woman might be, had seemed to delight in the interchange, regaling her with stories of his visits, the people he had met, and asking her about her own early years there. Deirdre, for her part, seemed lively and interested as well—the first time he had really seen her so in weeks. A vague somberness, almost a kind of resentment, had settled over her lately—but now that too, at least for the moment, seemed to have dispersed. She chattered like a girl, blushing at her mistakes but pushing on. He watched her, as he always watched her.

"John?" Suzanne was saying to them—"don't worry about him. He speaks a droll kind of gobbling talk anyway. I can hardly understand him myself. It's just as well that he stays quiet in his corner over there, the poor cripple. Don't you agree, John?"

"Yes."

"There. Don't you see? He's incorrigible."

It was difficult to know just what she made of them. At least the one thing he had feared most—an emotional scene complete with revelations and confessions—had not yet occurred, and from the look of things was not about to. Suzanne seemed remarkably calm and composed, amusing them with her wit and little stories, apparently reveling in the anonymity his reticence had provided her. Yes, today, for the moment, she was no more than that—a sweet little old French lady who had known their father. Martin and Deirdre, their relief and delight apparent on their faces, were appropriately charmed.

"And do have a little more coffee, both of you. And cookies too—I have lots more. And if you would prefer something a little stronger, Martin . . ." She winked.

"No, thank you. The coffee is just right. But do go on. You say the gendarmes were right around the corner?"

Yes, it had been much better than he ever expected. Indeed the only awkward moment, if even it could be called such, soon passed away without a ripple. Still, he wondered what had possessed her to bring it up.

It was just as they were leaving, rising from the table.

"John tells me that you are in the church—or perhaps only were?"

It was said in English, the first that had been spoken for nearly an hour, and the effect of the change of language was startling. Standing just opposite her, John had seen the familiar shadow of malice gathering in her dark eyes.

"Yes," Martin said, glancing quickly at John. "I was, but no longer."

"No, I don't suppose it's for everyone, the religious life. The demands it makes—on your spirit. But do you miss it sometimes, that sense of . . . commitment, I suppose you'd say?" The shadow lingered, darkened.

"Yes, sometimes," Martin said uncomfortably—then seemed to right himself.

"Are you a religious person yourself, *madame?*"

"Yes, I am," the old woman said, looking steadily, even defiantly into those disingenuous hazel eyes. "I was not always so, but now . . . Yes, I am a very religious person." She turned and led them to the door.

Yes, and that was all. They had descended together to the garden—Suzanne, her charm and straw hat restored, proudly showing off her flowers—and then they had taken their leave.

But no, not quite all. For there had been that puzzling last word too—when he had stopped for a moment with her while the other two walked to the car. It was simply said, with only the slightest trace of sadness about those dark, deep eyes.

"Oh, you poor, poor men," she had said, squeezing his hand. Then, without another word, she turned back to her flowers.

4

He hobbled across the yard and closed the gate, then headed slowly up the road. It was still quite warm, even at this late hour. The dark outline of the empty old bunkhouse, its front porch half collapsed now by neglect and winter snows, hulked off to his left, while up ahead the dipping shapes of bats could still be seen about the barn eaves. He watched their tumbling forms in the thin moonlight and tried to empty his mind.

It had been too much, this day. The trip with them, then Suzanne, then . . . all this. Yes, too much. He longed for his bed and prayed for sleep.

Passing the corrals and the dark tackroom, he pushed open his door and went inside. From the far wall the dim form of Lindbergh looked calmly out at him. He went over to it, pushed aside the wineskin hanging over one corner, and gazed intently at the young, confident face for a moment before, turning again, he went to the cupboard beneath the sink and took out a green gallon jug. Filling a glass, he went to the bed and sank down on the edge. His eyes were dark and tired, his expression utterly empty.

Yes, too much. He had tried to excuse himself from supper, pleading discomfort in his leg, but Kinsella had insisted, saying he had something important to tell them all. And so he had remained, helping Maria in the kitchen while they talked in the library, then going in to call them when it was ready.

They had been talking of Suzanne, of course. He had warned Kinsella beforehand of her wish to see them, and although the old man had offered no outright objection, it was plain that he was not at all comfortable with the idea. Now, however, satisfied that nothing untoward had been revealed, he seemed content, even pleased that they had met her.

"I'm glad you took them," he had said to John, drawing him aside as they proceeded to the table. "It's important for them now to know. But not too quickly, not all at once. Yes, this was a good beginning. Later . . . Well, we'll talk more of that, you and I. Come on along now."

And so it had gone, the old man radiating that aura of goodwill and contentedness which had so recently and unexpectedly become a part of his persona. The food was good, the wine was good, the talk was good, and judging from Kinsella's eyes, moving eagerly from one young face to the other, life was almost good as well. Until at last, the dishes cleared, the coffee and cognac on the table before them, it seemed the time had come for him to say what was on his mind.

"I didn't want to bother you about this right away," the old man had begun. "But now, I think it's time you knew. It has to do with this place, with both of you. It has to do with all of us here."

Sitting at the other end of the table, John had watched their faces—Deirdre vaguely glancing up, spoon arrested in midair above her coffee; Martin with that gentle, understanding smile he so often wore at table; and Kinsella himself, the pale blue eyes alight with anticipation.

"The place isn't what it once was," the old man had continued—"especially now with the water. But it's something; it'll always be something. And this house . . . well, it'll do—for this godforsaken country at least."

It was at that moment that he first had sensed it—where Kinsella was headed. With a sick, sinking feeling, he knew he did not want to be here. And yet there was no way to escape.

Kinsella lifted the glass of cognac to his lips, then went on.

"For a long time, when we were alone here, I thought that when I passed on it would all go to Deirdre—and that she, having discovered that there was a world outside, would simply sell it for a good price and go her way. I didn't mind. I'd had my time here—it was enough."

John, twisting in his chair, looked longingly out the window. A thin crescent moon had risen over the mountain.

"And then a few things happened that kind of set me thinking. One was last Christmas, when Deirdre came home for a few days. You seemed so happy then, honey, surprised that you liked it here so well after all. I could see it in your eyes, the way you were, the way you'd look when you came in from a long ride with John."

Quickly then, Kinsella had looked over at him, then just as quickly away. There had been a meaning in that glance, John sensed, but it eluded him in the swiftness of the moment. Was he to be spared—or was he to be put forward, proposed? He did not know.

"And then, of course, Martin, there was your coming—out of the blue. How I felt then, well I needn't go into that just now. But soon enough I could see . . . could see you were . . . my son." The old man's voice cracked, and he looked down at his glass a moment before he added: "Mine too."

Martin, his expression grown sober now, looked gravely, compassionately into his father's face as the old man lifted the glass, took a sip, and lowered it once more to the table. After a long silence, without raising his eyes, he began again. "Now, there's no way I can impose any of this on you, of course. And when I'm gone . . . well you'll do what you think best. But don't think I haven't noticed how the two of you get on—the . . . affection you have for one another. The way you talk, the way you just go off by yourselves sometimes. Yes, a lot of catching up to do, a lot of getting acquainted. It amazes me though—to think you never met until a month ago, and yet already . . . And it warms my old heart too, I can tell you, like a gift I never dreamed might come." He paused for a moment, clearing his throat, then hurried on. "And so if my own hopes, my own dreams, might count for anything . . . maybe someday you'd think about living here, the both of you. With me, if I'm still around. If not, well . . . It's a big house, you know, plenty big enough for two families to start with, and if you ever outgrew it, well, there's lots of room to build another. And who knows, springs have been known to come back too. It wouldn't be the first time. No, hardly the first time. Even without it there's plenty of water for necessities, all we'd ever need. And then there's wells, too, we haven't even tried that." He had been rushing, plunging on, the words tumbling from him in a way that John had rarely—no, never—seen before, but now he drew up suddenly. Again he coughed, clearing his throat, before he at last looked up, from one face to the other.

"Well, what do you think?"

Martin shifted uncomfortably in his chair, but the sober expression had not left his face. "I don't know," he said. "I'm kind of a city boy, really, but that could change, I suppose. I don't know. As for a family," he added, smiling, "I certainly don't have anything like that in mind right now."

"No, no, of course not," Kinsella rumbled. "This is just for the future. We're talking of the future. For now you have your career to sort out, Deirdre has her school. But then when that's done . . . who knows?"

"Yes," Martin said weakly. "Who knows?"

Kinsella had turned away then, looking vaguely out the window toward the western mountains. There was long, breathless pause before at last he went on.

"And as for family," he said gravely, "that'll take care of itself. That's the sort of thing you have to make your own choices on, out of your own world." He paused, then swallowed before he added: "But John will be here, honey. He'll always be right here."

Now the silence was complete. John, feeling a numbness pass through his body, looked only at Deirdre's face, paling now—the sudden, swift blinking of her eyes.

"What's that supposed to mean, Daddy?" she said at last, very softly.

"Mean? Doesn't mean anything," he barked, getting up. He walked to the hallway. "Maria!" he shouted. "How about a little more coffee in here?"

When he turned again to sit down his face was flushed, haggard. "All I'm trying to say is I've changed my will—so you both will get this place, together. All I'm doing is expressing a few things, a few thoughts I've had for the future. Anything wrong with that?"

"No, Daddy," Deirdre said. "Nothing."

"Good. Now the rest of it—there are a few other things too, a little money—all that will go mostly to you. Martin, I figure, was pretty well taken care of by his grandfather. That right?"

Martin nodded glumly.

Kinsella, with a violent movement, pushed his chair back from the table.

"Well, can't say that either of you seems too damn happy about it."

Deirdre sighed—a long, hopeless sigh. And then the telephone had begun to ring.

Sitting on his bed, the untouched glass of wine in his hand, John remembered the rest as if it had been a dream. The whispering of Maria's footsteps down the hall. The bewildered, wounded look on the old man's face as, vaguely nodding, he rose to take it in the library. And those two other faces, rigid as stone now, listening to the sound of his retreating footsteps, the muffled tone of his voice—talking, talking, until suddenly had come that shout: "For God's sake, man, you talk like it was my fault!" And again the footsteps, coming back—until there was only his face, ghostly pale now, framed in the doorway—looking straight into Deirdre's upturned eyes.

"That was Bob Fisk, from over across the valley. Looks like his boy's been killed."

5

He was just finishing his mid-morning meal, mopping the plate with a last piece of bread, when the knocking came. He took a sip of coffee, then went to the door. It was Deirdre.

"May I come in?" she said quietly. Her eyes were dark and hollow, as though she had not slept.

"Sure," he said, holding the door.

She stepped inside, then stopped, slowly looking around. He closed the door behind her.

"It's been so long," she said—"so terribly long since I've been in here."

"Not so long, really. Not even a year. Besides, nothing's changed."

She turned and smiled at him, a weak, weary smile that seemed to require all her strength. "Nothing's changed," she repeated vaguely—as though it meant something else. Then: "Do you have any more coffee?"

"Sure. But it's pretty strong. You remember."

Again she smiled, but this time quite differently, almost warmly. "I remember," she said. Then, glancing down at the neat gray blanket atop his bed: "Can I use your chair?"

"Sure," he said. Setting the coffee on to warm, he went over to the table. "I'll just clear off these things." He pulled out the chair and motioned her toward it. She sat down.

When he turned again from the sink, the coffee beginning to crackle now on the stove, she had not moved. Only her eyes seemed alive, searching slowly about the room—resting here and there, then moving on. He took the coffee to her, the cast ringing hollow on the floor.

"Thanks." Her smile was soft. He went to the bed and, sitting down on the edge, extended his leg out before him. There was silence, her eyes still moving about—as if trying to remember . . . or not to forget. Then at last she spoke.

"I wondered if we could go for a ride," she said.

"A ride? Sure. All three of you? Or just you and Martin."

"Just you and me. If you can, that is."

"You and . . ." He got up from the bed and went over to the stove.

"Why . . . sure," he said, pouring more coffee for himself. "This thing isn't that much trouble—I tried it out the other day, put on a big stirrup."

He turned to look at her, but again her attention seemed to be on the room—the picture on the wall, the books, the things over his bed. Then, quickly, she got up.

"Sorry," she said, looking at him. "I didn't really want the coffee, I guess. Could we go now? Right away, I mean?"

"If you like," he said. Putting down his cup, taking his hat and coat from the peg, he opened the side door and led her out through the shop, then continued into the tackroom.

"If you could just go out and catch your horse," he began— then realized she was not there. Thumping back toward the shop, he saw her standing at the workbench. He stopped in the doorway but did not speak.

"This is just where Booker used to stand," she said without turning. "All his tools."

"Yes."

"Wasn't he something?" she murmured, turning now. "Booker Goodman. Good-man."

"Yes, he was."

"I wonder if he ever really existed—if he wasn't just a dream after all. Sometimes . . . it seems he was only a dream."

He did not answer, and she did not go on.

"I'll do up the horses," he said at last. "I'll come back for you if you like."

"No," she said dreamily. "I'll be along."

He turned to go.

It was fifteen minutes later, the two horses almost saddled now, when she appeared at the tackroom door, then began walking slowly toward him.

"About done," he said, finishing off the cinch on her buckskin. "You ready?"

"Yes," she said, a calm smile on her lips. "All ready now."

"I'll be just a minute, then," he said, taking the empty canteen from the fencepost where he had hung it. He hobbled across the corral and into the tackroom, emerging a few minutes later with the canteen, his leather wineskin, and a small paper-wrapped parcel, which he proceeded to stow in the sorrel's saddlebag. Then, swinging the cast up over the horse's back, he mounted. They went out through the gate and headed up the creekside trail.

For nearly a mile they didn't speak, although they rode side by side. When the trail narrowed, however, she dropped back, the buckskin falling in behind—and something occurred to him he wished he had thought of before now. He drew up, then turned in the saddle to face her.

"But maybe you'd rather not go this way today," he said. "We could just head on up to the reservoir. Should be pretty full now—that spring is good this year."

"No," she said. "This is fine, just what I wanted. But not all the way. I'd like to go up on the ridge trail, way high on the mountain. Up where Booker took me . . . when we brought the sheepcamp."

"You've got a good memory," he said.

"Yes," she smiled. "For some things."

Soon they had passed the wooden bridge and, after proceeding abreast for some distance, turned off on the narrow trail to the right—the same that he and Kinsella had taken that first day, eleven years before. Again the sorrel led the way, threading steeply upward through the ever-thinning cedars until at last the dark flank of the mountain rose up before them. It was very clear, not a wisp of cloud to be seen in the wide summer sky.

They stopped at the ridge to let the horses blow. Beneath them, rising from the little hollow below the cave, the frosty green crowns of the two great cottonwoods shimmered in the gentle breeze. Beyond, over the low hills to the north, the vapor trail of a long-passed airplane curdled out into the pale sky. He watched her face, waiting for her gaze to move off to the left, across the valley, but it did not. She looked up at the fading trail in the sky for a long time, then turned the buckskin and headed off up the ridge. He waited until she was almost out of sight among the pinyons before at last he touched the sorrel and followed after.

Nearly an hour had passed before they stopped again. They were high up now, in the broad sweeping country of bunch-grass and low sage where, eleven summers before, he had first come to range the sheep. Further up, stands of pine and spruce darkened the steepening slopes, while further yet, beyond the treeline, the windswept tundra rose upward to the peak. They headed toward a little glen, where a stand of aspens had taken root beside a tiny, grass-choked rivulet, and here they stopped, dismounted, and took out the provisions he had brought.

They had been there perhaps ten minutes, she seated on a low rock by the water, the sandwich he had made her still un-tasted in her hand, when all at once she turned toward him, looking across to the log where he was seated as though it were a great, yawning distance. She smiled, then at last raised the sandwich and took a tiny bite.

"I think I'll be going away for a while," she said after a moment. "A little trip, something."

"I can see why you might want to," he said. "Does your father know?"

"Yes. We talked this morning. Last night . . . well, you know. You were there. But this morning . . ."

Yes, he had been there—had heard that sharp, sudden intake of breath, that little cry as she had risen to her feet, then bolted for the doorway, past an astonished Kinsella and out. And then, just as on that other evening a scant year before, had listened to the urgent rush of her footsteps on the stair.

"I went to his room early, woke him up I think. I sat on his bed . . . and we talked. I think he understood, finally. I hope so. I just have to get away now, for just a while. To let this sink in . . . somewhere else."

"Where will you go?" John said.

"I don't really know. Not far. Grand Canyon maybe. New Mexico. I don't know. Martin says . . ." She hesitated slightly, then went on. "I understand that New Mexico is very pretty, around Taos."

He nodded, remembering Levi Mondragon and his apples.

"There's more than a month, almost two, before I have to be back at school. Plenty of time to sort this out, come back here, and . . . Plenty of time for all of it."

"I suppose so," he said. "And with your new car now and . . . but you're not going alone?"

"No," she smiled wanly. "Not alone."

He didn't ask the rest.

"Could I have a little of that wine?" she asked after a moment. "You showed me how once—I think I remember."

He stood and carried the wineskin over to her, then watched as she raised it above her head.

"Oh, what a mess," she said, wiping a drop off her chin.

"You did all right," he said. "Anyway, you can just put it in your mouth. That works too."

Smiling, she handed it back. "Show me again," she said. He did.

"Good John," she said softly, looking up. He turned and went back to his log.

They were silent again for a while then, watching the shimmer of the leaves in the sun, feeling the breath of breeze on their faces. Through an opening to the sky he could see a single cloud, alone.

"Do you know why I wanted to come today, John?" she said at last.

"To tell me," he said. "What you're going to do."

"That's part of it," she said. "Another part of it . . . is just to be here, up here, before . . ." She did not finish, but soon went on.

"I wanted to talk to you," she said. "About what Daddy said last night—has said before. About us."

"Don't bother yourself about it," he said. "He has these ideas sometimes. Doesn't really mean anything by it."

She smiled across at him. "Doesn't he?"

"Well, even if he did . . . don't worry. I understand him, that's just how he thinks."

"Who else do you understand, John?" she said.

Blushing, he looked away.

"Do you understand me?" she pressed. "I think I understand you."

He did not, could not, answer. The wind rattled the leaves.

A moment passed before she said: "All I want to say is this, John. Whatever happens, whatever . . . you should know this. The things my father says are not always as foolish as they may seem."

Slowly, fearfully, he looked up. Her sky-blue eyes were full upon him. "Do you understand now?" she said.

"Not really." But he was smiling.

And now it was she who looked away, gazing down into the little grassy pool at her feet. She sat there, utterly motionless, for nearly a minute before suddenly she got up.

"But now I have to go," she said. "Martin will be waiting."

He followed her to the horses and they started down.

CHAPTER 4

1

He sat in the old rocker near the window. Outside he saw Maria moving across the yard, out to her cabin, leaving dark footprints in the new, fragile snow. From the nest of shadows across the room, beyond the massively carved footboard of the four-poster bed, came the even rale of labored breath. Occasionally there seemed to be a hesitation, a sigh, sometimes a kind of whimper or low cry—but then all at once it was there again, the heavy sound, regular as before. Another dream overcome, Cyril Kinsella slept on.

It had come at last the night before, this first dusting of snow. It was difficult to remember another year when it had held off so long. Christmas come and gone, the New Year now hard upon them, he had searched the skies and smelled the wind in vain, the gray-green sage flats and low hills no less naked than the peak itself—but then last night, utterly without warning, he had heard its soft arrival from his narrow bed, listened as the stealthy sound of its settling filled the open window above his sink. He had gotten up then, stood in the doorway watching for a long time, looking out as the broken roof of the old bunk-house grew pale before his eyes. Kinsella, he thought, must have heard, sensed it as well, for just as he had been about to return inside he had seen the light in the old man's room go on. It would remain on, he knew, until first light—and he had returned to his bed.

This morning, like most mornings of late, he had gone up to get the breakfast tray for Maria, then sat talking with him for a time. Soon, however, almost in mid-sentence it seemed, the old man had drifted off to sleep. It was not the first time this had happened, but today he had been in no great hurry to depart. The snow was very beautiful to look out at, a promise at last redeemed.

There was a sudden stirring of the shadows, then a harsh, hoarse cough.

"Huh," the old man said. "Must have drifted off. How long you been sitting there?"

"Not long. Maybe half an hour. It's nice from here, the snow. You can see so far."

"Not far enough," Kinsella said, and drew himself up against the pillows. The old man was silent for a moment, then pulled the blankets up over his shoulders. "It's cold as hell in here. Put on another stick or two, would you?"

He slowly rose to his feet and went to the low fireplace near the bed, added another log and a piece of coal to the grate.

"Well, guess I'd better get along," he said then. "Sure there's nothing else you can think of?"

"No, nothing. Just tell Lehigh I want to see him, that's all, soon as he can make it out here. No big hurry though, really. I'm not going anywhere just now. But ask him to bring two friends. He'll know what I mean."

"And Suzanne?"

"Just tell her I said hello," the old man said, settling back into the pillows.

He went over for the tray, looking down at the half-empty cup of coffee, the untouched egg, the single piece of toast, nibbled on one corner. "Done?"

"Yeah," Kinsella said vaguely, looking out the window. "Not too hungry today."

He picked up the tray and started for the door.

"You won't forget to check the mail?" the soft voice said at his back.

"No," he said, without turning, and started down the hall.

He drove slowly, savoring the whitened landscape as it moved by. Strangely, it had come as a great relief to him, this snow—as if he had really doubted that it would ever come at all. Indeed, some part of him must have doubted—the part of him that dreamed, for last week he had dreamed just that: an utterly dry winter, a sterile spring—riding through a dusty gray scene to stop at the creekbank, looking down . . . at nothing.

And yet even so he had known the meaning, or at least the source, of that dream. Things that were to happen but did not— that were to be but were not. Yes, it was all too clear. But now this, at least, had come.

It was over five months now since they had left. Aside from those two letters—the first only a postcard really, the one from Taos—there had been nothing. No calls. Nothing.

Not that he had been surprised—not after the letter, anyway. And yes, in a way he supposed Kinsella had known too, in spite of the face he had tried to put on it at the time.

"No reason to push things," the old man had said gamely. "Perhaps she *does* need a little more time, and a semester more or less . . . This way, when she's here at Christmas, it can be a new beginning, sort of. And like she says, she'll keep in touch."

No, the letter itself had not seemed to trouble him half as

much as the postmark. And yet even that he had tried so hard
to make right.

"Why shouldn't she go there, really—and if he had some
things to attend to, well, like she says, it made sense for her to
take him back. It's a lovely city anyway. You say you've never
been there?"

Yes, he had tried so very hard, Kinsella, perhaps even had
convinced himself for a few weeks. But then, when the silence
began to bloom . . .

He reached down into his inside pocket, touching the edge
of the envelope with his finger, then put his hand back on the
wheel. Yes, of course it was there, no reason why it should
not be. After the effort it had cost him to write it, he would
hardly have forgotten it. It had taken him a very long time—the
writing, yes, but the deciding so much longer. The idea itself
had come to him months ago, long before there was really any
need—and then when the need was there, or so he thought,
then the deciding, the putting off. But then, three days ago . . .
The address, of course, had been no problem; he had seen it so
many times now, neatly written in the upper corner of each letter, each of those many letters as they came. For she was really
the only one he could turn to now, the only one who might know
. . . Again he reached down, touching the edge, the square corner. Yes, it was written now, ready. He wondered if he would
really mail it.

He looked up at the mountains, the high, broad peaks to the
south, virginal and white.

"Tomorrow's out," Lehigh said. "Finishing up this trial. But
the next day . . . yes, probably could make it. You sure he's as
bad as all that?"

"I'm not a doctor. He said he wanted you, that's all."

"And two friends, that's what he said? You sure?"

He nodded.

The young man sighed, pushing his sandy hair back over his

ears. He took off his glasses and rubbed his thumb and forefinger across his eyelids, pinching the bridge of his nose.

"Okay. Tell him two o'clock," Lehigh said. "With friends."

He walked out through the waiting room and into the street.

Suzanne, returning from the bathroom, drew a handkerchief from of the sleeve of her sweater and blew her nose.

"I'm sorry," he said. "I didn't . . ."

"Don't be silly," she said. "One silly old person is enough. Two, rather." She wiped her eyes once more, then sat down. "More coffee?"

"I'm okay," he said. "But will you come?"

The old woman smiled, a gentle, forgiving smile.

"No, dear John. I won't. Even if he asked me himself, which of course he never would. You have such a good heart, John— but no. No. That time is over. We are ourselves now, each as he is. It's too late."

He bowed his head and was silent.

"You're worried to death about this, John, aren't you. Why not just let it happen? He's had enough." She paused a moment before she added: "We've had enough."

Again, he did not reply.

"But maybe I *can* do something for you," she said, getting up. She walked to the sink and looked out the window at the snow-dusted scene rising up the hill. "Not that, not what you ask— but something."

Now at last he looked up, his eyes resting on the narrow, sweatered back turned toward him. She had never seemed so small.

"You had a friend once," she said.

He felt his heart beating in his throat. "Yes," he said at last.

"Perhaps he might be of some use to you now. Anyway, I suppose he ought to know." Slowly she turned to face him. Her dark eyes dwelt on his face.

"That little motel behind the jail, the one just down from . . .

well, you know." She paused, then smiled softly. "Your friend bought it last week. He and . . . his lady. They should be there now."

Slowly, unsteadily, he got to his feet, then walked around the table to her. He raised his hand to touch her cheek.

"Thanks," he said softly. "I'll let myself out."

2

He drove slowly down the pitted street. The gray bulk of Suzanne's church, its lawn resplendent in the mantle of new snow, seemed somehow ominous to him as he passed, then continued on. He had almost reached the last block, the eternal neon of the brothels blinking against the snowy backdrop of the canyon beyond, when he drew to a stop and turned off the engine.

Below and to his left, set back a block from the main street, was a small, unpretentious motel. He had been looking down at it for several minutes when there emerged from one of the doorways, behind a hamper of sheets, a slim Indian woman of perhaps thirty-five. He watched as she guided the hamper down the little sidewalk and stopped before another of the rooms, its door ajar. Then she disappeared inside. Soon another figure, a stout, pale woman with graying red hair, burst from the office and, calling, set out for the same room into which the other had gone. He vaguely recognized the face, the voice, the walk—but of this one he could not be sure. From somewhere he could hear the sound of hammering, then the whine of a saw.

No one appeared again for perhaps five minutes. Then, from an open doorway across the lot, where a shiny new pickup truck was parked in the shade, there materialized a tall, heavy black man wearing overalls and a baseball cap. He listened as the man called out, watched as he walked across to the room where the others had gone, where he stood in the doorway talking. At last the two women emerged and, leaving the hamper on the walk, set out together for the office. The black man turned then, walking back to the room from which he had come, and soon the whine of the saw began again.

He sat quietly for several minutes, listening, looking out at the snowy hills and the canyon beyond. Then, with a long sigh, he started the engine and headed down.

As he parked the truck in front of the room he heard the sawing cease. Getting out, he went to the open doorway, but there was no one to be seen inside. The bed had been propped up against the wall and covered, and in its place was the saw, a plastic sheet beneath it deep in sawdust and chips. There was a sudden sound of hammering from the bathroom. He walked to the doorway and looked in.

The back had broadened, as had the girth, but the hand gripping the hammer was the same. He watched until the hammering ceased—and the big man, humming a tune beneath his breath, turned toward him.

For a long time, it seemed, neither spoke—although not five seconds must have passed in fact before Booker, slipping the hammer into the loop at his side, began to shake his great, graying head slowly from side to side, eyes downcast.

"John boy," he said. Only that. And then he sighed, sitting down on the edge of the tub. "John boy."

And John went to him then, putting his arm over the sagging shoulders and squeezing hard. Booker's head, pressed hard against him, still swayed from side to side.

There came a sound of quick footsteps on the walk, then in the room—then a high, familiar voice. "Come on now. It's all ready . . ." And then a sudden indrawn breath—and silence. He turned.

"Hi, John," Consuela said without a moment's hesitation. "I didn't know you were here."

"Hi, Consuela. Yes, I'm here."

"Good," she said. "Lunch is ready." She turned and headed

for the doorway. "Hurry along now, the two of you. Before it gets all cold."

They sat at the green formica table—or rather he and Booker sat, Consuela and Edna spending most of the time between stove and refrigerator.

"You don't really know me, do you?" Edna had said soon after they sat down, her old green eyes searching his face.

"'Course he does," Booker had said—just as he had said earlier, when they came in: "John, you remember Edna. She's been helping out this week."

"No," he had said to her then, when she asked. "I really don't. I should, I know. I seem to remember you from somewhere."

"From somewhere," Edna had smiled. "And just why didn't you ever come back to that somewhere? There was someone who kept looking out for you—but she's gone now."

Only then had it come to him. "I know you now," he had said.

"'Course you know her," Booker had said then. "You mean to say that . . . ?"

"Not once," Edna had said. "But enough of that. How you been, John?"

And so they sat at the green formica table, he and Booker, while Consuela and Edna moved about them. And Booker told what there was to tell.

"And so this is our third motel—would you believe it? I actually built the second, down in Tonopah, but then we were offered a good price and this one opened up. Kind of wanted to get back," he said. "Can't say just why."

"'Course he can," Consuela said. "Always thinking about that awful old man."

"Now Connie. We're closer to your mother too."

"I don't care. I don't want to see her. Not ever."

"Now Connie."

"I liked our place in Tonopah. Not here."

"Now honey."

"I'm going to finish off those rooms. You coming Edna?"

"Aw honey . . ."

But then she was gone, Edna bestowing a wink and a smile upon them as she followed. "I'm coming, no need to holler!" And out the door.

"She's okay, really," Booker said when they were alone. "You know how she is. But she's fine. Good with the people too— the guests, you know. Takes it real serious, all that. You'd be surprised."

"Maybe," John said.

"You would, I mean it. Anyway, we get along real well, she and I. No kids but . . . well, you can't have everything. Eleven years now. Just think of that."

"Long time," John said.

"You bet. And say, was that right what she said? Edna. That you never went back?"

"Yeah."

"You got another place?"

"No, just never got around to it."

Booker grinned, forefinger working in his wiry, fast-graying hair. "Well, no business of mine," he said. "Anyway, she's sold the place now, retired I guess you'd say. Still fills in sometimes, when the new boss lady's sick or gone or something, but mostly . . . well, she's got a nice little house down by the creek, a garden and all that."

"Nice lady," John said.

"None better. And Connie gets on with her."

Booker got up and went to the stove for the coffeepot. "Well, what about you?" he said when the cups were refilled.

"Not much. I'm still there."

"I heard," Booker said. "Could you stand a piece of pie?"

"Pie? Sure, I guess so."

Again the big man, big in all ways now, got to his feet. "Connie makes this peach custard pie that . . . well, I have a hard time keeping away from it, as you can see well enough."

He patted his belly, then took the dish from the refrigerator. In a moment he was back with two big pieces.

"I've heard a little since I got back. Suzanne, here and there —you know. That really so about the spring?"

"Yeah."

"Bone dry?"

"Yeah."

"Boy. The old man must have taken it hard."

"Yeah. He did."

Booker addressed himself to the pie.

"I could stand another," he said when he was done. "Not going to, though. She gives me a hard time about that sometimes. But you—you want another? I don't mind watching. Really."

"No, I'm fine," he said.

"Suit yourself." Booker refilled the cups.

They were silent for a time, Booker looking out the window into the parking lot.

"Well," he said at last. "How is he? Really."

"Not so good."

"Hmmm. This business about Deirdre—and that other one, the son?"

"Mostly, I guess. But just kind of . . . everything. That just pushed it over."

"Hmmm. I still think about him a lot, you know. Drives Connie crazy—well, you saw that. But I think about him anyway."

"Maybe he thinks about you too."

"Maybe. But anyway . . ."

"I expect he'd like to see you."

Booker was silent, gazing out across the parking lot. The two women were heading back.

"I don't know," Booker said softly. "The way we left it."

There was the clatter of the hamper on the curb, then the high sound of laughter as they burst in.

"Booker," Consuela sputtered, her red-brown face radiant in

the light—"Booker, Edna says the worst things. She's really *very* naughty!"

"What you been telling her now?" Booker smiled, looking up at the older woman.

"What business is that of yours? Just wipe the piecrumbs off your chin, you big lummox."

Consuela dissolved, collapsing into a chair. "See!" she shrieked. "She talks like that all the time! Lummox! That's what you are, Booker—a lummox!"

"Thanks, Edna," Booker said. "She'll get a lot of mileage out of that."

"Lummox," Consuela repeated as she went out the door to the laundry.

"Want some coffee?" Booker said then. "Should be a little left. Cold by now maybe."

"Believe I will," Edna said, going to the stove. There was the hiss of gas, then a puff as it ignited.

"Well, do you think," Booker began, turning back to John—"do you think it's so bad that he just might . . . ?"

"I don't know. I'm just real worried, that's all."

"Well then, how about Deirdre? If it's bad as that she ought to know—no matter what."

"I know."

"Well , . . couldn't we find her? There must be some way."

John was silent, looking down into his empty cup. The coffee sputtered on the stove, then hissed as she poured it.

"Only one way I could think of," John said at last. "I've written this letter." He reached into his coat and pulled it out, then handed the envelope across the table.

"Mmmm," Booker said, looking at the address. He scratched his head and laid the envelope softly on the table. "Yes," he said. "I guess she'd be the only one."

"Don't waste your time."

It was Edna, standing behind Booker now with her steaming cup of coffee.

"Or the postage." She sat down.

"She doesn't know," Edna went on quietly, looking straight into John's eyes. "Hasn't known for months. They were there for a week back in August, the two of them—but then she just up and left. An argument, I don't know. They didn't get along. And now . . . well, he's back home with Abby—but the girl, nobody knows. Nobody. There was some talk of drugs, you know, that sort of thing. Something about her having left the city, living in the country somewhere. Somewhere. But nobody really knows anything. She's gone, that's all. Vanished."

"And just how in the hell do you know all this?" Booker said sharply, turning on her.

"Cool down," she said. "We write, have written since high school. Abby and I, we go back a long, long time."

"And you never told me?"

"No business of yours," Edna said coldly. "My friends are my own business."

"Your own . . . ," Booker sputtered, then quickly got to his feet, knocking over the chair. He sighed, a long, heavy sigh, before he said: "I'll be getting on back to work." Without looking at either of them he walked to the door, opened it, and went out.

As he walked across the parking lot they could hear Consuela calling out to him from the laundry room.

"Lummox!" she cried. "You big old lummox!"

He kept on walking.

3

Huh. Who is it?

Sorry. For a minute I . . . Come on in. Come on.

No, I guess I didn't. Soon as you brought it I must have nodded off a little. Now . . . well it's cold, I guess.

No, don't bother. Didn't really want it anyway. But sit down a while. Let's have a little drink. Like old times. Know what they were saying on the radio this afternoon? It's New Year's Eve. Did you know that?

Well I sure as hell didn't. Hadn't even thought of it. And not a drop of champagne in the house, worse luck. Have to make do, I guess.

No, I can reach it from here. Been reaching it all afternoon, in fact, ever since that convention of owls cleared out. Maria tries to hide it—not very hard, but she tries. Sticks it under the bed when I'm asleep, you know, that sort of thing. Like she expects that if I don't see it I won't know it's gone. That make any sense?

Didn't think so. But come on over, bring that water glass. It's New Year's Eve, for chrissake.

There's a bit of a chill in here, don't you think? Ought to warm it up a bit for our celebration. Yes, good, that should do it. And now drag that chair over, right here beside me. I want to get a look at you, see you clear. Let's have a little talk . . . like in the old days.

Good. Now we're supposed to review the old year, tell about what we hope for in the new one. Isn't that about right?

I thought so. But anyway let's skip that part for now. Go on to the weather. It's always best to start with the weather. Still snowing outside?

Well, that's okay. We could use a little breather—for the New Year. The New Year . . .

I felt a little guilty really, having Lehigh and his bunch come all the way out this afternoon. Big enough nuisance without a snowstorm to contend with. But not a word of complaint from him. Nice young fellow. Knows his stuff too. Should make a name . . .

Well, that pretty much covers the weather, I guess. Didn't take long. Now I guess we move on to the news. Is there any news?

Didn't think so. Doesn't feel like there's been any news.

Well, I've covered the opening stuff. Now what've you got to say?

Is that all? Come on. You have to pull your weight too. Tell me some more about Booker, then, how he's doing.

Well, you went over all that yesterday. Chapter and verse. But . . . how did he look, for instance?

You jest. Booker? Well, that loony squaw of his must be taking some kind of care of him, anyway. Last person I would've expected . . .

Sure. Wouldn't mind seeing him either. No hard feelings, too much water's gone under . . . Anytime. You let him know, will you? No hard . . .

Who else you say was there?

Yeah, met her once or twice, I guess. Old-timer. Goes back a long way, all the way back to . . . Long way.

That what she said? Same class? Well, maybe so, maybe so. About the same age, I'd guess. Makes sense. But I never knew her that much anyway. Met her once or twice maybe, way back . . . Yeah, come to think of it now, might even have met her at their house. Reston's. Way back then.

Kind of ironic, considering the business she got herself into later.

Okay, just another little touch. Then you better hide it too, like Maria. I've got something important to tell you.

Ironic. Nice six-bit word. Ring to it . . .

You know I never was able to figure out what kind of person she really liked—in the way of women friends, that is. Or men friends, as far as that . . . Once or twice in New York I remember coming across them—girls from her work, that sort of thing—but they all seemed different to me. Some quiet, intellectual you might even say, then others just dippy dames with nothing in their heads but . . . nothing. Couldn't figure it.

The only real friend she had was her sister. Marcella. I never saw two women as close as that, the two of them. When they were together, well, you just might as well not be there. They had a kind of shortwave between them too—felt, sensed the same things. Over long distances too—she in New York, Marcella in Cleveland. It was amazing.

I remember that time in Mexico—hell of a long way further than New York, too. We hadn't been there more than three, four days, the knot barely tied, when that telegram came. Said not to go to the mountains, pleaded almost—and the funny thing was that we'd just hired a car for the next day to take us up there, up toward Zacatecas. Well, of course then she wouldn't go, not after the telegram—and a few days later we heard that the same car had taken someone else up there that day. And they were robbed—bandits, something. Woman raped, driver beat up. Could have been us. Would have been.

And there were plenty of other times too, before and . . .

Yes, and so we never got to those mountains, the high ones. Went on up to Chapala instead, a big lake they have there. We had a house by the water, a dock, a little sailboat. Used to go out in the evening sometimes, after I learned how to run it. Find a little cove, have supper maybe, sometimes a snooze . . . Long time ago.

It was amazing how she took to it, that place. Don't think she ever would have left if she'd had her way. She liked it all—the people, the climate, the food, everything. Spoke good Spanish too, not like me. We'd go into town, to the market, and there'd she'd be, chattering and bargaining with them like she's been doing it all her life. Curious . . . Ever been to Mexico?

No, I suppose not. But it's a strange place, can't say I cared for it much. Way they look at you sometimes . . .

We had a kind of houseboy—Miguel I think his name was. Just a kid—eleven, twelve, like that. He was all right, did what you asked with that big smile they all have, but sometimes I'd catch him watching me in a way that . . . Kind of fear and hostility and envy all rolled up into one. I don't know . . . But she got on just fine with him. Better than fine. Got it into her head to teach him English, in fact. They had a place out in the orchard where they'd go . . .

Now how the hell did I get off on this? I had something important to tell you, not this dreary business.

Where the hell'd you put that bottle? It's New Year's Eve, isn't it? We're supposed to be celebrating. The New Year.

Thanks. Make any resolutions?

You ought to be ashamed. Young fellow like you should be full of resolutions, ambitions, all that stuff. I was. How old you say you are?

Young. Not much older than I was when . . .

No, I'm all right. Just a little twinge . . .

But yes, she really did like Mexico—never would have come back at all if she'd had her way. I remember her telling me one day that a certain house further up the lake was for sale. Some writer she liked, forget his name, had stayed there a while once; just died, I guess, and she got the notion into her head that we should buy it, make it into some kind of museum or something, stay on a few years until . . .

We already have a house, I told her. Already . . .

No, no. I'll be all right. It's New Year's Eve, for chrissake. Drink up.

She hated this house, you know—from the first minute she laid eyes on it. Strange, because in a way she . . . But no, there was no doubt of it. As soon as we came over the hill—you know the place, where all of a sudden it's just there, in front of you—well right away I could . . .

And then her father, all that nasty business. Marcella heading out to tell him, break the news. The news. Half crazy with the waiting . . .

Might as well go out and give 'em a hand with the barn. Might as well . . .

Yes, and then the day. She seemed to have figured it out—that that would be the day. Somehow—that thing they had, the two of them. I remember taking her up the creek on that old roan, she behind holding on tight. All nerves, tight as a spring. Couple sage hens took off to one side of us and I thought she'd jump right out of her skin. But oh no, keep going, keep going, and so we did . . . until we reached that little clearing. You know the one. Where Tabby . . . Where you . . .

I wish you'd keep better track of that girl, damn it. Six years old and wandering about like some kind of a cat or a dog. I never know where to find her. And Booker, hell, he's just about as much help. Supposing a bale falls on her or something, way she burrows around like that in the barn. Just supposing. And nobody the wiser. At least this new fellow, the Basco, keeps some kind of track of her. Or her of him. When he's in the garden—or now working on his wagon— at least I can have some idea then where to find her. But pretty soon, when he goes, up there on the . . .

Ah. Must have drifted off again. Not so used to this stuff any more, I guess. Feel fine now though. First rate. Just give me a good kick next time. Rap on the noggin. Because I'm not kidding. There's something . . . But we were talking about . . . what was it?

Right. Yes. Right. Well, let's just forget all that, shall we? Now this other thing . . .

Yes, that clearing. Birches. Sitting down there by the creek. Not talking much, really. I remember just looking out at the water, watching it go by. And then . . . just that little whimpering kind of sound at first. But then when I looked over . . . hands pressed up against the sides of her head, and then the sound, louder, until it was a scream . . .

Yes, and then wetting something to put on her head, somehow piling her back on the horse, going back. Putting her to bed.

"Marcella," she kept saying, over and over again. "Oh, Marcella" . . .

Birches . . .

Well can't you talk some sense into that woman, damn it? I sure as hell can't but maybe . . . It just isn't right, that's all—taking off like that to God knows where without a word to anybody. At least she could tell you where she's headed—if she knew. That's the worst of it. She doesn't know herself. I've told the boys to keep an eye on her—not too damn close, you know, but watch her. Oh sure, the spring, she's always at the spring, they say—but I know for a fact she's not. Other day when I went up for the branding I spotted her myself, way up on the ridge. At least she's got that big gray, can trust . . .

Huh! Ah . . . sneaking out, ay? Not so fast. We're having a talk, remember? And I've got something . . .

But I was telling about her, I think. Her. And why not? No big secret. Tell it all. What the hell. But where had I got to?

Yes, the horse, heading back. Big roan it was, red-speckled, kind of. Strong as an ox. But dumb. That horse was really dumb . . .

She slept straight through until morning, never moved an inch. Fifteen, sixteen hours—and when she woke it all seemed to have passed. I went down for the coffee, the toast, and brought it up. But it all got cold . . .

Yes, she was crazy for it that morning—more than I had ever seen her. There was something about it, though. Scary, I don't know. Something that had nothing, or everything to do with me, I couldn't tell. Yes, and when at last it was over, the whine of the saw the only sound . . .

It was past noon then. She sent me out to the barn to tell them not to worry. She always did that, most of the time, took them out a lunch . . . Yes, and when I got back to the house it was almost ready. We carried the box out, she in her big straw hat, and sat with them in the . . .

It just wouldn't work, Suz—not now anyway. Besides, we're fine as we are, aren't we? Out there, well you'd just get lonely, that's all. Damn shiftless cowboys, haven't you had enough of them for one lifetime? Because that's it, all there is—six, seven cowboys, as stupid and crude as they make 'em, an old toothless Indian, and too damn many cows. No life for you, babe. I like you to look good, like you do. Nice little place like this, porch in the sun . . . But what's this thing about Denver? Your little brother . . .

Hey, I thought you were going to watch me, rap me upside the head. Can't count on anybody anymore. Any decent help. Well, that's okay. I'll just watch over myself.

And don't think I don't know where we'd got to, either. I know, all right. Out to the barn, that's where we'd got to . . .

Oh yes, she liked Tegelvik well enough—from the first minute there'd been no mistaking that. Can't say as I blamed her really, and the fact that he had a pretty little Swedish wife and two tow-headed kids in Salt Lake, why that had less than nothing to do with it. But up to then she'd managed to keep her admiration pretty much to herself. That day, though, when we took out the lunch, she . . . well, shined right up to him, if you know what I mean—and the more he squirmed, looking over at me, the more she just kept on. I looked over at the Indians, off to one side like they always were when she came. Oh yes, they were watching, looking worried and nervous, half scared.

Yes, I knew in my bones what it was all about. The same thing that dark business of the morning had been about. And now—I'd had about enough. She knew it too, could see it in my face, but she just kept on, pushing . . .

I remember I was just getting up, just reaching down for her hand to pull her up, march her back here . . . when I heard the sound of the car coming up the lane, rounding the corner, stopping in front of the house. Come on, I said. This'll be for you.

Yes, and when the car had gone she just stood there in the dust for a minute, looking down at that pale yellow envelope in her hand. She didn't say anything at all, until at last she turned and started up the stairs. I followed her into the parlor, then stood watching as she slipped that long fingernail under the flap, unfolded the yellow sheet. There was a little cry as she crumpled down on the couch.

I went over and took it from her, read the pasted words. DADDY STROKE STOP BAD STOP ARRIVING CREIGHTON FIVE P.M. TRAIN WILL SEND CAR FOR YOU STOP LEAVING TWO A.M. TRAIN SF STOP M.

I went into the library for a drink. After a minute she came in.

"I'm going with her, of course," she said.

"Of course."

"I don't think I'll be back," she said.

"No, you won't."

"I've made a mistake," she said.

"Yes, you have," I said.

I remember walking out to the barn then, the sun hot on my face. Take a month, I told him. Don't worry, I'll be in touch. There'll be a car coming later. Later . . .

Don't trust that Murchison kid one bit. Bad lot. Him and his fancy Chivvie. Did you see the way he looked at her, holding the door and all that? Bad lot, the bunch of 'em. Why don't you talk some sense into her like you used to? I can't do a thing with her anymore, but you always had a . . .

Ha! Caught you again! Not so fast. Come on back here now. That's right, sit down. I'll only keep you a minute. I promise. And you promise.

*Good. That's right. Because remember? I told you there was some-
thing important. Good thing I caught you too, sneaking out like some
kind of red Indian. Just be a minute, you'll see.*

*Good. Now listen, just do what I say. Put your hand under the
mattress here. That's right, a little further. Feel something? Good.
Now take it out.*

*Good. Just an envelope, that's all. Kind of fat but . . . see your
name there? And then what comes after?*

*Good. And that's just what it means. Not before. After. Under-
stand?*

*Good. And now it's your turn to promise. That when it's time,
and you open it up, you'll do what it says. Whatever it says. Promise?*

*Good. But wait, that's not quite enough. Not enough for Abra-
ham. Or Jacob. Or me . . . Listen now, come over a little closer.
That's right, over here, right close.*

*Good. Now take your hand and put it here. That's right, under the
cover, right there, under that scrawny cold thigh. Go ahead. Don't
be shy.*

Yes. Good. Stringy old turkey . . .

*But now, do you swear? Whatever it says? You'll be protected,
don't worry. No trouble, I've seen to that. But . . . whatever it says?
Do you promise me, no matter what?*

*Yes. You're a good fellow, John. The best . . . But go on along
now. I'm tired . . .*

*You got it with you? Good. Keep it safe. And don't you worry
about me. I'll be all right.*

4

Maria stood in the tackroom doorway, her bundled, motionless
form blocking the brittle early sunlight. He put down the saddle
soap and sponge, wiped his hands on the towel, and walked over
to her.

"You should come," she said. Her dark eyes searched his face.
"Come?"

"Yes." The old woman turned and, without another word, started back through the snow.

In a moment he had overtaken her. Turning to speak to her again, he was arrested by the heavy set of her jaw, the heedless constancy of her forward gaze. And then he was running.

The screen door slamming behind him, he burst through the kitchen and down the hall, caught himself on the banister post and, turning, headed two by two up the long, dim flight of stairs. Reaching the top, he stopped for a moment, gasping for breath, before he stumbled on.

The room was nearly dark, the shades drawn just as he had left them. On the other side a soft orange glow could still be seen in the grate. He stood in the doorway panting as his eyes adjusted to the darkness, then made out the gaunt, robed figure lying face-down on the bare floor, arms outstretched as if toward some receding shore.

He walked over, knelt on one knee, and laid his hand gently on the stubbled cheek. It was quite cold.

Rising to his feet, he went to the window and slowly raised the blinds. The brightness of the snow was jarring, intense, like a sudden shrill shout in the silence. He looked out, his gaze moving slowly down the distant ridge, from the virginal bulk of the peak to the jagged crags to the south. He could see the shape of a hawk, then two, as they circled in the clear cobalt sky.

At last he turned away and, kneeling down again beside the figure, carefully eased it over. It was already quite stiff. Then, quickly, he looked away. The face, frozen in a grimace, was not one he wished to recall. Like the body, it had already become an object.

Bending down, he lifted the stiff, robed shape from the floor. It was surprisingly light, like a sack of dry twigs. He carried it to the bed and, settling it as best he could there, pulled the blanket up over it and turned to go. He had almost reached the doorway when suddenly he drew up. For a moment he stood quite still, his brow rigid and furrowed, but then, slowly, he turned about and walked back to the bed. There he bent down and, drawing the blanket back again, pressed a kiss on the cold forehead. Then, replacing the cover, he turned and went out.

Maria was at the stove. "Shall I do anything?" she said, hearing him come in. She did not turn.

"No, not yet. I'll let you know," he said, going out.

He stood for a moment on the porch, breathing the sharp morning air deep into his lungs. The day was startlingly clear, the sky a deep, liquid blue above the bright ridges. There was no wind. From somewhere far across the valley came the faint bark of a dog, then, nearby, the whinny of one of the horses. He looked off to the southeast, where he had seen the two hawks. But they were gone.

Again he breathed in, feeling the air bite against his lungs. Then, with a long sigh, he descended the stairs and set off toward the barn.

Five minutes later he was seated on his bed, a half-finished glass of wine in his hand. On the blanket beside him, still unopened, was the bulky envelope Kinsella had given him only the night before. He looked down at it for what seemed a long time before, putting the glass on the floor beneath the bed, he reached into his pocket and took out his knife. Then, very carefully, he slit open the envelope and slipped out the single handwritten page. The rest, some money and another, smaller envelope, he left inside.

He had not seen Kinsella's handwriting for some time—at least had not noticed it—and he was struck by the clarity, the crisp authority of this. Small, erect, the lines so straight and close . . .

It was quite detailed, considering the fact that all was crowded on this single page. And very, very clear. Perhaps ten minutes passed before at last he laid it aside and got to his feet. He crossed the room to the little table and drew open its single drawer. Reaching in, he withdrew a neatly folded white handkerchief, which he carefully laid on the table and then, corner by corner, opened into a larger square. In the center was a small silver cross, set with coral stones, and a silver chain. He stood looking down at it, utterly still, for a long time. Then, extending his hand, he lay his palm softly upon it and closed his eyes for a moment before, carefully refolding the handkerchief, he put it back in the drawer.

He turned, put on his coat, and went back to the bed, where he returned the letter to the envelope and slipped it into his pocket, then went out, heading back toward the house.

"I have to make a call now," he said to Maria, passing through the kitchen.

"Do you want some coffee?"

"No, not right now. First I have to make this call."

He walked down the hall, through the parlor, and into Kinsella's library. There he drew up for a minute, looking at the long rows of books on the wall, before he continued to the desk and took up the phone.

"Consuela," he said when the answer came. "This is John."

He paused a moment. "Yes," he said then. "Beautiful out here. And the same to you too. Is Booker there?" Again there was a pause while he listened. "Yes, to wish him myself. Don't worry, I'll hang on."

It was ten minutes later when he returned to the kitchen. "Now I'll try that coffee," he said, sitting down.

"Anything else?" As she turned toward him he realized she had not looked at him since that first moment, out in the tackroom. He could have been mistaken, but it seemed she might have been crying.

"No. Just coffee. But you get some too. We have to talk, I guess."

She brought the coffee to him, leaving the pot on the table. Then, gingerly, she sat down, folding her hands before her. It occurred to him he had never seen her sitting before.

"Booker's living in town now, with Consuela," he said softly.

"I know," she said. "Boss told me yesterday."

"Good. Well, he's coming out for you."

"Don' know how that's gonna work. Consuela and me . . ."

"It'll work," he said. "Booker will take care of that. It's the best place for you now. Besides, you and she should be friends. You'll be surprised when you see her, how she's changed."

"Maybe," she said darkly, and looked away.

"He should be here inside of an hour, so maybe you ought to go out and start getting your things together."

"Won' take that long," she said. "Sure you don' want some breakfast?"

"No. But there's one other thing."

He reached into his pocket for the envelope and took it out, then withdrew the smaller envelope from it. "Boss wanted you to have this for now. It's some money, to help you get settled. There'll be something else later."

She gravely took it from him. "This too much," she said when she had opened it. "He still owes me for this month, but this too much."

"It's a present, Maria," he said. "He wants . . . wanted you to take it."

"But it's too much."

"He wanted it, Maria."

Scowling, she slipped the envelope into her apron pocket, got up, and went back to the stove.

"I'll be outside with the chores," he said. "I'll hear when Booker comes." He was almost to the door when he heard her voice again, quite softly.

"John?"

He stopped and turned. The broad back was still toward him.

"Can I go up, see him again?"

"Sure," he said. "Whatever you like." And he went out.

He had tended to the horses and chickens, gone out to check something in the shed, and returned again to his room in the barn when he heard the sound of the big new pickup coming up the lane. He put on his coat and went out, just in time to see it coming to a stop next to the side gate. Booker and the other man got out, then waited until he reached them.

"Thanks for coming," he said to the smaller man with the satchel. "I wasn't sure . . ."

"No trouble," the other said. "How's your leg been?"

"Fine," he said. "Just fine. Well, I guess you'd better just go on up."

They walked across the yard and into the kitchen. Maria wasn't there. "I'll just wait here," he said, and watched them go down the hallway. He went to the stove and warmed some coffee, then stood by the window drinking it. Outside, across the yard, the door to Maria's cabin was ajar. He could see her moving about inside.

There was the sound of a single pair of footsteps behind him approaching down the hall. It was the doctor.

"Shall I just send the paperwork out here to you?" he said.

"Yes, or give it to Mr. Lehigh."

"I'll do that. And as for . . . arrangements, well, I can send Duggan out if you like. But I suppose you've made your own."

"Yes," John said quietly. "Our own."

There was the heavy sound of Booker's tread on the stair, then coming down the hall. The big man's bare head, so grizzled now, hung low between his shoulders.

"Poor old guy," he said, only that, and walked out onto the porch. Across the yard, Maria had put two suitcases out in the snow. Booker looked out at her for a moment, then went down the stairs.

"Well, thanks again for coming," John said. "I know on this short notice . . ."

"These things sometimes happen on very short notice," the doctor said. He stopped in the doorway. "Glad your leg's not giving trouble."

"No trouble at all," John said, then watched him cross the yard.

Fifteen minutes later, Maria's things all loaded, he and Booker stood beside the truck. Inside, Maria sat like a rigid Buddha in the middle seat, the doctor next to her by the window.

"Sure I can't help you with anything?" Booker said, still looking worried.

"No. Nothing."

"I understand, I guess."

"Thanks," John said. "And I'll be in touch."

Then, for the first time, Booker smiled, the gold eyetooth flashing in the sun. "You forgot something," he said.

"What's that?"

Still the big man smiled, just as John had remembered. "To wish me luck," he said.

"That's so," John said, glancing inside the truck. "Good luck."

Then he stood aside, watching as the shiny new pickup turned and headed down the lane.

He drove slowly down the fenceline, the empty double horse trailer clattering behind. It had not taken as long as he had feared, these two trips, and now all four were safely in the little corral beyond the hayfield. They could surely spend the night there.

It was surprisingly passable, this little track, considering the infrequency with which it was used now and the weather they'd had yesterday. In long stretches the wind had blown it almost clear, and in the few places where there were drifts the four-wheel drive had easily taken him through, even with the two horses behind. It all seemed to be . . . arranged. It had all been set out so clearly, even the elements dared not interfere.

He closed the gate behind him and continued down toward the barn.

He had already moved the chickens to the little pen behind the bunkhouse, and he could hear their anxious clucking as he turned off the engine, then set out walking toward the house. Stopping in the empty kitchen, he warmed some coffee and took out the letter, spreading it flat on the kitchen table. He looked quickly over it once again, then stood at the window looking out as he finished up his coffee.

He was surprised at how alone he felt now. Looking out across the yard toward the empty cabin—Maria's, Tabby's, it no longer mattered—he realized that it was the horses more than anything. The chickens, well, they didn't really count, no more than sheep, but the horses . . . Yes, when he had shut the corral gate that last trip he had felt it for the first time, just a little twinge, but now it settled in upon him like a heavy shadow. He realized he was afraid.

Quickly he poured the rest of the coffee in the sink, filled the cup with water, and drank it down. Then he turned, walked around the table, and headed down the hall. The emptiness was everywhere.

He stopped only briefly in the library, where he took a large tin box from the desk drawer. For a moment he looked up again at the books, allowing his eyes to move slowly along the shelves, but then abruptly he turned, brushing the tall liquor cabinet as he went out. It had all been so very, very clear.

There was only one other stop to make then. Returning to the kitchen only long enough to leave the box on the table, he went back down the hallway and mounted the stairs, slowly this time. In the room the blinds were still open, the snowy landscape growing luminous now in the late afternoon light. He looked out, then briefly over at the covered lump on the bed, before he went to the bureau beside the fireplace and, opening a door, drew out a small, heavy safe. Then he walked out and down the stairs to the kitchen, where he gathered up the tin box and the letter from the table and, passing through the screen door, headed resolutely for the barn.

Ten minutes later he was headed back, walking very slowly now, a square, leaden-colored can tugging on his arm. At the picket fence he stopped and, resting the can on the top rail, stood looking upward at the big house until at last his eye came to rest on that small window, high up under the eaves, where he had seen Kinsella watching that day, so long ago now—the day before he had left for the mountains. For several minutes he remained looking up at it, his gaze seeming to flicker across the panes, before at last, lowering the can once more to his side, he continued on across the yard.

Reaching the porch, he mounted the stair and passed on into the kitchen. Here again he paused, standing quietly beside the long table for a moment while he looked about, just as he had done on that first afternoon. Yes, he thought, it was a marvel, the way it was put together. Not a nail or a screw. Not a nail . . . Then, shifting the can to his left hand, he gathered up an armload of kindling from beside the stove and hurried down the hallway . . .

He had been back in his room for perhaps twenty minutes when he first began to hear the sound. He sat very still a moment, his senses slowly absorbing it—the low, moaning roar, now and then a muffled thump, a squeal—before he slowly put down his glass and refolded the handkerchief, returning it to its place in the drawer. Then he turned, walked slowly to the door, and went outside.

He had not thought it would go so quickly. All the windows were out now, fountains of flame and smoke and sparks pouring out through the sockets and up into the darkening sky. He stood beside the barn and watched quietly, placidly, astonished at how calm he had become. Then, after a few moments, he started walking slowly toward it.

He had approached to within thirty yards, the high stone walls looming above him, before at last the heat became too much. He walked out through the brush and up on a little, snow-covered hillock. Far down the lane, where it disappeared over the rise, a faded blue pickup truck was just cresting the hill. He watched as it rolled to a stop and the driver, a thick figure in a bulky coat, got out. Then, satisfied who it was, he turned his eyes back toward the house.

It was dusk now. The broad, deepening sky, shot with pinks and grays above him, seemed almost to welcome the spark-laden column rising up into it. There was no wind, no sound but the fire, the insistent, sucking roar . . . and then, with a sharp, snapping report, it had begun—the upper floors falling inward, one upon the other. For a long time it seemed to go on, much longer than he expected—until at last, with a sudden rush of anguish, he lowered his face and turned away. He stood very still, his back to it, until the last crash, the last thump had faded, the low roar asserting itself once more. Then, his calm slowly returning, he raised his eyes, again looking across to the distant rise. Fisk's old pickup, turned about, was just disappearing over the hill.

For nearly an hour more he stood there—long after the slate roof had begun to sag, then suddenly collapsed, leaving a gaping rent in the northside wall—until finally the flames had seemed to slacken and withdraw, a soft glow lingering within the jagged shell. He remained in silence for a few minutes more, then set off through the snowy sagebrush toward the barn. The stars opened their bright canopy above his head.

Western Literature Series

■ ■ ■

Western Trails: A Collection of Short Stories by Mary Austin
selected and edited by Melody Graulich

Cactus Thorn
Mary Austin

Dan De Quille, the Washoe Giant: A Biography and Anthology
prepared by Richard A. Dwyer and Richard E. Lingenfelter

Desert Wood: An Anthology of Nevada Poets
edited by Shaun T. Griffin

The City of Trembling Leaves
Walter Van Tilburg Clark

Many Californias: Literature from the Golden State
edited by Gerald W. Haslam

The Authentic Death of Hendry Jones
Charles Neider

First Horses: Stories of the New West
Robert Franklin Gish

Torn by Light: Selected Poems
Joanne de Longchamps

Swimming Man Burning
Terrence A. Kilpatrick

The Temptations of St. Ed and Brother S
Frank Bergon

The Other California: The Great Central Valley in Life and Letters
Gerald W. Haslam

The Track of the Cat
Walter Van Tilburg Clark

Shoshone Mike
Frank Bergon

Condor Dreams and Other Fictions
Gerald W. Haslam

A Lean Year and Other Stories
Robert Laxalt

Cruising State: Growing Up in Southern California
Christopher Buckley

Kinsella's Man
Richard Stookey